It's Not What You Know

It's Not What You Know

Spiderwize
Remus House
Coltsfoot Drive
Woodston
Peterborough
PE2 9BF

www.spiderwize.com

A CIP catalogue record for this book is available from the British Library.

The views expressed in this work are solely those of the author and do not necessarily reflect the views of the publisher, and the publisher hereby disclaims any responsibility for them.

ISBN: 978-1-912694-07-5

IT'S NOT WHAT YOU KNOW

EILEEN WARD

SPIDERWIZE
Peterborough UK
2018

Acknowledgements

I would like to thank my friend and neighbour Dr. Kenneth Cully for all his help in proof reading and his encouragement in the writing of this book.

Also thanks to all my friends at the Driffield writing group for their support and enthusiasm.

Dedicated to my parents Stanley and Doris Dale.

Few people could have started out in life with less than Stanley and Doris.

Their burning ambition was to have their own farm. With no money, help or advice it seemed an impossible goal, but what they did have, was more than their fair share of Yorkshire grit, a willingness to work hard and an ironic sense of humour that saw them through the bad times.

They were just teenagers when they married in 1939 and they remained devoted to each other for the rest of their lives.

I count myself very fortunate to have had them for my parents and I know my sister Frances feels the same.

To begin with, I never really set out to write one book let alone two. My original intention was simply to record facts for my family to keep, but one thing led to another and I found myself writing it as a story.

Both of the books are based on fact and most of the anecdotes are true. I hope you will find them entertaining.

IT'S NOT WHAT YOU KNOW

CHAPTER 1

They hadn't known quite what to expect of the cottage that was to become their new home. But Stanley and Doris had certainly not expected to find the ceiling lying on the floor, in a tangled mass of lathes and plaster, with just the odd piece clinging to the gas light.

Never having had the opportunity to see inside before, they had come prepared to do some decorating and cleaning, but nothing like this. As they stood in the doorway staring in dismay at the scene, the removal man looked over their shoulders and sucked in a shocked breath. He swore softly and gave a whistle. Remembering the spotless little home they had just left behind he asked, "Do you want me to take you back?"

Doris exchanged glances with Stanley and together they shook their heads. "It took us long enough to get out of Winifred Road. There'll be no going back, will there, Stan?"

"Not likely," came the reply from Stanley, as he stepped into what would become their living room and began to push the mess to one side, thinking as he did so that he would need to have a word with his new employers who owned the cottage. If he didn't, Doris was likely to go storming across to the farm, and it wouldn't do to get on the wrong side of them at this early stage.

Working together, they dragged the fallen ceiling out of the house, across the narrow road and dumped it on the strip of grass at the other side, intending to deal with it later when the furniture was unloaded. The removal man charged by the hour, so the longer it took, the more expensive it would be. Stanley worked out the cost in his head, and knew that they were running close to their financial limit, so the furniture was unloaded in record time.

As the lorry left, Stanley put his arm round his wife and hugged her tight. "Well here we are, love. No regrets, eh?" and together they stepped into their new home and took the time to explore it.

The front door opened directly into the living room that now had exposed beams, thanks to the collapsed ceiling. Like most living rooms it was dominated by the large black stove and to the side of that a door led into a small front room. A third door led out into a kitchen, which was a lean-to building that looked as if it had been added as an after-thought. The ceiling was simply the underside of the pantiles on the roof, with plenty of gaps to allow fresh air in.

Just under the window was a brown stone sink that would have to be used for washing clothes, dishes, and bodies of course, as there was no bathroom. In fact, no water either, as the only tap was outside, near the gate.

Stanley looked at Doris, and took a deep breath, "Bloody hell, Dot," he said, "We're not going to want to spend much time getting washed in here in winter."

But there was a brick-built copper in one corner for boiling the dirty clothes on wash days, and Doris instantly thought that at least they had a means of heating water, even though every drop would have to be carried in by the bucket full, and ladled out again.

In the far corner of the kitchen, at the side of the sink, a low door opened into a pantry. Stanley lifted the latch and brushing away the cobwebs he bent down and peered inside. The walls had once been whitewashed but that had given up the fight to stay where it had been put and was now flaking away. A damp, musty smell hit them, and as their eyes grew used to the poor light they could see a flat stone slab, that was designed to keep food cold. On it was a plate containing something that had once been food, but was now some sort of foreign body that was concentrating on growing a fine green coat of mould. Pulling a face, Doris stepped down into the pantry and picking up the plate she carried it out at arms-length and dumped it in the garden.

A short length of stairs led out of the kitchen and up into the two bedrooms. Stanley tested the floor, bouncing on it tentatively at first, and then with growing confidence as it creaked but seemed able to bear his weight. As the ceiling below had lost its plaster there was now a clear view from the first bedroom floor, down into the living room through the cracks, but Doris said that wouldn't be a problem as she would begin making pegged rugs to cover the worst places. The second bedroom was reached through the first one and was in a relatively liveable condition.

The only means of lighting in the house was the single gas light in the living room which was now in a pretty sorry state due to the ceiling resting on it. Doris pulled a face but shrugged the problems away saying, "We'll manage. It's a good job me mam packed us some candles up."

Stanley nodded, "Aye, she's not as dizzy as she makes out is she? We'll miss her."

It was clear that however charming the cottage looked from the outside, the inside was a different story. Several of the walls were wet with damp and every window had wide gaps that would let in the wind and cold. Privately Stanley was doubtful if he had done the right thing bringing his wife and daughter to live in such a place, and wondered how on earth they were going to manage in such primitive conditions.

Outside, they made their acquaintance with the lavatory, which was an earth closet, and was housed in a tiny building that looked ready to fall at the first strong wind. Inside there was a raised area covered by a wooden board, worn smooth by the hundreds of bottoms that had sat on it over the years. There was a circular hole cut in the centre of it and the human waste dropped down into a deep pit below. All this was dug out by the dustbin men regularly every week and taken away with the rest of the rubbish. It stank of course, and Eileen held her hand over her mouth, appalled at the idea of having to use it, and thought that even Winifred Road had had a water toilet.

But none of these things mattered much to Stanley and Doris. None of these difficulties overshadowed their joy and they looked forward to a brighter future.

The garden was in the same state of neglect as the house, with waist high weeds flourishing. But here and there were signs that it had once been loved and cared for. Roses still bloomed among the nettles, and sticks stood at crazy angles, still supporting ancient dried up beans, and here and there a few self-sown peas were making a brave attempt to grow.

A path made of old bricks wound its way up the long garden, and Stanley pushed his way along it, through the overgrown grass and brambles that hung over the edges. Doris followed, almost treading on his heels, eager to explore. There were two large pear trees and an apple tree full of blossom at the top end of the garden, and there beneath them was a treasure they had never even dreamed of. There, in all its dilapidated glory was a stone built pig sty!

All of Stanley's doubts about the move disappeared, and in an instant he could visualise the tumble down building all repaired, and occupied by a large white sow, surrounded by at least ten young piglets that were rapidly growing into stock that could be sold. Giving a huge sigh of happiness he told Doris all about his idea. Inspired by his enthusiasm she went on to suggest that he could build a shed and they could buy chickens.

Stanley picked her up and whirled her around. " Dot," he said, "Everything's possible now. We just have to work hard and the future will be good. But first we've got to get the house liveable in." Hand in hand they walked back down the path and found the foreman, Bert Dunning, waiting for them.

He held out his hand in greeting and before Stanley could speak about the state of the cottage he began, "Aye Stan, Ah had no idea the house had been left like this, my wife's been ill and had to go into hospital, so I didn't get in to look at it till late last night." He gave a sort of sigh and blew out a long resigned breath, "Ah know it's put you both in a bad position, you've no alternative but to stay now have you?"

Stanley shook his head, and as he waited for Bert to continue, he looked at Doris, hoping she would keep her temper in check. Her lips were tight and her dark eyes were almost black, but thankfully she restrained herself and simply said, "We need some time to get it habitable, I can't do it all on my own, and if Stan's to start work on Monday he won't be able to do much will he?"

Bert shook his head, "I appreciate that Mrs Dale, and I've already had a word with Mr. Smith. He has suggested that if Stan would be willing to come in and just do the milking morning and night for the first two weeks, he can have the rest of each day to get the cottage in order, on full pay of course," he added hastily, as he looked Doris in the eye.

Appeased, Doris smiled at him, and for a moment Bert forgot what he was about to say as her beauty struck him. "Ah'm glad that's sorted out, Mrs Dale," he said quietly, and he held out his hand to her. She shook his hand and told him to call her Doris, then asked if the farm would supply them with some of the materials to paint the cottage. Bert smiled and recognised that Doris was a young woman who could hold her own with anyone.

Within an hour the materials had arrived. But in spite of the war being over, these were still difficult times, with paint in short supply, and all they received were packets of white wash and lime and some well- worn brushes, and they would just have to make them do.

Stanley set to work on the ceiling in the living room first. Wrapping a handkerchief around his mouth as a mask and dragging his oldest cap down over his eyes, he pulled out all the nails that had held the ceiling in place and brushed away the plaster. He emerged after a couple of hours coated in dust and coughing up the powdered plaster that had seeped through the handkerchief.

As he dusted himself down a neighbour appeared at the wall and introduced herself as Mrs Thomas. She was carrying a tray with a jug of tea and sandwiches on it, all covered with a white cloth, and she placed it carefully on the top stone of the gateway, and indicated to Stanley to take it.

"I'm from the next but one house," she explained and Stanley detected a faint Welsh accent. "The house next door is empty, ah can't see anyone taking it. It's in a worse state than this one. You've got plenty on sorting this lot out young man. The last lot of tenants were terrible. Dirty beasts they were. We were glad to see the back of them."

She waved away Stanley's thanks and disappeared as quickly as she had arrived, saying in a soft voice as she went, that she would collect the tray later. Calling Doris and his daughter from the upstairs rooms, they took the tray and sat under the trees at the top of the garden with blossom floating down on them and made their plans as they ate their first meal in their new surroundings.

CHAPTER 2

The training that Stanley had received at Teddy Downing's farm stood him in good stead. He had been appalled at the state of the cow-house when he had first seen it and had said as much to Bert Dunning, the foreman.

Bert had nodded in agreement and went on to comment that that was the reason the previous cow man was no longer employed, and why Stanley now had his job.

"Ah just couldn't get that bloke to do his job properly," he said. "He would have been out a lot sooner but the boss had taken him on as a favour to a friend of his mother's. He had warning after warning before Mr. Smith finally agreed he needed finishing. It was when his mother, Mrs Smith senior, found a lump of cow shit in the house milk, that brought matters to a head, and then, even she forgot all about any religious principles and said he had to go."

Bert had seemed to be having difficulty hiding a smile as he said these words and Stanley had given him a quizzical look waiting for more information, but obviously Bert thought that he had said enough and had left it at that.

Cows always seem to have loose bowels, especially when they have been eating fresh grass, which turns the contents of their bowels into liquid, and often erupts from their rear end in a stream, splattering anything and anyone who happens to be in the firing line.

Well, Stanley could see that the cows had certainly been on fresh grass. The evidence was lining the once white walls of the cow-house and lingering in the cobbles and the corners of the stalls.

This had to be put right, and although he had an agreement that he could spend the first two weeks sorting the cottage out when he wasn't attending to the cows, Stanley decided it couldn't wait.

So, as soon as the first milking session was over, he began by hosing the building from top to bottom. He found an unopened sack of lime in the store and poured it into a tub, trying not to inhale any of the cloud of white dust that drifted up from it. Then he added water a little at a time, and it bubbled like a witches brew as he stirred it with a stick until it became a thick, gloopy, white paste.

This could be dangerous stuff, and he couldn't risk a splash in the eye from it. Thankfully he found an old pair of goggles lingering on a shelf in the store. They were so opaque with age that he could barely see through them, but he wiped them with his handkerchief and put them on, then began the laborious job of painting the walls with the mixture.

By the time the tub was empty Stanley was covered with wet lime and as he could do no more until a further supply was available, he slipped off home to change his clothes and eat his dinner. He had expected words from Doris about leaving her to renovate the cottage alone but found her happily decorating the living room.

She had obtained a packet of bright blue distemper from the local shop and had devised her own distinctive style of decoration. Using a rolled up cloth she was gradually rag- rolling all the walls. Dipping the screwed up cloth in the runny blue liquid, she rolled it up and down the walls that had first been whitewashed, leaving weird patterns behind it.

Doris had wrapped a scarf turban-style around her hair that was now liberally coated with the blue distemper, as she had repeatedly pushed it back into place with wet hands that were now well and truly stained bright blue. She smiled happily at Stanley.

"Well, what do you think Stan? That's cheered the place up hasn't it? It only cost a shilling for the distemper." Actually Stanley preferred it with the plain white walls but knew better than to say so and he nodded in agreement as he looked around for signs of dinner.

Today, considering the state of the house and their finances, the only thing likely to be on offer was a cold lunch, but Doris never forgot his meals and there, under a tea towel was a cheese sandwich and a dish of left over stewed apple and custard.

Stanley, after a hard morning's work, would have loved one of his wife's meat and potato pies, but having been brought up in a large family he ate whatever there was without a word of complaint.

Before the two weeks were up, every inch of the cottage had been thoroughly scrubbed, whitewashed and decorated. Doris had worked her magic and created a cosy little home with their meagre belongings. The old black stove now looked magnificent thanks to the black-lead she had lavished on it, the horse brasses shone above the mantelpiece, and the whole house smelt of wax polish and flowers.

Even the earth closet had received a liberal coating of lime wash, and the seat had been well scrubbed with strong smelling Izal disinfectant. It had been emptied of the previous occupants waste and as Doris said, at least it was now their muck that they were sitting above every time they went.

Stanley had drilled holes in the door to let in fresh air, and it was now possible to watch if anyone passed by as you sat there waiting for nature to work. However, being able to watch out during the daytime was one thing, but visiting the closet after dark was a different matter altogether, as Eileen soon discovered and came to dread. With an old cycle torch as the only form of illumination the closet became an eerie place. As she sat watching out for spiders in the flickering light, she imagined unmentionable beings peering in at her while she sat on the cold draughty seat.

Oh yes, the closet was definitely a place to avoid after dark.

CHAPTER 3

They soon discovered that they would have no need of an alarm clock in their new home. The Northern Dairies stabled their horses and carts down the narrow lane near the old water mill, and every morning at five o'clock they passed within touching distance of the house on their way to the dairy, which was situated half a mile away on Tenter Balk Lane. The sound of the horses loud clip-clop, the rattle of the carts, and the voices of their drivers urging them to go faster would have woken the soundest sleeper.

They returned around mid-day, with their load of milk delivered and in a hurry to get the horses back to the stables. The horses needed little encouragement and were soon goaded into a full gallop anticipating the freedom of the field after their mornings work.

Bert had warned Stanley about them, and looking at Eileen he added. "Keep out of the way when you hear em coming," he said. "They haven't the sense they were born with. There'll be an accident one of these days, and we don't want you squashed under the wheels do we?" and he pulled her pigtails as he turned to go.

Less than a week after this conversation Stanley was walking towards home for his mid-day meal when he heard the sound. He stopped and waited. Round the corner going at top speed came one of the Northern Dairy horses pulling an empty cart.

The driver was standing on the cart, balancing, with feet planted wide apart, holding the reins in both hands, and laughing out loud, urging his horse to go faster. Less than twenty yards behind was a second horse and cart, and as it reached Stanley the first one glanced over his shoulder and made a gesture to his follower.

As a young man Stanley had done his fair share of reckless stunts, but this was sheer lunacy, and as they disappeared down the lane he shook his head in disbelief.

Before he had walked much further, another horse rounded the corner, and it was plain to see that this one was completely out of control. The driver was sitting crouched on the front of the cart, clinging on with the reins flapping loose. Without thinking Stanley dropped his haversack containing his flask, and began to run, gradually edging out into the road, faster and faster he went and glancing over his shoulder, he waited for the horse to come alongside him. Foam flew from the animal's mouth and Stanley could see the wild, frightened look in its eyes.

As it drew level, he reached for the reins, knowing he would only have one chance to get a hold of them. The horse seemed to be veering away from him but Stanley made a grab and took a firm hold, pulling the horses head sharply to one side, and kept pace, but gradually slowed it to a stop. He walked the horse and cart all the way back to the stables talking to him as they went, soothing the animal, and by the time they got there the only evidence of the near accident was the sweat and foam that lathered the horse.

It was not until the horse was calm that Stanley turned to the driver and told him to get a different job as he was not fit to be in charge of an animal.

But sadly, no lessons were learned from the incident, and two weeks later there was another runaway horse and this time there was no one to stop the animal. The driver jumped off the cart, and, completely out of control, the horse tried to turn into the stable yard, but was going much too fast. It ran headlong into the wall and one of the broken shafts of the cart acted like a spear and pierced its side. It had to be shot by the vet as it lay dying from its injuries.

News of Stanley's act in stopping the runaway horse soon spread through the village and for a short while he enjoyed a minor celebrity status. Doris said she was angry with him for taking the risk, "What would me and Eileen have done if you'd been injured?" she demanded, but secretly she was proud of his actions and wrote telling her mother, Edith, all about it. Edith in turn, told the story to one of Stanley's sisters when she saw her out shopping, and eventually it reached his father's ears.

By the time Harold retold the tale to his mates down the pit, it appeared as if Stanley had stopped a wild horse at a rodeo. His boasting about his son was overheard by Stanley's brothers and in due course they related the whole story back to him.

"Blood hell," said Stanley lapsing back into his strongest Yorkshire accent. "Bloody hell. Ar auld fella's been bragging about me down t'pit. That's a first. Wonders'll never cease."

But in spite of his words the fact that his father was now singing his praise meant a great deal to Stanley.

Praise was also coming Stanley's way from his employers. He had finished lime washing the walls in the cow house and now had everything as clean as it was possible to be in the old fashioned buildings. With the pan tiled roof there was little he could do apart from sweeping them to keep the dust and cobwebs away, but the walls were white and re-limed every other week.

He had been just about to begin the afternoon milking one day when he had unexpected visitors. As he wiped one of the cow's teats he looked up to see Mr Smith accompanied by his mother standing in the doorway. Mrs Smith rarely ventured into any of the farm buildings and left the whole running of the farm to her son.

As Stanley walked towards them she looked at him and said, "Now then young man, I've been hearing all about the work you've done and I have come to see it myself and I must say you've done a good job. Keep it up."

Evidently she had seen enough and turned to go, but not before she added, "I'd like to see your daughter at the chapel on Sunday. And maybe your wife would enjoy the sewing group on Wednesday afternoon."

To Stanley it sounded more like an order than an invitation and he just nodded and smiled, but promising nothing. Getting Eileen to go to the Sunday school would not be a problem; she would do as she was told, but Doris in a sewing group? He just could not see that happening.

He returned to his milking and pulled the three-legged stool up close to the old black and white Friesen and sat down, his long legs folded almost up to his chin. The cow her turned her head as far as the chain around her neck would allow, and stared at him, her jaws chewing with a steady grind, and her tongue licking round her mouth and she gave a snort as if to say 'get on with it.'

All the cows had names and this one was called Annie. Stanley pulled his cap to one side and placed it between her hide and his hair as he leaned his head into her side and reached for the two teats nearest to him, "Come on then Annie, let's get this done," he said, and he began to whistle softly as the milk flowed into the stainless steel bucket with a rhythmic swish, swish, and Stanley felt more at home and content than he had ever felt before.

CHAPTER 4

When Stanley acquired Meg, his collie, he had had visions of training her into a working dog to help him round up the animals on the farm.

The first time he took her with him to bring in the cows for milking she did exactly what a professional collie should do, stalking round the herd, slinking low, and making eye contact with them. Stanley was proud of her, thinking how naturally she did it.

The cows, if the truth be known, had they been able to unfasten the gate themselves, would have happily ambled along the road, down the farmyard and into their stalls in the cow-house without any interference or help from anyone. But Meg followed them all the way making a great show of her abilities and accepted Stanley's praise as if it were her due.

If there had been a beauty contest for collies there is no doubt that Meg would have won. With her long, black, silky fur and white ruff she was a very lovely dog. The little touches of tricolour around her face enhanced her appearance giving her a wide-eyed look. She seemed to have a constant doggy smile on her face and eyes that shone with eagerness to please. But looks are not everything as Stanley was finding out.

His job included looking after the large herd of bullocks. In summer, they were turned out into the fields to graze and fatten up, and they were rough and wild.

Meg stared at them in horror and her expression said, "Are you mad? I'm not taking those on," and she slunk round the back of her master for protection and stayed there, refusing all orders to go anywhere near them, and Stanley just had to accept the Meg was too timid to work the bullocks.

There was another collie on the farm, a male dog named Punch who spent his life chained up in the farmyard under the open barn. He was an old dog, long-legged with rough black fur that was matted and tangled with straw. He had his own wooden kennel and was fed every day, but his exercise was confined to the area that his chain would allow. He came out of his kennel whenever a stranger appeared and gave a few half-hearted woofs, and had regular slanging matches with the farm cats, but that was the limit of his dull life.

Now Meg may have been timid, but when she came into season she turned into a brazen hussy, and she went calling on Punch with courting on her mind, and Punch, who thought all his birthdays had come at once was only too happy to oblige. He brightened up considerably after that for a few days and put more effort into his barking.

Stanley was none too pleased with Meg but there was little he could do. It was too late and only time would tell if there would be any consequences from Meg's brief affair with the farm dog.

Stanley knew he would have to choose his moment to suggest to Doris that she might like to go to the sewing group but when he did, to his surprise she was all for it, and went off on the next Wednesday afternoon with the cushion cover she had been embroidering under her arm, looking forward to meeting some of the ladies who attended.

The happy mood did not last long however and Doris left early, went home and told her bewildered husband in no uncertain terms what Mrs Smith could do with herself, as there was no way she would be going again.

"I haven't time to sit around gossiping." she stormed, and Stanley pulled a face behind her back and kept quiet until her good humour returned.

As he expected there was no problem getting his daughter to go to the chapel services. Several of her new friends already attended the Sunday school and she simply joined them and slipped into the routine. The people running the chapel knew the value of bribery, and gave each child a card that was stamped with a gold star every time they attended, and at the end of the year a full card was rewarded with a book at Whitsuntide.

There were other benefits to being part of the Sunday school flock. Regular attendance meant you were allowed to go to the guild which was held on Wednesday evenings throughout the winter. It was a sort of gentle youth club, that began and ended with a short prayer, and in between everyone sat in a half circle around the roaring fire, listening to stories, playing Chinese whispers and competing in quizzes. Drinks of watered down orange juice appeared at half time and then the noisy and rowdy games began.

A favourite was a game in which every person was given the name of a railway station, and stood behind their allocated chair, before dashing across the room to switch places with someone else when called to change stations. It was really a complicated variation on musical chairs and Eileen thought it was the greatest fun she had ever had.

Orange and lemons was another frequent game, with the age old rhyme being chanted.

Orange and lemons, say the bells of St. Clements,

I owe you five farthings, say bells of St Martins,

When will you pay me, say the bells of Old Bailey,

When I grow rich, say the bells of Shore Ditch.

When will that be, say the bells of Stepney,

I do not know, says the Great Bell of Bow.

Here comes the chopper to light you to bed! Here comes the chopper to chop off your head

Chip chop chip chop the last man's dead!

A balloon could provide them with several minutes of energetic fun as it was batted between one team and another over a rope until it finally burst.

Sometimes they had high jumping contests, using a skipping rope, and the old wooden floor bounced and shook as it took a pounding.

It was all over much too quickly as far as Eileen was concerned, and then it was time to run home, down the poorly lit street, cringing from the shadows behind her as she hammered on the front door, and waited to be back inside in the warmth and safety of home where she could tell Stanley and Doris all about the evening.

In mid-summer it was time for the annual Sunday school outing when the whole flock of children were taken on a mystery trip, which always turned out to be Roche Abbey. Not much of a mystery, but these were children who were born during the war and any treat was good to them. Stanley said with a laugh that that was the only place the driver knew his way to, but they all had a good time anyway, with a picnic followed by games of hide-and-seek and rounders.

One year, as they waited for the coach to arrive, a game of chicken developed between two brothers who had recently moved into the street. They were rough, unruly lads, not the type that usually attended Sunday school, and they had a nasty habit of throwing stones at other children just for the fun of it.

There was little traffic at the time, but they waited until a vehicle appeared, and then dashed across the road in front of it. The younger of the brothers left it just too late and fell directly in front of a very smart, dark green MG sports car.

The driver slammed on his brakes, but it was too late, and everyone watched in horror as the car rolled on top of the boy's legs then slowly rolled off again. The boy sat up, then scrambled to his feet and ran to join his brother, none the worse for his accident.

The strange thing was, that for the rest of her life, Eileen longed to own a dark green MG sports car.

CHAPTER 5

Farm labourers were officially among the lowest paid workers in the country. At £4.10 shillings per week Stanley's wages were approximately a quarter of what his father and brothers were paid as miners. But even so, Stanley and Doris considered themselves better off than they had ever been before. It was the perks that went with the job that made all the difference to their living standards.

They were entitled to two free jugs of milk per day, which Eileen was sent to collect from the farm house every morning and evening as soon as the milking was done. Potatoes and turnips were free, and eggs now and then if Stanley was able to find the nests of the hens that refused to go into the hen house to lay.

The cottage, primitive as it was, at least had the advantage of being rent free, although, there were many times when Stanley declared his employers should be paying them to live in it as Doris battled to keep it clean and dry. There was not a wall that did not have a tide of damp creeping up it, causing the distemper to constantly flake and fall off. But the inside looked cosy enough thanks to Doris's home-making skills.

She had bought a square of coconut matting for the living room, and polished the surrounding floor every day with red wax floor polish until she had such a high gloss on it that it was treacherous to walk on. Stanley swore that it was like walking on a bloody skating rink, but nothing would persuade her to give up, and every surface in the house that could be polished, regularly received a coating.

Even if they had been able to afford carpet for the stairs, such items were still in short supply following the war, but Doris improvised by cutting old grey army blankets into strips and nailing them on to the wooden stairs. It was never a real success, and Doris thought longingly of the luxurious Wilton carpets that she used to sweep in the house where she worked before she was married.

Wash days meant a whole day of hard work, with every drop of water having to be carried into the house from the tap outside near the gate. Stanley spoke to Bert, his foreman, and asked that could they at least have the water piped indoors. Bert sympathised, and put forward his request which was turned down on the grounds that they had no plans to modernise the cottage, but they would not object to Stanley doing it himself if he wished.

Doris could not help thinking how ironic it was that her grandfather had owned a large plumbing business in Wath upon Dearne, and her own father was still employed in it. But obviously there would be no help coming from that direction as he never spoke to her.

Stanley was determined that they should have the job done before the summer was over and found a man who did plumbing jobs in his spare time. He turned up on an old shop bike with his bag full of tools in the carrier at the front, and set Stanley to work with a hammer and a chisel to make a hole in the wall, while he lit his blow lamp and began the job of joining the lead pipes.

He was a big man with a stomach so large that it inhibited his every movement. Puffing and panting, with sweat rolling down his face, he eventually got the pipes in place and attached the brass tap to the wall in the kitchen, almost two foot above the sink. "That's the best place for it, missus," he said to Doris when she questioned the position of it. "You need to have room to get a bucket under it don't you?"

Privately Doris thought he had put it there because he couldn't be bothered to weld another joint, but she held her tongue when Stanley gave her one of his warning looks and whispered that it would increase the cost if he had to use more lead.

He handed over the ten shillings that he had been quoted for the job and ignoring the man's grumbles that he was out of pocket with the work, he opened the gate and made it clear that he should be on his way.

Doris turned on the tap, and said what a treat it was to have water in the house, even if the high position of the tap meant it splashed all over the floor if it was turned on too fast.

The following week Stanley came home with news that the peas were almost ready and they would start the pea pulling within days if the weather stayed as it was. Doris questioned him about the work and Stanley explained that they usually paid two shilling per bag or two shilling and sixpence if the peas were very light.

Doris stood up and took the teapot from the hot shelf above the oven, and standing beside him she began to pour more of the strong brew into his mug.

"I think I'll go and have a few days pea pulling," she said. "We could do with some extra money."

Stanley looked up at her as he put his arm around her waist and let it slide down over her bottom. "Are you sure, Dot? There's some rough characters coming from down Adwick Lane tha knows."

Doris sat down and gave him one of her looks and tightened her lips, "Ah'm not frightened of them, ah can hold me own wi anybody."

Stanley nodded in agreement, "Aye tha can an all. Ah'll tell you as soon as Bert gives the word that we're starting."

If Doris felt apprehensive as she walked up Red House Lane to join the throng of pea pullers, she kept it well hidden. She was carrying just a bucket, a bottle of water and a sandwich for her lunch and had tied a scarf around her head turban style. The sun was just beginning to break through the early morning mist as she reached the field, and with relief she saw Bert Dunning who directed her to a position where she could begin.

"Nah then, Doris, looks like a good day for it and the peas are nice and heavy, so you should earn a few bob today. Ah good, you've brought a bucket to pull into, it makes it a lot quicker. Just pull a handful of straws up, strip all the peas off, and then throw the straws behind you."

He handed her a sack. "Once you've filled one of these take it to the scales over there," and he pointed over to the corner of the field where an empty cart stood beside the weighing scales. "They'll give you a ticket for every bag you fill. When we've finished for the day, hand the tickets in and you'll get paid. We're paying two bob a bag today."

He turned to go, then leaned over to speak quietly, "Watch the bags of peas that you're filling Doris, there's one or two sneaky buggers around here that'll pinch'em when your back's turned if you don't watch'em. Stan'll be here when he's finished the milking."

Doris nodded her thanks and began. She had set her mind on earning at least £1 that day. All she needed to do was fill ten sacks with peas and she set to work, pulling up the straws with her right hand, and stripping the peas off quickly into the bucket, then emptying it into the sack when it was full.

The workers were spread out in a line across the field and advanced slowly, gradually filling sacks with peas. Several of the farmworkers walked behind them, pitchforks in their hands raking the straws back into rows behind the pullers. Every now and then voices would be raised as one of the farm workers complained that all the peas were not being removed.

"Eh, pick em clean, missus. Tha's missing half of 'em."

For the most part they were talking to tough women who gave as good as they got and were not in the least intimidated by anything a farm labourer had to say. Doris listened, but intent on earning as much as she could, she took no part in any conversations, simply replying as briefly as she could to anything her neighbouring workers said.

By lunchtime her back was aching but she allowed herself only ten minutes to eat her sandwich, then carried on until mid-afternoon when she gave in and went down on her knees to fill the tenth sack. Her neck was burnt red by the sun, and she ached in every muscle, but Doris was triumphant as she walked unsteadily with that last sack in her arms to collect her £1.

Doris was no stranger to hard work, but this had been her first experience of field work and it had found muscles that she hadn't even realised she had. What she really needed was a long hot soak in a bath, but luxurious baths would not enter Doris's life for another few years yet, so when she arrived home she emptied the lukewarm water from the kettle into the enamel bowl in the sink, drew the curtains, locked the door, and strip washed her body piece by piece.

If Eileen had been at home she would have called her into the kitchen to wash her back while she held a towel around her breasts for modesty. But she had noted from the school dress hung over the arm of the sofa that her daughter must have come home, put on her old skirt and gone to the farm to help Stanley with the cows.

It was her regular routine every day now, and normally Doris didn't mind, but today she could have done with her at home to run to the shop and get some Sloan's liniment for her back.

Sloan's liniment was a white lotion and came in a ridged glass bottle with a picture of a be-whiskered old gentleman on the front label, who boasted that the evil smelling contents would cure all types of pains and rheumatics known to man. It attempted to achieve this by using an ingredient so hot, that it made the patient forget about any pain they had as they endured the torture of their stinging, burning skin. But Doris was desperate for some relief from her aches and pains and was willing to try anything.

Stanley arrived home in due course with his young daughter sitting on the seat of his bike while he pushed it. Eileen was barely through the door before her mother pushed money into her hand and sent her off to the shop at the end of the village.

"Don't forget," Doris instructed, "Ask Mrs Sneap for Sloan's liniment, and bring three fancy buns if she's got some. Don't be long. Don't go into the park. Go straight there and back, and don't nibble at the buns or you'll get none for tea."

Eileen ran all the way, repeating the message with every step, but even so by the time she stood in front of the counter she asked for Sloons linent. The shop keeper, Mrs Sneap, leaned on the counter with her elbows, put her head in her hands, stared at her young customer and wrinkled her brow.

"Sloons linent? I think you've got it wrong, love, go back home and bring a note."

"But Mam says I have to be quick. It's for her back, because she's been pea pulling."

All became clear then and Mrs Sneap smiled as she reached up to the top shelf and brought down the glass bottle. "I think this is what you want, love. Anything else?"

It was no effort to remember the fancy buns and three pink iced ones were chosen and went into a brown paper bag and were carried home very carefully along with the liniment.

Stanley applied the liniment to Doris's back at bed time, rubbing it in as gently as he could with his rough calloused hands. The strong smell of it rose and surrounded them.

"Bloody hell, Dot, it's making my eyes water," commented Stanley, and jokingly let his hand slip on to the top of her thigh. He received a sharp elbow jab from his wife as she rolled away from him.

"Don't you dare, Stanley Dale. You watch where your hands go with that stuff on them." She jumped out of bed, forgetting her aching back when Stanley advanced towards her making a pretence of grabbing her.

"No, no, Stan that's enough, I'm not kidding. Get off downstairs and wash your hands or you're sleeping on the sofa."

Stanley did as she said, laughing all the way downstairs and calling as he went that she was just being mardy.

Doris may have had an aching back but she was determined to carry on with the pea pulling, and was up early the next morning and off by 7.30, leaving her daughter with strict instructions to get to school on time.

With each day that passed the work seemed easier as her muscles became more accustomed to the work, and the thought of the money she was earning kept her going. By the end of the week she had almost eight pounds tucked away in her savings tin and Doris knew exactly what she was going to do with it.

A gas cooker and a gas washer/boiler were on her shopping list, and as soon as Stanley finished work on Saturday lunch time they set off to walk to the gas showrooms at Carcroft.

They took the path down Mill Lane, past the Northern Dairies stables and the mill house, and along the banks of the mill stream which had once been a fast-flowing waterway that had turned the water wheel underneath the house.

It was now a sluggish stream that meandered slowly through the weeds that had flourished for lack of cleaning out, but at least the water ran clear, unlike the canal they had been used to seeing back in Wath upon Dearne. Life was good since they had made the move to Adwick and they viewed the future with hope and optimism.

As they walked, the steam train went past at top speed on the nearby rail line, smoke and steam belching out of it. The driver raised his arm in greeting as he leaned on the door and they waved back as delighted as children. Stanley said that sometimes the Flying Scotsman passed through Adwick station, he had seen it the previous week and they wondered if they would ever be able to afford to travel on it.

At the gas showrooms Doris chose a reconditioned gas cooker and a new gas washer/boiler and paid all the money she had earned from her week of pea pulling as a down payment They signed the paperwork which said they promised to pay the rest over the next two years. Doris tucked the payment card into her bag feeling very nervous that they had taken on a debt but was quite determined that it would be paid in record time.

CHAPTER 6

The motto, LIVE TO WORK, WORK TO LIVE could have been written especially for Stanley. He was quite prepared to toil every minute of every day in order to make a better life for himself and his family.

In what little spare time he had after work at the farm was finished, he had tackled the garden. Every inch had been dug and raked and now had neat rows of vegetables and flowers.

He had taken up the bricks that had formed the old curved path, cleaned them and re-laid them in a straight line up the centre of the garden to the pig sty. And now here he was in late July leaning on the fence staring into space, imagining a fine large white sow in the pen with at least eight young piglets with her.

That was Stanley's plan. If only he could acquire a sow who hopefully would produce a good litter of piglets he could keep two for his own use, and sell the rest at market for a profit; then have the sow serviced with the boar pig and start the whole procedure again.

He had been attending the pig market at Doncaster whenever possible, taking in the scene, watching, listening and learning.

On the last weekend in July he had a rare Saturday off and took the chance to make another visit to the market while Doris did the weekend shopping. It would be his last opportunity for a few weeks. The harvesting was due to begin and all the men would be expected to work every available hour apart from Sundays until it was all gathered in.

The market area was divided into squares by metal rails and

gates tied up with string. Each square held pigs of varying breeds and ages that were all up for sale.

The auctioneer started at one side of the market, standing on the middle rail of a gate so that he could see all around. He held a clip board in one hand and a measuring stick in the other. First he gave a brief description of the stock he was selling, and who owned it, and then he began by asking for a high starting price which he knew perfectly well would be ignored by the farmers surrounding him.

"Come on then, tell me where you want to be with this. I don't have all day to waste. This pig will have turned to bacon if you lot don't get a move on."

A finger twitched and a ridiculously low price was mentioned. With an exaggerated sigh the auctioneer began, speaking rapidly; taking bids here and there from a nod of a head or a wink of an eye, until finally the auction was won by the highest bidder, and the stick was slapped down on the clipboard, and the auctioneer moved on the next pen.

Stanley moved along with the rest of the crowd making sure he never made any movement that could be misconstrued as a bid, but his eyes followed the movements of the farmers who were bidding and he memorised the names of the stock breeders who sent in the best pigs, while he dreamed of the day when he would be in a position to buy his own breeding sow.

A dig in his back alerted him to the fact that Doris had joined him, and she squeezed herself through until she stood by his side and slipped her hand into his but remained silent. She was not the only female to stand by her man's side but she was the most beautiful and drew sidelong, admiring glances from the dour Yorkshiremen around her.

As always, when ladies were present these rough men curbed their language and treated them with respect. But today was to prove the exception and as Doris stood there she felt someone fondle her bottom.

Without saying a word or turning around she stepped back a pace on to the man's toe with the heel of her shoe and at the same time delivered a sharp jab with her elbow. Doris heard the sharp intake of breath and the man backed away out of the crowd. She moved closer to her husband but said nothing about it until much later when the sale was over.

As usual, Stanley spent some time at the Irish market which was where the horses were sold. For this sale the auctioneer stood on a raised platform while the horses were led into the area one by one. Most of them were heavy working horses held by Paddy, a tiny Irishman who had a Woodbine in the corner of his mouth as a permanent fixture. As one burnt to a stub he lit the next one from it and with the cigarette smouldering he trotted the animal he was holding up and down the market.

With tractors being used on the land more and more, many of the magnificent creatures were redundant and going for knock-down prices, many of them ending up in the knacker's yard as horse meat.

There was a shop selling horse meat nearby in Silver Street that displayed great slabs of red haunches in the window, and Stanley shuddered as he thought of these animals with their flowing manes and tails being destined for pet food or someone's dinner plate.

As a farmer he had no false sentimental feelings about animals being bred for slaughter but horses were different.

No farm labourer was happier to see mechanisation coming onto the farms than he. It meant less back breaking work for everyone, but surely, he thought, the horses that had toiled and sweated alongside man for so many years, deserved better than to be led away to the knacker's yard.

As they walked back towards the bus stop at the North Bridge they passed through the fish market. The kippers laid out on one stall reminded Stanley of his step brother Herbert, and he told Doris again about how he used to eat a whole kipper, bones and all between two slices of bread. He chuckled as he retold the story but there was a lump in his throat as he thought of Herbert's tragic death down in the depths of Cortonwood Colliery. Even after all the years that had passed it still had the power to hurt him.

Doris gripped his hand. She knew how he felt and she pulled him close and steered him towards the tripe stall. "Come on Stan," she said, "Let's get some tripe for tea, I got a nice new loaf from

27

the market and there's some best butter in the pantry. It'll go down a treat."

Stanley agreed, then at the last moment decided on a cow heel instead, and chose one with a generous amount of jelly clinging to it and looked forward to sprinkling it well with salt and eating it.

They stood for a few minutes listening to the busker performing outside Woolworths in Baxtergate. Today it was a man who sang just like Stanley's favourite singer, Josef Lock. His powerful tenor voice echoed down the street as he sang, 'Take me home again, Kathleen,' and the audience that surrounded him clapped and dropped coins into his cap as the song came to an end. The words and the melody imprinted themselves on Stanley's brain and he sang the song himself for years afterwards whenever he was happy.

On almost every corner of the streets in Doncaster there were ex-servicemen standing with trays hung around their necks containing matches or shoe laces, or any kind of small commodity they could buy with the hope of reselling for a tiny profit. All of them were injured in some way, either physically or mentally by their time serving in the war. There was one man on the corner of the market place with an empty sleeve where he used to have an arm. Stanley dug in his pocket and bought a pair of shoelaces that he didn't need, handing over the sixpence and telling the man to keep the penny change.

"Poor bugger," he said to Doris as they walked away, "Bloody fine reward he's got for serving the country, having to stand on street corners, scratching out a living. That's the thanks the men have got for ruining their lives. They should be living in luxury for what they've been through."

Ex-servicemen standing on street corners were not the only reminder of the war so recently ended. There were still some ex-prisoners of war working on many of the farms. Two of them were employed at Smiths farm where Stanley worked, and he had become friendly with one of them. Both were called Toni, but as one was tall and the other short they had become known as big Toni and little Toni.

Now that the war was over, they were of course, free to return to Germany, but they chose to remain in England as displaced persons rather than return to their families, who now found themselves living under harsh Russian rule in what had become the Eastern Block.

The two Toni's continued living in the Nissen huts where they had lived during their prisoner of war days but were now free to come and go as they pleased. A bus collected them every morning along with several other Germans and dropped them at the farms where they worked, just the same as they had during the war, and then picked them up again in the evening. The difference was that they were now employees and were paid a wage.

Big Toni was a handsome man with fair hair and blue eyes. He had a stern expression and spoke only when he had to. Stanley suspected that he understood a lot more English than he pretended and treated him with caution.

Little Toni, however, was completely different in every way and had a good knowledge of spoken English. He talked as he and Stanley worked alongside each other, telling him how happy he had been to be taken a prisoner of war. "I do not want to fight, it is not good to kill," he said. "In England I grow food same as when I was in Germany before the war."

And then he confided that he now had a girlfriend in a nearby village and although her parents had been against their relationship they were gradually coming around to the idea.

"I never go back to Germany now. We will marry next year and soon I will work on the farm where her father works and there is a cottage for us. So, soon I will say goodbye, Stanley. You are a good friend."

Stanley was touched by his words and he talked about him to Doris that night as they prepared for bed.

"You have to feel sorry for some of them lads, Dot," he said. "Most of them are just the same as us. They didn't want to fight any more than we did. It's the bloody politicians every time that cause it. The lads are sent away whether they like it or not. They have to leave their homes and families, then kill or be killed. What's the bloody point of it all?"

Doris agreed as she snuggled up to him and just as he was

drifting off to sleep she murmured that they should ask Toni to come for tea. "Mmm," came the sleepy reply before the gentle heavy breathing signified that he was already in dreamland.

The next day, after milking, Stanley set about preparing the reaper for the harvesting. Toni joined him armed with a tub of grease, and together they dismantled the cutting blade and sharpened it, then oiled the old machine and greased all the moving parts. Stanley stood back and looked at it.

It was the most ungainly machine, and lethal looking too, with the long blade at the front and the wooden sails that moved round and flattened the straw so that it fell at the right angle to be cut. It was horse drawn and so only moved at the walking pace of the horse.

The moving parts that tied the string around the sheaves of straw were notoriously temperamental, and much time was lost retying them with improvised bands of straw, the way it had been done for centuries when scythes were used.

"These things have had their day, Toni. When they were first invented, they must have been a big improvement on scything the corn, but they're out of date now. Combine harvesters are the modern way. I've been reading about them in the Farmer and Stock Breeder. There are some being brought out called the All-Crop harvesters. They're tractor drawn and do the whole job in one operation right there in the field. They use them in America. It's about time we got up to date."

Toni laughed, "I think you need talk to the boss, Stan." He picked up his tub of grease and began to walk away.

Remembering Doris's words, Stanley called him back, "Just a minute, do you want to come to our house for tea tonight?" Toni nodded but said he would need to wash before he ate with them, and at finishing time he disappeared into the cow-house and stripped off his shirt before washing his face and upper body under the cold water tap. With his hair still damp he walked across the road with Stanley looking nervous and apprehensive.

But Doris had prepared a meal and made him feel welcome. Eileen was overcome with shyness and kept even quieter than usual, but listened to every word their foreign visitor said. He spoke very little about Germany, except to say that he had no reason to go back there. Doris asked him about his family.

"No family," he said, "No one for me in Germany, this is home now. I have girl-friend here. We will marry soon." He left soon afterwards, shook hands with Stanley and thanked Doris politely for the meal before he left to catch the bus back to the camp.

Stanley looked forward to seeing him again after the weekend but Monday morning came and there was no sign of either of the ex-prisoners of war and he never was able to find out why.

CHAPTER 7

Since they had moved to Adwick-le-street, Stanley and Doris seemed to have a continuous stream of weekend visitors. Harold and Cyril often turned up on Sunday afternoons, roaring down the road on their shared motorbike.

Harold usually drove with Cyril riding pillion on the wobbly square sponge seat behind him. The house was instantly turned into a place of noise and fun as Cyril entertained them with one funny story after another, while Harold shook his head at him through his laughter.

"Can't take him anywhere can tha, Stan?" he'd say and then proceeded to try to outdo him with tales of what had happened down the pit and who'd said what.

Even Stanley's parents, Ada and Harold came to visit, taking the Doncaster bus from Wath and navigating their way across the town to the North Bridge station where they caught the bus to Adwick.

Stanley took his father to the Foresters Arms, which was the local pub in the centre of the village and bought him a pint. Harold sat and looked around at the full-sized billiard table and the dart board on the wall and nodded his approval.

He stated that the pint was 'not bad,' and that was great praise from an expert drinker. Stanley smiled to himself as he rightly guessed that all his father's collier mates would soon be hearing an exaggerated version of how good his son's local pub was.

Ada declared herself impressed with the cottage but was much less enthusiastic about the earth closet. "By heck, Doris, this is a bit primitive isn't it? Can't Stanley's boss put you a water toilet in?"

Doris shook her head, "No, he says he doesn't want to spend any money modernising the house. We've got used to it now. I put the ashes down it so it smells a bit less."

Ada nodded sympathetically, "I think you should get on to the sanitary inspector, Doris."

Doris agreed and pointed out that the council offices were less than thirty yards away just across the narrow lane outside the cottage, and she resolved to take Ada's advice as soon as possible.

Their favourite visitor was Edith, Doris's mother. They had all missed her since moving away from Wath, and Edith certainly had not forgotten them. Every Thursday like clockwork a parcel arrived from her, full of whatever little treats she could find. Bars of chocolate, boiled sweets, magazines, underclothes for Eileen, socks, padded pan holders that she loved making and often a half crown tucked inside to help with her daughter's housekeeping.

Edith was a prolific knitter and churned out jumpers and cardigans, usually in bright colours and original styles, but the problem was that Edith never used a pattern, and often the neck of a jumper was so tight that it almost removed the recipient's ears trying to get it on and off. The sleeves were often different lengths but what did that matter? They had been knitted with love and when they were so short of clothes a few problems with the fit of a garment didn't really matter.

The week after harvesting had begun, there was a letter in Edith's parcel telling them that she would like to come and stay if they could put her up. She was due a week off work, and wanted to come the following Saturday.

Reading between the lines Doris guessed that she needed to get away from her brother William, or Willie as he was usually known. He was a difficult man and expert at making life unpleasant for both her and his mother. Patient as Edith was, and much as she loved her brother there were times when she needed to get away for a while.

Instantly Doris began planning. Her mother could have Eileen's bed and she would make up a mattress on the floor in the corner of their own bedroom for their daughter to sleep on. Like all children would, Eileen treated the suggestion enthusiastically. It appeared a great novelty to her to sleep on the floor and to be truthful she would have happily slept anywhere at all if it meant she would be seeing her grandmother.

In the letter, Edith said she would be catching the ten o'clock bus, and would Doris please meet her at the Waterdale Bus Station in Doncaster, as she didn't think she would be able to find her way across the town alone.

Now, Edith had her own methods of travelling, and just because she said she intended catching a certain bus, it didn't mean that she actually would. Not that she would be late. Edith was seldom late. The problem was that she was frequently very early.

Saturday came around, and Edith was up an hour before her usual time, and at the bus stop in the centre of Wath anxiously waiting among the early morning shoppers at nine o'clock; and so when the Doncaster bus came along she reasoned that she might as well get on and be there an hour sooner. Assured by fellow passengers that, 'yes' she was on the right bus Edith sat down and took some deep breaths to calm herself.

The last few weeks had been hectic. She worked in the kitchens of the convalescing home in Sandygate. It was a good job, and probably the best paid she had ever had, but it was hard work.

Added to that, she was taking on an increasing amount of the house work at home. Although her mother would never admit it, her age meant she was slowing down, and could no longer do as much as she used to.

So now, all the washing and most of the cleaning was done by Edith. The washing alone was a full day's work, with the copper to be filled and the fire under it to be lit. Then everything had to be scrubbed and the whites boiled, dipped in dolly blue, and starched, before she put them through the wringer, and then carried them up the garden steps and hung them on the line, hoping that they would all dry outside.

The coal for the fires had to be carried up the rough path from the coal house, which was situated more than fifty yards away at the back of the row of cottages. There was not a single convenient thing in the house. Nothing that could be called labour saving, and Edith coped with all of it; but it was William's constant grumbles and bad temper that got her down. She thought about him now and not for the first time she wished she was more like Annie, her eldest sister, who squared up to him and told him straight what she thought of him.

Edith looked at her reflection in the bus window, and worried that she might have applied too much Ponds face powder, she took out her handkerchief and carefully dabbed her face with it, hoping to wipe off any surplus. She was wearing her new brown felt hat today and she gave the brim a tweak to pull it slightly to one side, and deciding that she looked quite smart, began to feel excited about her little holiday.

Of course, because she had caught an earlier bus, there was no one to meet her when she eventually reached Doncaster, but that was not a problem, she merely had to find someone to leave her case with, and then she could go to a café and enjoy a cup of tea.

There was a newspaper seller in the corner of the station, a middle aged lady, who, even in July, wore an assortment of skirts and jumpers, and a brown woolly hat to combat the wind that blew around the bus station no matter what time of year it was. Edith, trusting as always, asked her if she would look after her suitcase while she went for a cup of tea. The woman nodded and indicated that Edith should put it down at the side of her seat.

"It'll be safe there, love. Fetch it before twelve though, or I'll be gone." Edith dropped sixpence into her hand that was stained black by newspaper print, and told her that she would be back in an hour.

Crossing the busy road outside the bus station brought her to a parade of shops and a selection of three cafes. Edith was in seventh heaven. Her idea of a treat was tea in a café and she chose the one with the large window and two matching plant pots outside the open door. Making her way to the table nearest the window she ordered tea and toast, and settled down to enjoy herself.

In the meantime Doris was setting off towards Doncaster, and estimated that she had time to do a little shopping. Many commodities were still in short supply following the war, but the government were releasing army surplus goods and the place to buy them was in one of the army and navy stores that had opened up in various parts of the town.

The one in French Gate just opposite the impressive Guild Hall had advertised in the local press that they would have army blankets for sale this week, and Doris hurried there the moment she got off the bus with Eileen struggling to keep up with her. In Doris's pocket were the fifteen shillings she had saved from her housekeeping, and she was intent on buying two blankets before the supply ran out.

As they entered the shop, to her relief there was still a large pile of the rough grey blankets on the floor. Doris picked one up from the top of the heap and smelt at it. Watching her, the manager of the shop came forward.

"They are all new," he said, "They've never been used by the troops. These have all been held in reserve in a warehouse. They might smell a bit fusty but all they need is a good wash. They'll last for years. 7/6 each; you'll not find em cheaper anywhere. This lot 'll be gone by dinnertime."

Doris rummaged among them, and gave a tug at the two she had chosen. The manager was none too pleased that she refused to take the top two but looking at her determined face he beckoned to the youngest lad from behind the counter, and instructed him to get them out and pack them into Doris's bag.

Well pleased with her purchase, she turned her mind back to meeting her mother. As they crossed the road at clock corner Doris glanced up and realised they were running late if they were to be there to meet the bus on time.

Urging her young daughter to hurry she increased her speed but was hampered by the weight of her shopping bag, and felt annoyed with herself for not leaving the blankets at the shop to be collected later. Eileen complained that she had a stitch in her side but got little sympathy, "Come along, if we miss your granny's bus lord knows where she will go wondering off to. We'll never find her, come on and stop complaining."

They arrived at Waterdale just as the Barnsley bus was pulling into the station. Heaving a sigh of relief Doris slowed down and took out her handkerchief to wipe her face. A trickle of sweat was making its way down her back and her feet in her court shoes were hot and uncomfortable. The sun was full out now and temperatures were reaching into the high seventies.

The passengers began to alight from the red single decker bus, and Doris watched for the familiar figure of her mother until Eileen tugged at her hand. "Look Mam, that's granny's portmanteau?" she said, using Edith's old fashioned term for her suitcase, and she pointed to the navy blue leather case at the side of the newspaper seller. Doris gave it an irritated glance, and turned her attention back to the bus, then, slowly she looked at the case again and stared hard.

Approaching the woman she asked if the case had been left by someone. "Oh yes, love, she'll be back soon. She's gone over the road for a cup of tea, you must be her daughter, you can leave your bag with me if you want to go and find her."

None too pleased, Doris had little alternative than to accept the offer and go off in search of her mother.

As she re-crossed the road and headed towards the cafe, Edith was just on her way out. Spotting her daughter she waved and smiled broadly, so pleased to see her. However, Doris was too irritated to return the smile and began to rebuke her mother. "What were you thinking of, Mam, going off and leaving your belongings with a stranger?"

"Yes it's nice to see you too." For once Doris received a sharp answer from Edith. "If you're going to be like that, I might as well get straight back on the bus and go home. I haven't come here to have you shouting at me. Ah get enough of that from our Willie," and her lips tightened in a determined way, but she was not far from tears.

Realising that she had upset her mother Doris backed down and tucked her arm into hers and kissed her cheek. "Sorry Mam, ah just got worried and ah'm so hot. Let's get off home, ah want to get Stan's dinner ready."

The next day was a Sunday and due to his employer's religious beliefs there was a lull to the grind of the harvesting, much to Stanley's relief. Only the absolutely essential work was allowed to be done on the Sabbath. The men took it in turns to milk the cows and feed the livestock and as this was his weekend off he had a whole day without work.

Always used to early rising Stanley was still up at his usual time, but enjoyed a leisurely breakfast and then took his mug of tea outside and sat on the bench overlooking the garden. Edith joined him, lit her cigarette and offered one to Stanley.

"No thanks, Mam, ah gave up when we moved here. Ah don't think they do you much good."

"Ah think you're right, Stan, but ah usually only smoke when ah'm washing up and ah don't think the odd one will hurt." Changing the subject Edith commented on how good the garden looked and Stanley pointed out the renovated pigsty.

"All we need now is the pig to go in it." said Stanley with a sigh, and told her all about his plans to breed and sell the pigs.

"How much do they cost?"

"For what ah'm looking for; probably about thirty quid. So far we've managed to save ten. Ah'll have some overtime to come next week, but the way we're going we'll be lucky to save enough by Christmas."

Edith touched his arm, and looked at him, "Ah can lend you some money Stanley. Ah've some saved up in the post office. How much do you want? Ah've got my post office book with me, ah can draw some out tomorrow."

As usual when anyone tried to do Stanley a favour he was overcome with emotion, and he swallowed the lump in his throat. "Well that's good of you, Mam, but ah wasn't hinting for a loan. We can't take your money."

"You're not taking it Stan. Look, you're as good as a son to me and ah know you'll pay me back. If it makes you feel better let's call it a little business loan and you can give me the interest that the money would make."

Stanley took her held out hand and hugged her to him. Suddenly the tiredness that he had felt recently drained away, and he was full of enthusiasm again, realising that by this time next week there could be a large white sow occupying the pig sty.

Edith was as good as her word and by Monday afternoon she had been to the post office and drawn the money out. At teatime she opened her purse and placed six large white five pound notes on the table.

Stanley had never seen so many five pound notes at once. For him they represented almost seven weeks work, and he was completely overwhelmed that his mother-in-law trusted him enough to loan him that much money.

As his blue eyes met her dark brown ones, he held her gaze and reached for Doris's hand as he said, "Thank you, Mam, I'll never forget this. I won't let you down."

CHAPTER 8

Now that they had the capital that they needed to invest in a breeding sow Stanley couldn't wait to go to market to buy one. But being in the middle of harvesting meant that he would have to work every Saturday for the next few weeks.

The only possible chance of a free Saturday would be if it rained. All week he scanned the sky for signs of a break in the dry weather, but it continued hot and sunny. He had almost given up hope, but then, on Friday afternoon, although the sky was cloudless, he caught the faint rumble of thunder in the distance. They finished cutting the wheat in the top field next to the Great North Road at mid-day, and by evening all the sheaves were neatly stacked in stands of six, all leaning against each other like miniature pyramids.

"Nice and dry these," commented Bert, "Let's hope that storm that I can hear holds off or misses us, then we can have this lot in on Monday. It's a pity Mrs Smith won't let us work on Sunday. That extra day would make a difference to us being able to get the harvest in."

Stanley didn't reply but gave a slight nod while privately praying for a torrential downpour. Wind, rain, hail, anything would do as long as it meant he wouldn't be able to work the next day.

He didn't often get his prayers answered and goodness knows he had tried many times in the past, but when he was woken in the middle of the night by an enormous clap of thunder followed by a flash of lightening that lit up the room, he looked up and said under his breath, "Thank you Lord, I promise to have more belief in future," and he smiled as he heard the heavy drops of rain hammering on the pan tiled roof and the water gushing down the old metal drainpipes.

He could hear several drips coming from the direction of the staircase and knew the water was finding its way through the broken roof tiles in the lean-to kitchen and didn't care in the slightest. All Stanley was thinking about at that moment was getting to the market to buy his sow the very next day. He turned over and curled around Doris, and as he breathed in her familiar scent he drifted off to sleep again.

The next morning the cut up blankets that Doris had made into stair carpeting were wet and bedraggled, and water had seeped through the coconut matting and formed puddles just out of sight on the uneven floor and squelched to the surface when they were walked on. Fortunately the new cooker had escaped a soaking but it was small comfort, and Stanley assured Doris that he would speak to the boss about the leaking roof as soon as he saw him.

Doris was not easily appeased and insisted, "We can't have this, Stan. The least he can do is mend the roof. Ah am not putting up with it. Ah'm going to have to take all this lot up and dry it. Ah'll go and see him myself. Ah'll tell him a thing or two"

Stanley sighed, "Yes ah know, Dot. Don't go on about it. Ah will be on to him as soon as ah can, you know he's away in Scotland till next week. Now can ah have some breakfast and get off to t'market." He was becoming agitated himself, what the heck did she expect him to do at this time in the morning he wondered, and he figured the best solution was to get out of the house as quickly as possible.

Half an hour later as he was walking through the village, towards the bus stop, he saw the new man who had recently been set on working part time at the farm. He was cycling towards him with his heels on the pedals and his knees at an angle that made him look bow legged. The old Wellingtons with turned down tops did nothing to improve the look. He drew to a halt as he reached Stanley.

"Nah then, Stan, Ah'm just off to do t'milking." Stanley looked him up and down, taking in his unwashed appearance, stubbly chin and dirty clothes and wondered what on earth had made Bert set him on. He and Doris had nicknamed him Harry Baskin after a scruffy character in a book they had just read, and more than once he had called him Harry to his face by mistake instead of his real name which was Eric.

When Stanley was in a good mood he described Eric as a character, but more often he said he was like a bag of shite, but not half as useful. One of Eric's duties was to do some of the milking and feeding to relieve the regular men for the harvesting. But Stanley was not impressed with the state that he had left the cow-house in the previous day, and this morning he was not inclined to mince his words. Ignoring Eric's greeting he told him not to leave the cow-house like a shit hole.

"Aye tha don't need to worry, Stan, tha'll be able to eat of the floor when ah've finished wi it."

Shaking his head Stanley thought he had better be on his way before he said something he would regret, and he turned his thoughts back to his pig buying as he made his way along the street.

When he arrived at the market the pig pens were already half full and the rest filling up quickly. It seemed that many of the breeders were taking the opportunity of the enforced break from the harvest to get some of their stock into the market. Stanley walked among the pens making mental notes of the pigs for sale. Each one had a number chalked on their backs to identify them.

Taking care not to show too much enthusiasm for any particular one he took out his notebook and wrote down the numbers, twenty one, thirty, and thirty three. The middle one was his favourite but he decided that if the first one was a good price he would bid for it. He strode over the fences and discreetly ran his hands over each one. The last on his list was a young female pig, a gilt, who was expecting her first litter. They often went cheaper due to them being untried and inexperienced mothers.

The auction was due to begin in less than ten minutes and Stanley was feeling nervous, but he tried to look casual and as unconcerned as if he had bid before. It was at that moment that he saw the one man that all the buyers in the market hated.

He was known simply as Bassa, and he was in the habit of running up the bids without having any intention of buying. If he suspected that someone was interested in an animal he would keep putting in a bid every time the hammer was due to go down. Of course sometimes he slipped up and he found himself the owner of a pig that he didn't seriously want, but it never seemed to bother him. He had several allotments at Brodsworth and kept an assortment of stock in poor conditions. It was rumoured that he was in the pay of several of the regular sellers who benefited from his habits.

Stanley positioned himself opposite the auctioneer and moved along as the sales progressed. He was wasting no time today and within half an hour was standing at the side of number twenty one.

"Now then, gentlemen, this is a fine pedigree animal from Mister Prendagast of Norton, a tried and tested breeding sow, you all know the quality of his stock so let's have sensible bids." There was silence. "Come on then, where do you want to be? Am I bid twenty pounds?"

There was a nod of a head from somewhere in the crowd and they were off, with the bids going up ten shillings at a time. Stanley had set himself a limit of thirty pounds and the bids soon went past that and finally settled at thirty nine.

He heard the two farmers behind him commenting that the price was high and one of them nudged him. "Is tha after buying today, son?"

Stanley gave a nod but said nothing else for fear of missing the auctioneer's words. He had never seen him work so fast and it needed all of his concentration not to miss what was going on.

Before he knew it, lot number thirty was reached, and as the bids went up, he put in a few himself, and the price reached twenty nine. Taking the plunge he went all the way to thirty five and thought he had won, but just at the last minute another pound was bid.

"Lot thirty to Mr Barry Norman," came the announcement and he heard the men behind him say, "Ah, Bassa again. He came unstuck that time, serves him bloody right." One of them bent forward and in a low voice said, "Bad luck, son."

Stanley was disappointed. He had pinned his hopes on that particular sow, but then he reasoned with himself that he had bid more than he could actually afford and he set his mind on lot thirty three.

There were fewer buyers around at this stage in the selling and Stanley felt more confident. The price began at fifteen pounds and the bidding was slow. Not many of the buyers there were willing to take on an animal that had no breeding record. The auctioneer kept his eye on Stanley who was making regular bids. When the price reached twenty four pounds he held his breath and could hardly believe it when he was asked for his name and realised he had won the auction.

He was about to leave and go to the market office to pay his bill when he noticed the two young pigs on their own in the next pen. They looked tiny at the side of the full grown gilt that he had just bought and he estimated they were probably in the region of ten weeks old. They each had a number thirty four chalked on their backs indicating that they were to be sold as a pair. They had not been washed or prepared for the market and both looked underweight.

"Now then, gentlemen, ah have a couple of nice little porkers here. Come on now, what are they worth. What about a fiver for the pair?" There seemed to be no takers and the auctioneer was growing impatient. Stanley, without thinking, put up his hand and the stick went down.

"There we are. Sold. Mr. Dale of Adwick isn't it?" Stanley nodded and did a bit of quick mental arithmetic to check that he had enough money. When he had paid for the pigs and their cartage home he would barely have the bus fare left, but his spirits were sky high and he couldn't wait to see Doris's face when he arrived home with not only a pregnant gilt, but also two young pigs for fattening.

There was a small group congregated outside the market office and Stanley, thinking they were just talking, was about to walk around them and enter to pay for his pigs, but a hand on his arm detained him.

"Ah wouldn't go in there if ah were you. There's a bit of business going on." The speaker tapped his nose. "They won't be long."

Stanley waited for an explanation and looked around at the men. Almost all of them wore the same type of cloth caps, some placed at a jaunty angle and some straight with the peaks pulled low. Several were so thick with grease they were guaranteed to be waterproofed by it. One of the men gave a knowing shake of his head at Stanley and winked as he said, "There's a bit of poetic justice being handed out in there, best let em sort it out between themselves, they won't be long."

And the words were hardly out of his mouth when Bassa came out of the office trying to avert his gaze away from the audience that were gathered, but it was clear to almost everyone that he was suffering from a bleeding nose. He was closely followed by a very tall man with a florid complexion who Stanley had seen around the market several times and he was obviously well respected by the men as they parted like a wave to allow him to pass through.

"Sorry to keep you all waiting lads," he said, "It's all sorted now. See you next week."

And with a flourish he took off his cap and doffed it as if he was greeting a lady.

"That was Juddy Newton," the man next to Stanley explained, "Bloody hell, ah wouldn't like to get t'wrong side of him. Ah reckon Bassa gorr off light wi a bleeding nose."

He went on to explain that not only did Bassa keep upsetting buyers, he was also a bad payer and he had obviously picked on the wrong person to owe money to. Juddy Newton had cornered him in the office, shooed everyone else out and locked the door. It hadn't taken him long to extract the money and dole out some retribution.

Stanley joined the queue, and handed over the six crisp white five pound notes and in return received a chit as proof of purchase which now gave him the right to collect his livestock and take them home.

As soon as he left the office he turned left, intending to go to look for a carter to take his pigs home when he heard someone call him.

"Nah then, Stan, is tha looking for transport for thee pigs?" Turning to see who had spoken, Stanley looked straight into the eyes of a small, wiry old man who was waiting expectantly for an answer.

"Well, aye ah do, but how much will it be and how did yer know me name?"

"Eeh, word travels fast in t'market. Jungle telegraph rules here. Lot thirty three and thirty four you bought. It'll be Adwick we're going to isn't it? Will ten bob be ok? Have yer got yer chit? What did yer reckon to that business wi Bassa?"

Without waiting for answers he introduced himself as Bob Winters.

"Best rig in Doncaster ah av. Best quality trailer. Ask anybody. Everybody knows me. Ah've been doing this job since before tha were born. Ah know Donny like the back of me hand. Trust me, ah'll do a good job."

Well, Stanley decided there was no point in arguing with that, and nodded his head as he tried to make sense of all the questions and statements that came from his new acquaintance.

Within half an hour the pigs were herded into a rather dilapidated trailer that seemed to depend largely on baler twine to hold it together. So much for the best trailer in Doncaster thought Stanley.

Bob indicated for Stanley to get into the passenger seat at the front of the old van, which he did after moving a collection of bottles and empty paper bags. He shared the front seating area with a dog of dubious parentage who greeted him with a glare and a low growl, but Stanley was less worried about the growl than the fact that the dog constantly scratched itself vigorously.

"Has this dog got fleas Bob? It's doing a lot of scratching. Ah don't want its bloody fleas. Can yer put it in t'back of t'van."

"Eeh tha's a bit fussy in't tha? What's an odd flea or two?" Grumbling, Bob opened his door, grabbed the dog by the scruff of his neck and bundled it into the back of the van. "Gerrin there Bob," he said, as the dog bared its teeth at him.

Stanley hid a smile as he wondered why he had given the dog the same name as his own, and as Bob got back in the van he asked him why.

"Well," he said slowly, as he revved the engine and ground the gear stick around in an effort to find first, "Well, ah thought ah'd remember it better if it were same as mine."

It was going to be an uncomfortable journey. That was obvious from the beginning, with Stanley starting to itch from the imagined dogs fleas crawling inside his shirt, and the fact that Bob, far from knowing Doncaster like the back of his hand, seemed incapable of even finding his way out of the market, and only managed to get onto the North Bridge because Stanley had resorted to shouting instructions at him.

Even then he took the right fork just past the River Don instead of staying left and heading straight down the Great North Road. So they were now driving through Bentley, and rather than risk instructing him to turn around Stanley directed him every inch of the way, and they eventually arrived in Adwick from a different direction.

Poor Bob was now completely lost. So much so that his questions had dried up, but he kept up a constant muttering about never having been this way before and didn't know how he would find his way back.

While Stanley had been off on his pig buying expedition, Doris had been busy. She had cleared the wet blanketing from the stairs and the coconut matting from the kitchen floor and hung them to dry and was now in a better mood.

Instead of sending her daughter for their daily jug of milk, Doris went herself, and as the milk was being measured out she told Mrs Smith all about the leaking roof and the mess she had just had to clear up, and she was assured that it would be attended to as a matter of urgency.

And so, by the time Stanley arrived home, Doris had recovered her good humour and the news that they were now the owners of not one pig, but three, turned the wet kitchen into a distant memory.

That evening there was not a more optimistic couple in Yorkshire than Stanley and Doris as they leaned over the wall of the pigsty and scratched the back of their very first breeding pig and christened her Eleanora.

CHAPTER 9

There was a row of buildings that ran the full length of the farm yard and above them were interlinked rooms that had once been used as granaries. They were all connected to each other by low doorways and steps, and were now mostly used to store a variety of abandoned farming equipment.

Empty hessian sacks that were waiting to be patched found their way up there, old bridles and saddles, frayed halters, buckets, huge hampers for carrying feed stuffs, wicker baskets used in the potato picking season, and several patent seed sowing machines that had been bought in the hope of making the work quicker, and then dumped up there when they proved useless. There were broken ropes and rusty chains, three legged milking stools that were now only two legged, zinc baths with holes in them and a large collection of dusty bottles that had once held elixirs that would cure any animal disease, or so the labels said.

Among the motley range of items were many discarded tools, some were broken beyond repair and some riddled with woodworm, but there were a few that had survived and were still strong and usable, with handles worn smooth and silky by years of use. If they could have spoken they would have told of the men and women who had used them, and were now all gone, worn down by backbreaking work.

To Stanley, that granary was a treasure trove, and he selected some of the still serviceable tools, and borrowed them on a sort of permanent basis, and gave them a good home. They were cleaned and oiled every time they were used, and were destined to be still in good order at the end of his working life many years later.

With animals to feed, Stanley and Doris needed a supplier of meal and grain and on Bert's recommendation they contacted 'Otleys', a feed stock merchant in Doncaster. It was to be one of the best decisions they had ever made.

Each week on Thursday evenings their rep, a Mr. Shilito, would call to take their order. He was a tall dignified gentleman, with silver hair, who removed his trilby as he walked through the door, and treated his new customers with as much respect as if they were the most important people on his books, in spite of the very modest orders they placed.

It was he who put forward the idea that they possibly had room for chickens as well as pigs, and offered the name and address of a company that supplied day old chicks for a very low price. He suggested they buy fifty and as Doris looked at him aghast at such a large number he hastened to explain.

"With day old chicks, Mrs Dale, you are bound to lose a few but they are very inexpensive; especially if you buy them unsexed. That means you receive them just as they have hatched out and you take pot luck what sex they are. As they grow and it becomes obvious which are male and which are female, you can sell the surplus and keep some laying birds. You could also keep some cockerels and fatten them up for Christmas. You would find a ready market for the birds if you are prepared to pluck them and prepare them for the table. There's a good profit to be made."

Doris nodded eagerly at Stanley, "Let's do it, Stan, write the address down in your diary."

"Slow down, Dot, we need a shed first and don't forget they need to be fed. Let's have a think about it." But Stanley was as excited as Doris and he carefully wrote down the address.

They were already stretched to the limit financially buying feed for the pigs, but the chicken idea was too tempting to resist, and within the week, a postal order had been obtained from the post office and the chicks were ordered. By return of post came a receipt, and news that the chicks would be arriving at Adwick railway station on Wednesday, on the six o'clock train.

In the back yard of the cottage there was a brick-built building that had once been a stable. The roof leaked in several places but

Stanley selected a dry spot inside and built a small square enclosure and rounded the corners off with strong cardboard. This was to be home for the baby chicks for the first few weeks. The rounded off corners were necessary to prevent the chicks, who, as everyone knows, are not well endowed with brains, and given the slightest opportunity will crowd into corners and smother and trample each other.

They still needed some form of heating to get them through the first couple of weeks, and once again the treasures of the granary were investigated. There, hidden away in a corner, liberally coated with cobwebs was exactly what they needed; a small round paraffin heater, with a central chimney that was slightly battered and rusting around the rim but Stanley could see no reason why it would not light and give off heat.

Taking it home, he sent Eileen off to the hardware store at Woodlands with an empty can, and instructions to buy a gallon of paraffin while he set about cleaning and renovating the heater.

When it was clean and filled with paraffin, he struck a match and at arm's length he touched the flame to the wick. For a moment nothing happened, then with a great whoosh, there was a flash, and a flame and a cloud of smoke rose from the chimney before it went out. Stanley grinned and pulled a face at his daughter.

"Better than bonfire night isn't it?" then added, "Now you see why I said stand back."

Eileen nodded back at him and retreated another step. The second attempt was more successful and the flame regulated itself and soon began to send out gentle warmth. It also sent out a noxious smell which worried Eileen.

"Dad. Won't it gas the baby chicks?"

"No," he said, "It'll be fine when it settles down. We'll leave it running for a bit. We're all ready now, but we can't leave Meg in here all night with baby chicks, she might think they're for her supper. She'll have to sleep in t' house for t' time being till we get her a proper kennel sorted out."

The dog looked up at him as if she understood, and gave a little wag of her tail and certainly didn't give any appearance of being worried about sleeping in the house. She sidled up to Stanley, who felt her stomach, and said she was most definitely in pup following her brief liaison with Punch, the farm dog. Excited at the news, Eileen wanted to know when these puppies were likely to appear but had to be satisfied with her father's answer that he would consult his diary.

At 5.30 on Wednesday evening after a hasty tea Stanley was on his way to the railway station with his young daughter to collect the day old chicks. They took the shortcut down past the mill house and along by the stream, then up the stone steps and over the bridge to the station.

Right on time the huge steam train came hissing and clanking into the station, blowing steam and smoke over the few people waiting on the platform. Some were passengers waiting to climb aboard, but most, like Stanley, were there to collect deliveries.

A motley collection of goods appeared from the luggage compartment. First a pram, then a cycle, and various parcels all wrapped In brown paper; then very carefully, a stack of four sturdy brown boxes all tied together were handed down. The moment all the deliveries were on the platform the porter slammed the doors shut and blew his whistle, and releasing a cloud of steam, the wheels of the locomotive slowly began to turn and the train left the station on its way to its next destination.

As quiet descended on the platform again Stanley let go of Eileen's hand and walked towards the station master.

"Ah think you have my chickens among your deliveries. Mr Dale's the name." He pointed to the brown boxes and without waiting for confirmation, he picked them up and peered through the round holes in the sides to check if there was movement inside.

Little balls of yellow fluff with black eyes stared back at him and chirped their greeting. The boxes seemed to have taken on a life of their own as he felt the movements inside. Stanley stood up and instructed Eileen to hurry, as they needed to get the chicks home and into warmth as soon as possible.

He strode out, trying his best to keep the boxes as steady and level as he could, knowing that tipping them to one side could cause them to crowd on top of each other, and probably result in many of them to dying of suffocation.

They were home in record time and relieved to find that all but two had survived the journey. Doris claimed the job of unpacking them, and as she delighted in the feel of the delicate little bodies, she carefully lifted them out of the boxes and into the enclosure. The paraffin heater gave off a gentle heat and an unpleasant smell while the baby chicks walked and stumbled around it and accustomed themselves to their new home.

Three weeks later it was a completely different scene. The numbers were now down to thirty. The others had managed to commit suicide by one means or another, but Stanley and Doris had expected losses and now hoped they were past the most dangerous stage.

With the baby fluff gone, the remaining chickens were rapidly sprouting feathers and a different attitude. No longer content in the enclosure, they made constant attempts to take over the whole of the building, and so it was just as well that Stanley had finished their makeshift shed and run and they were moved into it.

It was becoming easier to sort the males from the females now and Stanley stated with more confidence than he actually felt, that they had a dozen hens and the rest were cockerels. If he was correct that was perfect said Doris. Twelve laying hens would do very nicely and they would fatten the rest up for Christmas.

As they stood looking at them Doris slipped her hand into her husband's, and said how glad she was that they didn't have to worry about the likes of Jack Jackson, who, they believed, had stolen their chickens when they lived at Winifred Road in Wath upon Dearne.

Stanley agreed, but pointed that there were some shady characters not too far from where they lived now who were not above stealing, and they would have to keep a close watch on their livestock, especially as they got closer to Christmas.

"What we need," he said, "Is a good guard dog. One that will make plenty of noise if there's anybody about at night, and it's no good relying on Meg. She'd probably go and hide at the sight of a stranger, or go and welcome them."

Doris laughed and turning to him she wrapped her arms tightly around him. My Stanley she thought, she loved him with every fibre of her passionate nature. He bent and kissed her and they stood with arms entwined until Stanley remembered how hungry he was.

"Go and make us some supper, will you, Dot? Ah'm famished. Is there any of that potted meat left? Ah'll have some on that new bread from Cooplands."

Releasing him Doris turned to go, "Stanley Dale," she said, "Ah don't know where you put all t'food. Look at you, as skinny as that post. Kettles on t'boil, it'll be ready in five minutes."

He puffed out his chest. "What do ya mean skinny?" and he gave one of his favourite jokes another airing. "Look at this. You too can have a body like mine. And live!!"

Doris was right. He had always been lean, but Stanley had lost so much weight this year he had to rely on braces to hold up his trousers. She was worried about him and she had said as much to his mother, at the same time assuring her that she always made sure he had a good cooked dinner every day.

Ada had said that he looked fit enough. "He never did carry much weight, Doris. He's working such long hours it's no wonder he's thin. Don't worry, he'll fatten up a bit in winter. Give him plenty of stew and dumplings as soon as t'weather turns cold. He likes that."

While Doris went indoors to prepare the supper Stanley took a final walk up the garden to check on the pigs. As he walked, he looked around and thought back over the previous year. He could hardly believe that they had achieved so much. A year ago they had been in despair; desperate to find a way out of Winifred Road, and now here they were, with a large garden, chickens, two pigs for fattening up, and a gilt about to give birth. He could hardly believe their good fortune. Granted the cottage was very basic, almost primitive, but they could put up with it and hopefully persuade Smiths to improve it as time went on.

The two pigs he had bought at market to fatten up were growing rapidly and eating bucketful after bucketful of food that Doris mixed up for them. Not a scrap of leftover food was wasted. Even the tea leaves out of the teapot found their way into the swill bucket that Doris kept under the sink. The neighbours brought their leavings to add to the bucket in the hope of some pork when the time came for the pigs to meet the butcher.

They looked content now, snuggled down together under a blanket of straw, but they raised their snouts hopefully as Stanley leaned over the fence. He carried on the next few yards to check on their main investment, Eleanora.

She looked restless, shuffling about and taking up mouthfuls of straw. She grunted as Stanley stepped into the pen and bent to examine her teats. They were swollen and he ran his hands over her belly. "Now then," he said, "What's the matter old girl?" He talked softly to her as she rolled about and grunted repeatedly, obviously uncomfortable.

"Looks like your babies are on their way. You would start at bedtime wouldn't you?" He rubbed her bristly back and patted her haunches as he said, "Take it easy old girl, ah'll be back in half an hour."

He was back in twenty minutes, carrying a lighted stable lantern, walking quietly up to the pig sty. In the twenty minutes that had just passed, Eleanora had changed from a docile gentle animal into a raging beast, frothing at the mouth and making angry warning sounds as Stanley approached her. Knowing that she was bewildered by the pain she was experiencing for the first time, Stanley held the dustbin lid in his hands as a shield in case she attacked him and settled himself on a wooden stool as far away from her as possible. He took a deep breath. This was going to be a difficult night.

He sensed rather than saw Doris outside the pig sty and whispered to her to go to bed. The less people there were around at the moment the better it would be, and for once in her life Doris didn't argue but whispered back to call her if he needed her.

Stanley settled down to wait and watched Eleanora. She seemed to be calmer now. The lantern gave off a soft light that accentuated the uneven stone walls and made the darkness outside seem blacker than ever. The two pear trees behind the building rustled in the wind and the branches tapped with eerie regularity on the roof tiles. Leaning back, he rested his head against the wall, his eyes felt dry and gritty and he closed them for a moment.

When he opened them again there were four tiny piglets in the straw behind their mother and she was straining to deliver more. Instantly Stanley's tiredness left him and he was as alert as if it were morning rather than the middle of the night. By the time he left the new mother, she had eight babies, and all of them had suckled their first essential portion of milk. Now they were clean and warm, snuggled together in soft chopped straw behind the safety rails he had installed.

He left the lantern hanging in the pig sty and hoped it would stay lit until morning. Walking down the path towards the cottage he looked up at the stars and knew this would be a night he would never forget.

Inside the cottage, there was a dim, flickering light from the candle on the mantelpiece. Doris had gone to bed but had left his nightshirt hanging on the fireguard and the kettle full of still warm water on the hearth. Bringing the washing up bowl from the kitchen he placed it on the table and poured the contents of the kettle into it. The water only half filled the bowl but it was enough, and he washed himself from head to foot, folded his clothes and pulled on the warm nightshirt.

Meg looked up at him from her bed behind the front door, gave a feeble wag of her tail and went back to sleep. Blowing out the candle he felt his way into the kitchen, and bending over the sink he took a drink of water straight from the tap, then went up the stairs wincing and smothering a swear word as he stood on one of the protruding tacks that held down the makeshift stair carpet.

Slipping into bed beside Doris, he curled himself around her and whispered the news that Eleanora had eight babies. But Doris was too deep in slumber land to care and simply mumbled in her sleep as she took his hand and moved her legs away from his cold feet.

Awake at his usual time the next morning Stanley had a vague feeling that something good had happened the previous day and as the mists of sleep left his brain he remembered! Eleanora had given birth! She had done them proud; eight piglets were way beyond their expectations for a litter from such young gilt.

Doris slept on, breathing lighter now, and he knew she would be awake within minutes, but leaving her comfortable in bed he made his way down the stairs, put the kettle on the gas stove for tea and a mug of water to shave with. He dragged on his work clothes and was on his way up the garden path long before the kettle boiled. As he reached the pig sty he could see that the lantern had gone out, but there was just enough daylight for him to make out the shapes of the animals. There she was, good as gold, laid out full length on her side with her babies lined up suckling for all they were worth.

'Whatever had he been worrying about?' he thought. 'She's a natural mother,' and he felt proud that he had been able to spot her potential when he had bought her at market just the month before.

Beginning at one end he counted up the babies. Seven! He decided he must have counted wrong and went through them again. Still there were only seven and he opened the gate and went inside, checking carefully where he put his feet in case he accidentally trod on the missing one. But the missing eighth one was nowhere to be seen and he came to the conclusion that the mother had laid on it and crushed it.

As if to put his mind at rest Eleanora stood up, shaking off the suckling babies and looked innocently at Stanley. He checked underneath her, swishing his hands about in the straw and that's when he uncovered the tiny tail, and he knew instantly what had happened.

 In the moment that he realised she had eaten her own baby, Stanley could quite willingly have taken a stick and beaten her, but what good would it have done? He had to content himself with swearing at her and pushed all the babies under the safety rails hoping they would get the message that that was where they were supposed to go when they weren't feeding.

Slamming the door shut after him Stanley stared at Eleanora; in his mind he could see her chomping her way through all their profits, and he shook his fist at her, and told her in no uncertain terms that she would be off to the f------butcher if she so much as thought of snacking on another one.

"Ah wouldn't mind if she was hungry," he told Doris as he got his razor out and scraped the night's stubble from his face, "But there's still half a bucket of best meal and chopped turnips in the trough."

"Ah can't believe she's done that," said Doris, "Ah'll keep going up and checking on them," and she handed him a slice of thick bread liberally smothered with some of the blackberry jam that she had made the previous week.

Eleanora managed to dispatch another one of her babies by rolling on it and squashing the life out of it and as Stanley told his visiting brother, Harold, that weekend, it just would be the best one in the litter, but thankfully, after that, she seemed to get the hang of motherhood, and reared six healthy young pigs to maturity.

In all the excitement of their first litter of pigs being born and the extra hours he was working, Stanley forgot to check his diary and work out exactly when Meg was due to whelp, but Meg didn't forget and nature took its course, and one night, without any fuss or problems she produced five puppies.

It happened on the very night after she had returned to her regular sleeping quarters in the outbuildings. She had gone straight to the large sack filled with straw that Doris had prepared for her, and settled down with relief as if it was exactly what she had been waiting for. Laying her head on her paws she had closed her eyes, then opened one and looked at Stanley as he closed the door as if to say, "Thank goodness, now I can get some sleep."

When he opened the door again next morning Meg was calmly suckling five puppies. Going slowly across to her Stanley praised her, "Well Meg," he said softly, "Aren't you a clever girl? And you've managed all by yourself."

Meg lowered her head, looked up at him and lifted her back leg to show her babies off. It was clear to see how proud she was of them, and Stanley stroked her head, before he gently looked at each puppy as they stumbled against their mother and searched for her teats.

Eileen gained in popularity at school that day as she disclosed the news of the puppies and suddenly there was a competition to be her best friend. But the offers of friendship depended very much on whether they would get viewing rights to see the puppies. When it was made clear that Eileen's mother would definitely not allow it, the popularity faded as fast as it had started.

The puppies grew at an amazing rate as puppies do, and as they grew, Meg seemed to shrink, losing weight and condition. She was no longer a young dog and the strain was beginning to tell on her so Stanley was eager to find new owners for the pups.

Four of them were images of their mother with silky coats and beautiful markings and they were spoken for very quickly but no one seemed to take to the fifth one and it was true she had not the charm of her siblings but something about her appealed to Stanley and he decided that they would keep her.

They christened her Lassie and found, as she grew, that what she lacked in looks she made up for in character and courage. She had inherited the same long legs as her father, the farm sheepdog, but her fur was short and rough to the touch. Her head looked ever so slightly small for her thick neck and Stanley discovered that it was almost impossible to keep her on a leash due to the fact that her small head meant she was able lean back on the collar and pull it straight over her head. But on the plus side she walked obediently at his heel with barely any training and followed him like a shadow.

Where her mother, Meg, was timid, and refused to go anywhere near the bullocks, Lassie was fearless, and at command would herd them into a corner with no regard for her own safety and slipped in and out among them, dodging their kicks and attempts to stand on her.

She dispatched rats as quickly as any terrier and was soon in great demand on threshing days when the vermin were disturbed from the stacks of straw.

She was very territorial and Stanley hoped she would make a good guard dog and so she would have, if it hadn't been for the fact that she refused to bark. Instead she lay silently in wait for any intruders. Her other great fault was that she was inclined to slip over to anyone she took a dislike to and give them a quick nip on the ankle. Stanley never was able to cure her of the habit and in the end she had to be left at home in her kennel guarding the livestock.

CHAPTER 10

The next big event in the farming calendar was the potato harvest and in the early hours of a misty morning in October it began. For the first time at Smiths, a tractor and spinner had been hired. As the machinery made its way up the field the plough sank into the soft earth and the spinners behind it scattered the potatoes to the surface. Bert watched and nodded his head in approval, and turning to Stanley and his fellow workers, he commented that it was a great improvement on what they had previously used, and then he went on to give them their instructions. They were to set large wicker tubs out at fifty yard intervals right around the edges of the field.

"We're tackling it different this year," he said, "The tubs mark stints. Two women are to work together. They just keep going from one stint to the next and empty the potatoes into the tubs. The machine will keep moving constantly, they'll soon get the hang of it."

No sooner were the words out of his mouth than the lorry pulled into the field. On the open back of it were seated around twenty women of various ages and sizes. Many of them were miner's wives intent on earning some extra money for themselves. Almost all of them wore a headscarf wrapped around their heads turban style, covering hair that was tightly wound onto steel curlers. They wore a variety of old clothing that was deemed suitable for nothing else but rough land work. A loud cheer went up from them as they saw the tractor and spinner, knowing that the modern machinery would make their work much easier.

Individually, each and every one of them was kind, generous, and polite, but in a bunch they were formidable and raucous, and capable of embarrassing any new young male worker. As they spotted Stanley the bawdy comments and innuendos began, but coming from a mining area, he had heard it all before, and he grinned as he let it wash over him.

Each one of the women was given a basket and directed to their position in the field. The autumn mist hung over the land but it promised to be a good day once the sun broke through.

By ten o'clock they had made good progress, and they stopped for what was known as snap time. Stanley found himself seated on the ground next to Florrie, who was the unofficial leader of the gang of women. As she lit a cigarette and took a deep drag at it she asked Stanley how long he had worked at the farm, where he was from, and if he was married.

He watched her as he answered her questions and wondered when the smoke would reappear. Somehow he managed to work into his reply that he was fattening some cockerels up for Christmas.

At that news, all the long lost smoke came streaming down her nose and through her mouth and wreathed its way around her head as she began laughing. Waving to two of her nearest mates she shouted,

"Hey up lasses, Stan here is going to have some fat cocks at Christmas. How about it? Anybody want one?"

Stanley laughed with her but held up his finger and shushed her. "Keep it quiet. Ah don't want all bloody Adwick to know. Ah might have some pork an all. Ah've got a couple of pigs that will be ready at Christmas.

Being serious Florrie said, "Ah get yer Stan. Ah'll have a word with t'lasses at dinnertime."

Stanley handed her a piece of paper and a pencil from his haversack.

"Here, anybody who's interested, tell them to write their names and addresses down and ah'll get in touch with 'em nearer Christmas." Then he added with a wink and a twinkle in his blue eyes, "That's if any of 'em can write."

"Cheeky young bugger," she said, and taking a last drag at the cigarette, she nipped it out, placed it in an old tobacco tin and dropped it in her pocket.

"Leave it wi me Stan. There'll be plenty of customers. Just you make sure it's worth me while."

Stanley held out his hand and they shook on it before Florrie returned to her teasing self and pretended to kiss him in front of all her potato picking companions.

Meat was still strictly rationed and although the government had generously decreed that anyone could keep and kill two pigs per year for their own use, they did not allow anyone to actually sell the meat without a licence and a large amount of red tape.

Stanley saw absolutely no reason for the government to have a share in his hard work, or benefit from the financial risk he had taken in borrowing the money to buy the pigs in the first place. He figured that he paid quite enough tax, and would be doing no worse than millions of others in selling, on what was known, as the black market.

And so he went home elated that night to tell Doris that they had ready-made customers for their pork and cockerels. As he told Doris all about it he remarked that the potato harvest had brought them good fortune and it was about to bring them more.

After the potatoes had been picked it was usual to harrow the field which brought more to the surface that had been missed. Any that were left in the soil would keep growing in the following years and add to the risk of blight developing, so it was important the land was picked clean of the old potatoes.

Stanley offered to pick the 'harrowings' in one of the smaller fields if he could keep the potatoes himself, with the intention of using them as feed for his pigs. His offer was accepted and on Saturday afternoon straight after dinner they began. It was to be a team effort and their daughter, at eight years of age was to be part of the team.

Taking a strip of approximately ten yards each they set off across the field with Eileen in the middle, laboriously picking up every rogue spud that lay white and exposed by the weather and the harrowing of the soil. At first Doris tried to make it into a game for her daughter but Eileen was not fooled and protested at having to work when she would have preferred to have been at the park with her friends. Her mother soon lost patience and told her in no uncertain terms to shut up whining and get on with it.

They had finished by late afternoon on the next day, and had twenty sacks of potatoes to show for their efforts. Doris went home to light the fire and feed the animals, leaving Stanley to decide how to transport his load home. Normally he could have borrowed a horse and cart but there was the strict ban that his employers imposed on working on Sundays, and that included the horses. He had asked Bert if there was any chance that he could borrow the horse and cart just this once but he had held up his hands.

"Well ah'd like to say yes, but you know Mrs Smith's stance on working Sundays, so ah can't say yes officially. So let's say that ah know nothing about it. We haven't had this conversation."

Stanley took that to mean that if he borrowed it and was found out, Bert would say he knew nothing about it. It would have to be his own responsibility.

With the possibility of frost that night it was imperative that he got the potatoes into shelter or all their work would have been wasted and Stanley soon came to the conclusion that what his employers didn't know wouldn't hurt them.

So muttering 'bugger Sunday' to himself he walked back to the stables and collected a halter and a handful of horse nuts for Daisy, the general purpose horse, who was running free in the little field at the top of the farm yard.

Now Daisy was perfectly willing to come to him and eat the nuts he held in his hand, but at the sight of the halter she took off to the other side of the field. Stanley sighed, why did everything have to be extra difficult when he was so tired? All he wanted to do was get the potatoes home then put his feet up for an hour before bedtime.

He walked towards her again holding out his hand with a few nuts on it, but she looked at him sideways and tossed her head as if to say, "You're not fooling me, matey," and she turned sharply around and kicked both heels in the air as if she was young foal instead of a staid old lady.

"What's up, Daisy?" he said in a calm voice, "Don't tell me you've turned religious an all." Under his breath he was cursing their part time man Eric (or Harry Basskin,) as Stanley had nicknamed him. Each time he returned the horse back to the field he took off the halter and slapped the horse with it. So naturally each time Daisy saw a rope she associated it with being slapped and was reluctant to go near it.

Stanley and Geoff, the regular horse man on the farm had both tackled Eric about the practice but he continued to do it and not for the first time Stanley wondered why they employed him at all.

It took him a good hour before he was able to catch Daisy, get her harnessed and backed into the cart. Leading her, he left by the top entrance, well away from the farm house and eyes that could spot him using the horse and cart, and worked at top speed to load the potatoes. There was around one hundred weight of potatoes in each sack and after tying them up, he got down on his knees and hoisted each one on to his shoulders, then slowly rose up and slid it on to the cart.

By the time he had them all loaded he was sweating in spite of the cold that was now beginning to creep in. In the gateway the soil had been churned into deep mud and ruts filled with water, and calling to Eileen who was sat on top of the sacks on the cart, to 'hold tight,' he urged the horse to, "Get up Lass," and they sloshed their way through it, "Well done old girl," he said and patted her neck as he praised her.

Once out of the field they set off down the road trying to be as quiet as possible, but it was no easy feat when the big iron wheels rumbled and the horse's shoes clip clopped, echoing in the late Sunday afternoon quiet. As if that wasn't bad enough, the rest of the farm horses in the big field nearby began whinnying their greeting as they heard their companion, with Daisy calling a loud reply. Stanley put his hand on her mouth and told her to shush, and couldn't help looking back at and grinning at Eileen who was trying not to laugh.

The evening service at the chapel would be due to begin at six o'clock, and the last thing he wanted was to be taking the horse back just when Mrs Smith was walking up to chapel with her prayer book in her hand.

It's doubtful that Stanley had ever unloaded anything as quickly as that load of potatoes, and he was so relieved that he could have cried when he got the cart back into its position under the barn, and Daisy back in her field munching a generous handful of her favourite nuts as a reward. He left the farm by his usual weekend exit which meant climbing through the fence at the back of the barn. He dusted himself down roughly and was walking towards home when he spotted Mrs Smith approaching on her way to chapel. She gave him a knowing look as she said,

"Ah, good evening Stanley. Have you been to check on the animals? I'm afraid they need looking after even on Sundays, don't they?"

Stanley touched his cap, "Oh yes," he said, "We can't neglect their needs. They are all settled down nice and comfortable. Good evening." And he went on his way, thinking that it would be a miracle if no one reported that he had just been using the horse and cart for his own needs.

But thankfully, miracles do sometimes happen and nothing was ever said about it, and Stanley told the tale to his brothers, Harold and Cyril , when they came visiting the following week.

CHAPTER 11

The cottage next door was still unoccupied and the garden completely overgrown. But it had something that Stanley coveted. Right at the top of the garden, adjacent to their own was another pigsty and a tall, dilapidated building that he believed he could repair.

In November, he contacted the owners who agreed to rent him the top half of the neighbouring garden complete with the buildings, for half a crown a month. It would be a drain on their already strained finances but it would mean they could keep more stock.

Doris was doubtful but Stanley was optimistic, "If we can just get through to Christmas," said Stanley, as they sat at the table after their evening meal, enjoying the last cup of tea in the pot, "If we can just get through to Christmas we'll be fine. Once we get the cockerels sold and the pigs butchered we'll have spare cash to invest and pay your mam back." Then he added, "Don't forget we're sending three of Eleanora's pigs in to market this week."

"Ah don't think ah will forget," said Doris, digging him in the leg, "You've hardly talked about anything else all week." She was right, Stanley had been looking forward to sending his very first lot of pigs into market and there wasn't a prouder man there as he heard the auctioneer say, "Now then, gentlemen, look at these, did you ever see more promising stock? They've been reared by Mr Dale; who is standing right here beside me. What am I bid?"

Stanley looked around. Bidding was slow today and he wondered where Bassa was when he was needed to run the price up. But Bassa was nowhere to be seen. Rumour had it that he was selling up after his scare in the market office. 'Good riddance,' was the general opinion, but right now Stanley would have made him welcome.

Then suddenly just when he thought that there were no bidders and he would be forced to pay to have the pigs taken home again, someone called out a figure. It was a price that was unbelievably low, an insulting price, and Stanley held his breath, but quickly the price rose and he began to breath normally again. When the auctioneer's stick slapped down on the clip board Stanley was well satisfied with the price and he couldn't help the smile on his face.

As he travelled home with the money in his pocket his head was full of plans for the future. His first priority was to make sure that Eleanora was serviced by the boar pig and he looked through his diary for the telephone number of Len Beardsley who owned a pedigree large white boar, and made a lucrative business out of transporting him around to service many of the lady pigs in the area.

He got off the bus near Sneap's shop and called in to buy a few sweets as a treat for Doris and Eileen. The shop owner, Mrs Sneap, knew all about his pigs going to market, and wanted to know how they had done. Stanley was happy to report his good news, but was in a hurry to make his telephone call and saying a quick cheerio, went across the road to the red telephone box.

Pushing two pennies into the slot, he dialled the number and waited. He could hear the loud ring at the other end and impatiently under his breath he urged Len to answer it. He was beginning to think there was no one at home and was about to push button B to get his money back when he heard Len's voice. Breathing a sigh of relief he pressed button A which connected him.

"Is that Len? Len Beardsley?" he asked. When the answer came that it was, Stanley talked all in a rush, aware that time was passing and his two pence would soon run out, "Nah then, Len. It's Stanley Dale here, ah've got a sow needs servicing as soon as possible, can tha oblige?" Ignoring the comment that he couldn't, but his boar probably could, Stanley continued, "Look, ah've no time to waste, can tha bring t'boar round as soon as possible before she goes off heat again?"

"Aye ah reckon that can be arranged. It'll cost thee ten bob. It'll have to be cash, of course. Is that ok wi thee? Ah can bring him round in about an hour. What's the address?"

Relieved, Stanley gave him the address and went home for tea. True to his word Len was there in an hour as promised. As he dropped the rear door of his trailer down to act as a ramp, there was a snorting and grunting as the enormous boar pig turned around and prepared to descend. As he lumbered down the wooden slope, he paused and tossed his head so that his ears swung away from his eyes momentarily, and he held his snout in the air. His tusks at either side of his mouth looked menacing but Len reassured Doris and Eileen who were watching from a safe distance.

"He's as gentle as a baby Missus, his name's Billy; just don't get in his way when he smells the lady he's come to see." As if he had understood, Billy walked slowly past them, with his man baggage swinging at his rear end, then broke out into a slow, stiff legged run. "Eh, he's off, get that door open, Stan, and keep out of t'way."

With the mating business successfully concluded, Billy was coaxed back down the garden path and into his trailer, where he tucked into his reward of half a cabbage that Len had left him. As he fastened the trailer door and secured it with the metal peg, Stanley handed him a ten shilling note and asked him if he knew of a butcher who would slaughter his pigs.

"Aye ah do, Stan. There's one lives right next door to me. He's a good bloke and a fine butcher. Does tha want me to pass a message on."

"Well, yer could tell him that ah'll have a ride up on me bike tomorrow if he's at home and make arrangements."

Lifting his cap as a goodbye, Len double checked on his boar, and told him solemnly that he could have a rest now. Then taking the starting handle, he inserted it in the front of the van and swung it a couple of times before it fired up. As he left in a cloud of foul-smelling smoke Stanley looked at Doris and put his arm round her shoulders, and drawing her close he kissed her. "Today's been a good day, Dot," he said, with a contented sigh.

The next day after his stint at the milking was done, Stanley set off on his bike to see the butcher who lived at Five Lane Ends just off the Great North Road, and made arrangements for him to come and slaughter his pigs on the last weekend before Christmas.

With only four weeks to go, Stanley and Doris made their plans and prayed that the weather would be cold enough to prevent the meat going off. Doris said that the cold pantry with its large stone slab would be fine, and Stanley said if need be, he would go and see the fish man, who was known locally as Fishy Poole and buy some ice from him.

In the meantime their finances were stretched to the limit buying feed for all the animals. As there was no overtime in the winter months they were on basic wages of four pounds ten shillings per week. But then, Stanley had an idea, and asked Bert if Mr Smith would be willing to let him do some of the turnip chopping on piece work.

A price of five pound per acre was agreed upon and Stanley began on Saturday afternoon after he had finished milking. He worked until the daylight went and as the field was out of the sight of the farm he was able to work most of Sunday. He finished it the following weekend and collected the much needed five pounds.

It was time to write to Florrie informing her of the date that the pork would be ready and he sent her a letter hoping that she would keep her word; otherwise, as he said to Doris, they would be salting all the pork and turning it into bacon. But Florrie was true to her promise and wrote back by return post telling them that she would be there with the rest of the potato picking gang on the arranged date.

The day before the butcher was due to dispatch the pigs, they set about preparing the cockerels. Tackling them in fives, Stanley wrung their necks, and then they began the laborious job of plucking them. It was something Doris had never done before, although she had watched her grandmother do it many times; and it was not a job she relished, but it had to be done. She was a quick learner and before long they had worked out a system. As she remarked to Stanley, money is a great incentive and they looked with pride on the plucked and dressed birds neatly laid out on the stone slab. Each one had been weighed and priced, and Doris's quick brain had worked out exactly how much they were worth.

Mr Savage, the butcher, was due to arrive at eight o'clock the following morning, and he was there on the dot as the church clock began to strike. Stanley opened the gate for him and noted his clean navy blue boiler suit and the black Wellington boots, and thought that he looked more like a dustbin man than a butcher. He was viewing the day with some trepidation. It was one thing to wring the necks of chickens but slaughtering a large animal was something he had no experience of.

However, Mr Savage, in spite of his appearance, was a professional, and immediately took charge. First he went to inspect the building next to the house where the pigs were to meet their end, and nodded with approval at the clean floor and whitewashed walls. He inspected the strong oak beam that ran across the ceiling and pulled on the ropes that hung from it.

"Right ," he said, and opening the old tartan shopping bag that he carried, he took out a bundle of knives all rolled up in a length of brown hessian, and placed them carefully on the windowsill. He selected one and put it by the side of the others but separate. Then delving into the bag again he pulled out a hammer and gripped it firmly, and swung it back and forth a few times.

"Come on then, Stan; let's get down to the job in hand. Have you ever done this before?"

Stanley shook his head and found that his mouth and throat were dry.

"There's nothing to it lad. Tha's not one of them that faints at the sight of blood is tha? A squeamish pig farmer's got no future tha knows."

"No ah'm fine, let's get on with it," replied Stanley and straightened his back.

They brought the first pig down the path and he came willingly enough, hoping the bucket that Stanley carried held some treat for him. Steering him into the old stable he bent to put the bucket down and heard a dull thud. Looking up he was astonished to find the pig already on the floor stunned, and as quick as he had delivered the blow the butcher had picked up the knife and deftly cut its throat.

A shudder ran through Stanley, but there was to be no time to reflect on what had happened. Mr Savage was busy tying ropes around the pig's back legs, and swinging the ropes over the beam, he beckoned Stanley to help him. Together they hoisted the body into the air and slid the old zinc bath underneath to catch the blood.

"There we are, that's one down, one more to go. Next one might not be so easy. They get the smell of blood tha sees." He was right. There was no coaxing the second one out of the shed and Mr. Savage sighed.

"Ah well, ah thought this might happen. Just hang on there a minute. Ah'll get a barrow." When he returned he was pushing a low flat cart and had the hammer protruding from his pocket. The pig retreated as far into the shed as he could and backed into a corner giving out a high pitched squeal as the butcher entered the shed and closed the door behind him. The pig looked around and tried to run but quick as a flash the hammer found its spot and down he went.

"Come on, quick, Stan, give us a hand before he comes round." Stanley felt like a traitor as he took hold of the pig's legs and helped to swing him on to the flat cart. Within a matter of minutes the job was completed and pig number two had joined his friend swinging from the beam with his life blood draining away.

In the kitchen, Doris, as instructed, had a large quantity of water at boiling point in her washer/boiler. It was needed to help shave all the hair and bristles from the skin of the pigs and Mr Savage wanted it doing as soon as possible.

Filling jugs, they poured the hot water over the pigs, and with sharp knives they scraped them clean.

"Nice pigs these, Stan," commented Mr Savage, "Is there any chance of a mug of tea, we could both do with one."

Stanley nodded and managed a smile. He didn't feel so bad now, and was beginning to appreciate the size of the pigs and anticipate the revenue they would bring in.

The rest of the day passed in a blur of activity and Eileen was allowed out of the house now that the killing was over. She had tried to watch through the keyhole but the view had been limited. So now she went to the doorway of the stable and watched in morbid fascination at the pigs hanging there, but soon ran away as the butcher slit the bellies, and all the innards came tumbling out, filling the air with a foul aroma.

By mid-day most of the butcher's work was done and the carcases were clean and cut in two, with the heads removed. Before he went Mr. Savage gave Stanley instructions on the best way to cut the joints and finally asked if he could take the liver of one of the pigs as a bit of a perk, in addition to his fee.

As Stanley handed it to him, wrapped in greaseproof paper, the butcher said, "My Missus has been told by the doctor that she's anaemic and recommends that she eats plenty of liver. Trouble is, she hates the bloody stuff, but what can you do? Doctor's orders have to be obeyed, so she'll just have to get it down her."

Stanley was anxious for him to be off now and handed him the two pound fee he'd been quoted, telling him as he went, that he would call on him again if and when he needed him.

Alone after he had gone Stanley looked at the carcases and tried to remember what Mr Savage had told him and after sharpening his knife, he took a deep breath and began.

As each joint was cut Doris carried it into the kitchen, weighed it on the old spring weighing scales, and worked out the price before she arranged it to its best advantage on the sheets of paper that covered the old copper. Eileen found her niche writing the price tickets and generally running errands. By the time all the meat was cut and displayed, there was not a single inch of working surface left in the kitchen or the pantry. Thankfully, the weather was bitterly cold and the kitchen was as cool as a fridge.

With no form of communication apart from the post, they had no way of checking that their customers would be arriving as arranged and Stanley and Doris spent an anxious night hoping and praying that they would turn up.

Stanley had a day off work owing to him so he was able to be at home the next day, and it was just as well seeing that his nerves were so on edge; and Doris was no better. So much depended on the pork and the cockerels being sold, and as people do when they are stressed they snapped at each other. Doris's fiery temper blew up and battle commenced.

Doris stormed and said that there was no way they would turn up and it was all Stanley's fault anyway, and added, 'What did he expect from miners wives who smoked and went out on lorries potato picking.'

White with rage at her unreasonableness Stanley shouted at her to stop being so bloody stupid and told her to bugger off back to Wath if that's what she was going to be like every time there was a problem.

Eileen took the opportunity to grab her coat from behind the door and slipped out unnoticed. It was only four days until Christmas and she had been so looking forward to it and now it was all ruined. Tears slid down her cheeks as she walked along the lane until she stopped to stroke the dappled pony in the field next to the Northern Dairies. He listened to her troubles while she fed him handfuls of grass, taking it gently from the palm of her hand with velvet lips. She brushed away the tears, said goodbye to him, and went to see her friend Mary who lived at the mill house.

Back in the cottage, war was still raging between Stanley and Doris, and so intent were they on their argument that they failed to see the black cab that had pulled up outside the house, and also failed to hear the knock at the door. A second louder knock reached their ears and Stanley, in a stage whisper, told Doris to shut up as they were here.

He opened the door to find Florrie on the doorstep surrounded by some familiar faces he had come to know during the potato picking harvest. Apart from their faces, everything else about them was different. No hair in curlers and old clothes now. They were all smartly dressed, wearing make-up, and carefully styled hair.

Florrie smiled at him, "Good morning Stan. Sorry I had to knock so loud. I couldn't make you hear." Then lowering her voice she pulled a face and said, "Having a bit of a row are you Stan? It happens to us all at times. Is it convenient for us to be here?"

Stanley flushed, feeling embarrassed, but managed to recover enough to raise a smile as he opened the door wide and invited them all in.

"We came in a taxi,Stan. Have a look outside. We're travelling in style today."

He clenched his teeth and gave Doris a glare as he went to the window. There in all its stately glory was an old black London taxi cab.

"Newest addition to Askern is that, Stan, so we thought we might as well make use of it. Better than the back of a lorry, eh?" and she shot a meaningful look at Doris who had forgotten her bad temper and remarks, and was now all grace and politeness. But Stanley who knew her so well could detect the slight bristling in her manner, and expected derogatory remarks as soon as they had gone.

But for now it was down to business, and the women exclaimed at the quality of the meat and lost no time in choosing their joints of pork and cockerels, not only for themselves but also for friends and relatives all eager to buy the unrationed meat.

Doris sat at the table with pen and paper and took the money, and with every note that went into her apron pocket her humour improved. By the time the women left every joint and every bird was gone and they would have taken more if it had been available. Doris was thankful that she had hidden some away for their own Christmas dinner.

In the quiet after they had gone Doris had the good grace to apologise and wrapped her arms around her husband.

"Ah'm sorry, love," she said, "Ah don't know what gets into me sometimes. Friends again?" and she held up her face to be kissed.

As usual Stanley hugged her "Ah don't know what gets into you either, Dot. You don't make things easy do yer? Come here, yer little spitfire."

With amends made they sat at the table together and Doris emptied out the contents of her apron pocket and counted the money out. They sat looking at it for a while, barely able to believe that their first business venture had paid off.

Stanley put fifteen pounds to one side to pay back what they still owed to Edith, then eight pounds to finish the repayments on the gas cooker and the washer/boiler. He pushed four pounds towards Doris and told her to buy whatever they needed for Christmas.

"The rest," he said, "We should re-invest. We've done well, Dot, but this is only the beginning. We'll show em. We won't be living in a tied cottage forever."

"No we bloody won't," she agreed, "One day we'll have our own farm," and she tucked the four pounds into her purse as she spoke. "Ah need five bob of this to finish paying for that teddy bear for Eileen. Mr Pinder at the post office has had one laid away for me for ages now. Ah bet he thinks ah don't want it. Our Eileen's been looking at them bears in the window every day since he put them in there." Doris paused and looked at the coats hanging behind the door. "Where is she by the way?"

Christmas 1947 was the best that the family had ever had. Stanley's brother Harold came to stay with his beautiful new wife Marion and they brought Eileen a book of Grimms Fairy tales. That and the teddy bear were presents beyond anything she could have imagined.

Doris roasted a large joint of pork and one of the cockerels in the big fire oven for their Christmas dinner. After all the long austere years of rationing it was a feast. There was no Christmas pudding due to dried fruit still being difficult to obtain but Doris had made one of her famous apple pies and a jug of thick custard to go with it.

Harold, who was just as lean as his older brother, sat back in his chair after he had swallowed the last spoonful of pie, and extending his stomach, declared he had become as fat as a barrel and would be unable to eat another thing until teatime.

Later on, as they took a walk along the village street and into the park, Harold turned to Stanley and said, "By heck, Stan, tha made a good move coming here. Ah envy you."

On New Year's Eve,Stanley and Doris looked back on the year, and marvelled at the way their lives had changed and the progress they had made. Stanley had a glass of milk stout and Doris a tot of whisky from the small bottle that Harold had left them.

It was just before ten o'clock, but they toasted each other and went to bed, as Stanley said, "New Year will have to see itself in. Ah have to be up early for milking tomorrow." Doris lit a candle and turned out the gas light and they went up to bed, full of happy anticipation that 1948 would be good.

CHAPTER 12

In late January there was talk among Stanley's fellow employees that the herd of cows were to be sold, and the dairy side of the farm given up. Stanley heard the news and tried to dismiss it as rumour, but the man who had imparted the news assured him that it was true; he had overheard the boss talking to Bert the foreman.

He worried about it all day and resolved to tackle Bert about it at the first opportunity. In the meantime he would say nothing about it to Doris until he was sure of the facts. 'Just my bloody luck,' he fumed as he worked. Just as they had got livestock and things were improving for them financially, it looked as if he might be out of a job and a home.

Any other day he would have seen Bert several times during his work, but typically, because he so desperately wanted to talk to him, it appeared that Bert had been summoned to the other farm at Hooten Pagnell for the day.

That evening Stanley could bear the suspense no longer, and walked down the lane and across the fields to Bert's house, then knocked on the door. In answer to his question Bert looked him straight in the eye, "Well, it's on the cards Stan. Ah was going to have a word about it tomorrow, sorry you had to hear it that way."

Stanley's heart sank. He was boiling up with anger, and struggling to hold himself in check, "Where does that leave me then Bert? Am ah going to be out of a job? We've just got settled down, and done a lot at the cottage. Ah expect we'll get thrown out, won't we?"

He turned his head away, and clenched his teeth, trying hard not to lose control. 'Bloody farmers,' he was thinking, 'Sweat your guts out for em and they'll turf you out without a minute's thought if it suits em.'

Bert shrugged his shoulders, "Ah honestly don't know Stan," he said, "The boss values you as a worker but with the cows gone we could be overstaffed and it's a case of last in first out ah'm afraid, and then there is the matter of your cottage. As you know it's barely fit for habitation and if it is declared as such, there is no other place available so it's possible he will let you go. But, this is between you and me in confidence, Stan."

Stanley pointed out that in fact, Eric was the last person to be employed but Bert said that as a part timer he didn't count and would be going anyway. Again he shrugged his shoulders and said, "I am sorry, Stan. I really am but it's out of my hands. There's nothing I can do."

As he walked back home Stanley felt as if the bottom had dropped out of his world. This was exactly what he had feared when he had taken the job with a tied cottage. If the job went, the house went. Everything they had been striving for would come to nothing. The pigs and chickens would be sold and they would be back to square one. He swore out loud and picking up a stick threw it into the stream disturbing the moorhens and the ducks.

He was dreading telling Doris. 'Bloody farmers' he thought again, 'They kick you in the teeth whenever it suits em.' He went to bed that night bitter and despondent, and he still hadn't told Doris.

He dreaded her reaction if his job went. He had no doubt at all that she would stand by him, 'But, oh my God,' he thought, 'She will go on and on about it.'

But, Stanley was about to be thrown a life line, and it appeared in the shape of a Fordson Major tractor. The very next week, on the day that he was officially told that the dairy herd was definitely going, he also heard that they would be taking delivery of a new tractor and they would need a man experienced in driving.

Stanley immediately made a verbal application to the foreman, and smiling, Bert held out his hand and said, "The job is yours, Stan, and ah couldn't be happier about it."

Now that Stanley knew he would still have a job when the cows went, he was quite happy to see the back of them and an end to the early morning milking sessions. They were keeping on just two of the cows to provide milk for the farmhouse and the worker's portions of milk. Eric, after all, had been kept on as a part timer to look after the two cows and keep the garden tidy.

Stanley instructed Doris to boil all the milk that came from the farm before using it.

"I wouldn't want us drinking anything that that dirty bugger has had his hand in without it being sterilised first." he said. "I'm surprised Mr Smith has let him stay on. He's useless."

He began work in his new capacity as tractor man first thing the following week. There were several fields waiting to be ploughed, and he set to work on the one nearest to the farm, carefully striding out an equal distance at the top and bottom of the field and then hammered in stakes as a guide for his first furrow. It was essential that the first one was correct or the whole lot would be wrong and it was a matter of great pride that all the furrows should be straight. A field with crooked furrows would come in for a lot of criticism and derogatory remarks from fellow workers and employers alike.

Stanley lined up the big blue Fordson and took a deep breath as he revved the engine and put it into gear. As the plough share bit into the ground and turned the soil over Stanley reflected on how easy it was in comparison to following the horses, and was soon thinking how much colder it was.

As he sat for hour after hour, driving up and down in the freezing cold with his hands and feet completely numb, he remembered how he had sweated walking after the horses and manhandling the plough. 'Bloody hell,' he thought, 'With one method they try to work you to death, with this they try to freeze you to death. You just can't win.'

He got off the tractor every now and then and stamped around, trying to get his circulation going and held his gloves over the exhaust chimney of the tractor to give them a little warmth before he set off again.

It was lonely work out in the fields alone, but that had never bothered Stanley, it gave him time to think and plan the future. He thought now about the article he had read in the local newspaper. It had been written by a man called James Harris who was the leader of the local branch of the farm workers union. The place and the date of the next meeting were listed and Stanley decided that he would attend it.

There were many farmers who disapproved of the union; and some farm labourers were forbidden by their employers to attend the meetings or become members, and were under threat of dismissal if they disobeyed. As Stanley pointed out to Doris that night, the farmers could not actually sack anyone for being in a union but they could always find an excuse to get rid of them if they really wanted to, leaving the worker not only out of a job but out of a home too.

He was only too aware that there could never be a nationwide strike of farmworkers to attain better standards of pay and conditions. It would never happen with such small units of men employed by so many different people, but there had to be a way to improve things for the thousands employed on the land for such low pay, and Stanley was determined to be at that meeting.

He was not sure what stance his own employers took about trade unions but reasoned that if he didn't tell them about it there wouldn't be a problem. And as much as he liked and respected Bert, the same applied to him. He did discuss unions briefly with some of his fellow workers without letting on that he was thinking of joining, but they all seemed to be of the opinion that it was a waste of money.

It was on the tip of Stanley's tongue to say, 'Yes, but you will all be happy to accept the increased pay if the unions are able to negotiate it,' but he bit back the words, and kept it to himself.

On Wednesday the following week Stanley left his warm fireside and cycled the five miles to Carcroft where the union meeting was to be held. There were less than a dozen men there and none of them were familiar to him. Conversation was slow to begin with as they eyed each other up and down, but slowly they began to relax and reveal where they were from, although, he noticed that none of them actually said where they worked, only the villages they had come from.

The union leader arrived slightly out of breath, carrying a battered brief case, with his trousers still wrapped tight around his ankles and held in place with cycle clips. As he pulled the clips off and slipped them into his bag he apologised for his lateness and introduced himself as James Harris and quickly took charge.

After giving them details of how they could become members of the farm workers union, he went on to explain that if they decided to join they would be given a union card, and membership would cost one shilling per week, to be paid when they attended the monthly meetings.

"Any questions?" he asked.

"What if one of us was to get the sack for being a member?" asked the man sitting next to Stanley.

"Well the employer would be acting illegally and could be taken to court," came the answer. There was a ripple of disdainful laughter at that.

"And where would any of us have the money to do that? It's taking me all my time to feed my family on the wages my boss pays me."

"The union would fight your case, Things are changing. We have to stand together to improve things. None of you would have come to this meeting if you did not want better wages and conditions," said James firmly.

There was a murmur of agreement at that and nods of approval. Stanley cleared his throat and spoke up thinking of his own recent experience.

"What if we lose our job through no fault of our own? If we live in a tied house we're out of a home as well as a job, can the union help in a case like that? And what about a decent living wage for farm workers? How does the union plan to bring that about when we can't strike?"

"One question at a time please. First. The position of tied houses. The farmers can terminate their labourer's employment at a week's notice, some can and do, and that's bad enough. But to lose your home at a week's notice cannot be tolerated. It's unfair, unreasonable and medieval. I must admit it is rare that that actually happens nowadays. Few farmers are that heartless. The union is lobbying the labour Member of Parliament for this area for more rights for workers living in tied houses, and the same applies to wages. We have to stand together to get better wages and conditions for farm workers. We have lagged behind for too long. Now who would like to become a member?"

Stanley cycled home with a membership card in his pocket and his union dues paid up for the next month. He worried about the extra expense, but if he could only have seen into the future he would have known that it was money well spent.

The front light on his bike flickered and he crossed his fingers that the battery would last until he reached home. There was certainly not enough light from it to show him where he was going, but hopefully it would satisfy the local bobby if he came across him on his evening patrol.

'The damned batteries don't last long,' thought Stanley, 'But then, it does get a lot of use.' It was the only light they had to go out to the lavatory with in the evenings, and Eileen seemed to be out there for ages. He'd grumbled at her many times about using the bike lamp for so long. If he had but known it, once she got out there in the dark she was afraid to unbolt the door and come out, but would never have admitted it.

He reached the top of the railway bridge just as the battery gave out completely and he cruised down the hill in the gloomy light and decided to take the short cut down by the mill stream. Hoisting his bike on to his shoulder, he felt his way cautiously down the stone steps, holding on to the wooden hand rail. It was pitch black now that he had left the road with its street lights, but gradually his night vision improved, and he was able to make out the well- trodden path. It passed along the banks of the mill stream and through three fields and involved climbing over two wooden styles.

As he approached the first one he could hear the sound of voices. He stopped and listened, there it was again, the murmur of low voices. He thought about retracing his steps, reasoning that anyone hanging about behind hedges in the dark was probably up to no good and Stanley had no wish to cross swords with some of the rougher characters that lived at the other side of the railway bridge in the area that was known as Adwick Lane.

'But then,' he thought, 'It might be just a courting couple,' and convincing himself that that was the most likely reason he carried on, walking as quietly and carefully as he could, and almost stumbled into the herd of Friesen bullocks asleep near the style. One of them staggered to its feet and gave a low grumbling call that awakened the rest of the herd.

Stanley knew cattle well and had no intention of being accidentally trampled by a herd of confused bullocks and before they could all stand up he walked quickly through them with his bike on his shoulder and began to climb the style. It was just as he stood astride it that he heard the shout.

"Bloody hell it's the copper. Run." At that moment it was doubtful who was the most shocked, and Stanley was very relieved to see four shadowy figures running away from him and towards the railway line. He wasted no time himself in crossing the next field and didn't pause until he was through the final gate near the mill house and heading down the lane towards home. As he recounted the story to Doris he admitted that he would not be using the shortcut after dark again in a hurry.

CHAPTER 13

It was Mr Shilito, their feed merchant rep who gave them the idea that was to change their lives again. He had taken a real liking to the young couple and often spent extra time chatting to them on Thursday evenings. He gave them all the news on the farming front and suggested to them that the time might be right for them to apply for a West Riding smallholding.

Stanley and Doris exchanged glances and gave him their absolute attention.

"I'm sure you will have heard of the West Riding properties," he said, " I could give you the name and address of where to send a letter of application if you like, but don't tell Bert or Mr. Smith, I wouldn't want them thinking that I was encouraging one of their workers to leave their employment. It wouldn't be good for my business. You understand? This is strictly between you and me."

Stanley waved his hand, "Of course, they won't hear anything from us." and Doris produced the writing pad and waited while Mr. Shilito wrote the details down in his beautiful hand writing.

After he had gone Stanley looked at Doris and put his hand on her knee. There was such a fizz of excitement running through him, "Do you really think we would have a chance, Dot? It's worth a try. Pass me the writing pad and I'll write a letter."

The remains of their meal were left on the table while the letter was drafted out. It took several attempts before one was written to their satisfaction with no mistakes or crossing out. But eventually it was done and the envelope addressed to the chairman of the committee in Wakefield. It sat on the mantelpiece behind the clock until the next day when Doris walked to the post office, bought a stamp and touched the letter to her lips before she dropped it through the letter box.

It was almost two weeks later that the letter produced any results. Early on Friday morning a large brown envelope dropped on to the mat and Doris slit it open carefully and pulled out the wad of forms that would have to be completed.

At dinnertime Stanley held them in his hand and looked through them, "Bloody hell, Doris, they want to know some stuff. This is going to take some filling in."

Doris was busy cutting the thick crust on the pie she had made, as she lifted it towards his plate the steam rose and the delicious smell distracted him as he watched her carefully deposit a large portion on to his plate.

She ladled gravy on top of it and said, "We can do it, Stan, we'll make a start on it tonight and have it back in the post tomorrow."

Stanley shook his head as he paused with a fork full of pie in his hand, "Ah don't think so Dot. It's more complicated than that. They want names of employers and references. Ah don't want Mr. Smith knowing. He's not going to be very pleased if he thinks I'm planning on leaving is he? And they want to know how much money we have in the bank. Our bank account is not very impressive is it?"

Doris put her hand on his knee, "Yes, but don't forget we've got the pigs and the hens, so we would have some stock to start a small holding with wouldn't we? Mam will lend us some money again if we need it."

Stanley finished his dinner and pulled his chair as close to the fire as he could get, and held his mug out for a refill of tea. He looked at the clock, and shuffled through the forms again.

"I guess they are not so bad, Dot, They just look a bit daunting at first glance. I'll sort out the references." He drained the mug and stood up, pulling on his coat and scarf, preparing for another few freezing hours on the tractor. He gave Doris a kiss and said, "Well, ah've got all afternoon to think about it, see you at tea time."

By the time the afternoon was over he had come to the conclusion that he had no alternative but to take Bert into his confidence and ask him for a reference. In addition he had the ones he had received from Norman Flint and Teddy Downing in Wath.

As he drove into the farmyard, dusk was falling, and he spotted Bert, his foreman, walking up the yard towards him. He reversed the tractor into the old cart shed and the engine came to a stop, leaving the low roofed shed full of paraffin and petrol fumes.

Bert appeared in the doorway as Stanley, stiff legged with cold, climbed down from the tractor, "Now then, Stan, how's it going? You'll have nearly finished the twelve acre won't you?"

Stanley nodded and taking off his gloves rubbed his hands together to get the circulation going, "Aye, ah've just got the headlands to do. It's turned over well. Erm, ah was hoping to see you Bert, ah wanted a word with you. In confidence like."

Bert looked at him and waited while Stanley dug in his pocket and produced his handkerchief. His nose was so cold he could barely tell if it needed blowing or not, but he had no wish to risk speaking to Bert with a dew drop hanging on the end of his nose.

"Well it's like this," he began, and explained his need for a reference. "It's not that ah don't like working here Bert, but ah don't want to be a farm labourer all my life. Ah need to make a better future for my family, and ah'm worried about Mr Smith knowing. Ah don't want to put my job at risk, you understand?"

Bert drew in a deep breath between his teeth and pulled a face. "That puts me in a funny position Stan. Strictly speaking I am supposed to keep Mr. Smith informed on these kind of matters but ah can see that you and Doris are ambitious and ah admire that." He hesitated, "So yes. Ah will write it for you. But keep it quiet. It's just between me and you."

He held out his hand and Stanley shook it and thanked him before adding, "Just one thing. Ah want to get the application forms off as soon as possible, so could ah av it tomorrow?"

Bert gave a wry smile, "Don't push it, Stan. Aye go on. Ah'll write it tonight. Now get off home for your tea and get warmed up. You look frozen."

"Aye, you can say that again. One day somebody will invent a heater for tractors to keep the poor drivers warm."

Bert laughed, "Good idea, Stan, but ah can't see it ever happening. See you tomorrow."

After tea, Doris took away the pots, and brought out the pen and ink, whilst Stanley spread the forms out on the table directly under the gas light. He took a deep breath and in his best handwriting began with the first page, blotting each piece carefully as he went along.

When it came to the part that involved their bank account Stanley stared into space, recalling that at the moment their Midland Bank account held exactly four pounds fifteen shillings, which was equivalent to one week's wage. They had twenty pounds hidden away in a cocoa tin under the mattress, but most of the money they had made from the pigs and chickens at Christmas had been reinvested in more stock. He bit the end of the pen, and then before Doris could argue with him, he wrote down that they had one hundred pounds in their bank account.

Doris sat up straight, "But what if they want to see the bank book, Stan?"

Stanley gritted his teeth emphasizing his strong jaw line, "Well in that case, we'll just bang every penny we have into the bank and borrow some from your Mam again. It's got to look as if we have something behind us Dot, or we won't stand a chance."

"Mmm, ok." Doris agreed, and got up to put another log on the fire, "We'd better go to bed when this has burned Stan, we're running low on wood."

He turned towards the fire, the log looked wet and hissed as it struggled to ignite. "It's not much bloody good is it?" he said, indicating the few remaining logs in the hearth. "Ah'll see if ah can find something better at the weekend. That was the only good thing about Wath, at least we could always get hold of some cheap coal."

He folded the form carefully and slotted it into the envelope. He stared at it for a moment before placing it on the mantelpiece to wait for Bert's reference to be included, and picking up the kettle he took it into the kitchen to have his nightly strip down wash.

A single candle flickered in the kitchen and Doris called to ask if he wanted her to light the oil lamp.

"Nah, its ok, ah'm a big lad, ah know where me arms and legs are. Ah don't need a light to find 'em." He picked up the red carbolic soap and began to wash his face, taking care to avoid his eyes with the lather, knowing from bitter experience exactly how much it could sting them.

Bert was true to his word and handed the reference over the next morning, and by the afternoon the forms were in the post and on their way to Wakefield.

For the next couple of days Stanley and Doris were in a buoyant mood and full of excitement; until the letter arrived from Edith. The moment it dropped on the mat Doris had a sense of foreboding and turned the letter over in her hands several times before tearing it open.

Dear Doris and Stanley,

I don't want to worry you both but I think you should hear what I have just been told. Doris, it appears your father has left Wath and gone to live in Scunthorpe and the house that was willed to you has been sold. There has never been a sale sign up but the new people are already living there.

I think you need to see a solicitor about it as soon as possible. I don't know how they have been allowed to do it. They have gone against the will. Sorry to have to write with this news as I know how upset you will be but I knew you would want to know.

Love Mam xxx

Doris read the letter again, her lips tight. Her instinct was to put her coat on, go straight to the bus stop and catch the bus to Wath right there and then. Her emotions swung between anger, deep, deep anger that boiled inside her, and a need to sit down and cry.

Bitter thoughts went through her head. Why would her father do that to her. She had never done anything to him and now he had taken her inheritance away. He had actually sold the house that her grandfather had bequeathed to her. He couldn't be allowed to get away with it.

She sat on the hard wooden chair and laying her head on her folded arms, she wept, and as the tears flowed, she remembered all the times when she had longed for her father to acknowledge her, and all the times he had walked past her in the street without so much as a glance. She thought of all the times she had passed the big house in the centre of Wath and seen her grandmother sitting in her rocking chair in the bay window watching her as she walked by and given her not the slightest sign of recognition.

But gradually the anger took over and she washed her face and began to plan. She could hardly wait for Stanley to come home for his mid-day dinner break and she met him at the kitchen door. Thrusting the letter into his hands she demanded, "What do you think of that, Stan? It came this morning. We'll have to go to Wath tomorrow and see the solicitor."

Stanley threw his ex-army overcoat on to the settee and sat down. Like Doris, he read the letter several times while she piled the food on to his plate and hovered at his side waiting for his comments. He looked up at her.

"They can't do this, Dot. It's illegal. It says in that will of your grandads that the house is yours when your Dad dies. He only has the right to live in it during his lifetime. Maybe your Mam's got it wrong, love. Don't get upset." He got up and wrapped his arms around her. "Come on, love, buck up. Our Eileen will be home from school in a minute for her dinner. You don't want her seeing you like this do you?"

Doris wiped her face on her apron, put her daughter's dinner on top of the oven and sat down to try and eat her own.

It was clear that they would have to make the journey to Wath to find out for themselves if Edith had got her facts right and also to see a solicitor if it were true. Arrangements were made for Stanley to have a day off work on Thursday of the following week. In exchange, Bert had agreed that he could make up the time by putting in extra hours every evening.

Thankfully it was now late February and the days were lengthening so he was able to put in an extra hour before darkness fell. As he reached the bottom of the field he spotted the small figure standing near the gate and realised that it was his daughter waiting for him to finish work. He stopped the tractor and beckoned to her to climb up and take her usual seat on the mudguard by his side.

"Hold tight, love," he said, "Just one more round then we can go home, Are you cold?"

She smiled at him and shook her head, refusing to admit that her feet were frozen and her hands numb on the cold metal mudguard. It was well worth suffering them to be able to ride on the tractor with her Dad.

As they left the field Stanley opened up the throttle and slipped into top gear. The tractor surged forward and suddenly they were both laughing with the exhilaration as the wind blew in their faces and cold hands and feet were forgotten.

On reaching the top of the farmyard Stanley leaned forward and turned the little brass tap that switched off the paraffin and allowed the carburettor to empty. Doing that ensured that it could be filled with petrol the next day and the engine started and warmed up before converting back to paraffin.

Meanwhile Doris had spent her day fretting about the prospect of their visit to Wath, and worrying about their appointment with the solicitor. Thursday could not come quickly enough for Doris and she had gone over and over the possible outcome until Stanley was heartily sick of hearing about it.

He didn't really care about the house much himself, he had never been able to envisage Doris actually inheriting it, but he was well aware of what it meant to her. It wasn't just the value of the house. It was the sense of rejection that hurt her and the fact that her father thought so little of her that he would take what was rightfully hers.

By Wednesday evening Doris was as tense as it was possible to be and she snapped at Eileen and Stanley every few minutes, her face grim and lips pursed ready for a fight with anyone who got in her way. Eileen was sent to bed and Stanley wished it was still daylight so that he could get out into the garden. Eventually bedtime came but of course neither of them were able to sleep and they were thankful when the alarm clock rang.

The pigs and chickens were fed in record time and Stanley and

Doris set off at eight o'clock to catch the Doncaster bus. Eileen had been given strict instructions to set off for school at the usual time, and to come home at lunch time and eat the sandwich that Doris had left in the pantry for her. The key was to be left in the shed under the dog's bed and it was impressed on her to make sure that she locked the door again afterwards.

Eileen said "Yes, Mam," and gave a sigh of relief when they set off. She could hear her mother's shoes tapping as she walked along the road outside the cottage with her arm through Stanley's and behind the safety of the net curtains Eileen pulled her tongue out at her mother and felt much better for it.

Once in Doncaster, they walked to the other end of town to catch the Barnsley bus which made slow progress passing through Conisbrough, Denaby and Mexborough, picking up passengers at every stop until there was standing room only. Stanley gave up his seat to an old lady who was carrying two bags of dirty washing, which, she informed Doris, she was taking to her daughter's house as she had 'one of them new-fangled washing machines.'

"Have you got one, love?" she asked Doris. When Doris just shook her head, hoping to discourage further conversation she continued, "You want to get your husband to buy you one, then you can sit down while the machine does it all for you."

Curtly, Doris told her that as they didn't have electricity in the house, there would be no point in buying one of the machines, and in any case she had more important things to spend money on, and she turned her head away pretending to be absorbed in the passing scenery.

The old lady tutted and muttered about her being a stuck up cow and fortunately got off at the next stop, standing on Stanley's toe as she passed him in the struggle to get to the door with her bags.

It was almost ten thirty when the bus pulled into Wath. Their appointment with the solicitor was for eleven o'clock so they had a good half hour to spare, and although they had no agreed plan they automatically walked towards the house in Bridge Street. With no hesitation Doris walked right up to the door and taking hold of the shining brass knocker raised it several times, banging it as loud as she could, then turned her back on the door and stared down the familiar street.

Stanley had seen her in some rare old tempers but he had never seen her look so angry as she did at this moment, and as she turned back towards the door again he felt sorry for whoever answered that knock.

He took her arm, "Steady on, Dot," he said quietly in her ear, "Keep that bloody temper of yours under control. Try and stay calm. You'll get nowhere with a shouting match."

But Doris was in no mood to be reasonable and she shook his hand away. At that moment the door was opened and there stood a young boy about the same age as their own daughter. That was the last thing that Doris had expected and her temper cooled instantly.

"Hello love," she asked, "Is your Mam or Dad in?"

The boy sniffed and held his handkerchief to his nose, "No missus. Me Dad's at work and me Mams gone to t'shop. Ah've got a bad cold and ah can't go to school."

Doris smiled at him and Stanley marvelled that her mood could change so quickly. "Ah can see you're poorly, love. Will your Mam be long?"

"No she won't. She's here. Who wants to know?" Stanley and Doris turned towards the voice and saw a tall well-dressed woman standing right behind them, with her hand on the gate. "Yes?" she continued, "Can ah help you?"

Recovering herself Doris stood up as tall as she could. "Yes, I am looking for Mr. Bramham. Mr. Larrett Bramham. I'm his daughter."

"Oh. Well, ah'm sorry, but they left and moved to Scunthorpe. Didn't he tell you?" she asked suspiciously, staring into Doris's eyes, "We bought this house from him a month ago."

So, it was true. Stanley and Doris looked at each other and instinctively joined hands. Stanley felt there was no point in going any further with the conversation and tried to draw his wife away, but Doris was not finished yet and declared, "Well it was not his to sell. It's my house not his." Her voice was becoming louder with every word, and people were gathering at the gate, eager to listen in, loving a diversion to their usual dull routines.

Stanley pulled Doris firmly away and nodding to the crowd told them to clear off and mind their own business.

From there the couple went straight to the solicitor's office and stood outside for a few minutes while they composed themselves. Unsure if they should knock or just walk in, they hesitated, staring at the brass plaque on the wall that declared that these were the offices of Smith, Morgan and Morgan with several letters after their names. Taking a deep breath Stanley squared his shoulders, grasped the handle and opened the door.

They entered into what was obviously a waiting room. The only occupant in the room was the receptionist sitting behind a highly polished oak desk. She looked up as they entered and peered at them over the top of her steel rimmed glasses.

"Yes? Do you have an appointment?"

"Mr and Mrs Dale," replied Stanley in his firmest voice. He recognised the woman. He had delivered coal to her back in the days when he had worked for Flint's and remembered that she was always a slow payer.

'So,' thought Stanley, 'Don't you put airs and graces on with me lady.' Of course he said nothing aloud but looked at Doris and raised his eyebrows.

"We have an appointment with Mr Morgan, senior," said Stanley, holding himself at his tallest and giving her one of his steely blue eyed glares. It was clear that she had not recognised him as she indicated for them to be seated on the hard leather chairs that lined the wall facing her, and they sat down, silent and tense.

For ten minutes they sat waiting, listening to the loud tick of the clock and the scratch of the woman's pen. A fire smouldered in the grate at the far end of the room giving off little heat in its struggle to stay alight. It was bitterly cold in the room, with an icy wind blowing under the door and Stanley and Doris looked at each other, and then at the fire, and each knew what the other was thinking.

The buzzer on the desk sounded loud, startling both of them, and the woman stood up and told them to follow her, as Mr Morgan senior would see them now. Unlike his receptionist, Mr

Morgan was full of charm and old fashioned courtesy and half rose from his seat giving a sort of little bow. Stanley almost expected him to kiss Doris's hand, but she was not prepared to be charmed or pacified, and came straight to the point as she sat on the chair facing him across his desk.

"We've come about number seven Bridge Street. It was left to me in my grandfathers will. My father was allowed to live there in his lifetime then it was to pass to me." She stopped then, her voice shaking.

"Ah yes, Mrs Dale. I remember your grandfather very well."

Stanley interrupted, "Can you tell us why her father has been allowed to sell the house?"

Mr Morgan fiddled with the papers on his desk for a moment before replying. "I can assure you, Mr and Mrs Dale, that the will has been followed correctly, but the executors have used their discretion and allowed the house to be sold on condition that some bonds were purchased from the sale. They will eventually become yours, Mrs. Dale." He paused as he took off his glasses and began to polish them. "After the death of your father of course," he added and Stanley noticed that there was a tiny trickle of sweat running down the side of his face in spite of the coolness of the room.

After further indignant questioning from Doris he admitted that any interest accrued from the bonds would be paid to her father during his lifetime.

Doris sat on the edge of the chair, her whole body giving off signs of indignation. Her dark eyes were almost black with rage and for a moment, as the solicitor looked at her, he could see the likeness to her grandfather, who had sat on that very seat several times consulting him on business matters, and he drew back as he took a sharp intake of breath.

Anxious now to bring the meeting to a close he looked pointedly at the clock and stood up.

"There's nothing more I can say on the matter Mrs. Dale. I have given you the facts. If you wish to contest the will I am afraid I would not be able to act for you as I am the solicitor for the executors of the will.

Doris faced him across the desk, "I think you mean you are hand in glove with them don't you?" she said as she struggled to control her voice.

"I am very sorry that you feel like that Mrs Dale. I can only suggest that you see the executors yourself if you are not happy about it." He gave a little nod as he held out his hand which both Stanley and Doris ignored, and he continued, "There will not be a charge for this consultation."

Stanley took his wife's arm, "Don't worry, you wouldn't be getting paid even if you sent a bill."

Leaving the office they walked to the bridge over the canal and sat on the low wall with their backs to the black still water beneath them. Stanley put his arm around Doris's shoulders and pulled her close. They were both too stunned and emotional to speak and both knew that they were in no financial position to think of employing a solicitor to act for them and well aware that it would be a waste of time approaching the executors of the will.

As the cold from the stone wall began to creep through their clothes Stanley turned to Doris. Tears were running down her cheeks and he wiped them gently away with his thumb. "Come on love, let's get the next bus home," he said quietly, and they walked arm in arm through the High Street and were just in time to see the Doncaster bus approaching.

It was such a relief to be on the bus and know they were heading out of Wath and Stanley nudged Doris as they were about to pass the top of Winifred Road.

"At least we're out of there, love," he said, and Doris brightened a little and gave him a wobbly smile.

"Well, that's that then," she replied, referring to the interview with the solicitor. "To tell the truth, ah'm not surprised, I always thought he'd find a way to fiddle me out of what should have been mine," and she gave a deep shuddering sigh.

It was late afternoon when the bus dropped them off at the end of Village Street in Adwick. The sight of that pretty street with its stone walls and overhanging trees raised their spirits and Stanley steered Doris in the direction of Sneap's shop on the corner.

"Come on, love," he said, with the air of a man about to treat his wife to a big night out, "Ah'll buy us some spice for tonight and we'll have a game of cards after tea."

"Aye," she replied as she gave his arm a punch, "And no cheating this time."

He thought for a minute, "Tell you what, Doris, ah think we deserve a treat. Let's go to t'pictures tonight. There's Bud Abbot and Lou Costello on, we could do with a laugh. Our Eileen's been on about it all week."

They walked the rest of the way home hand in hand, passing the lovely old St. Lawrence's Church on one side and the well-kept park on the other. Even in late February it was attractive, with masses of snowdrops and clumps of crocus pushing their way through like stars in the grass.

There was a surprise waiting for them at home. There on the table was the letter they had been waiting for, in a long brown envelope with a Wakefield post mark over the stamp.

With a little trepidation Stanley slit it open and looked at the contents, with Doris peering over his arm. They read it together, then grinned at each other. It was from the West Riding County council confirming that they had received their application and they had been accepted on to their list. In future would be invited to apply for any suitable smallholdings that became vacant.

CHAPTER 14

Rising early the next morning, Stanley set about feeding the pigs before he went to work. It was just beginning to get light, and as he closed the door on the huge black sow who was the latest edition to their stock he paused and looked around.

Their garden and the plot they rented from next door resembled a mini smallholding. Every inch had been put to use. They now had two breeding sows, four store pigs that were being fattened up to butcher and sell, and a small flock of hens that were producing enough eggs for their own use and some left over to sell at the door.

They also had ten cockerels that were being fattened up and Stanley reflected that the sooner they went the better. The older they got the more aggressive they became, and they regularly chased Doris and Eileen down the path with their wings outstretched.

Stanley looked at them strutting about in the run and gave them a warning. "Don't get too big for your boots, you lads. You'll be in an oven before very long," and then he had a quick glance around, hoping that he had not been overheard by any of the workers on their way to the council yard just down the lane.

The cockerels had the freedom of one side of the garden during the day and he knew that Doris would let them out later on, and grinned as he had a mental picture of her running down the path with the birds in hot pursuit, and he thought to himself that there was no doubt her language would be colourful.

Just time now to take a look at Eleanora, who was due to have her third litter and her bulging sides promised a good number of piglets. She had managed to resist eating any of her offspring when she had had her last litter, but she was quite the clumsiest pig he had ever seen and had trodden on two of her babies and then laid on top of them, squashing them flat. And he contemplated that if she did the same again he would send her into market while she was still a young sow. He would talk it over with Doris later.

But there was no more time to waste admiring his own stock, he was due at work in five minutes and he picked up his ex-army haversack and walked across the road to begin his working day.

He arrived at the entrance to the farm just as Eric came cycling along in his own unique bow-legged fashion with his heels on the pedals and his knees splayed. As usual he was wearing his turned down Wellington's that were liberally coated with dried cow muck and a filthy tweed jacket with no buttons. He had a half inch of stubble on his chin and his dirty grey hair straggled below a greasy cap.

Stanley looked at him in disgust. He had completely lost patience with him and given up all pretence of politeness.

"Hey up Stan," Eric called, "Ah'm helping you wi t'tatie riddling today."

"Oh aye, and is tha planning on doing any work then or is tha going to spend all day dodging it as usual?"

His blunt words were lost on Eric, he was quite immune to insults and he slid his feet along the ground as he came to a halt and swung his leg over the seat of the bike as he dismounted. As he did so he displayed the rip in the crutch of his trousers that exposed his slack underpants and gave a brief glimpse of what they failed to cover.

Stanley put his hand over his eyes and exhaled a long breath. "Bloody hell, Eric," he said "That's not a sight anybody's prepared for at this time in a morning. Pull thee self together man," and he walked away grinning to himself and thinking how Doris would laugh when he told her about it.

He was pleased they were riddling potatoes today. It would be the last of the previous year's crop that they would be sorting, and Bert had said that he could have the ones that were damaged or too small to sell to the wholesalers as ware potatoes. They were known as pig potatoes, and that was exactly what Stanley intended to use them for.

They had to be cooked before they could be fed to the pigs of course, so Stanley had removed the top of a round five gallon oil drum with a hacksaw, and attached handles made from wire rope. After giving it a good scrub it was perfect for cooking up large amounts of potatoes and whatever other waste food they could find. To begin with he had made a fire pit out in the garden to use for boiling up the pig swill, but Doris reasoned that it was a waste of fuel when they had a fire going in the living room.

Every morning as soon as the fire was glowing red, she carried the drum into the house, pushed it on to the bars and as far into the fire as it would go, then topped it up with water and left if there until the potatoes were thoroughly boiled. Carrying the drum into the house was hazardous enough, and carrying it out again full of boiling pig swill was much worse, but Doris managed it every day, and considered it well worth the risk and the effort for the saving in the feed stock bills.

For a while Stanley had had an arrangement with the fish and chip shop at Woodlands to take all their waste; and the pigs had loved all those tasty fish bits. He had made a little trailer to fit at the back of his bike and rode up there after work twice a week to collect it all from the back door of the fish and chip shop. But it had had to be boiled along with the potatoes and the smell was indescribably disgusting and spread into every room, and Doris refused to have it in the house. No one was more relieved than Eileen when that arrangement was cancelled.

Stanley opened the door of the tractor shed and breathed in the aroma of petrol and paraffin as he set about his routine of checking the fuel and water before he cranked the engine with the starting handle. As it burst into life clouds of smoke belched from the chimney, filling the low, old fashioned building that had once been a cart shed, with enough fumes to make Stanley cough and choke, and he quickly went outside to take a few deep breaths of fresh air before he returned to climb aboard and drive the tractor out of the shed.

Once he had hooked up to the trailer and loaded the heavy scales and all the equipment needed for the job, he set off for the field. Geoff, the horseman, went with him, and stood on the drawbar at the rear of the tractor exchanging news with Stanley in a loud voice to make himself heard above the sound of the engine. They got on well together and Stanley gave him a description of the state of Eric's trousers and the views of the dirty, loose underwear that it would be better to avoid.

"Bloody hell," said Geoff as he laughed, "It doesn't bear thinking about. God knows what his bits are like, the last bath he had was the one the midwife gave him."

Once in the field, Stanley and Geoff set about uncovering the potatoes that had been preserved there since they had been picked back in September. First they had to scrape off all the covering soil to expose the thick layer of straw that had been keeping the potatoes free from frost for the last few months.

It was hard work and in spite of the cold weather they were both soon sweating and they cast off their coats, laying them across the back of the trailer, well away from the pile of dusty sacks. The sun broke through the clouds, transforming the surrounding countryside and reminding Stanley that spring was well on its way. A robin sang in the nearby tree and Stanley had one of those moments of pure joy and happiness and he sang softly as he worked.

"Tha sounds happy, Stan, has tha come up on t'pools?" asked Geoff.

Stanley laughed, "If only," he said, "Every bloody team ah pick on t'pools seem to have players with two left feet, they couldn't score a goal if t'posts were fifty foot apart. No, ah reckon ah'll always have to work for what ah get. But ah'll tell you what, yesterday me and Doris had to go to Wath on business, and it reminded me all over again how pleased I am that we got out of it and live here."

He went quiet for a minute or two concentrating on the rat's nest that they had just uncovered. "Watch out for rats, Geoff, we could have done with t'dog here," As he spoke a large rat made a dash down the pile of potatoes, went straight under the trailer and disappeared into the dyke. Geoff scooped up the nest and threw it as far into the field as he could. "Ah hate them bloody things," he said with a shiver.

Stanley agreed and then continued their previous conversation as if nothing had happened. "Aye, if only t'cottage were in a better state. It's been that damp this winter; it looks as if a tides creeping up t'wall. Our Eileen is badly half the time; she has one cold after another. She's off school now, poor kid. The whole house needs modernising, but they won't spend a penny on it."

Geoff nodded, "Ours is not much better Stan. It looks good from the outside but inside is a different kettle of fish; but at least we've got electric in and a water toilet. It's wet through wi damp though."

He lived in an attractive stone built cottage alongside the Great North Road at Woodlands and although it was more up to date than Stanley and Doris's cottage it still left a lot to be desired and Geoff's wife struggled to bring up their five children in it.

Putting his head on one side, Stanley declared that he could hear Bert coming with the horse and cart, which meant that the women would be arriving with him to begin work sorting the potatoes. He walked to the hedge and craning his neck looked over at the road.

"Aye they're on their way. Ah'd better get the riddle going. Bert won't want the women standing about doing nothing."

By the time Bert pulled Daisy to a halt beside them the engine on the riddle was running smoothly and Stanley slipped it into gear, sending the metal bars shaking and rotating round and round like an iron conveyor belt.

The women arranged themselves around the machine, two to each side ready to begin sorting. Geoff stood at the end with sacks attached on hooks waiting to be filled and they were ready to begin.

Stanley lifted the first batch of potatoes onto the riddle, shovelling them up with a large scoop that was like a blunt edged fork and known as a sippet. It was impossible to hear over the noise of the engine and the rattle of the riddle and they worked in silence apart from instructions or warnings that were occasionally shouted out loud.

Sometimes Stanley counted how many times he bent down and lifted the heavy sippet full of potatoes in a minute, and from there he worked out in his head how many per hour, and then per day, but he gave up when the numbers began to run into thousands and thought he would rather not know. He looked forward to morning break time when he would swap jobs with Geoff. It was certainly no easier bagging up the potatoes and stacking them on the cart, but at least it gave them both a change.

Just as the engine was switched off ready for the break, Eric was spotted walking into the field with a big grin on his face, and a cheer went up from the women. Stanley went over to Geoff and said, "For God's sake Geoff, don't let him start climbing on and off the trailer. If the women see the state of his trousers they'll have a field day. They'll torment the life out of him."

Geoff looked at Eric. The rip in his trousers had extended and was clearly visible. He beckoned Bert and pointed it out. For a moment Bert stared at him and his lips twitched and he sighed as he shook his head and said, "Bloody hell, he's going to have to go, the silly fool's a liability," and taking Eric to one side he uttered a few words in his ear.

Still cheerful and unperturbed Eric gave them all a wave before he trudged off pushing his bike and whistling tunelessly.

Stanley went home that night with several sacks of potatoes for pig feed and the news that he had sold all the cockerels to the women he had been working with. Doris was delighted and said she would be more than willing to prepare them for the oven. "That'll teach em to chase us down the garden," she said as Stanley wrung their necks, and she was already calculating how much they would weigh when they were plucked and ready for the oven.

Over the past few months, from the profits of the eggs that Doris sold at the door, she had saved enough to buy a gas water heater for the kitchen and thought it the height of luxury that they no longer had to boil every drop of hot water they needed in the kettle. And that was not their only indulgence. A radio had been purchased!

There had been great excitement on the day that they went to Fox's, the electrical shop in Doncaster and came out carrying a large box containing a modern radio with a light wood surround. They had hardly been able to wait to get it home and listen to it. But it proved to be a temperamental piece of equipment that slipped off the station at the slightest excuse, producing obscure hissing sounds, interspaced with the odd foreign word now and then that no one could understand, and it needed the most delicate of touch to return it back on to the programme they had been listening to.

It also used up batteries at a faster rate than they could afford to replace them and so the times they listened to it had to be strictly rationed. Doris became a follower of Mrs. Dale's Diary, which came on at four o'clock every day for fifteen minutes but she switched it off the minute the programme ended.

The episodes of Dick Barton, Special Agent, at a quarter to seven were listened to avidly every evening, and the plays and comedy shows gave their life an added lift. Previous to the arrival of the radio their entertainment had been mostly reading and playing cards, and the occasional visit to the cinema.

Doris had always been a great reader and had been delighted when she discovered the local library at Woodlands. It was a good two miles away but Doris looked forward to her regular Friday night visits to renew her books.

It was the distance she had to walk and the time it took that persuaded Doris to accept Stanley's challenge that she should learn to ride a bike.

"You could get there in a quarter of the time Doris. Come on, have a go," urged Stanley, several times, until eventually, she agreed, but made the condition that she should try in the meadow at the back of the house.

Stanley sighed and pointed out, "But it's rough ground in the field, Dot, and it's full of cow shit. Tha'll end up falling in a cow pat. It'd be a lot easier down the lane."

But Doris was adamant and stated, "Ah'm not having everybody watching me, Stan, and that's that."

So Stanley shrugged his shoulders and lifted the bike over the fence into the field, wondering why Doris had not learned to ride a bike when she was a child like everyone else. He was very soon to find out why.

He held the bike steady while Doris got herself into position on the seat and adjusted her skirts on the crossbar of the man's cycle. "Right, start pedalling, Dot," he called, as he gave her a push. "Don't worry, ah'm holding you. Go on. Pedal. Pedal." and he ran alongside holding the back of the seat, "Keep going, tha's doing well. Keep to where the grass is short. Go on. Keep going."

Doris, for her part, pedalled as fast as she could, her face grim with determination and kept calling out, "Don't let me go, Stan."

But Stanley had already let go, and was standing still, watching and panting from the exertion. Doris carried on for a good twenty yards before she realised that she was riding on her own and promptly fell off. Unable to help himself Stanley bent over, put his hands on his knees and laughed until tears ran down his face.

The scene was repeated several times until Doris was frustrated at her lack of success, and Stanley was exhausted by running at her side. It all ended when a blazing row developed and Doris stormed off, saying that she had managed this long without riding a bike, and she didn't need to ride one now, and finally ended by telling him what he could do with the bike and where he could put it.

He had more luck teaching his daughter to ride and she was soon wobbling up and down the lane on the much too large man's bike. By stretching her long thin legs she was just able to reach the pedals with her toes, and began dreaming of owning her own bike, but it would be some time before that vision came true. In the meantime she used her father's bike to run errands for her mother and the only time she fell off was when she came around the corner too fast, crashed into the wall and acquired a bump the size of an egg on her head. She never did it again. Pain is a good teacher.

CHAPTER 15

It was in the summer of 1950 that Stanley and Doris decided it was the right time to increase their family and they were soon looking forward with great excitement to a new son or daughter. The baby was due the following March and Doris began collecting all the clothes and equipment they would need.

Edith, Doris's mother, after recovering from the shock of becoming a grandmother for the second time, went into a frenzy of knitting, and in her own style produced many baby cardigans of varying sizes in lemon or white, and even impressed everyone with her ability to knit a lacy pattern.

On one of her shopping trips at Woodlands, Doris saw a pram advertised in the window of the newsagents and memorising the address set out to look at it. Navigation had never been Doris's strong point but by asking directions numerous times, she eventually arrived at the right house which was in the middle of a large estate that had been built for the miners who worked at Brodsworth Colliery.

The moment Doris saw the large, black Silver Cross pram she fell in love with it, but managed to remain nonchalant and examined the hood as if seeing faults. The seller looked on anxiously and wheeled the pram back and forth a few times as far as the crowded room would allow. She picked up her little girl and jiggled her on her hip.

"She's grown out of a pram, she just needs a push chair now. But ah've always looked after it as you can see. We really need the space, these rooms are so small."

Doris said nothing for a moment, and then hesitantly said she would think about it. Just as she reached the door she turned and looked back, "How much did you say you wanted for it?"

When informed that the asking price was seven pounds she looked sad. "Oh, it's a bit more then I can afford to pay for a pram. I can only spend five pounds. What a shame. I do like it. I could have taken it right now. I've got a five pound note in my purse."

The woman nudged her husband who sat reading the racing paper, totally oblivious to the negotiations that were going on right beside him. "What do you say, George? Can ah let it go for five pounds."

Looking up from his paper he sighed, "Ah don't know. Do as tha likes. Tha usually does. Don't involve me in it. It's nought to do wi me." And he raised his paper again and shook it in annoyance at being disturbed.

His wife looked at Doris and raised her eyebrows and gave that look that all women understand. "Men," she mouthed silently. Then aloud she said, "Aye, ok you can have it for five. Ah want it out of the way."

Doris walked home pushing the pram and admiring the way it bounced gently as she went up and down the curbs and felt so pleased with the bargain she had struck. She smiled as she thought that Stanley would be very proud of her.

And of course Stanley was extremely proud of her, but not because of her bargaining skills, although he had to admit they came in useful. Every time he looked at her he was struck by her beauty, and never more so than now, when she was carrying their second child. But more than anything else it was her strength of character that he admired and he knew that she would work alongside him and support him to her dying day.

Arriving home with the pram Doris positioned it in the corner of the living room behind the front door that was rarely used and stood back to admire it, promising to herself that she would give it a thorough clean and polish the following day, but for now she switched on the radio and listened to Mrs Dales Diary while she laid the table for tea.

As Stanley walked in after finishing work he was struck by the size of the pram and the amount of space it took up. But seeing how delighted Doris was with her bargain he rocked it a few times and said complimentary words of admiration before he sat down and leaned back in his chair. Doris stood by his side watching him, knowing he would not be able to resist making some droll comment; and she was not to be disappointed.

With a grin on his face he put his arm around her waist as he said, "Bloody hell, Dot, Ah've seen smaller cars than that. "What's tha planning on putting in it? Triplets?"

Doris laughed as she gave him a pretend punch and told he would just have to wait and see.

The next morning a letter postmarked Wakefield dropped through the letter box. Doris was suffering from a little early morning sickness but it vanished as she held the envelope in her hands. She propped it up against the blue striped milk jug on the table and looked at it as she plaited her daughter's long hair into two thick plaits and tied them up with the checked ribbon that had spent the night curled into a roll on the mantelpiece.

The letter was addressed to Stanley but as soon as she had shooed Eileen off to school with instructions not to dawdle in the park, she sat down and slit the letter open. Her heart seemed to miss a beat as she read the words.

The council, was inviting them to apply for a smallholding of ten acres. There was a black and white picture of the house on the second page of the letter and already Doris was imagining them living there and visualising all the stock they could keep in the buildings attached to the house, and dreaming of all the fresh vegetables they could grow on the land. Enough to feed themselves and plenty left over to sell thought Doris.

She could hardly wait for Stanley to come home from work and see the letter that had arrived, and she went about her chores in automatic mode as she dreamed of the future. It was not until mid-morning when she was collecting the eggs that she realised she had not noticed exactly where the smallholding was.

She could not believe she had been so lax and hurried back to the house and opening the letter again she scanned down until the address leapt out at her. Goldthorpe! The smallholding was in Goldthorpe a well-known mining village and she threw the letter down in disgust.

With her pregnancy playing havoc with her hormones and emotions Doris put her head in her hands and cried tears of disappointment and even the sight of the elegant pram standing in the corner could not raise her spirits.

Meg crept close to her and laid her chin on Doris's knee and nudged her hand until she stroked her. As Doris sniffed and wiped her eyes Meg stood on her hind legs with her front paws on her knee and wagged her tail as she gave a little woof and a doggy smile as if to say 'cheer up'.

By the time Stanley arrived home for his dinner at mid-day Doris was back on form, and as she showed him the letter she explained where the smallholding was situated, eager for him not to suffer the same disappointment that she had experienced, but at the same time she could not help the agitation she felt at the thought of moving back into another mining area.

"We're not going there Stan. Ah'm not going and that's that."

"Calm down, Dot. We're not going. Don't get in such a state. Ah' don't want to go any more than you do." He pulled a face as he studied the letter and sighed. "Ah well," he said, "At least it shows they have not forgotten us. Ah'll write back tonight and tell them we won't be applying due to the location."

Eileen arrived home from school for her dinner at that point and, sensing the mood, sat down quietly at the table. Doris plonked her plate in front of her and Eileen stared in dismay at it. Today's dinner was beef stew and her plate seemed to consist mostly of large uneven chunks of onion which she hated. Pushing the onions to one side she ate the rest, and still hungry, looked to see what the pudding was.

Doris produced a large apple pie from the oven. It was usually one of her specialities but today's effort was an exception and even Stanley who normally ate anything she put in front of him, stared at the thick slab of pastry with a small amount of apple in the middle of it.

"Bloody hell, Dot," he said, "Tha's gone a bit mad wi t'headland today. Is there any custard to soften this lot?"

He turned and winked at Eileen and she grinned at him while Doris's back was turned and made a face at the pie on her plate.

There were just ten minutes to spare before Stanley was due back at work and he put his arm on Doris's shoulders and kissed the top of her head.

"Come on, love," he said, "Let's go and have a walk round the estate and see how t'pigs are gerrin on." Walking up the garden path after dinner was something they did almost every day and Doris pulled on her cardigan and followed him outside, calling to her daughter to wash her face and hurry back to school or she would be late.

Eileen was sitting on the sofa lost in another world as she read her library book but her mother's words seeped through, bringing her back to reality and with a groan she put the book under a cushion and wiped around her mouth with the dishcloth, before putting on her coat and setting off for the afternoon lessons.

Stanley was pitching his idea to Doris. "What we need, Doris," he said, "Is some transport. We could afford a second hand car now. We really need one, Dot. If the right place comes through from the West Riding we'll need some transport to go and have a look at it. They're not all on a bus route are they?" He paused and waited for her reaction.

Doris's face was set and her lips pursed in the manner that she had when she was thinking something over. "Oh, ah don't know, Stan. How much would it cost?"

"Well, ah reckon we need at least £80 to get something reliable, but ah'll have to get back to work now, I'm going to be late. We'll talk about it tonight. Have a think about it," and he set off at a fast walk then broke out into a run as the church clock began to strike.

Left alone, Doris walked slowly back down the garden path deep in thought and ignored the chickens clamouring at the wire netting expecting a few treats from her. A car! Could they really afford to buy a car? Her quick mind was adding up the funds they had, and calculating how much the latest litter of pigs might fetch at the market.

She stopped off at the lavatory and sat down on the smooth wooden seat, automatically noticing that the squares of newspaper hanging by a string were almost used up and she made a mental note to remind Eileen to prepare some more from the softer pages of the Farmer and Stockbreeder magazine.

At the same time her mind had moved on to thinking of the advantages of having transport. They would be able to visit her mother and Stanley's family, and then she thought of having trips out to the coast on Sundays and she gave a happy sigh as made her decision. She would tell Stanley that she agreed with him.

Doris was not given to singing when she was happy, but today she hummed softly to herself as she went back into the house and began to clear away the remains of the dinner. She gave a little shiver of excitement at the thought of herself and Stanley actually owning a car.

When Stanley returned home from work that evening, Doris was waiting on the doorstep, with a smile on her face. "Well?" he said, not needing to say more.

"Ah've had a good reckon up, Stan, and I think we can just about afford a car and still leave something in the bank to show the West Riding council if they come up with a smallholding for us."

She grasped his hands. "It's going to make us a bit short of cash though, until we can send another litter of pigs into market." Doubt flashed across her face. "Maybe we should leave it, Stan."

"Make your mind up, Doris. Do you think we can afford one or not." Disappointment made him speak sharply. "Look. Ah've had a word with Bert and he's agreed I can contract to chop the last couple of acres of turnips. That'll bring us an extra ten quid in, and the two store pigs are about ready to go. The hens are still laying, so we've got some eggs to sell. Surely we can afford a cheap second hand car." He pushed past her and went to the sink to wash his hands and sighed as he lathered the red carbolic soap into them.

He stared out of the window for a moment before he said in a voice throaty with emotion. "Ah work every hour God sends, Dot, and so do you, surely we're entitled to a bit of pleasure now and then. Ah think we should go ahead and get the car."

Immediately Doris realised how low he was feeling, and went across the room, wrapped her arms around him and laid her head on his back as he stood at the old brown sink.

Eileen, who had been following her father into the house, stayed just outside and observed the whole scene, and deciding her presence was not needed, disappeared up the garden path and out into the field with the two dogs.

By the time they all sat down to tea, order had been restored between Stanley and Doris and with big smiles on their faces they told their daughter that they would soon be getting a car, but she was not to tell anyone until they had actually bought it.

She couldn't fathom out any reason for it to be a secret but knew when to obey, and kept thinking happily to herself what her mother had said about them being able to go to the seaside in it. She could hardly wait for the sleek, shiny car that would soon be standing outside their house waiting to take them out on trips.

In 1951, second hand cars were still in short supply due to loss of production during the war. Stanley soon discovered that the only car they were going to be able to afford was likely to be a very old one. But he was quite prepared to accept that and was full of happy anticipation as they set off the following Friday evening for the motor auction at Sprotborough, with their money securely fastened in his inside pocket.

The motor auction had only recently been set up and was held every Friday evening in a large ex-army Nissen hut. Getting to Sprotborough proved easy enough and they would have arrived in good time if only the bus conductress had not put them off two stops early, informing them that this was where they needed to be.

Stanley had a nasty feeling the moment they got off the bus, and asked the first passer-by where the motor auctions were held.

"It's about a mile in that direction, mate," came the answer to his query. "You should have stayed on the bus for another two stops. It's a long walk. The next bus will be here in about an hour."

Stanley looked at Doris, "Bloody hell, Dot," he said, "That's messed things up. We'd better call it off for today. It's too far for you to walk." and he looked down at her feet and added, "Especially in them shoes."

Doris was now seven months pregnant but still insisted on wearing her court shoes. "Rubbish, Stan," she replied, "Come on, ah'll be fine," and hooking her arm through his, they set off walking.

Stanley looked down at her, smiled, shook his head at her stubbornness, and matched his steps to hers. They arrived just as the auctioneer took his place behind the high desk with a clipboard of papers in one hand, a gavel in the other.

"Now then you ladies and gentlemen," he began, and Stanley reflected that most of the auctioneers he knew seemed to begin proceedings with exactly the same words, and wondered to himself if they had all been trained at the same place.

Both ends of the Nissen hut had large doorways that were opened to allow each vehicle on sale to be driven through for the buyers to view. Unfortunately it turned the building into a sort of wind tunnel, and the potential customers shivered in the icy blast that whistled through the corrugated iron building. They stood pressed up close to one side with the auctioneer opposite them and watched as the motley collection of cars and vans were paraded in front of them.

Stanley stood as close as possible to Doris to protect her from the worst of the wind and she smiled at him but he could see how cold she was and bending towards her he whispered, "Are you ok, Dot? Do you want to go home and leave it for another day?"

As she shook her head he removed his scarf and wrapped it around her shoulders and turned his collar up high. The first car through was an old taxi cab that sent out clouds of black smoke from its exhaust and had large patches of rust clearly visible around the doors. The man behind them remarked that it looked as if it ran on coal and nutty slack judging from the amount of smoke that it sent out. But to Stanley's amazement the bidding was brisk and it was soon knocked down for just over one hundred pounds.

As it left the auction another vehicle entered the tunnel. A van this time, that was in an even worse condition. It made thirty pounds and as it left with its engine spluttering it back fired twice and stopped, leaving the new owner to push it out, with the help of a couple of onlookers.

Stanley's spirits were sinking as one weary motor after another passed through, each one leaving a cloud of smoke to add to the cocktail of fumes that hovered near the top of the building. Stanley could now see the advantage of the open doors at each end. Without them they would probably all been overcome by the gas.

Just as he was about to abandon all hopes of acquiring a car that day the auctioneer announced, "And now, folks, we have a delightful little Austin seven, in good running order. A 1932 model. Well looked after as you can see. She's very economical, and perfect for a small family. Here she comes. Now just look at this, ladies and gentlemen."

Before the words had left his mouth, the Austin appeared at the end of the building and was slowly driven to the front of the bargain hunters. In no way could it be described as streamlined. Modelled like a square building block, it showed its age and had obviously been hand painted in a rather bright shade of blue, but its engine ticked over evenly and there were no rust patches as far as Stanley could see, and a bubble of excitement churned inside him. This could be just what they had been looking for!

"Come on then, you good people." called the auctioneer, "Let's get this over and done with, then we can all go home. Come along now, we've got a right little cracker here. Who's going to start the bidding?" There was complete silence and he gave an exaggerated sigh. "Everyone's asleep are they?"he said.

The wise cracker behind Stanley quipped, "No they're all bloody frozen stiff." When the laughter and mutterings of agreement died down the selling began again.

"Come on then, start me off at twenty quid," and the hands began to go up. But Stanley refrained from bidding until the price reached fifty pounds. Then he put up his hand and soon there was only himself and one other person bidding.

The price crept up slowly, ten shillings at a time until the seventies were reached. His mouth was dry and he swallowed knowing he was nearing his limit of eighty pounds. Doris was gripping his arm so tight he thought she would cut off the blood supply. He knew she was silently telling him not to go above the agreed price and he glanced quickly at her, noting how cold and tense she was. He looked back towards the auctioneer and gave a slight nod to him. Seventy five pounds and ten shillings he had bid. The other bidder shook his head and the hammer went down.

The car was theirs. He could hardly believe it, and he put his arm around Doris and led the way out through the crowd towards the makeshift office. He carefully counted out the money and received the paperwork for the Austin in exchange. He also received a key which, he was told, would only work for the driver's door. The passenger door could only be secured from the inside.

"Ah'm not sure if it works," Stanley was informed by the man behind the office desk, "A spot of grease might sort it out," then added under his breath as he turned away, "Tha won't need to lock it up no one's likely to pinch it." but he gave Stanley a cheery thumbs up sign as he glanced back.

As far as Stanley was concerned it really didn't matter if the car was old. It was theirs, bought and paid for, and he opened the door for Doris with as much pride as if it had been a Rolls Royce.

The engine was still warm and started easily at the first swing of the starting handle, and he folded himself into the driving seat of the tiny car with his long legs almost doubled up under the steering wheel.

He pressed the accelerator and the little engine revved feebly. Stanley let in the clutch and set off. The lights flickered and a dim beam lit only a few yards of the road in front of them, but thankfully, the moon was out and the lights were barely needed.

As they had no tax or insurance for the car, Stanley decided it would be prudent not to go home through Doncaster town centre, and instead, chose the back route out of Sprotborough, via the quiet country roads that would eventually bring them out onto the Great North Road just a few miles from Adwick.

The flaw in the plan was that the back road out of Sprotborough led them down a steep hill at one side of the River Don; and that was where he discovered just how bad the brakes were. With the brake pedal pushed to the floor boards the car still continued far too fast down the hill and Stanley sent up a silent prayer that there would be no on-coming traffic when they reached the sharp corner at the bottom.

Doris had complete confidence in her husband's driving ability, but she soon picked up on his anxiety, and saw the grim look on his face. Realising that they were going very fast she gripped the sides of her seat and drew a sharp intake of breath that verged on a scream.

But their guardian angel was watching over them and they rounded the corner and drew to a halt on the iron bridge that crossed the River. Doris reached over to Stanley and gripped his hand, and they were both silent for a moment as they looked across the river towards the waterfall that made such a beautiful picture in the bright moonlight.

"Bloody hell, Doris," Stanley commented, "That made the hairs on the back of my neck stand up. Ah'll have to have a look at the brakes. They probably just need new brake pads."

"How much will they cost, Stan?" she asked, forever mindful of their finances.

"Oh, ah should be able to get some for a couple of quid," he said, bluffing, as he had not the slightest idea how much brake pads cost, but he was eager to divert Doris away from realising just how close they had come to having a serious accident.

However, the hill at the opposite side of the river soon took their minds off the rapid descent they had just made, and also made them forget about the cost of repairing brakes.

As they left the bridge the road turned to the left and they were straight on to a hill that climbed sharply up out of the valley. Immediately the engine began to fade. Frantically Stanley went down the gears until he was in first, but it was clear that the engine would never carry the car and two passengers up the hill and they quickly ground to a halt.

That was bad enough, but worse was soon to follow when it became clear that the brakes were just not capable of holding the car and they began to roll backwards.

Stanley had never been a religious man, but he sent up his second prayer of the evening and happily someone must have been listening, as they met no one on their backwards descent down on to the bridge again.

As they rolled to a halt, Stanley closed his eyes and said a thank you. Then full realisation of their situation hit him, and between clenched teeth he cursed his luck, the car, the hill, the weather and anything else that he could think of.

Now that they were under the trees it was much darker, with only a thin glimmer of moonlight lighting the inside of the car, and probably it was just as well that it was too dark to see the expression on Doris's face. But, he could certainly hear the anger in her voice as she let blast about him having bought a car that was useless.

"You've wasted all our money, Stanley. Turn round, we'll take it back and ask for our money to be refunded."

Stanley gave a biter snort of laughter, "We can't do that, Doris. It was an auction. You buy as seen. Talk sense. They don't give refunds. You know that."

But Doris was in no mood to listen to reason. "Well turn the bloody car round and we'll go back the other way through Doncaster."

He sighed and swallowed, trying in vain to stay calm.

"Doris, shut up a minute will you? Don't you realise we can't turn around and go back. If the car won't go up this hill, how the hell do you expect it to go up the one we have just come down? It's just as steep as this. Be quiet will you, while I think."

"Oh bloody hell," said Doris, "What are we going to do?"

The ideal solution, thought Stanley, was for a lorry to come along with a nice friendly driver who would give them a tow up the hill, but that was hardly likely to happen at this time of night. He was just going to have to go and get help, and he put the idea to Doris.

"You'll just have to stay here with the car Doris, while I go back and get some help."

Doris however, was having none of that, "Not bloody likely, Stanley. Ah'm not staying here on my own in the dark. Ah'll come with you."

"Don't be silly, Dot. I might have to walk all the way back to where the auction was held, it's much too far for you in your state."

"Ah'm not staying here and that's that, Stan," and he knew it was a waste of time arguing with her.

"Well, there only one other way, Dot. Ah'm going to have to reverse it up the hill. But it won't carry both of us. Can you manage to walk up it?"

Doris said nothing more but got out of the car and slamming the door behind her she began the slow walk into the darkness carefully picking her way in her court shoes along the edge of the road, flinching at every rustle in the trees.

Stanley turned the car around and gradually inched his way up the hill backwards, going only slightly faster than Doris's walking pace. He held his breath most of the way, only dragging in a heavy, shuddering mouthful when he had to.

He thought he had never felt so relieved in his life when he reached the top, and parking the car on the first level piece of ground he could find, he ran back down to rescue his wife.

Doris was almost crying when he reached her, and was so thankful to have him by her side that she forgot her anger for the time being.

"Don't you ever do that to me again, Stanley Dale," she said, and then added, "Well, at least it's warmed me up, except for my feet. Ah think they are frozen solid"

"Ah'm not surprised in them shoes. You should get some boots for winter, Doris."

In spite of her cold feet Doris looked at him in disgust, "You know what you can do with boots, Stan. Ah won't be wearing them." And she wriggled her cold feet out of the court shoes and rubbed them.

Stanley had other things on his mind. He was worried about the car and as much to himself as to Doris he said, "Don't worry about the car, Doris. It just needs a bit of sorting out."

That turned out to be a vast understatement and many years later they were able to laugh about it, but it was no joke at the time.

CHAPTER 16

Stanley spent the rest of the winter evenings gradually taking the car to pieces and reassembling it. He began with the brakes, patiently taking them apart on the living room table directly under the gas light, on a thick blanket spread out to protect the highly polished wood. He cleaned each one and reassembled them and assured Doris that they would now work much better. Doris received the information with a derisive, "hmm," but Stanley knew he would win her over once the car was in running order and they were able to take the long awaited trips out in it.

He had discovered that the two rear tyres were almost without tread and showing the canvas in several places and he knew they would have to be replaced. He imparted the news to Doris and watched her expression. He knew what was coming but he had chosen his moment well and picking up his haversack he pulled on his cap and said he would have to get off to work, leaving her to rant and fume about 'how much the damned car was costing them.'

By the time March came around, the car was almost ready to use and Doris was nearing her confinement. She was heartily sick of feeling heavy and clumsy, and couldn't wait for her baby to be born.

The midwife, who visited her every week now, had said that her blood pressure was too high and instructed her to rest more. That was like expecting a bird not to fly and Stanley threatened to tie her to the sofa if she didn't sit down and take things easy. Doris did try to rest but it was against her nature, and the sight of a piece of fluff on the floor or a film of dust on the furniture had her jumping up to clean it.

Stanley had now taken over the hens and all the other outside chores that his wife usually took care of, and work on the car had gone on hold for the foreseeable future. It stood looking forlorn in the back yard, with its rear axle propped up on bricks until the day came when they could afford the new tyres.

Doris's mother, Edith, came to stay for a few days and set about the washing that was piling up. She thought that her daughter's gas washer/boiler was a marvellous invention, in spite of the heavy agitator inside the machine that had to be turned manually back and forth for at least ten minutes with every load of clothes.

The water inside the washer was heated by a gas burner that was situated under the tub and the gas was supplied to it through a rubber pipe. The gas point was at the opposite side of the room and it meant stretching the pipe as far as it would go. It had to be strode over in order to get to the sink, but it was a small price to pay for having the convenience of a modern gas washer/boiler and so far no one had fallen over the rubber pipe.

Edith had very different cleaning methods to her daughter. Doris was a tin of polish and a cloth person, and polished everything in sight, while Edith believed that a scrubbing brush and plenty of hot water was the right way to go. It was not long until Doris began to get irritated. She snapped and grumbled until even her good natured mother had had enough and went home a day early leaving them to fend for themselves.

It was in the early hours of the 9th March that Doris began to feel twinges of pain in her back, but said nothing to Stanley as he set off for work. The baby was not due for another week but by late morning she realised she was definitely in labour and when Stanley arrived home for his dinner he found his wife curled up on the sofa waiting for a contraction to pass.

"Bloody hell, Doris. Why didn't you send for me? Let's get you upstairs and I'll go and get the midwife."

Stanley pedalled his bike as fast as he could up Tenter Balk Lane to the midwife's house. As he went he recalled the last time he had done the very same thing when Eileen had been born, and he remembered how hard their lives had been back then and how they had worried about the cost of having to have the doctor. At least now, thanks to the new free health service, they wouldn't be afraid to call the doctor if he was needed.

Checking that he had the right address, he knocked on the door and waited impatiently for an answer. He took off his cap, wiped the sweat from his forehead and took a few paces back and forth praying that she would be at home and not out on a call.

He was in luck, the door opened and he doubted that he had ever been so glad to see anyone in his life. Receiving the news that his wife was in labour, the midwife smiled calmly and with maddening slowness said, "Ah, it's Mr. Dale isn't it? You go back home. I'll be along very soon," and she smiled again and nodded at him reassuringly as she closed the door on him.

Stanley had just arrived back home when his daughter walked in, expecting to find dinner on the table as usual.

"There's no dinner today, love," he said, as he filled the kettle and put it on the gas ring. "Get yourself some bread and jam and we'll have a cup of tea. Your Mam's going to have the baby today."

Eileen gave a little "Oh," then thought about it. "What time?" she asked, "Will it be soon? I've got to go back to school at one o'clock."

She was aware that her mother would be giving birth and needed the nurse to help her but was very hazy about the actual facts.

Stanley sighed; he was not very good at this sort of thing and wondered why Doris hadn't explained things more clearly to her.

But he was saved from any more questions by the arrival of Nurse Metcalf, the midwife, who breezed in, full of matter of fact confidence, patted Eileen on the head, and told her that she would soon be getting a little brother or sister, and wasn't it exciting? Without pausing for breath she added, wasn't it time she was off back to school?

So for the first time in her life Eileen was sent off to school with a jam sandwich in her hand and she sat on the swings in the park to eat it, wondering as she munched, if the new baby brother or sister would have arrived by the time she went home at four clock.

Back home in the cottage Doris was being examined by the midwife, who told her cheerfully that she would be in labour for a few more hours. "Nothing is likely to happen just yet, Doris, you rest and let the pains come and go," she said, and bent down to peer through the tiny windows. "My word, these windows let a draught in, and no wonder, there's a half inch gap here. "

Draughty windows were the least of Doris's problems at that moment in time, and she groaned as another pain struck. The midwife made soothing noises and checked the new baby clothes waiting in a neat pile on the dressing table.

"Now, Doris," she said "I need to pop round and see one of my new mothers who gave birth yesterday. You'll be fine. Nothing's likely to happen for an hour or two. Just keep timing the contractions and try to relax into the pain. Don't worry. I'll be back very soon," and she picked up her black bag, waved her hand casually and went down the stairs grumbling as she went, that Doris's makeshift carpet was a death trap.

Stanley in the meantime had been across to the farm and informed them that he would not be at work that afternoon due to his wife being in labour. It was his employer's mother, Mrs Smith who took the message and she clasped her hands together anxiously.

"Oh dear me, Stanley. I hope she delivers safely. If you need the doctor you can use our telephone. Just ring the bell. You will let me know when the baby arrives won't you?"

As always, when Stanley received unexpected kindness, a lump developed in his throat and he could only stammer a thank you, as he tried to keep up his normal front.

Nurse Metcalf was loading her black bag on to the basket at the front of her bicycle as Stanley arrived home. He stared at her in dismay. "Where are you going?" he asked bluntly in his straight forward Yorkshire manner.

Quickly she brought him up to date, "Oh your wife will be fine for a few hours yet. I'll be back soon. There's nothing to worry about. You stay and look after her just in case," and before Stanley could reply she wheeled the bicycle out of the yard and rode away leaving him standing at the kitchen door. In two strides he was at the foot of the stairs and leapt up them three at a time and burst into the bedroom. Doris lay resting between contractions. She was calm but sweat stood on her forehead.

"Oh thank God you're here, Stan, hold my hand, love."

Stanley sat on the side of the bed and took her hand as he leaned over and kissed her, "Doris, the midwife's gone. What do you want me to do? Shall ah go for the doctor? What's she bloody playing at? She's supposed to be looking after you. She's gone off on her bike."

Doris took a deep breath and looked at him. "Aye ah had noticed she wasn't here, Stan. Calm down, she said she won't be long. Can you help me? I need to pee."

Once out of bed Doris stood up straight, her hand held around her stomach and with her husband's help lowered herself gingerly on to the commode, and sighed with relief.

"Thank God ah borrowed this from Mrs. Franks, ah couldn't have managed on the jerry, ah don't think ah would have been able to get up again," she broke off as another contraction began.

"Oh my God, Stan. Bloody hell. Ah'm never going to go through this again. How the hell did your mother manage to go through it so many times?" and she gripped Stanley's hand so tight he thought she would crush the bones. As the pain eased he helped her back into bed and sat holding her hand. White faced he looked through the window.

"Where the hell is that midwife? She's supposed to be here looking after you." he said.

"She's here," a voice came from behind him. "Ah told you ah wouldn't be long. Now calm down Mr Dale. Getting impatient will only upset the mother. Now go downstairs and make a cup of tea. Make sure there is plenty of hot water available, that's all you have to do. Then stay out of the way."

Relieved, Stanley kissed his wife and left them to it. He took a long drink of cold water straight from the tap and filled the kettle. As he waited for the kettle to boil he sat on the bottom step of the stairs and inhaled some deep breaths to steady his nerves, and tried to reassure himself that Doris would be ok.

'After all,' he reasoned, his mother had given birth many times. But his mind rampaged off into dark places, and he imagined her bleeding to death. Women died having babies even in these modern times. What on earth would he do if anything happened to Doris? He shook his head and pushed the thoughts away.

'Keep busy,' he told himself, 'Keep busy, don't think, just work.' He stood up as the kettle boiled and made the tea. Pouring out two mugs of strong brew, he took them upstairs and tapped on the door. He could hear Doris moaning softly and the nurse briskly reassuring her.

"Leave the tea on the step, Stanley," the midwife called to him, and in spite of his anxiety, he couldn't help thinking, 'Oh, we're on first name terms now are we?"

In a voice that sounded so unlike his own he said, "Ah'm just going to see to t'pigs. They need feeding, shout me if you need me."

Inside the bedroom Nurse Metcalf wiped Doris's forehead, "Ah don't think we need a man here do you, Doris? It's better if he stays out of the way. We're managing very well aren't we? That's right, Doris. Relax into the pain. We'll soon have this baby out."

But the hours crept past with no baby ready to pop out and greet the world. The midwife kept repeating with every contraction, "Relax into the pain, Doris, relax."

There was no doubt that had Doris not been in dire need of Nurse Metcalf's help she would have told her exactly what to do with her relax into the pain idea.

At seven o'clock Eileen was sitting on the sofa with Meg's head on her knee. The dog looked up at her with big brown eyes that said she understood what was happening. Stanley was as tense as it was possible for him to be, and he sat staring into the fire as they listened to the sounds from the bedroom above. Through the cracks in the wooden floor that formed the ceiling they could see movement as the midwife walked about and hear her voice as she coaxed and cajoled Doris.

The tick of the clock on the mantelpiece had suddenly become very loud and they watched as the logs on the fire sizzled and burnt away. Stanley shook his head and gritted his teeth. He looked across at his daughter and saw how close she was to crying. He remembered how he had felt when his mother was giving birth. Not for the first time he wondered how she had coped and how his father had dealt with it. Had he felt remorse for putting his wife through the ordeal of child birth so many times?

Well he couldn't stand his wife going through this ordeal again and he swore to himself and God, who he didn't really believe in, that it wouldn't happen again. Their family would be complete when this child was born.

He was so lost in his thoughts that the call from upstairs startled him and he was half way up the stairs before he realised he had moved. The bedroom door opened and Nurse Metcalf, looking quite red in the face, filled the opening.

"I think we had better let the doctor take a look at your wife, Mr. Dale," she said calmly.

'Oh my God, we're back on formal terms again,' thought Stanley. 'There must be something wrong,' and he stared at her in dismay.

"Don't worry," she reassured him, as she saw the expression on his face, "Doris is fine but I'd like the doctor to take a look at her just in case. Can you go and ring for him, then come back and tell me what time he is likely to get here? When you've done that," and here she paused as if waiting for it to sink in, "When you've done that, I want you to go up to my house and collect the gas and air machine. Doris is a little tired, and the gas and air will give her a bit of relief. Off you go and be a quick as you can," and she withdrew back into the bedroom and closed the door.

Thankful to have something positive to do Stanley turned, and almost skidded to the bottom of the stairs on the loose blanket that served as stair carpet.

"Someone is going to break their bloody neck on this thing." he said, aloud, and with one yank pulled up the whole length of the ruffled fabric, sending the polished brass stair rods, that were Doris's pride and joy, clattering down into the kitchen.

As he pulled on his jacket he gave Eileen instructions to pick up all the rods and look after the house while he was away. "Ah won't be long, love," he told her and he was off, running across the road to the farm to take up Mrs Smith's offer of use of the telephone.

The farm house was in complete darkness apart from a faint light showing through the frosted glass in the front door, and

Stanley guessed that everyone would be in the rooms at the rear of the house.

The door-bell was operated by turning a knob clockwise and gave a tinny sort of ring. He turned it several times and heard the sound echoing down the long empty passage that led to the kitchen and living rooms, and for good measure he knocked hard on the glass, then stood back, waiting impatiently, clenching and unclenching his hands.

Remembering his manners, he removed his cap as the light inside was switched on and the door opened. It was Mr. Smith's brother in law who Stanley knew only slightly but was aware that his name was Mr. Thirsby. He looked at Stanley, his eyebrows raised questioningly as he recognised him as one of the farm workers.

Stanley explained as quickly as he could that they needed the doctor and was shown into the kitchen, where the big black telephone lived in a position of importance, on a shelf of its own with two notebooks beside it. Indicating for him to make use of the phone Mr Thirsby returned to his study and left Stanley to it.

He took a deep breath to calm himself and picked up the receiver. Looking at the piece of paper in his hand he dialled each number, watching as the chrome wheel on the dial turned and then slowly returned to its basic position ready for him to dial the next one.

Stanley had only ever used the red telephone box at the end of the road for his previous calls, and was familiar with the pay procedure with its slot for the money, and the buttons A and B to press, and for one surreal moment he almost forgot that he was using a private telephone, He was in such a turmoil about Doris that he was taken by surprise when a voice spoke into his ear almost immediately.

"Hello, this is Doctor Thompson, who's speaking?"

Hastily Stanley gave his name and asked, "Can you come quickly please," and would have put the phone down and returned home, but the doctor's voice came through calm and steady, "Just a moment. I think I need the address, don't you?"

Feeling a like fool, Stanley gave a nervous laugh as he apologised, before giving the doctor his address and felt unbelievably emotional when the doctor told him that he would be there within ten minutes.

Arriving back home he shouted up to the midwife that the doctor was on his way and he was now going to collect the gas and air machine. As he turned to go he almost fell over his daughter who was standing close behind him. He looked at her white face and saw that she had been crying. But there was no time to sit down and explain, and he told her briefly to listen out for the doctor, and to keep the dog fastened up.

She nodded and went back to the sofa in the living room and listened to the sounds from upstairs and the loud tic of the clock. Meg shuffled close and put her head on Eileen's knee and repeatedly nudged her hand, insisting that she stroke her head, and stared at her with her brown soulful eyes.

Meg's daughter Lassie was out in the garden in her kennel guarding the livestock. As a guard dog Meg would have been as much use as a kitten, and was permanently excused outdoor duties. She spent much of her time in the house looking like a very glamorous show dog. Stanley had often said that she was much too beautiful to be of any use as a working dog, but nevertheless she earned her place by always being in tune with the family's moods, and gave comfort to anyone who needed it, and tonight Eileen was very glad of the dog's companionship.

As Stanley left the house he glanced across the yard at his car, still standing on its piles of bricks and felt more annoyed than ever that he had not managed to finish the repair work. Shortage of time and money for parts had held the project up and he wished he had been able to finish the old 'jalopy' as Doris called it.

But, there was no point in regrets at this moment, and he pulled his old bike out of the shed and set off. There was a layer of ground fog that floated at waist height and gave an eerie feel to the cold night. The light on the front of his bike began to flicker and Stanley swore as he gave a groan. 'Fine bloody time for it to run out,' he thought. But this was no time to abide by the law and he carried on riding into the darkness and fog at top speed, breathing heavily from the exertion of the uphill ride.

Ten minutes later he was hammering on the door of the midwife's house and rubbing his cold hands together while he stood on the doorstep praying for there to be an answer to his knock.

Warmth and light floated out as the door slowly opened and a man whom Stanley presumed to be the midwife's husband stared at him. He was evidently used to anxious looking men knocking at the door, and he beckoned Stanley in and pointing to the machine said, "Ah expect that's what you have come for. There it is. It's heavy. Have you got transport?"

Stanley looked at Mr. Metcalf, taking in the expensive wool cardigan and checked felt slippers. He was holding his pipe in his hand and took a slow pull on it as he watched Stanley pick the machine up and hoist it on to his shoulder, and as he did so informed him that, 'yes, he had got his bike as transport.'

"Ah well," came the reply, "You'll be ok then. I would have run it down for you in the car but it looks a bit foggy and I am just going to listen to the news. Cheerio."

Stanley glanced at him and his expression said it all. He strode out without another word being said, and it was just as well that Mr Metcalf could not hear what he was being called as Stanley set off. Thankfully it was downhill all the way and he went much faster than he should have done with the gas and air machine balanced precariously on his shoulder, steering with one hand.

The doctor was already there in the bedroom when he finally reached home and carried the machine up the stairs. He was about to open the door when Nurse Metcalf appeared blocking his entrance.

She took the machine from him and seeing the anxiety in his face said in a soft voice, "The doctor is examining your wife now, Mr Dale. I'm sure he will have a word with you very soon. You look cold. I should go and have a cup of tea. Don't worry, Doris is a healthy young woman, she'll be fine," and she backed into the room, closed the door with her foot, and left Stanley standing looking at the dull green painted door.

As he stood there he realised just how cold his hands were and put them under his armpits to try and thaw them out as he turned and went back down into the kitchen. He slipped off his heavy khaki jacket and hung it on the peg and going into the living room went straight to his chair by the fire and held his hands out to the welcome heat.

"You'll get hot aches, Dad," a quiet little voice came from the sofa, and he smiled at his daughter, she sounded just like Doris. Looking at her he realised what an ordeal it was for her too and beckoned her to him.

She came and stood close to him with her hand on his shoulder and could smell the old familiar aroma on his working clothes, a mixture of animals and paraffin from the tractor.

"Well," she continued, "That's what me Mam says when I come in out of the cold. When will baby be born, Dad? It's taking a long time," and as a tear slid down her cheek, she brushed it away quickly with the back of her hand.

Before he had time to reply the doctor tapped on the door as he opened it. He smiled reassuringly at them both and said briefly that Mrs Dale's delivery was progressing normally and he would expect the baby to be born within the hour.

"She's in safe hands," he said, "Nurse Metcalf is very experienced," and with those brief words he left, explaining that he had another patient to see.

The next hour seemed endless to Stanley as he stared into the fire, willing the baby to be born and swearing to himself that they were never going to go through this again. Two children would be the limit for him and Doris.

With only the thin wooden boards separating the living room where they sat from the bedroom upstairs, the sounds of the midwife talking to Doris and the long groans were only too audible. And then suddenly it came. The sound they had been waiting for, the unmistakable sound of a baby's first cry.

Eileen put her hand over her mouth and looked at her father. Their eyes met and he held out his arms to her. "There, love, baby's been born, we'll be able to see it soon. Do you think it's a boy or a girl?" She shrugged her shoulders and bent to fuss Meg who seemed to sense the excitement and stood on her hind legs with her paws on Stanley's knee.

They waited impatiently until at last Nurse Metcalf called,

"Come along then you two, there's someone here for you to meet." Stanley stopped with his foot on the bottom step and looked up expectantly at the midwife.

"It's a girl, Stanley, another healthy daughter for you," and holding out her hand to Eileen she led her into the bedroom and instructed her to sit in the chair. "Hold your arms out, me dear, aren't you a lucky girl? A little sister for you to look after."

Eileen sat in the hard wooden chair with her feet only just touching the floor and shyly held out her arms. As she felt the weight of her baby sister, she held her tight and felt the bond between them that would last for ever.

CHAPTER 17

Stanley and Doris's second daughter had been born on the 9th of March and she was to be called Frances Mary.

Having a new baby in the family was like a new beginning. A fresh chapter was opening and they were all happier than they had ever been.

With the spring arriving the garden was coming to life and Stanley began planting up for the coming year. He sang as he worked and was full of optimism for the future. The chickens were laying and producing enough eggs for their own use and some left over to sell, and the pigs were bringing in a steady income to supplement his low wages.

The one thing that marred their contentment were the living conditions in the cottage which had deteriorated during the last winter. With no damp course the walls actually felt wet to touch. They were still living with no electricity, no bathroom or water toilet, and a kitchen roof that allowed snowflakes to drift through the loose fitting pantiles in winter.

Doris was becoming increasingly discontented with the house, and despaired of trying to keep it clean and warm and at the same time cope with a young baby under such conditions.

Stanley approached his employers again and asked for the cottage to be repaired and brought up to date, but just as before, he was told that they had no intention of spending any money on the house as it was just not worth it.

They discussed the situation night after night until Doris, tired after a day trying to soothe a teething baby and at the same time cope with the distemper that kept flaking off the damp walls, finally snapped and decided that they would apply for a council house.

When Stanley asked her what they would do with all their animals in a council house and how they would afford the rent, she lost her temper and shouted that she didn't bloody care, she couldn't continue living in this dump.

Stanley did what he usually did when she lost her temper. He looked at her, his mouth tight lipped and his blue eyes cold as ice, and told her not to talk so bloody stupid. Then he picked up his cap and went off to work.

By the next morning Doris's temper had cooled but she was determined to carry out her intention to put their names down for a council house, and strapping the baby into the pram she set off for the housing offices at Woodlands.

As she walked with the big Silver Cross pram bouncing along the uneven pavement, Doris began to imagine them living in a brand new council house, something like the one her cousin Les and his wife lived in. How marvellous it would be she thought, and in her mind's eye she could see the nice bathroom, upstairs of course, and the modern kitchen, and a back boiler behind the fireplace that would produce all the hot water they needed. There would be electric lights all through the house, and best of all, no more damp walls and flaking distemper.

Stanley could get an allotment and they would keep their animals there. Lots of other people kept a few chickens and even a pig down on their allotments. Well, she thought, they could do the same. She would suggest it to Stanley that evening, but in the meantime she had arrived at the council offices, and tucking the blanket firmly around Frances, she put the brake on the pram and went inside.

She looked down the long corridor that stretched away in front of her and at the row of people sitting on the hard, wooden bench just inside the door.

The woman nearest to her smiled encouragingly, "Knock on there, love," she said, indicating the frosted glass sliding window, "It's no good ringing the bell, it doesn't work."

Nodding a thank you Doris pulled her coat straight, checking that all the buttons were fastened and tapped politely on the glass. "You'll have to knock louder than that, love, give it a good hammering, ah think she's bloody deaf, or she's gone for a cup of tea," came the voice of the woman on the bench.

If there was one thing that Doris hated it was being told what to do and she gave the woman one of her looks as she knocked on the glass again.

The window opened almost immediately and she was confronted by the receptionist who looked at her condescendingly and raised her eyebrows as she said, "Yes?"

She seemed vaguely familiar to Doris and she tried to remember where she had seen her before. 'Blondie, that's it,' thought Doris, and she recalled seeing her in the 'Foresters Arms' public house in Adwick several times, and with a different man on every occasion.

Stanley had christened her 'Blondie,' which was an ironic nickname as her hair colour was so obviously out of a bottle judging from the half inch of mousy brown hair showing at her scalp.

Doris's lips twitched as she remembered Stanley nudging her and making derogatory comments about the woman in her ear, and she would have loved to have told her that it was time she got her roots done, but managed to just say politely that she had come to put her name down for a council house.

The woman smiled showing the bright red lipstick that had stuck to her teeth, "Oh yes, you and all these other people too. You'd better take a seat and wait. Mr Jameson will see you shortly when it is your turn," and she slid the glass window shut again.

Doris looked at the small amount of space left on the bench and remained standing, wondering if she should wait or return on another day. She opened the door to check on Frances who had begun to cry and decided to bring the pram inside where she could keep rocking it and hopefully get her to go back to sleep again.

By the time the big pram was inside the waiting area there was very little room left and everyone stared at it and then at Doris, obviously weighing her up, and without a word being spoken they all shuffled along the bench leaving her just enough room to sit down.

It was at this point that Frances's low grizzling turned into a full blown bawl and no amount of rocking would pacify her.

At the far end of the bench the man sitting there groaned, "Bloody hell," he said, " Ah get enough of this at home. Can't tha shut it up, love. It's making my bloody head hurt," and he got up, pushed his way roughly past Doris and left.

He was quickly followed by the two other men waiting on the bench but at least they had the good manners to make an excuse, and say, above the sound of the baby's wails that they were late for work and would come back another day.

The moment the door closed behind them the crying stopped and Frances gave her mother a gummy smile.

The woman still seated on the bench touched her hand lightly, "By heck, love," she said with a wink, "You've got her well trained. You'd better go in next before she decides to start again. Leave the pram here, I'll watch it for you."

Within minutes Doris was in the office with Frances in her arms, facing the man in charge of allocating the council houses. She took the seat facing him across the desk, and noticed, according to the brass name plate, that she was dealing with Mr Jameson, the housing officer.

Looking up from his paperwork he smiled at her, "Ah, Mrs Dale, I see from your form that you are currently living in a cottage that goes with your husband's job. That sounds idyllic."

"Yes, but," began Doris and before she could say any more Mr Jameson continued, "In that case, Mrs Dale, you will not be entitled to a council house as a priority. I have to make that quite clear. Let's see, how many children do you have?"

"Two, but," and again, before she had time to say more, she was interrupted and told firmly that their names could go on the list but it would probably be years before they stood any chance of a council house.

He gave her another smile and shuffled the papers on his desk.

"We'll keep your names on the list, Mrs Dale. Ask the next person to come in as you leave."

And that was it. Doris bundled her daughter into the pram and wheeled it out, smarting with indignation. All the way home she went over and over the interview thinking of what she should have said and hadn't.

She expected Stanley to say, "I told you so." And he did. But seeing how upset she was he put his arm around her and tried to cajole her.

"We don't want their bloody council house, Dot. We should get a smallholding soon."

Doris's reply was a sceptical, "Huh," and Stanley knew what was coming next.

"I shouldn't have to be going cap in hand to a jumped up official to beg for a council house. I should have had my own house that my granddad left me if my father hadn't fiddled me out of it. I hate him, and all the rest of the family too. They were all in on it."

Stanley sighed and shrugged his shoulders. What could he say? She was right, and there was no doubt that life would have been much easier for them if Doris had inherited what had been intended for her.

"Stuff em, Dot," he said. "They can stuff the council house and your Dad and his family can all rot together. We'll make our own way, Dot. Don't you fret. We"ll show em," and he took her face in his hands and kissed her slowly, before taking his handkerchief out of his pocket, and after shaking the dust from it, he made as if to wipe the tears from her cheeks.

Just in time Doris saw the state of it and backed away. "What the hell have you been doing with that, Stan? It's blacker than the fire back."

He held it up and examined it, "Ah think that's a bit of tractor grease, and look, there's a bit of snot. Come here and let me wipe your face with it," and he chased her around the table with it until she ran outside laughing.

So Doris had to resign herself to the fact that there would be no nice shiny new council house for them, but summer was beginning and conditions in the cottage were always better when the weather was fine.

This was the first year since they had moved to Adwick that Doris had not been able to earn some extra money pea pulling, but she took over more of the work of caring for their pigs and stock, leaving Stanley free to contract more piece work in the evenings.

At this time of the year the turnips and sugar beet were growing so fast that it was difficult to keep pace with them.

The seed was sown thick and as soon as the crop reached a couple of inches high it was considered ready for 'striking.' Using a hoe, the surplus plants were pulled out; leaving little bunches approximately nine inches apart. These 'bunches,' then had to be singled out so that only one healthy plant remained, and that was known as 'singling.' It was tedious work that meant bending over or crawling up and down the field on hands and knees.

Stanley took on an acre at a time to strike and single a measured out piece, which he worked on after his day at the farm was finished. The lengthening evenings gave him the extra daylight hours he needed and now he had a helper. At twelve years of age Eileen was considered quite old enough to work and joined her Dad to help him complete his contracts whenever her school hours allowed.

It was an exciting day when Stanley declared that the repair work on the Austin Seven was complete, and they all piled into the car for a trial run. At some time in the car's long life someone had thought it a good idea to repaint the exterior a bright shade of blue, and they had done it using an ordinary paint brush that had left faint ridges all over the bodywork. But Doris had set to work with her tin of Mansion furniture polish and now at least the rough paintwork shone. On the worn out rear seat she had placed a folded up blanket that her mother had knitted with small balls of wool left over from her many knitting projects. Stanley said it was like Joseph's coat of many colours, but it was warm and cosy for Eileen and baby Frances to sit on.

Now that the car was in running order Doris had forgotten all her rants about it being a waste of money and sat regally on the front passenger seat eagerly anticipating their first trip out.

Stanley swung the starting handle and the engine spluttered into life. He breathed a sigh of relief as it began to tick over, and allowed some time for it to warm up before he cautiously edged the car down the narrow passageway with only a couple of inches to spare on either side and out through the gate and on to the lane. He turned to Doris and gave her a grin as he squeezed her knee.

"Right girls," he said, "We're off. Hold tight." He revved the engine and turning his cap back to front he bent over the steering wheel and gripped it tight like a comic racing driver.

Doris laughed and told him to behave as they reached the end of the lane, and pulling his cap back around the right way, he looked along the village street, checking that it was clear and waved proudly to a couple of neighbours as he set off.

"Let's just go up Red House Lane and back again. Ah don't want to risk the Great North Road today. Ah want to see how she runs first." Doris nodded in agreement and gazed around at the scenery, which, she declared, looked so much different when passing it at such a speed in a car rather than walking.

"Well we're not going fast, Dot. Ah reckon we're going about twenty five miles per hour," he reassured her. It was a guess as the speedometer wasn't working, it was one of the things that he hoped to get sorted at some time in the future, but in the meantime it didn't matter much, they were unlikely to break any speed limits. He checked the amount of petrol they had with a sort of dip stick that gave him a rough estimate of how much fuel was In the tank, and he resolved that in future he would carry a small amount of petrol in a can just in case they ran out.

With the engine running smoothly there was no more talk of making just a short run and they headed north until they reached Wentbridge which was situated in a steep valley.

Stanley was still not quite prepared to trust the car completely, still not confident the brakes would hold them and also doubted the cars ability to tackle steep hills. Deciding not to push his luck any further that day he drew the car to a halt and they admired the view, before turning around heading for home.

The little car made a great change to their lives. That summer they were able to make trips to the seaside on Sunday afternoons. Cleethorpes, on the Lincolnshire coast was their usual destination. Not only was it the closest seaside resort, it was also a mostly flat run with no steep hills on the journey for the engine and brakes to struggle with.

They soon realised that there was a sort of unofficial 'Austin Seven Club' and on the rare occasions that they saw another car of the same model there was much waving and lights flashing as if they were old friends.

Once in Cleethorpes, Stanley usually parked near the swimming pool, in what Doris decided was the better part of town and they spread an old blanket on the soft sand and enjoyed a few hours of leisure.

A nearby kiosk sold large jugs of tea for sixpence. A deposit of half a crown was charged for use of the jug, but that was refunded when the jug was returned. Doris usually took a picnic of rough, chunky sandwiches and an apple pie. She spread it out on a tablecloth while Stanley lay back on the blanket, and as the sun soaked into his work weary bones he said he couldn't have been happier if he had been the King of England.

The very best visits to Cleethorpes were the ones when Stanley's brother, Harold, joined them, having driven from Wath upon Dearne, in the black Ford that he shared with Cyril. In the passenger seat beside him was his wife Marion, a beautiful girl with delicate features and a cloud of dark wavy hair that framed her face.

Living all their early lives so far away from the coast, neither of the two brothers had ever had much chance to enjoy the sea side when they were young, and so they made the most of it now, and rolling up their trouser legs they began to race each other along the beach to the sea.

The tide went out a very long way at Cleethorpes and they ran first across the soft sand that seldom saw water, then on to the sand mixed with mud that was hard and flat until eventually they were running through almost pure river silt that formed ridges with salty water in the hollows. Curly worm casts littered the beach and squeezed through their toes as they ran, until at last they reached the sea and stopped; and allowed the rippling water to wash over their feet.

As they stood, with hands on hips, panting, Harold gazed out across the estuary to where they could see the opposite north bank in the distance, and he breathed in the salty air. Eileen caught up with them and ran straight into the water splashing her father and uncle until she was told to pack it in as they didn't want their Sunday suits spoiling.

The muddy water swished over their white feet as they all turned and looked back at how far they had come from the beach. Doris and Marion were miniature figures so far away that they were barely distinguishable among the other day trippers until they waved.

"Bloody hell, Stan, look how far away they are. We could do with binoculars," said Harold, as he shaded his eyes from the sun. "It's no wonder they have pony and traps to take the trippers down to the sea."

They sauntered slowly back with Harold bringing his brother up to date with the family news.

"Ah'm supposed to keep this quiet, Stan," he said with a grin, "So don't let on that ah've told thee."

Stanley turned all his attention to Harold and gave his head an inquisitive lift, "Go on then, let's hear it."

"Well tha'll not be surprised to hear our auld fellow went to t'races last Saturday," he said, referring to their father. "He had a big win on an outsider then put it all on another one and ended up with £100."

Stanley looked at him incredulously, "£100! Bloody hell that's a first for him in't it? He usually backs horses wi three legs. What did me Mam say when he got home with that sort of money? Ah bet she was off to Barnsley for a new three piece suite the minute she got to know."

"Aye she would have been, but he reckons he got his pocket picked on t'way back to t'bus stop."

"Huh. More likely he went to t'pub and got a skin-full of ale and lost it. That's if he won it in the first place," retorted Stanley as he laughed in disbelief.

"Oh aye he won it, cause Uncle John saw him with it. Can tha imagine that, Stan? He had all that cash in his hands and managed to lose it."

"By hell, ah could have put it to good use. Does tha realise, ah'd have to work for twenty weeks to earn that sort of money, or chop twenty acres of turnips on piece work. That puts in into perspective doesn't it?"

"Will tha be following me father's racing tips in future then, Stan?"

"No ah bloody won't, it's probably the one and only time he's ever won. Ah don't reckon naught to gambling. You don't see many hard up bookies do you?"

Harold agreed and then said, "Be careful what you say about bookies to Marion, her Dad runs a bookies tha knows, all on the quiet of course; he runs that business in the back room of his grocery shop. Local copper knows all about it but he bungs him a few bob now and then as a sweetener and he turns a blind eye. Tha'd be surprised how much her Dad makes out of t'gambling. Ah reckon he's worth a few thousand quid."

Stanley nodded, "Good luck to him. Ah admire him for it. But he won't see any of my money. Gambling's a mug's game."

As they drew nearer to the parked cars and the picnic that was laid out waiting for them, Stanley thought what a perfect picture Doris and Marion made. They were both dark haired and beautiful but suddenly he was stuck by the delicate, also ethereal appearance of Marion in contrast to Doris's rosy cheeks and glowing health, and a little shiver of foreboding ran through him. But this was no time to be having gloomy thoughts and he put his arm around Doris as he joined her on the blanket and was thankful for her sturdy good health.

They sat on the blanket and ate the picnic and then spent half an hour playing cricket until it was time to pack up and go home.

For all of them, that summer was one of the happiest in their entire lives; when they were young, and looked to the future with all the confidence and optimism of youth.

CHAPTER 18

As the summer drew to a close, a wet autumn began and with the rain the dampness in the cottage increased and their living conditions were worse than ever.

The final straw came in November when there was a violent storm and the overloaded drains and sewage system completely failed. Rain water mixed with sewage burst out of the manholes, lifting the lids and spewing down the street in a fast flowing stream to settle at the lowest point, which just happened to be around the cottage. Thankfully the deluge stopped just before their home was flooded but as the water drained away it left behind all the waste and effluent which had floated into the yard.

The mess and the stench were indescribable and as Stanley and Doris stood and stared at it Doris burst into tears of anger and despair.

"That's it, Stan, I've had enough. What's next? We haven't got a toilet ourselves and now we've got everybody else's shit in our back yard. You can go and tell your bloody boss that we're not putting up with it any longer. I'm going to get the sanitary inspector round. They can't expect us to put up with this."

"Doris," reasoned Stanley, "This is nothing to do with Smith's. This lot is down to the council, it's them that have built all the extra houses and not improved the drains. It's them we need to complain to."

"Right, Stan, first thing tomorrow morning I will be round there to complain." Her tears had now dried and Doris was in fighting mode and Stanley thought to himself that the council officials would wonder what had hit them when Doris confronted them the next morning.

He sighed as he pulled on his Wellington's and raincoat and collected the hose pipe and yard brush to begin clearing away the mess.

The council offices were situated just across the lane and Doris only needed to walk around the corner to be at the main entrance and she knew exactly which was the department she needed to go to.

First thing next morning as soon as she saw the lights go on in the building. Doris brushed her hair and put on her best coat. Then with baby Frances in her arms, she walked across the lane and through the main doorway prepared for battle. Straight down the corridor she went, till she reached the door with the brass plaque that stated it was the office of Mr. Senior, Sanitary Inspector.

Doris was still seething with an anger she had nursed all night, refusing to allow herself to calm down, and had been rehearsing her speech in her head for the last three hours, ever since she had woken at dawn. Knocking sharply on the door, she opened it without waiting for a reply, and walked straight in.

Mr Senior as seated at his desk looking through the Monday morning post. He was a quietly spoken gentleman with old fashioned manners and he rose and began to smile as he recognised Doris. But the smile froze when he saw the expression on her face.

"Ah. Good morning, Mrs Dale. Is there a problem? Do sit down," and he indicated the chair.

"No. I think I will stand thank you," Doris swallowed, "I want to know what is going to be done about the drains." In spite of the speech she had ready she was too angry and upset to speak coherently.

Mr Senior's politeness had cooled Doris's anger and she found herself almost sobbing as she described what had happened.

"That's terrible, Mrs Dale," he sympathised. "We really can't have that happening, it is most insanitary. Look, you go home and see to your work and I will come round in half an hour. You can show me exactly what happened and how far the contaminated water reached." Opening the door he ushered her out, reassuring her that he would be there as arranged.

Back home, Doris strapped Frances into her pram and tucking her in firmly she pushed her outside and parked her under the shelter of the pear tree at the top of the garden and crossed her fingers that she would go off to sleep.

Shoving the bucket full of soaking nappies under the sink she covered it with a towel and washed the breakfast pots that were stacked in the enamel washing up bowl. The hearth was swept in record time and the beds hastily made. Thinking to herself that she was glad she had emptied the chamber pots earlier she went downstairs and began to dust.

By the time Mr. Senior knocked on the door all was clean and tidy. Doris took a deep breath and began to show him around. It was almost an hour later when he left with his note book under his arm, complimenting her on her beautifully kept home. He raised his hat as he bid her goodbye and assured her that he would be giving the matter urgent attention.

When Stanley arrived home from work at midday for his dinner Doris told him all about it in great detail, informing him that Mr. Senior had said in his opinion it was not the new housing estate to blame, it was more likely to be the Northern Dairies further up Tenter Balk Lane that had caused the problem with their increased output and if it was, it would be within his powers to put a stop to it.

"And," she said triumphantly, "He examined all the walls in the house and saw how damp they were. He even looked in the pantry."

Stanley had been just about to take another forkful of potatoes covered in thick gravy as she spoke. He stopped and replaced it back on his plate and stared at Doris.

"Bloody hell, Dot. Don't tell me he went poking about in the pantry?"

As she nodded, he asked, "What did he say to all the bacon salted on the slab," He waited for her reply, his eyes troubled.

"Well he didn't say anything much, Stan. He just commented that he could see we had been killing a pig."

"It's to be hoped that he didn't look too close, or he'd have thought it were a funny sort of pig, seeing as there are three tails laid out there on the slab."

Stanley went back to work a worried man, and all afternoon as he ploughed up and down the fields, he kept thinking, you never knew quite where you stood with council officials, you never knew what they were observing and taking note of.

Every day for the next few weeks he expected to see a policeman arriving and demanding to know if he had exceeded his quota for slaughtering pigs, and accusing him of selling unlicensed meat.

Happily the phantom police officer of Stanley's nightmares never materialised, and the long damp autumn gradually gave way to a cold, dreary winter that sapped everyone's spirits. But, in the middle of December a very welcome letter arrived from the West Riding Council informing them of a smallholding to let in Guisley and inviting them to apply for it.

It was everything that Stanley and Doris had been searching for and the application form was completed and posted back the very same day. Then they waited. All through Christmas they waited, watching every day for the post, hardly daring to hope that their application would be accepted.

Then at last on the fifth of January the letter arrived. Slitting it open Doris scanned through the first page, and hardly able to believe what was printed there she read it again, and danced around the table clutching the letter to her face.

They had been shortlisted for the tenancy of the smallholding and were instructed to attend the interviews on the twenty second of January. The letter advised them to go and view the property in person before that date to ensure that they would be willing to take up the tenancy if they were selected.

There was certainly no question of their willingness, they were so anxious to get the tenancy and so burning with desire for the twenty acre smallholding that they would have taken it no matter what condition it was in.

It was nine o'clock when Doris read the letter, and unable to wait until lunchtime to tell Stanley the news, she put Frances into her pram, donned her Wellington's and an old coat and set off in the rain to walk up Red House Lane to the field where she knew Stanley was ploughing.

She was wet through by the time she reached him but it was worth it to see the expression on his face as he read the letter. They huddled together beneath the tree at the entrance to the field. Water dripped from Stanley's cap, and trickled down the turned up collar of his khaki ex -army coat, but his eyes were shining with hope.

"Ee Dot. Ah can hardly believe it, but you shouldn't have come out in this lot," he said, as he indicated the rain that was increasing. "You hurry up home. Ah'm off back to t'farm now. It's not fit to do this job today, ah'll get bogged down if I carry on."

He kissed her and climbed back aboard the tractor and watched Doris hurrying back towards home pushing the pram.

From his position high on the tractor he looked around. The rain was pouring down with flecks of sleet among it and the wind lashed the bare branches of the tree above him, but at that moment he didn't care what the weather did, they finally had a chance,

If only they could just be successful at the interview, he thought, and he allowed himself to dream of all they could achieve as he steered the tractor homewards.

That evening they carefully spread out their old road map on the table under the gas light, and Stanley smoothed out the folds and hoped that Guisley wouldn't happen to be in one of the many holes in the map.

He was in luck and found it to the north of Leeds. Tracing with his finger down the line of the Great North Road till he reached Adwick, he informed Doris that it should be fairly easy to find.

"But how far is it, Stan?"

He made a quick calculation, and said probably about fifty miles, and quickly added as he saw Doris's face, that it was no further than them going to Cleethorpes. Just in time he stopped himself from saying that it was much more hilly.

But Doris knew him too well and had seen the doubt in his face.

"Stanley, are we going to be all right in the car? Is it going to make it up the hills? Is that what you're worrying about? I think we should go on the bus."

"Doris, we're not going on the bus when we've got a car. Have you any idea how many times we would have to change buses to get there? We'd never make it there and back in the day. We're going in the car and that's that," and he glared at her, his jaw clenched tight, daring her to challenge him.

Doris however, was willing to be persuaded, and simply said, "Ok." Knowing he had won the argument Stanley immediately softened his attitude, and pulling her towards him he cuddled her and said, "Stop worrying, Dot, the car will be fine." Then silently he mouthed the words "I hope," and crossed his fingers.

As he prepared his tractor for work the next morning his foreman, Bert, walked into the shed.

"Now then, Stan, do you think it's going to keep fine today? If you manage to get the big field finished come straight back here will you? The boss wants the grass field ploughing up now that he's got the grazing rights at Bentley for the bullocks."

Stanley nodded and cleared his throat before he asked if he could have Friday off, and seeing Bert's doubtful expression felt bound to tell him the true reason he wanted time off.

"You know that Mr Smith won't be very happy about that."

Stanley hastened to explain that he would make the time up by working all day Saturday and Monday evening.

Bert lifted his cap and scratched his head, "Aye go on then. Hopefully t'boss will be away in Scotland again and won't be any wiser, but if he asks, tell him you've had to go on family business. Ok? Keep it to yourself. This is just between you and me." As he turned to go he gave a little salute with his forefinger and said, "Good luck Stan."

By the time Friday came around all the preparations had been made. The car had been checked over, and the tank filled with petrol. Stanley also had a spare can of petrol wedged behind his seat, along with a bottle of water for the radiator and a brick in case he had to park on a hill.

Eileen had been given a day off school to look after her baby sister and had received long instructions about what to do and what not to do while they were away for the day.

She was to collect the eggs while Frances was to sleep in the afternoon and was told several times not to sit reading and let the fire go out. If they were not back by dark she was to make sure that the hens had gone into the shed and lock them up.

"And make sure you change Frances's nappy," Doris reminded her for the third time as she filled a hot water bottle and Thermos flask to take with them. With no heater in the car it would be a long, cold journey.

When they finally left, Eileen stood at the window with Frances in her arms and waved to them until they were out of sight.

Within ten minutes Stanley and Doris were on to the main road and heading north towards Leeds. Doris had tucked the woollen blanket around her legs and sat regally admiring the passing scenery. Like Stanley, she was filled with a sense of adventure until suddenly a thought struck her.

"Stan," she said, "Will we have to go through Wentbridge?" Geography had never been her strong point.

He glanced sideways at her wondering if she was serious, "Aye, ah reckon we will, unless they've moved it that is," he paused as he negotiated his way around a stationary bus. "Of course we've got to go through Wentbridge, you know the Great North Road goes directly through it."

"Ah, but the other week you said the car might not go up the hill and you were worried about the brakes."

"Yes, but since then I've put new spark plugs in the engine and fitted new brake pads. It should be fine now."

He spoke with more confidence than he felt, his mouth was dry and his hands gripped the steering wheel tight when they eventually reached Wentbridge.

He looked at the steep road that wound down into the bottom of the valley and into the picturesque village way below. At any other time he would have appreciated the stunning view, but today, he had other things on his mind and changed down into a lower gear as they began their descent.

There was a lorry in front of them and it lumbered slowly downwards with its brakes letting out a high pitched whine, and Stanley consoled himself that his wasn't the only vehicle with less than perfect stopping ability. But they reached the bottom safely and he pulled the car to a halt in the first lay-by he could find.

"What have you stopped for, Stan? Is there something wrong?"

"No." He shook his head and flexed his fingers that were stiff and cold. "You see that lorry in front? He's got a heavy load of sand on and ah'm going to let him get well away from us, then ah can hopefully get a good run at the hill."

As the lorry disappeared round the bend Stanley set off, going at a good speed to begin with, but was soon forced to double his clutch and go down the gears until they were in bottom and travelling at a slow walking pace. Without realising he was doing it Stanley was making a back and forth rocking motion, willing the engine to keep going, and as he looked at Doris he could see that she was doing the same.

He grinned at her and winked, "Are you ready to get out and push, Dot?"

"No ah'm bloody not. It had better keep going or it'll be off back to the car auction next week."

As if the car had heard her, its little engine kept grinding slowly onwards until they reached the top and Stanley patted the dashboard and said "Good lass, ah knew you could do it."

The rest of the journey was straight forward, with just a slow steady climb as they passed the signposts for Leeds, and eventually arrived in Guisley. Doris had imagined it as a little village but was pleasantly surprised to find that it was more like a small market town.

"Oh look, Stan, there's a good few shops, and look there's a Woolworths, and lovely wide streets."

Minutes later they were standing outside the place they had come to see. It looked so much better than anything they had expected and as Stanley gazed at the stone built house and the wide farmhouse gate at the side it he could hardly believe that they had a chance of living there. Doris slipped her hand into his and he knew she was thinking the same.

Holding their paperwork in his hand he knocked on the door and waited, wondering what sort of reception they would get.

Half an hour later they got back into the car having been shown around by the present tenants. It was icy cold in the car and their breath blew out in front of them like faint clouds of mist.

Doris reached into the bag, brought out the Thermos flask and poured two cups of strong hot tea into the plastic beakers. Thankful for the warmth it gave, they slowly drank it, each in deep thought about the smallholding they had just viewed.

In unison they both heaved a big sigh and turned to look at each other.

"What are you thinking, Stan?"

"The same as you of course. If only we can get the tenancy. I really want this place, Dot. I really do."

She put her hand on his knee and with a choke in her voice said, "We'll just have to wait and see. Try not to get your hopes up too much, love," and she smiled at him, "If anyone deserves it, you do."

Stanley nodded and handed her the empty cup, "Aye, we'll just have to hope the interview goes well," and getting out of the car he retrieved the starting handle from under his seat.

The engine spluttered into life after a couple of turns and as it warmed up they set off home. Being early January, it would be dark by four pm and Stanley had no wish to be travelling on a busy road with such feeble lights and he pressed the Austin faster than he had ever done before.

Doris was becoming more and more anxious about the children at home and worried that Eileen might not have been able to cope with her baby sister for a full day. Her imagination was working overtime and she pictured one tragedy after another until by the time they pulled up into their back yard she was just about as tense as it was possible to be.

The house was in complete darkness and Doris was out of the car and stumbling across to the back door on legs that were stiff with cold almost before Stanley had switched the engine off.

Bursting through the door it took a few moments for her to take in the scene. The fire glowed and the table was set. Frances lay asleep in her pram and Eileen jumped up from the sofa in surprise at the sudden entrance of her mother.

"Why are sitting here in the dark? Why didn't you light the gas?" In her tense state Doris spoke more sharply than she had intended.

"But you said I was never to touch the gas light, Mam," Eileen was on the point of tears, it had been a long lonely day coping with her young sister and now it seemed she was in trouble for not putting the gas light on.

Stanley walked in and looked from one to the other and instantly weighed the situation up. "Ah think she's done well don't you, Mam? She's collected the eggs and locked the hens up."

Doris put her arm round her daughter, "Ah'm sorry, love. You have done very well. Has Frances been awkward today? Here look, you run to Mrs Sneap's and get some buns for tea," and she took some change from the tin on the mantelpiece and held it out. "There's enough to get three buns and some toffees for tonight, off you go, run as fast as you can. We'll tell you all about the place we've been to look at later on."

It was half past four and almost completely dark and Eileen needed no urging to run fast, especially past the church with its ugly stone gargoyles that hung from the square stone tower. Every local child knew for a fact that they came alive after dark and followed anyone who dared to look at them. So keeping her eyes firmly downcast she ran at full pelt and arrived at the corner shop panting and out of breath.

"Now then, what can I get for you today?" Mrs Sneap smiled at her, "You've been running haven't you? Frightened of the church are you, love? You don't want to take any notice of the stories they tell you, it's all rubbish, there's nothing about the church that can hurt you."

Too shy to confide in Mrs Sneap, Eileen just blushed as she nodded and held out the money for the buns and toffees, and in spite of the shop keeper's advice she passed the church warily, with the hairs on the back of her neck prickling, and was greatly relieved to reach home without one of the gargoyles chasing her.

That evening, exhausted by their long drive, Stanley and Doris settled down by the fire and shared out the toffees. They had gone over and over the day's events until Stanley thought they were just repeating themselves and switched on the radio just in time to catch the beginnings of a play.

Doris turned off the gas light and they sat listening by the light of the flickering fire. Eileen had curled up on the old fireside chair and said not word hoping that no one would notice that it was well past her bed time.

The only sound apart from the radio was the crackle of the logs as they burned away and shifted position in the grate. Stanley leaned forward and stirred the fire with the long poker sending showers of sparks up the chimney.

He looked at his daughter and winked as he held up his hand with his fingers spread out and mouthed "Five more minutes." He settled back into his chair, closed his eyes and thought of the smallholding in Guisley.

It was then that he became aware of another sound, a faint scraping and crunching, that at first, he thought was coming from the radio. He looked across at Doris who dozed in her chair intent on following the play and then he looked at Eileen and saw her expression as she gazed at the ceiling just above the table behind him.

For a moment, he could see nothing until his eyes adjusted to the different shadowy light away from the fire, and then it dawned on him what was happening. A mouse was gradually gnawing its way through the layers of paper that Doris had pasted over the many holes in that part of the ceiling.

Murmuring to himself, "Cheeky little bugger," he took off his slipper and stood up ever so slowly. Signing to his daughter to keep quiet he moved to the back of the table and waited, poised with slipper raised ready to strike.

Oblivious to the danger it was in the mouse continued to gnaw, and soon had the hole enlarged. Pushing its head through, it looked around taking in the cosy room and evidently decided to join them.

Wriggling its front quarters through, it gazed around again cautiously, its whiskers twitching. And that was the moment that Stanley's slipper struck with deadly accuracy and the mouse dropped to the floor.

Doris jumped, brought awake by the noise, and Meg raised her head from her paws and gave a wag of her tail as if to say, "Well done."

"What the hell are you doing, Stan? You made me jump," grumbled Doris, and then as the sound of crying came from upstairs, she sighed, "Bloody hell, Stan, you've woken Frances up, It'll take me ages to get her settled again."

But Stanley was busy moving the table and bending over to retrieve the dead mouse. He came upright, holding the rodent by its tail, and waved it about triumphantly.

"Look at this cheeky little bugger, Dot," he said and he waved it in front of Meg, "You're supposed to catch em, not let em come to live in the house.

Meg managed to look insulted and turned her head away. Stanley couldn't help smiling at her expression and threatened to replace her with a cat, as he took the mouse outside and threw it into the garden.

Doris, however, was not amused, and sighed again as she said, "It's just one thing after another with this house, Stan, now we've got mice to contend with. Ah'm going to have to repaper over the hole it's made. Ah've had enough of it, ah really have."

Putting his hand on her knee he looked into her eyes, "Calm down, love, it was only a mouse. Ah'll put some poison down tomorrow and set a few traps in case there's any more. Let's hope we won't be here much longer."

CHAPTER 19

It was less than two weeks till they were due to attend the interview for the tenancy, and Stanley could think of little else as he worked for long hours alone in the fields. Over and over he went through the questions that they were likely to ask, and mentally prepared the answers. He thought about it until he was sick of thinking about it, and grew short tempered with Doris whenever she brought the subject up.

But, at last the day arrived, and they prepared to set off for Wakefield where the interviews were to be held. Stanley was wearing his freshly pressed Harris Tweed suit that he was so proud of. He had bought it just after Christmas from the fifty shilling tailors in Doncaster. It was the first suit he had ever had made to measure but the fit left much to be desired and Stanley tugged at the sleeves that were just a little shorter than they should have been for his long arms.

"Ah reckon that bloody tailor needs to buy a new tape measure, Dot, the one he's got must have a few inches missing" he grumbled, "Does it look ok?"

Doris looked stunning in her dark maroon wool coat and black court shoes. She had fixed her hair into an elaborate roll at the back of her head and had a deep wave at the front and trusted to lavish amounts of Amami setting lotion and a handful of hair grips to hold it all in place.

"Do I look alright?" she asked, "Are my stocking seams straight?" she turned around for him to check.

Stanley looked her up and down and declared that she looked

like, 'A fifty bob hoss all decked out for the show,' and added that she would have the council committee members mesmerised.

Doris laughed and told him to stop messing about as Stanley kissed her and whispered to her that she looked lovely. They went out to the car carrying the knitted blanket for Doris to wrap around her knees and the paperwork that they would need for the interview safely stashed in a large brown envelope.

They waved to their elder daughter standing in the doorway holding her baby sister as they set off. As before, Eileen had been given the day off school to act as nursemaid, and was none too pleased to be missing two of her favourite lessons but she jiggled Frances up and down and persuaded her to smile and wave to her mum and dad as the little blue car carried them away.

They arrived in Wakefield almost an hour before their interview was due and stood on the steps of the town hall feeling conspicuous in their best clothes while the people of the town bustled around them intent on their everyday business.

Stanley was never good at waiting and he was becoming decidedly twitchy. It didn't help that the Harris Tweed suit was rough, and irritated his skin, and he said quietly to Doris that it was like wearing a hair shirt.

"Well I did say in the shop when you bought it that the material felt rough," retorted Doris, "But you said it would be alright. You'll have to wear long Johns underneath it in future."

"Mmm, but that's not much help now, is it?" and he sucked in his breath as he eased the trousers away from the back of his knees where his skin was particularly tender. He looked up again at the clock above the door, "Come on, it's time to go in and let them know we're here."

They were directed up to the top floor where the interviews were to be held, and sat in the cold waiting room on the wooden benches with the hard leather tops that were provided for the waiting interviewees.

Their voices echoed around the large empty room and they spoke in whispers, overawed by the surroundings. Stanley took out his papers from the brown paper carrier bag and shuffled through them again.

There were the references from Teddy Downing and Norman Flint, and the one that Bert Dunning had written for him the previous week. He glanced through them then looked at their bank statements and the receipts for some of his sales at the pig market. His confidence dropped as he thought that there was little to show and prove that he was worthy of the tenancy of the smallholding in Guisley.

As if she read his thoughts Doris squeezed his arm and smiled at him and he leaned over and gave her a quick hug and a kiss on the cheek but sprang away as the door opened.

In walked one of the biggest men Stanley had ever seen. He was not just tall but also broad and seemed to fill the whole doorway. As if afraid of banging his head he stooped slightly and ran his hand through his unkempt hair and hitched up his baggy trousers.

Stanley nodded to him and tried not to stare, but with a sidelong glance he took in his heavy paunch that hung over his waistband and he nudged Doris. He gave her a quick look and raised his eyebrows before he turned his attention back to his rival for the tenancy and was just in time to see the man's wife come hurrying into the room.

She hoisted herself onto the seat beside him and swung her feet back and forth, as a child would who couldn't quite reach the floor, but stopped when her husband put his hand on her knee, waved his forefinger at her and shook his head. She looked as if she would start crying and gave her feet another little swing before she placed them on the spindle.

"Good morning," she called to Stanley and Doris in a squeaky little voice. "Have you come for the interviews?" Her husband gave a slight grunt and whispered in his wife's ear as he hitched up his trousers again in an attempt to cover some of the flab. Stanley took it that the man had no intention of having any conversation with them and simply gave a nod to the woman and looked away.

With just one minute to go before the interviews were due to begin, the door opened again and almost as if he expected a drum roll the third candidate walked in. He was so obviously of a military background that he might as well have had army stamped on his forehead, and he marched into the room swinging his arms, stopped beside the benches and looked closely at every person in the room.

"Ah good morning everyone. Captain Davies is the name. Very nice to meet you all. May the best man win and all that. Eh?"

The interviews began at eleven o'clock on the dot, with the giant and his wife being the first to be called in. They were gone for a full twenty minutes while Stanley's tension slowly mounted. But at last they returned and went back to their seats.

"Mr and Mrs Dale?" called the receptionist. "The committee will see you now; go straight through the first door on the left."

Looking at his wife, Stanley stood up, and together they entered the interview room and took the seats indicated to them that faced the long desk. There were three men from the West Riding committee waiting to ask them questions. They sat evenly spaced along the opposite side of the desk.

Each one had a highly polished brass name plate in front of them. Stanley looked at each one, memorising the names. The two at either end, a Mr. Tingle and a Mr. Wainright were complete strangers to him, but the man in the centre looked vaguely familiar. His name plate announced that he was chairman of the committee and named Mr. Molton.

He stared at Stanley, his expression unsmiling and then he turned his gaze to Doris. There was something about him that Stanley took an instant dislike to and it seemed that the feeling was mutual. From that very first meeting they were set to antagonise each other whenever they met.

Mr. Tingle, who was seated closest to them, rose from his seat and shook hands with the young couple. He thanked them for attending the interview and did his best to put them at ease. Looking at the references he commented that his previous employers had thought well of him. He made a neat stack of the papers and passed them along the table to Mr. Molton who, without so much as a glance, slid them along to his colleague.

Mr. Wainright agreed that the references were excellent and

added that he appeared to be doing well with his stock breeding. He nodded approvingly as he examined the sales sheets and invoices and murmured, "Very good, Mr Dale, You seem to be experienced in all aspects of farming."

He turned to the chairman, "Do you want to examine the paperwork?" he asked. At first it seemed that he would refuse but then he took the bundle and shuffled through them without speaking, then picking up the bank statement he looked directly at Stanley and said, "I take it then, that this is the sum total of your capital?"

Stanley took a deep breath before he replied, "Yes it is."

"And do you think that £100 is sufficient capital to begin farming a smallholding of this size?"

"Well, we already have some stock," replied Stanley, "We have two breeding sows, six store pigs and poultry besides the money in the bank."

"And what do you intend using to farm the arable land on the smallholding? I believe most of the land is used for crops. Or perhaps you have a tractor and implements hidden away somewhere." He gave a snigger before turning left, then right, to look at his two colleagues."

It was obvious that he was trying to rile Stanley, but he managed to keep his cool, and answered in as calm a voice as he could. "I will of course buy a tractor as soon as I am able and in the meantime will hire one, or offer my services to a local farmer in exchange for the loan of one."

Stanley's voice was hard and tight and he would have loved to have put his hands around the chairman's flabby, red neck and shook him till his teeth rattled.

With a "Hmm," Mr. Molton shoved the references into an untidy bundle and pushed them across the desk.

"Interview over," he said, "You will receive a letter informing you if you have been successful. Tell the next person to come in. I think you'll find it's a Captain Davies."

With as much dignity as he could manage Stanley gathered up

his papers and walked out of the room with his head held high and a very angry Doris by his side.

With his hand on Doris's arm he steered her straight outside into the fresh air. "Aren't you going to tell Captain what's his name to go in?" she asked.

"No ah'm bloody not. Ah'm not his lackey. He can go and tell Captain bloody Pugwash himself."

Despite her own anger at the derisive way they had been treated, Doris recognised the hard look in her husband's eyes and the jutting of his chin, and wisely kept quiet as they walked back to the car.

It was two weeks later that the letter arrived from the West Riding County Council. It stated briefly that they had not been successful in their application for the smallholding in Guisley, but invited them to apply for any other property that might become available in the future.

Stanley swallowed hard as he read the letter. He was bitterly disappointed and went over and over the interview in his head. He thought of the other two candidates and knew he was better qualified than either of them. He seethed with anger as he thought of the chairman of the committee who had obviously been against him from the moment he had set eyes on him.

He talked it over with Mr. Shilito, their feedstock merchant representative.

"It would be interesting to know who did get the tenancy, Stanley," he said, "I dare say I will hear sooner or later." He replaced his trilby on his head as he bid them goodbye and promised to make a few discreet enquiries.

The information filtered back to Stanley less than a week later that Captain Davies had been given the tenancy. He also discovered that he was connected to a relative of the chairman. Stanley fumed with anger at the news.

"It's the same old story, Dot," he said, "It's not what you know, it's who you know," and he stormed off to work and spent the rest of the day ploughing and turning the matter over and over In his mind until the bitterness began to drain away, and his natural optimism renewed his good nature. But deep inside him the resentment against the chairman of the council smouldered.

It was early in March when Doris saw the advertisement on the notice board at Woodlands. She made a point of looking at the board every week to see what bargains people were trying to sell. This one caught her attention right away. 'TO LET,' it said, and went on to advertise a 4 berth holiday caravan at Marton Road, in Bridlington for £7 per week.

Doris looked in her purse and counted the money. She had just over two pounds, enough to pay a deposit on the caravan. As luck would have it Doris would be passing the house of the caravan owner on her way home and as she approached it, her feet slowed to a halt and she stood still, trying to decide.

She hesitated. Could they afford it? Neither of them had ever had a holiday before. What would Stanley say? Before she had time to change her mind she decided to take the plunge and rang the bell.

As she walked home she could hardly believe that she had gone ahead and booked a week's holiday in Bridlington in late June. Despite her reservations about Stanley's reaction, excitement began to mount inside her.

Just imagine, a whole week at the sea side. It would do them all good, especially Stan who had been in low spirits since they had been turned down for the smallholding. Anyway, she reasoned, it wouldn't matter what he said, she'd booked it and that was that and he'd just have to get used to the idea.

She waited until Stanley was eating his dinner to break the news. He stared at her, different expressions passing across his face.

"Bloody hell, Doris, What if I can't have the time off work?"

"Well you're entitled to a week's holiday with pay now."

Stanley sighed, "Aye ah know, but ah can't just take it whenever ah like."

Quick as a flash Doris retorted, "If it were left to Bernard Smith, you'd be taking your bloody holidays in the middle of winter."

Stanley nodded as he picked up his pork chop and took a bite out of it. He couldn't argue with her about that. Given the chance, his employer probably would have all his workmen take their holidays in winter.

He munched on his pork and thought it through. "And when have you booked this holiday for then?"

Doris got up from the table and refilled his mug with tea as she said, "Last week in June."

"Mmm. Well the sugar beet hoeing should have finished, but the peas will be ready. Ah can't see them letting me have that week off. I wish you wouldn't do this sort of thing, Doris. You should have checked with me first."

With her best stubborn look on her face Doris said, "Well it's done now, so you'll just have to get the time off." She should have known it was the wrong thing to say but she couldn't help herself.

Pushing his plate away, all appetite gone, Stanley's own temper flared, "No, I'll tell you what's going to happen, Doris. I'm going to have to go cap in hand and ask if I can have that week off and if the answer's no, you'll have to go and get the deposit back."

Leaving the table he walked outside and up the garden while his temper cooled. He stood leaning on the fence looking at their latest batch of store pigs. Meg appeared as if from nowhere and leaned against his leg, nudging him gently. When no response came she stood on her hind legs with her paws on the fence at the side of him and gave a soft whine.

Stanley put out his hand on her head and gently stroked it. "What's up with you then, Meg? It's alright for you, you've got no troubles, have you?"

He turned as he heard Doris approach and held out his hand to her. She slipped her hand into his and looked up at him, "Don't you want us to have a holiday, Stan? It won't cost much."

"Course ah want us to have a holiday. Ah'd love to have a whole week off work and spend it at the seaside. But you know what it's like, ah've told you often enough. Ah have to see when ah can get time off before we go booking holidays. You've put me in a really bad position, Doris."

But Doris still had that stubborn look on her face and Stanley knew it was a waste of time to try and reason with her, so he turned away, gave a quick wave and said he was off back to work.

He was ploughing in one of the fields near the Great North Road that afternoon, and as he worked his way up and down, turning the soil over and leaving behind him the perfect furrows that gleamed in the weak winter sunshine, his mind was occupied by the problem of the holiday.

He dreaded having to ask another favour of his foreman Bert, but there was no alternative and his opportunity presented itself as he came face to face with him at tea time when he returned to the farm yard.

"Nah then, Stan, how's the ploughing going?"

"Ah, it's turning over a treat, ah should have it finished by tomorrow afternoon at the latest. Ah'm glad ah've seen you. Ah wanted to ask you about holidays."

"Aye. Now then. Mr Smith wants me to have a word with you about the holidays. It's a bit awkward suiting everyone and the only week ah can let you have off is the last week in June. Would that suit you?"

Stanley could hardly believe his ears, and he struggled to stop himself from grinning. He sucked in his breath and tilted his head to one side as if thinking about it.

"Yes," he said slowly, "Ah think that will be alright. Put me down for the last week in June."

"Very good." said Bert. "Ah knew ah could rely on you to be amenable." He took out his notebook and scribbled names and dates in it. "That's it then, all sorted. You get off home now Stan, You look frozen. See thee in t'morning."

Five minutes later Stanley walked into the living room, picked Doris up and whirled her around. "Well, ask me who's going on holiday the last week in June then?"

"Oh, have you fixed it then, Stan?" He nodded as he went into the kitchen and hung his coat behind the door..

"Yes I have," he said. "It took a fair bit of negotiating but Bert agreed in the end. Don't ever put me in that position again, Doris," and he smiled at himself in the mirror that hung above the sink as he washed his hands and thought that he would tell her the truth later on, and then again maybe he wouldn't.

CHAPTER 20

They began making plans for the holiday immediately. Doris sold the big Silver Cross pram and managed to make a small profit on the price she had paid. In its place she bought a second hand, low, black pram that could be converted into a push chair. For such a small pram it weighed a lot, but Stanley said he would be able to strap it to the roof of the car when they went on holiday.

The phrase, 'when we go on holiday,' was uttered several times a day and Doris thought to herself that it had worked out just as she had intended. The prospect of a week at the seaside had raised the spirits of all the family.

Preparations began. Into a box, each week, went an item of food for the holiday. Tins of corned beef, spam, peas, beans, condensed milk, tea and sugar and even a precious tin of pink salmon were squirrelled away until Stanley realised how heavy the box was, and had to call a halt to it, pointing out that they had hills to climb, and 'Bluebird' as they had christened the car would never be able to carry everything.

Doris protested, saying it was only a few tins, and they would need all of them as everyone had told her that the shop on the caravan site charged extortionate prices. But Stanley stood firm, "No more, Doris," he said, "That's enough. We can easily go into Bridlington to get what we need."

They set off on the last Saturday in June. It was doubtful that they could have packed another item into the car. The bedding that was needed was laid across the back seat and Eileen sat on top of it all with Frances on her knee. The box of groceries took up half of the seat and their clothes which were packed in various shopping bags wedged it firmly into place.

Stanley had strapped the pram on to the roof, and he gave the straps a tug before he took the starting handle and turned the engine into life. It ran smoothly and he slapped the bonnet before he folded himself into the driving seat and crossed his fingers that the car would carry them safely to Bridlington.

Of course as with all toddlers, Frances soon became restless and was passed back and forth like a hot parcel between her mother and sister in an effort to keep her quiet.

When they reached Market Weighton, Stanley estimated that they were about half way there and the seven horse power engine was purring away in spite of the heavy load. But just ahead lay the first steep hill that climbed up on to the Yorkshire Wolds and Stanley knew it would be a challenge.

To begin with it was just a gradual climb and he changed down the gears until he was in second and sat tense in his seat willing the engine to pull. Half way up, the gradient increased and Stanley double-clutched down into bottom gear. There was nothing else he could do now, except to keep his foot on the accelerator and pray that the engine kept going.

They were barely moving faster than a walking pace and just ahead a cyclist dismounted and began to push his bike up the hill. He stopped as they slowly approached him and gave them a thumbs up sign.

Everyone in the car returned his greeting with a little wave as they drew alongside. Stanley was sure they would grind to a halt, and through gritted teeth told Doris that she should never have packed all those groceries. But just in time the road began to twist, first to the right, and then the left reducing the steepness of the hill. They were nearly there now, just a few more yards and then the final hump and they had made it. He patted the dashboard as if the car was a living creature, and then stuck his head through the open window.

"By, the air smells good up here," he said, as the engine returned to a normal sound and gathered speed, "There's a prize for the first person to see the sea."

"What's the prize, Dad?" asked Eileen.

"It's a Mintoe," laughed Stanley, and fishing in his pocket found the lump of minty confectionery wrapped in the crumpled white wrapper with red lettering that declared it was a Nuttall's Mintoe. It was Stanley's favourite sweet, but his wife and daughter did not share his enthusiasm and groaned in unison.

"You can keep that yourself, Stan, We're sick of them aren't we, love?" and she turned in her seat and looked at her daughters.

Eileen had found a half chewed piece of Liquorice root in her bag and offered it to Frances, who sucked on it even while she pulled a face at the strange taste and texture.

"Don't give her that, Eileen. We can get enough dirty nappies without giving her liquorice." But the warning was unnecessary. Frances had decided she had had enough of it, handed it back, and demanded to go to her mother.

With the back seat and the grubby looking stick of liquorice root to herself, Eileen settled back on the pile of bedding and admired the scenery. It was another hour before they reached Bridlington and eventually found the caravan site. They drew to a halt at the side of the shop just inside the gateway, and no one was more relieved than Stanley that they had arrived.

The caravans were lined up neatly in rows, each one identified by letters of the alphabet and each caravan numbered. Standpipes for water and drains were situated haphazardly here and there and even in the sunshine it was clear that there was a good sized muddy puddle around every one.

The caravan that Doris had hired was number 6 on row G at the top end of the site where it backed on to open fields. It was a dusty shade of blue with small windows and had a split stable type door that opened outwards. It was a big step up into the van but the thoughtful owner had provided an upturned beer crate with a piece of wood on top to serve as a step.

As Doris opened the door her heart sank. It was so small inside and had a damp, musty smell in spite of it being such a warm day.

"It looked much better than this on the photograph that the

woman showed me," began Doris, "Bloody hell, I thought it would be better than this."

Stanley stood beside her and put his arm on her shoulders, "It'll be ok, Dot. We're only going to sleep here. We'll be out most of the time."

"But where am I going to wash the nappies, Stan? That's no good," and she pointed to the tiny bowl set into a block of wood that served as a kitchen.

"You don't have to wash 'em in there, Dot. Look it says here on this piece of paper that we got with the keys." Opening it out he read aloud, "There are clothes washing facilities in the central washing block," and he pointed to the red brick built building no more than fifty yards away. "Come on, love," he said, "Don't spoil things. We're on holiday."

Doris took a deep breath and looked around again. She decided it was not so bad after all and actually really quite cosy. There were seats and small tables at either end that converted into beds at night. Cooking facilities were provided by a tiny cooker with a kettle and one saucepan on top of it.

To be truthful it would have been small for one person but for a family it was a very tight squeeze. Stanley shook his head as he looked around, it felt claustrophobic and he resisted commenting that he now knew exactly how a sardine felt. He'd just got Doris calmed down, there was no point in setting her off again, but he prayed the weather would be kind to them.

It began to rain during the night, a steady pattering on the metal roof that was quite soothing but within minutes it became a loud hammering and as dawn broke the wind shook the little van and the rain poured down. Stanley opened the curtain and looked out. The happy sunny holiday scene from yesterday had changed dramatically.

A man dressed in black oil skins and southwester sloshed his way towards the shower block with his towel under his arm, while another in similar wet weather gear filled a bucket at the standpipe.

Doris sat up in bed and peered out at the scene with him and felt thankful that she had had the foresight to fill the buckets the night before. As she wiped the steam and condensation from the glass she gave a heavy sigh and said, "Well, it looks like they've come better prepared than us, Stan, ah never thought about needing wellies and waterproofs."

It was not a good start to the holiday and spirits were low as they contemplated being confined to the caravan till the weather brightened up. They were all irritable. Stanley and Doris snapped at each other and Frances decided she was not going to wear shoes that day and took them off as fast as her mother put them on, until Doris tapped her leg and established who was in charge.

Eventually, order was created in the overcrowded space, the beds were stashed away and tables replaced and set for breakfast. The caravan rocked slightly as they moved about and tilted quite alarmingly if they all sat at one end. Stanley banged his head several times until he got the hang of automatically ducking down at either end of the van due to the arched shape of the roof.

Stanley sat back and began to relax. For the first time in his life he could contemplate a whole week with no work and as he thought about all those days of leisure in front of him, the rain stopped and the sun came out as if a light had been switched on.

Instantly, everyone's mood lifted and they began to make plans for the day, and Eileen was impatient to be off.

"Can we go to the sands, Dad, like you said? Can we go now while the sun's shining? Frances wants to go now don't you, Fran?" and obligingly Frances who had only just learned to walk, struggled to her feet and stood there wobbling, with her coat in her hand.

"Put her in the pram and take her for a walk round the caravan park while I get this lot sorted," instructed Doris, as she began to gather up the breakfast pots.

So, with Frances strapped in her pram Eileen took her on two full circuits of the caravan site bumping over the rough grass, and only stopped to examine the goods for sale in the window of the camp shop.

There was an assortment of dusty souvenirs, mostly cheap ornaments with 'A present from Bridlington' stamped on them, and a pile of shells that had never seen a British beach.

But it was the brightly coloured buckets and spades stacked outside that caught Frances's attention, and she reached over, grabbed the handle of one and pulled over the entire stack.

Mortified, Eileen prised it from her hand and tried to put everything back in its place but looking up saw the shop keeper standing in the doorway watching. "Did you want to buy one," she asked. She glared at Eileen whose face was crimson and she shook her head.

"Well don't handle the goods if you don't want to buy," snapped the woman and tossed her head sideways in a way that meant they were to go away.

Eileen took no further bidding and almost ran along the path and lived in dread of being sent to the shop on an errand for the rest of the week.

It was ten o'clock when they finally set off walking down Fortyfoot Road and along the sea front till they found a sheltered spot on the beach. They had a good hour enjoying the sun and fresh sea air before the clouds slid over the sky again and they had to seek shelter in the nearby amusement arcade.

But with only one pound per day allocated for food and spending money Stanley had no intention of parting with much of it in the arcades, and the moment the rain passed he led them out again. They strolled along the promenade to the harbour, where he promised he would take them out on a sea trip on the YORKSHIRE BELLE before they went home.

That day, weather wise, set the pattern for the rest of the week with heavy showers spoiling the sunshine several times a day. By Thursday, the novelty of living in the tiny caravan had completely worn off for them all, and as much as they had enjoyed the sea air and their trips to the beach, both Stanley and Doris were ready for home.

Their conversation constantly turned to what they would do in the future. Doris said that she really could not stand another winter in the cottage and thought that Stanley should begin looking for another job with a better house, and added that she was losing faith the West Riding council ever allocating them a smallholding.

But Stanley had a more drastic solution than that. One that he had been turning over in his mind for the last two weeks, ever since he had seen the advertisement in the 'Farmer and Stock Breeder' magazine. The more he thought about it the more it appealed to him and seemed to offer many opportunities.

It was as they were travelling back from a day in Scarborough, heading towards another night in the cramped beds of the caravan that he first voiced the idea. Feeling relaxed and refreshed after their few days holiday, with the car purring along down the coast road he took a deep breath.

"I've been thinking, Dot. What would you say to us emigrating to Canada?"

Before Doris had time to reply disaster struck with a loud bang. Immediately the car lurched to one side and Stanley knew what had happened. He pulled the car onto the side of the road and stopped the engine.

"We've got puncture, Dot," he said, "Sounds like a blow-out. Bloody hell! There's always summat!"

As he got out of the car Doris said, "It'll be ok won't it? We've got a spare wheel haven't we? Can you change the wheel?"

Of course Stanley could change the wheel, but he was aware of something that Doris wasn't. Doris had no idea that the tyre on the spare wheel was in such bad condition that it would be unlikely to last long enough to get them home.

The wheel was quickly changed and they cruised down into the hill into Bridlington with the magnificent view of the town and the bay in front of them. At any other time he would have admired the scenery but at that particular moment his mind was occupied by the ruined tyre and the cost of replacing it.

Back at the caravan he broached the subject. "We're going to have to buy a new tyre, Dot. How much money have we got left?" Doris emptied her purse out on the little table and Stanley turned his pockets out. They had four pounds and five shillings.

"I've got to buy some food out of that Stan. I'll need at least two pounds to keep us for the rest of the week." Stanley put the two pounds to one side and then added enough to buy petrol to get them home. It was obvious that what was left would not buy a tyre.

They had one hundred pounds in the bank. That was to remain untouched. It was what they called their farm fund and was not to be used except in an emergency. 'Well,' thought Stanley, 'This is an emergency.'

"We'll have to borrow out of the bank Dot, and pay it back in later."

As he looked at his wife's face he knew. He knew exactly what she was going to say.

"You haven't brought the bank book have you?" he said, hoping against hope, that he was wrong.

Doris shook her head, "I thought it would be safer at home. I didn't want it to get lost." She stared back at Stanley challenging him to contradict her and Stanley was ready to rise to the occasion

"Well that was a bloody clever thing to do. I left you in charge of the money because you always insist on it. Now we're in a right bloody fix. That tyre will never run for seventy miles. It's nearly threadbare now."

Doris slammed her hand on the table, "It's not my fault, why didn't you get a new one before we set off."

Stanley, as always, slipped back into his broadest Yorkshire when he was angry.

"Why? Why? Tha knows why, because tha kicks up a stink every time ah spend a penny on the car. But tha's keen enough to enjoy riding in it. Tha makes me so bloody mad, Doris."

And so battle commenced. Eileen picked up her little sister, put her in the pram and set off walking. Round the caravan site again they went, calling in at all the toilet blocks and peering inside to see if they were different to the one they used, doing everything she could to pass some time. She even risked looking in the shop window, but this time made sure that Frances could not reach the seaside buckets.

Back in the caravan, there was a sulky silence, a frosty atmosphere with each refusing to speak to the other. Stanley sat staring out of the window watching the clouds gather ready for another downpour, and he wished they were all safely back home. He wondered briefly if the manager at the Midland bank in Bridlington would let them draw money out without them having their bank book and was just about to suggest it when another idea came to him.

He picked up his cap and turned it around in his hands. He looked across at Doris who sat with that familiar pursed lips look that she always had when she was angry. At that moment in time she appeared completely unapproachable. But Stanley knew her well and knew how to coax her round. As often happened, he decided humour was the best way to ease the tensions.

"Well, that's it then, Doris. There's nothing else for it, we need the money so ah'll auction thee off to t'highest bidder. Although ah would have to admit to any prospective buyer that tha's got a terrible temper."

In spite of her determination to remain angry, Doris's lips twitched and she sat down beside him and put her head on his shoulder, sighed and said, "What are we going to do, Stan?" Then, as a thought struck her, she sat up straight and said, "I know, if we go home now, we won't have to fork out for any food and that two pounds will get us a tyre won't it?"

"Only just Doris, even if ah could get a second hand one. But listen, ah've had an idea. What would you say to us going pea pulling tomorrow? When we were coming back here ah noticed a field just up Scarborough Road that had a board out advertising for workers for tomorrow. What do you think?"

Doris's face lit up, "Yea, that's a good idea, Stan, we'll easily earn enough between us. Our Eileen can look after Frances. Where have they gone?"

"Well, ah don't think they're hiding under t'beds, Dot. Ah think they went out when we were arguing. Ah'll go and look for em while you get tea ready." He hugged her to him and kissed her, holding her so tight she could scarcely breathe. "Early to bed tonight. Dot." he said.

"Ah don't think so, Stan. That bed is so narrow we can hardly move in it. I expect the damn thing to collapse every time I turn over, and anyway the caravan would rock every time we moved."

"Don't flatter yourself, Mrs Dale, I was only meaning we need to get to bed early so we can get rested ready for work tomorrow." He patted her bottom and nibbled her ear as he passed her and gave her a wink as he went out of the door.

So that was it, the holiday was more or less over, but neither of them really cared about that; if anything they viewed working in a field near the seaside as a bit of a novelty, and they were up early the next morning and on their way before half past seven. They were almost the first pickers to arrive and Stanley walked along the headland and cast an expert eye over the field, noting where the crop was heaviest.

Wasting no time they began, each one competing against the other to fill the bags first. Stanley grinned at his wife and admitted that she was much faster than he was.

"Yea of course I am," replied Doris, "I'm a woman aren't I? Women are much better at this than men. Come on Stanley Dale, let's see how fast you can go."

Doris's hands flew, pulling up the pea straws with her right hand and stripping off the heavy pea pods with the other. By four o'clock the work was over. The field was bare and the workers began to leave the field and make their way home, walking wearily, but all of them happy to have earned some extra cash. And none of them were happier than Stanley and Doris, now that they had enough money to buy two new tyres and still have a few shillings left over.

It was obvious that their promised sea trip on the Bridlington Belle would have to be postponed for the time being, but instead they took one last walk down Fortyfoot Road and along the promenade, stopping at the amusement arcade to watch the laughing policeman in his glass case obligingly bursting into loud jolly laughs every time anyone popped a penny in the slot

The lights flashed and the background music blasted out creating a carefree atmosphere and Doris declared that she would never get Frances to sleep that night; but she was wrong. Tired out by the fresh sea air she was asleep before they got back to the caravan for their last night in the lumpy narrow beds.

Travelling back home was almost as exciting as their outward journey and certainly a good deal more comfortable for the girls on the back seat now that they were no longer sharing it with a box of groceries. Stanley had been much impressed by one of the songs that had been played over and over in the arcade the previous night, and from time to time he burst into song.

"Auf Weidiseine, we'll meet again, the time has come to part. With love that's true I'll wait for you, Auf Weidiseine, sweetheart."

Sometimes he got the words wrong and improvised. The tune had got into his head and it was a lovely melody that suited Stanley's voice but half a dozen times were enough and Doris dug out a stick of rock, broke a piece off and handed it to him.

He took it, laughing, "Is tha trying to tell me summat, Doris?" he asked. "Ah thought you liked me singing?"

There were no steep hills to climb on the way back home but plenty of downhills to negotiate and the inefficient brakes turned the drive into a dangerous adventure but they arrived home safe and sound and felt as if they had been away for a month rather than a week.

CHAPTER 21

Doris could hardly wait to get into the house to see if they had any post but was disappointed to find only her mother's weekly letter. There was no sign of what they had both been hoping for. No letter with a Wakefield post mark that would raise their hopes of a small holding.

That evening their thoughts turned again to Stanley's suggestion that they should think about emigrating to Canada. He searched through the previous week's copy of the 'Farmer and Stockbreeder' and found the article that had caught his attention.

"Look here it is, Dot. They are offering assisted passages to people who meet their conditions and we do that easily. We're young and healthy, we have no criminal record and we have some savings. I've got several references and plenty of experience. According to this, the Canadian government would be more than willing to take us."

Doris read it through carefully and then looked at her husband. Her eyes shone with excitement. "This could be just what we need, Stan. Just think. A complete fresh start in a place where there's plenty of opportunities. Bloody West Riding Council can keep their smallholdings. " As she spoke, she opened the top drawer in the sideboard and produced the pen and ink and their best writing pad.

She put them down in front of him. "There you are, Stan. Don't let's waste time. Write to the address on the top of the page. I'll post it tomorrow."

The following week a large brown envelope dropped through the letter box. It was post marked Canada House, London. Doris picked it up and stared at it, excitement rippling through her. Inside were pamphlets with job vacancies, details of housing available and a handful of application forms to complete.

After a whole evening pouring over the contents of the envelope Stanley rubbed his eyes and yawned. "That lot gives us food for thought, Dot, but ah can't look at them any longer tonight, ah'm much too tired. Let's go to bed and sleep on it."

Stanley fell asleep almost as soon as his head hit the pillow. Eight hours working on the farm took its toll on him every day, and this week was particularly hard. They had collected all the dried pea straw and were leading it into one of the barns ready to use for winter feed for the animals. It was heavy to handle and full of dust and when Stanley woke early the next morning he still ached in every muscle.

As he turned over he glanced at the clock and found with relief that he still had another half hour in bed until he had to get up. He fluffed up his pillow and turned on to his back and thought about the job vacancies in Canada.

One of the pamphlets had an impressive full colour picture of a train on the front and advertised job opportunities on the railways. It had caught his attention straight away but he had pushed it to one side. Now, in the lull before his busy day began, he thought more deeply about it.

Doris stirred and turned towards him. Stanley took her hand and squeezed it, "You awake, Dot?" he said, and without waiting for an answer, he continued.

"Ah've been thinking, Doris. When ah send the application forms back ah'm going to apply for a job on the railways."

Until he had actually spoken he hadn't really made his mind up, but as the words came out of him he realised that was exactly what he wanted to do.

"What?" asked Doris, "Did you say you were going to apply for a job on the railways? What's brought that on? Ah thought you always said the only thing you ever wanted to do was farm?"

"Aye it was, but ah'm beginning to think ah've had enough of working myself into the ground. As long as ah don't have to go to work down a mine ah could settle to do other things, and the railway seems very attractive to me and a lot better paid."

Doris put her arm round him and snuggled into his side. "It's up to you what you do, Stan. Now, how long have we got before you have to get up for work."

Stanley walked home that evening feeling weary. He was covered in dust and thankful that they had finished leading the pea straw. He stood outside in the yard, took off his cap and banged it against the wall to rid it of dust, then did the same with his working jacket.

Doris came to the door and picked his haversack up from where he had dropped it, "Come on love, get your hands washed and have some tea, you'll feel better with some food inside you. I've made an apple pie. The pigs have been fed you can have a rest tonight. You look worn out."

"I am, Doris, I've been thinking about those forms, and today has made my mind up. Ah'm going to go for the railway job. It must be an easier way to earn a living than slogging away like I've done today.

Doris was worried about her husband. It wasn't like Stanley to grumble about the work on the farm. Normally he took it all in his stride no matter how hard it was, but he had been looking gaunt and tired lately. The long hours he worked were taking their toll, and she resolved to buy him a bottle of tonic from the chemists out of the next week's housekeeping.

A nice hot bath would have gone a long way to relieving Stanley's aches and pains but of course he had to make do with a strip down wash. As he stood at the kitchen sink and washed himself bit by bit he began to feel better and by the time he had eaten his tea, with a large slice of Doris's apple pie covered in evaporated milk to finish off, he felt refreshed and ready to complete the emigration forms.

They had told no one about their thoughts on emigrating. "Time enough to spread the news if and when it comes to anything," said Stanley and with that thought in mind Doris walked up to Woodlands post office with the large envelope addressed to Canada house and posted it there, rather than use their little corner post office just along Village Street where prying eyes missed nothing.

And then the waiting began again. A week went by and then another and Stanley swung between being optimistic one minute and downhearted the next. He went over and over the answers that he had given on the form and constantly worried that he may have made mistakes on some of the statements he had written.

It was probably his preoccupation that made him forget his own strict rules on personal safety. Working on the farm with machinery and animals could be dangerous and over the years he had developed rules that up to now had kept him safe, apart from a few minor scrapes and bumps. He had stressed these rules to his daughter and one of his strictest instructions was never to walk close to the back end of the heavy horses.

"Always give them a wide berth, never walk close enough to be in kicking distance," he had told her many times. It was a rule he observed himself until one evening when Geoff, the horse man was late finishing, and Stanley had gone to the stables to help him feed and bed the horses down.

It was a job that Stanley loved. There was something so satisfying about settling the big heavy horses; leading them down to the water trough where they drank their fill, then taking them into their stalls and watching them pull at the sweet smelling hay in the racks while he brushed them down. His final job was to sweep the cobbled floor behind the horses and it was then that he grew careless and walked too closely past the only bad tempered horse that they had on the farm.

If the horse had taken deliberate aim he could not have hit Stanley harder. His massive foot flew out fast and made contact with Stanley's leg just below his knee. It hit him with such force that he fell to the floor. Instinctively he rolled away from the horse's feet and that action probably saved him from being stood on.

Geoff ran to help him but Stanley was already struggling to his feet and insisted that he was ok. The horse turned his head as far as the rope on his halter would allow, and later Stanley swore that he was sure he was laughing.

Geoff was usually such a mild, amiable person and seldom swore, but seeing his friend and work mate in pain he cursed the horse, whacked him with the brush and assured him that he would be the first one off to the knackers yard when the new tractor came on to the farm. Maybe the horse understood, maybe he didn't, but he tossed his head in a 'Don't care,' manner and continued eating his hay.

Stanley pulled himself up on to the box where they kept some of the spare equipment and waited for the waves of pain to ease.

"Ah think ah'm going to need some Sloan's Liniment on this, Geoff," he said, trying to smile. "Ah'd better get off home before it starts to stiffen up."

It was obvious the following morning that Stanley was going to suffer much more than just a stiff leg. He had gone to bed with a liberal handful of liniment rubbed into his leg and wrapped it up in bandages to try and keep the embrocation off the bed clothes. By morning after a sleepless night all the bandages had slipped down to his ankle, which was just as well seeing that the whole leg had swollen and turned a violent shade of purple.

He shuffled his way down the stairs into the living room and sat down on the wooden chair facing the fireplace and looked at Doris, "Ah'm not going to be able to work with this, Doris. Pass me some paper and I'll write a note to let Smiths know. Can you take it across to the farm? They'll not be very pleased." He rubbed his leg and winced with the pain. "I should be ok in a couple of days."

"From the looks of that, Stan it's going to be more than a couple of days. I think you need to see the doctor."

"No, it'll be alright, Doris, don't make a fuss." But inside he was worried. Would they still pay him his wages, he wondered.

Doris pulled on her coat and checked that she had some coins in her pocket. She planned to take the note then go straight to the red phone box at the end of Village Street and phone for the Doctor to call.

As she stood outside the door of the farmhouse waiting for an answer to her knock she read the note that Stanley had written, and wished she had written it herself. Stanley sounded almost apologetic for having time off. After all, she reasoned, it was the farm's horse that had caused his injury. She had said as much to

Stanley the previous evening and Stanley had sighed and said that she didn't understand.

"Don't you see, Doris," he said, "It's my own fault, I should have kept my wits about me. I know only too well that I shouldn't walk too close to the back of a horse, especially one that's known to be bad tempered, but I got careless. I can't blame anyone else."

"Well, I just hope they are going to pay your wages."

Stanley had replied that if they didn't he would take it to the union and see what they had to say, and Doris had retorted that he had more faith in the bloody union than she had, and then seeing her husband's expression had gone into the kitchen to wash up.

Now as she stood on the square stone step with these thoughts going around in her head she was almost shocked when the door opened and she was faced with Mrs Smith. She was dressed as always in her long black dress and matching jacket and looked immaculate even at this early hour.

In her usual gracious manner she said. "Ah. Good morning, Mrs Dale. What a surprise. Is everything all right? You look upset. Come inside."

As Doris explained she held her hand to her mouth, "Oh my dear, I am so sorry to hear that. Poor Stanley! Has he seen a Doctor?"

Doris shook her head and told her that she was just on her way to ring for the doctor from the telephone box.

"Oh there is no need for that, Mrs Dale. You can ring from our phone. Would you like my daughter to do it for you?"

If the truth was told Doris was extremely pleased that the telephoning had been taken out of her hands. She had never actually had to use a public telephone before and had been dreading doing battle in the red phone booth with the buttons A and B, and the printed instructions saying which slot to put the money in.

Doris was soon being reassured by Mrs Smith's daughter that the Doctor would be calling to see her husband later and Bert the foreman would also be round to see them very shortly.

While Doris had been out, Stanley had claimed one of Doris's sweeping brushes and covered the bristles with an old piece of cloth. Turning it upside down he demonstrated that he could use it as a crutch to help him get around.

"There, see, at least ah can get out to the lavatory now." he said, and then asked her how they had taken it across at the farm.

Before he received a reply there was a knock at the door and Bert, his foreman had arrived.

"Now then, Stanley," he said in his usual brisk manner, "Been having an argument with one of t'horses have you?"

"Aye you could say that," replied Stanley and he rolled up his trouser leg as best he could and showed him the injury. The swelling had now extended down into his foot and even his toes were changing colour.

Bert exhaled a deep breath, "Bloody hell, Stan. Ah bet that's painful. You're not going to be able to work with that for some time."

Stanley nodded. "That's what's worrying me more than anything. What about wages. Ah've got a family to think about. Ah've never been off work before, Bert, never had so much as a day off with bad health. Even when ah've been full of cold, ah've worked through it."

Bert took a deep breath. If it had been left to him he would have paid Stanley's wages for as long as it took him to get fit again. But he had to abide by his employers rules.

"Well it's like this, Stan" he said, "Boss usually pays full wages for two weeks to anyone who is off work sick, after that it goes down to half pay for a month."

"What?" declared Doris as she jumped up from her chair. "He's been injured at work and he's going to lose money through it. He's going to have his pay cut. Never mind cutting his pay, he should be given some compensation for all the pain he's in."

Stanley shook his head at her, this attitude was not going to do any good, although he had to admire the way she stood up for him. For a moment he was reminded of her grandfather, who Stanley remembered from years ago, and had been well-known as a formidable character in Wath upon Dearne.

"Doris is right, Bert. I received this injury at work. So surely that makes a difference." Stanley swallowed hard. Partly due to the pain, he was having difficulty speaking evenly, and he tried to get his emotions under control. "Let me get this straight. I get full wages for two weeks, then half wages for a month. And then what?"

Bert looked acutely embarrassed. "Well to be truthful we've never had a case quite like this, Stan. It will be different for you because you were injured at work. It's not like a normal illness."

"Go on. Tell me what usually happens if someone is off work long term due to illness?"

"Well," Bert continued hesitantly. "Say if someone was ill for a long time, eventually they would lose their job and would have to move out of the house. But don't worry, Stan, it won't happen to you. Try not to worry. I'll talk to the boss. You concentrate on getting that leg better. I'll pop in again tomorrow and see what the Doctor has said."

He picked up his cap, bid them good day and walked out. At that moment he hated his job and didn't feel too kindly towards the man that paid his wages as well as Stanley's.

It was almost mid-day before the Doctor arrived and he was obviously in a hurry, he took one look at Stanley's leg and announced that it needed an x-ray. "We'd better have it checked, Mr. Dale, just in case there is a fracture," he said. "You need to get it examined at the hospital today. Have you got some Aspirin for the pain?" He picked up his bag and prepared to leave. "Must get on," he said, "I've several more patients to see before afternoon surgery."

With that he was gone. Stanley looked at his wife. She knew what he was going to say and reached for her coat from the hook behind the door. "I'll go and ask Mrs Smith if she can ring for an ambulance, Stan."

"Ah don't really think ah need to go to hospital and ah don't want to be going in an ambulance, Doris. Ah think it will be ok when ah've rested it a bit."

Doris picked up Frances from the floor. "No arguing, Stanley, the doctor said you needed an x-ray, and how else do you think you're going to be able to get to the hospital."

"If ah could just manage to get to the car ah think ah could drive myself there."

"No you won't, Stanley Dale. I'm going to ring up now." and

before he had chance to say any more she was out of the door carrying Frances and calling over her shoulder that she would be back soon.

Left alone, his thoughts turned instantly to the conversation he had had with Bert, and he turned over in his mind what he had said about anyone with a long term illness. What if his leg was broken? He could be in plaster for weeks. What if he lost his job and they were turned out? And then common sense prevailed and he thought of the farm workers union that he had been a member of for a few years now. They wouldn't stand by and let him be thrown out of a job and his home, would they? Workers had rights now.

While Stanley was churning these thoughts over in his head, Doris was already at the farm speaking to Mrs Smith's daughter, Mary Thirsby, who said straight away that there was no question of Doris ringing for an ambulance.

"I will drive Stanley there myself, Mrs. Dale. Just let me get my coat and leave a note to say where I've gone. I will be across in five minutes."

Stanley had long admired Mary Thirsby's car and any other time he would have thoroughly enjoyed a drive in it, but under the circumstances he felt uncomfortable and obligated to her and it was a feeling he didn't like. Doris sat in the back with Frances on her knee; he glanced back at her and could tell instantly that she felt just the same as him.

He felt he had to say something to ease the tension; so he swallowed and began, "This is very good of you, Mrs Thirsby, I really appreciate you taking me to hospital."

"Oh, nonsense, Stanley. If it wasn't for our horse you wouldn't need to go, and besides, to tell you the truth it gives me an opportunity to drive the car, usually my husband gets behind the wheel and I don't get the chance to have a go."

Stanley reached out and touched the walnut dashboard and nodded admiringly, "This is stylish," he said, "I've always admired the Rovers," and then he found himself telling Mary all about the cars he had driven when he worked for Dysons in Wath upon Dearne, and realised that she was very knowledgeable about motors.

The car surged forwards when they reached the Great North Road and for once there was little traffic. Mary turned to look at him and smiled as the powerful engine carried them effortlessly towards Doncaster.

"What do you think to it, Stanley?" she asked. "How does it compare with a Daimler?"

"It's very good, Mrs Thirsby," he said, and seeing her smile he added, "I'll do you a swap for our little Austin Seven any day, a straight swap, I wouldn't want any money."

"Yes I bet you would, Stanley, I bet you would, I'll suggest it to my husband tonight." She laughed, and from that moment the atmosphere became easier.

Within minutes they were passing over the North Bridge and driving along Frenchgate. The policeman on point duty on Clock Corner waved them through and they were soon drawing to a halt outside the hospital.

Stanley got out of the car, and with the aid of his makeshift crutch made his way into the x-ray department. Waiting had never been his strong point and knowing that he was also keeping his employer's sister hanging about didn't help. By the time his name was called he was so tense and twitchy that he could barely keep still, but eventually he had his leg examined and was greatly relieved to be informed that there was no fracture.

Happy to find that his leg was not broken, Stanley expected the swelling to go away within days and optimistically told Bert that he should be back at work the following Monday morning. Bert looked sceptical as Stanley limped to the gate with him and just said "We'd better wait and see, Stan. We might have to get some temporary help in from the other farm."

That worried Stanley. He hated the thought of someone else doing his job and driving the tractor that he regarded almost as his own. He was desperate to get back to work but as he examined his leg he knew that there was little chance of it being back to normal by Monday.

He had a surprise visitor at the weekend. It was not unusual for his brother Harold to turn up unexpectedly and as he heard the familiar rev of the Norton engine he pulled the curtain to one side and peered through the tiny windowpane.

He could hardly believe his eyes. There was his mother, Ada, climbing off the pillion seat, where she had been riding dressed in her long black coat and her hat tied in place with satin ribbon. She looked a little windblown but otherwise was as neat and tidy and dignified as normal.

Shoving Meg out of the way from her position behind the front door, he opened it with the big iron key..

"Now then, Stanley, you didn't expect to see me today did you?" Ada asked, "What you been doing with yourself," she had a scolding tone to her voice and Harold, who was standing behind her, winked at his brother and tipped his head to one side in a manner that meant, 'Stand by, you're in for an ear bashing.'

"Had an argument wi a bad tempered horse, Mam, and he came off best, but never mind that, what you doing riding pillion? Ah never expected to see you on the back of Harold's bike."

"Ah wanted to come to see how you are, Stanley, and this was the quickest way to get here. But ah might have to get myself one of them ex RAF flying suits from the Army and Navy Stores if ah'm going to make a habit of this. It gets mighty cold and draughty on them motor bikes you know. The wind gets everywhere. Ah'm fair frozen. Has your Doris got the kettle on?"

While Doris made the tea, Ada examined her son's leg. "By that looks nasty, Stanley." she said, "You sure it's not broken?" Ada touched it carefully, "It's very hot, Stanley."

She sat back and nursed her cup of tea. "Maybe some Comfrey would help heal it. Have you got any in the garden?"

Stanley thought about it for a moment, "No, but I think there is some down by the stream towards the Willow Garth."

"Do you know where that is, Doris? We'll go and pick some now. We'll have to hurry up though. I need to be back home by teatime."

Stanley looked at his brother Harold, "Does me father know you've brought me Mam on the back of the bike?" He pronounced father with the flat A in the way he usually referred to him, and raised his eyebrows."

"No, he doesn't, and he doesn't need to know," interrupted Ada. "What he doesn't know won't hurt him will it? Come on, Doris, let's go and find this Comfrey. You lads get a big pan of water boiled ready to make a poultice."

Harold gave his elder brother a look and said, as his mother closed the door behind her, "Well ah'd rather thee than me, Stan, when me Mam gets that poultice made. She's got a habit of slapping it on while it's still hot. She says it works better that way."

Harold went outside and stood on tip toe to see over the hedge and watched his mother and sister-in-law hurrying across the field in search of the Comfrey. A lump came into his throat as he observed his mother walking unsteadily in her shoes that were totally unsuited to trekking across rough grass. He suddenly realised how much older she was looking and how frail she seemed compared to Doris's healthy build.

He returned back into the house and said as much to Stanley and had to stop the catch in his voice as he described her walking determinedly across the rough field in search of the herb.

"What's up, Harold? Are you worried about her? There's nowt wrong with Mam is there?"

Harold shook his head, "No. Well not as far as ah know anyway. She just suddenly looked so frail. Ah'm like you, Stan, ah think the world of me Mam."

"Aya, ah know, she's not had an easy life has she? She must think a lot of me Father to put up with him."

"Don't be too hard on him, Stan. He's just the way he is. He's just the same as a lot of colliers, he likes his beer a bit too much, but he's a glutton for work tha knows. Never misses a shift."

Stanley nodded thoughtfully; he had to admit that he had a much better relationship with his father these days, but was not yet ready to say as much, even to his brother. He leaned forward and poked the fire under the pan of water that was beginning to boil and pushed it into a safer position on the fire.

He glanced across at his brother, and for a moment thought

what it a wrench it would be, leaving him and Cyril behind if they went to Canada. He almost told him about his application but at the last minute he held back.

'I'll wait until we know something definite.' he thought. 'Don't want to look a fool if they turn me down,' although he did tell Harold about the conversation he had had with Bert.

Harold was incredulous, "What, do you think they would actually sack you, and turn you out of the house? The boss wouldn't do that would he? It's bloody medieval. He couldn't do that in this day and age."

Stanley shook his head, "Ah don't think it will come to that. Ah'm sure the union would have plenty to say about it and would probably take it to court. Anyway, ah'll be back at work next week, even if I have to go on crutches. But ah can tell you it's caused me some sleepless nights. The sooner we can get out of living in a tied cottage the better."

Before the conversation could go any further Doris and his mother walked through the door. Ada sank down on to the sofa and gave a weary sigh as she eased her shoes off. "By, that was a rough walk, it's not done my corns any good walking across the field in these shoes. But look, we got the Comfrey. Just let me have a rest for a minute and then we'll get the poultice made. We'll have you right in no time, Stanley."

Doris had a brown paper carrier bag full of fresh green Comfrey leaves and on Ada's instructions dropped a large handful into the pan of boiling water.

"That's it Doris, just push the leaves down into the water, but don't leave them in too long. Right, take it off the heat now and strain the liquid into a bowl. He can use that to bathe his bad leg and the leaves can be wrapped in a cloth and applied to his leg while it's still hot; and then bandage it up. Keep doing it every day until it's better."

Ada pulled her hat on tight and tied it on with the satin ribbon, "Come now, Harold, get me home before your Dad wants his tea, but don't go so fast this time, and no leaning over when we go round corners."

Harold grinned, "She loves riding pillion really, she's just a speed queen aren't you, Mam?"

Ada pushed him out of the door, "Go on, you cheeky young devil. Tha's not too big for a clip round the earhole tha knows." But she smiled as she said it and winked at Doris.

Stanley was more than a little sceptical about the Comfrey but knew better than to contradict his mother and allowed Doris to carry out the treatment. The next morning he could barely believe how much easier his leg was, and how much the swelling had gone down. After three days it had almost gone and the multi coloured bruising was fading fast.

The letter from Canada House arrived on the same day that Stanley went back to work. Doris handed it to him as he sat down for his dinner. He turned it over in his hands and took a deep breath. Using his knife from the table he carefully slit it open and withdrew the papers inside. They had returned his references and Stanley laid them on the table well away from the food and the risk of spillages, and began to read the letter.

His face lit up before he reached the bottom of the page. He looked up and met Doris's eyes as she waited. "They've accepted me, Doris. They said yes."

"What? When?" began Doris, but Stanley was engrossed in the contents of the letter.

Forgetting how hungry he was and how much he had been looking forward to his dinner he left it to go cold while he read the letter again and again. He passed it over to his wife and said, "Here you read it, Doris."

"Ah can hardly believe it," he said. "They're offering me a position on the railways and there's a house available that's not tied to the job. Look just there." He pointed half way down the page. "Look at the wage they're offering, and, we can get assisted passages. It'll be a completely new way of life, Dot. They say that there are plenty of opportunities out there."

"It sounds like you've made up your mind already, Stan. You really are sure about it?"

"Well we'd be fools not to take it, wouldn't we? What have we got

184

to lose? We're getting nowhere with the smallholding idea. We get knocked back every time we apply. What's the point of us staying here? Ah don't want to spend the rest of my life slogging myself to death for a pittance. If we move to another farm job we'll be no better off. They're all low pay for hard work. We'll always be poor. There no bloody future in that is there?"

Doris rubbed her hands together, then clasped them together. "Oh Stan, ah'm so excited. Just think, us, off to Canada." She stopped for a moment, and then said, "What shall we do with our furniture? And what about the dogs? What shall we do with Meg and Lassie?"

"Calm down, Doris, one thing at a time. Let's talk about it tonight. Look at the clock, ah'm due back in ten minutes and ah've not eaten my dinner yet."

There was one thing that bothered both of them and took the edge off their excitment, and that was telling their families. Doris dreaded breaking the news to her mother Edith and her Grandma, both of whom would be devastated at the idea of her emigrating. Even her Uncle Willie, who she often quarrelled with, would be incredibly sad at losing her, and as she thought about his reaction she knew he would stomp up to his garden and pretend he didn't care, and then spend the next few weeks in a bad mood making life miserable for everyone around him.

Stanley expected that his mother would be upset and no doubt there would be tears, but he thought to himself that she would cope with the idea of one of her brood leaving the country, and his father wouldn't really care much one way or the other, it would be something to boast about down the pit and at the British Legion if he had a son living in Canada

So at the weekend, before they had told anyone else, they set off to Wath. Much to Eileen's disappointment they left her at home looking after her baby sister, telling her that they couldn't do with the two of them that day as they had business to discuss, but promised they might go to the seaside next day, which was a Sunday.

It was decided that they would go to see Doris's family first, and as they drew to a halt in Sandygate near the blackened stone steps that led up to the cottage, they looked at each other. They got out of the car slowly, putting off the inevitable as long as possible.

They stood and gazed at the view down Sandygate which had been the scene of so many of their earlier days and they linked hands.

"You tell them, Doris, it's your Mam and Grandma," said Stanley, "They'll take it better from you."

Doris met his gaze and bit her lip, "Come on then, let's get it over with," and hand in hand they walked up the rough path, avoiding treading on the fresh ashes that had been thrown down that morning in an effort to fill in the pot holes.

The door stood wide open as they reached the top of the path and they could see that Edith was sitting on the black wooden dining chair with her feet up on the opposite one. Her shoes lay beside her and Doris rightly surmised that she had just finished her morning shift at the convalescing home just across the road where she worked. She was intent on reading the Weekly News and didn't hear them until they reached the doorway. Stanley gave a light cough and Edith lowered her paper and looked up.

Her face lit up at the sight of them and she roughly folded the paper and pushed her feet into her shoes.

"Doris and Stan! What a surprise. Didn't expect to see you today." She shook her mother's shoulder, "Hey wake up, Mam, look who's here."

Doris's Grandma had been enjoying an after dinner nap and looked startled at Edith's words.

"What are you waking me up for, Edi? I was having a nice little sleep then. What's the matter?" She turned her head and as she saw Doris exclaimed, "Why didn't you tell me our Doris was here?"

Edith made a face and whispered, "Your Grandma's hearing is getting worse. You'll have to shout a bit. Come on, sit down, I'll make a cup of tea." Picking up the kettle she pushed it on to the bars of the fire grate. "Where are the girls?" she asked as she thrust the poker into the fire and stirred it into life.

"We've come on our own, Mam. We've got something important to tell you. Where's Uncle Willie?" Edith's face instantly took on an anxious look and her mouth quivered ever so slightly. Her gaze went from Doris and then to Stanley and back again.

"Whatever is the matter, Doris? Has something happened to the girls? Is that why you've come on your own?"

William walked in at that moment, and seeing that Edith was upset he went towards her. Now William, could be the most irritable person you would ever wish to meet and frequently made Edith's life a misery with his bad tempered outbursts, but when the chips were down he always stood by her side and would have fought anyone who dared to hurt her.

"What's going on? What's the matter, Edi? "and glaring at Stanley said, " What have you upset her for?"

Of course it needed very few words from William to get Doris going, and she waded straight in. "That's bloody good coming from you. You're always on at her, shouting and throwing your weight about, aye, and throwing your dinner about an all come to that. Ah've seen you plenty of times."

Stanley shook his head. This was exactly what he had dreaded happening; Doris hell bent on going into a slanging match with her uncle. It only needed half an excuse to get her going.

He put his hand on her arm and slid it down till he could take hold of her hand, "Now steady up, Dot. Don't start. There's no need for all that."

Stanley had little liking for Doris's uncle but turning to him said as calmly as he could, "Don't jump to conclusions, William, we haven't said anything yet, we were waiting until you came, so that we could tell you all together. Right, Doris, you tell them the news."

He stood back and looked at her. She was wearing the red coat that she had made herself and he had to admit she looked beautiful in it, but he was sure the colour didn't help her temper, she seemed more inclined to fire off whenever she went out in it and he thought to himself, 'Talk about red rag to a bull, that's Doris all over.' And he decided that the next time she needed a new coat he'd try to get her to buy a nice pale blue one. Maybe she'd be calmer wearing blue.

Doris took a deep breath and went and sat next to her mother on the couch, "Stanley's got a new job, Mam."

"Oh is that all? Is that what you were going to tell us? Is it further away from Wath? Ah won't mind love, ah can always come and stay with you for holidays."

"Yes it is further away, Mam. A lot further away. It's in Canada."

There was complete silence for a few seconds, and then both Edith and William spoke at once. "Canada?" they echoed. Doris's Grandmother sat up straight. "Where did you say? Conisborough? Well that's not far away. But you'd be better off staying at Adwick, Stanley, it's a lot nicer there,"

"No, Grandma, we're going to Canada," explained Doris.

"What the heck do you want to go to Canada for? It snows a lot there you know and they're over run with bears." Tears began to trickle down her wrinkled cheeks. "We'd never see you again." And she bent over and pulled her apron over her head and sobbed quietly, rocking herself back and forth.

William stood up. "Now look what you've done. You know how much family she's lost in her lifetime, and now you two plan on buggering off. You are so bloody selfish you two, you think of no one but yourselves." He walked out of the house, and both Stanley and Doris knew that he had gone to seek solace in his garden.

Edith tried her best to put a brave face on her feelings but Stanley knew her well enough to realise that she was just holding herself together until they had gone and then she would break down. Doris and her family were her life and he suddenly realised just how much their going would affect her.

Doris tried to be bright and encouraging, "You'll be able to come out and have holidays with us, Mam," she said. Edith looked from one to the other. She knew the words were empty and just an attempt to pacify her; and what Stanley wanted to say was, "Don't talk daft, Dot, it takes your Mam all her time to find her way to Adwick. How the hell would she be able to get to Canada, even if she could afford the fare?"and he felt the dream of the new life in Canada begin to slip away from him.

They left shortly after that, unable to bear the sight of Edith's woebegone face and her efforts to try to look normal. As they walked down the path together Stanley gave a huge sigh as if he had been holding his breath for hours and Doris echoed it.

They were both very apprehensive as they tapped at the door of Stanley's old family home at 93 Oak Road and entered the kitchen.

Ada was standing at the sink washing pots and smiled at the sight of them and gave them her usual welcome. "Well ah don't know, look here, it's our Stan and Doris." She invariably used the same words every time they arrived and then put the kettle on.

Stanley gave her a smile and a quick hug but instantly Ada knew something was wrong and looked at him closely, "What's the matter, Stanley?" she asked.

"Come on through, Mam, we've something to tell you," said Stanley, mentally squaring his shoulders, and he walked through into the crowded living room with Doris close behind him. He had been hoping to catch his Mother and Father alone but there was slim chance of that on a Saturday afternoon.

His Father, Harold, was sitting at the table that was covered with a snowy white tablecloth, and set with Ada's best crockery, a plate of boiled ham, thickly sliced bread and butter, and of course the blue patterned jug in the centre containing several sticks of celery.

Stanley marvelled at the warmth of his father's greeting. He seemed to have become more and more popular with Harold as the years had passed, and it was taking some getting used to. He kept expecting him to revert back to the harsh character he remembered from his childhood days.

"Nah then, Stan and Doris, we didn't expect to see you two today. Move up you lot," and he waved his hand in the direction of the sofa where two of his daughters sat with their boyfriends. "Let our Stan and Doris sit there, we don't see 'em very often."

Stanley held up his hand, "No we're ok, leave em be. Doris can sit here on the sofa arm and ah'll stand. We're not stopping long. We have to get back. The animals need feeding."

Ada sat down, she was looking at Stanley expectantly, "Hurry up, Stanley, what have you got to tell us, you're worrying me."

Using Doris's words when she had told her family, he said quietly, "Ah've got another job. But it's in Canada."

Harold's face was a picture, his jaw dropped as if he had been struck and Ada went pale, and she repeated her son's words.

"You've got a job in Canada? Do you mean you're emigrating? Oh, you can't do that, Stanley. We'd never see you again. Please don't do that, Stanley, ah couldn't bear it." She began crying and the tears rolled down her face.

Stanley was taken aback, he had expected that she would be upset, and probably shed a tear or two, but his mother had always seemed to be able to take everything in her stride and cope with whatever life threw at her.

"We'll be able to write to you, Mam, and it's a really good chance for us to have a better life," he reasoned, and looked at his father hoping for some sign of support but found that he looked only one step from breaking down himself.

His younger brother, Cyril, jumped up from the cushion he had been sitting on close to the fire. "Did you say you were going to Canada, Stan? Aw that sounds brilliant, wait till our Harold knows. Ah might come with you."

Stanley laughed at his words, but stopped short when he saw his mother's face and decided it might be a good time to leave.

They were quiet on the way home, both lost in thought. Stanley brought the car to a halt in Brodsworth and switched the engine off. They were in the prettiest part of the village that had tall beech trees on each side of the road and rockery flowers hanging over the old stone walls. He wound down the window and listened to the wind stirring the leaves and they sat quietly staring into space for a moment or two.

He turned to Doris and taking her hand he rubbed her golden wedding ring round and round her finger. "Well that was awful, Doris. I hate upsetting the family. Ah even felt sorry for your Uncle Willie and God knows there's not much love lost between us."

Doris nodded slowly, "Ah know it's your dream, love, but maybe we should think a bit more about it."

"Aye, we'll sleep on it eh?" Stanley sighed and got out of the car with the starting handle, and turned the engine back into life. "There's one thing, Dot, if we decide not to go we won't have to worry about what to do with the dogs, and there be no frantic rush to sell the pigs and chickens."

"It sounds to me that you have already made your mind up, Stan. You're not going to take that job are you?"

Never one to make snap decisions, Stanley put the starting handle back under his seat and shook his head. "Ah think we need to study it out a bit more, Dot, it's a big decision. Ah think ah might have got a bit carried away. Ah must admit to underestimating how much it would affect other people. Ah was totally unprepared for how upset your Mam and mine would be."

He took a deep breath and smiled at her, "Come on love, let's get off home and see if our Eileen has sold her sister to the gypsies. I saw some hanging about up Red House Lane yesterday."

When they arrived home Eileen was waiting on the doorstep holding Frances by the hand and was clearly very glad to see them back home. Doris scooped her youngest daughter into her arms and hugged her tight.

"Has she been good?" she asked.

Eileen said "Yes," as she crossed her fingers behind her back and gave Frances a sharp look. "There's a letter for you, Dad," she called, "I think it's important. It's got a Wakefield stamp on it," and she disappeared around the corner before another chore was found for her.

Stanley and Doris almost raced each other into the house and there it was on the table, a long brown envelope, post marked Wakefield. Doris would have torn it open in her rush to see what it was about but Stanley picked up the butter knife and carefully slit it open.

That letter was to be the deciding factor in their dilemma about Canada.

Apparently there was a twenty five acre smallholding available in Wickersley, and as usual the words of the committee were that, 'they were invited to apply for it.'

"What do you want to do Stan? Do you think we would have a chance?"

"Well, Dot," he said, as he looked upwards and raised his eyebrows slightly, "We've got as good a chance as anyone else, as long as the chairman hasn't got any more bloody friends or relatives that are after a place."

There were four letters posted early on Monday morning. There was one to Edith, one to Ada, one to the Wakefield County Council, containing their completed application, and finally one to Canada House turning down the offer of a job on the Canadian railways.

It happened to be the time of year when one of the jobs on the farm was pulling the wild oats out of the crops of wheat and barley just before they were due to be harvested. It was mostly a very solitary occupation and one that gave plenty of thinking time, and Stanley spent much of the day wondering if he had made the right decision.

CHAPTER 22

Life settled down again into a routine. The harvesting began, and every day Stanley and Doris waited for a reply to their application for the smallholding in Wickersley.

They had been shortlisted for almost every smallholding that they had applied for and Stanley felt confident that this time they would succeed; so it came as an unpleasant surprise when their application was rejected.

As he read the letter he was filled with regrets that they had not gone ahead with their emigration plans, and he threw the letter on to the table, stamped outside, and went up the garden path to lean over the fence looking at his stock, until the anger and disappointment settled down.

"Ah'm going bloody backwards instead of forwards," he muttered to himself, and he kicked the fence in frustration. It must have been the kick that disturbed the rat that was busy gorging itself on the best quality pig meal out of the trough. It quickly retreated into a corner of the pen beneath pig's bedding, and the moment Stanley stepped out of view it had the audacity to return to its feasting.

Stanley had known that they had vermin hanging around the stock but this was the first time he had actually seen a rat. All his anger focused on it and he crept quietly away from the pen and back down to the shed, looking around for a suitable weapon to kill it. He found a lightweight hammer that he could swing easily and gave it a few imaginary swipes before he walked very quietly back up to the pig sty, hoping it was still intent on eating its fill.

Yes, there it was, with its back to him and Stanley could not help a shiver of horror running through himself, but this was war, and putting his hand on the top rail he leaped over the fence. The rat saw him and made a dash across the pig pen with Stanley in pursuit, it reached the wall and without a moment's hesitation ran up the rough stones heading for a gap near the ceiling; Stanley swiped at it with the hammer but the rat was too fast, and it disappeared into the hole head first with its long tail trailing behind.

Dropping the hammer, Stanley grabbed its tail and held on to it, forgetting his revulsion in his determination to catch the rodent. He gripped it as tight as he could and pulled, but the rat had a firm foothold and continued its desperate effort to escape and Stanley found himself clutching just the skin of the rat's tail as its owner disappeared from view. He looked at the skin in disgust and threw it away with a shiver of loathing and went back to the house to wash his hands thoroughly.

For a short time at least, the incident with the rat had taken his mind off his disappointment but now it hit him again, and he barely spoke to Greg and Bert as they worked together in the field of barley. But by teatime he had come to the conclusion that there was little they could do except carry on as before and hope that another chance came their way.

As the year wore on it was obvious that they would have to spend yet another winter where they were. Stanley asked again if they could have electricity and a bathroom put into the cottage, but was met with the same answer as before. Resigned to it, they began to stock up with logs and bought another twenty young cockerels to fatten up for the Christmas trade.

In the second week in December Stanley woke early and decided to feed the pigs and chickens before he had his breakfast. As he opened the back door, Lassie, his youngest dog, came sneaking in with her tail between her legs and the hairs standing up on the back of her neck. Her coat was wet and cold and she had obviously been out in the open for some time. She slunk around the back of him sneaking sideways looks and he knew something was badly wrong.

Bending down he stroked her rough fur and said, "What's up, Lassie? What's wrong?" and he picked up the torch and went outside. It was still very dark and the feeble beam from the torch showed only a limited view, but as he walked cautiously up the garden path with Lassie following, he realised that the chicken shed had been broken into. The gate swung loose in the wind and the water trough was up turned. Fearing that all his cockerels had gone he shone the torch into the shed and thankfully found them all roosting safely on their perch.

'But what was Lassie doing loose?' he wondered. Her kennel was situated between the two chicken sheds, almost out of sight. As he looked at her and she began wagging her tail Stanley guessed what had happened. It was well known that Lassie had a talent for slipping her collar over her head and never wasted time barking but would go straight in and bite if the need arose.

As he told Doris later, "I bet whoever it was, got the shock of their bloody lives when Lassie appeared out of the dark. I hope she managed to bite them."

"Do you think there would be more than one person then?" Doris asked. Stanley nodded as he stroked his dog and told her that she may not be the bonniest dog he'd ever had but she was certainly the best.

"Ah do Doris, they would need at least two or maybe three to carry the birds. They're heavy now. Ah bet it's that bloody gang from down Adwick Lane. Do you remember them, Dot? I almost stumbled into em one night when I took the mill stream path coming back from the union meeting. The thieving swines. Everyone knows em, and t'bobbys know what they are up to most of the time but they never seem to be able to catch em.

The following evening Stanley brought all the fattened birds down into the old stable near the house and placed Lassie's kennel just outside the door. As an extra precaution Meg was also stationed in the yard. Stanley knew there was no chance that she would tackle anyone but hoped she might just put a little effort in and do a bit of barking.

Thankfully, the would be thieves stayed away, and Doris said she hoped it was because they had septic legs from Lassie's bites. They were all thankful when the birds were sold and the profit from them safely in their pockets.

Had they but known it, that winter was to be their last one in the cottage at Adwick, It was in the middle March 1953 when everything changed for them. Stanley was preparing the seed bed for a new crop and he was at his happiest. The newly turned soil had a sweet fresh smell, the leaves on the trees were just beginning to unfurl, the birds were singing and Stanley was full of optimism and hope on the day that he saw Bert striding across the field towards him.

It was not unusual for Bert to come and accompany him on a couple of circuits of the field, riding on the drawbar at the rear of the tractor while he discussed work that needed doing on the farm. But today there was something about his expression that made Stanley apprehensive, and he stopped and waited for his foreman to reach him.

"Now then, Stan." "Now then, Bert." That was their usual exchange of greeting, but today there was no smile to go with it from Bert. He looked solemn and very serious and Stanley began to wonder if he had done something wrong.

"Ah need a word with you, Stan. But first ah need you to assure me that you will keep strictly to yourself what I'm going to tell you," and he looked Stanley in the face and waited until he said, "Of course, Bert, whatever you say is completely private. You know that I never repeat our conversations."

"But this, Stanley, is different. It concerns Mr Smith and I could lose my job over what I have to say. I need your word that you will not disclose where you have got the information that I am about to give you."

Stanley offered his hand and they shook on it. Bert took off his cap and rubbed his hand over his thinning hair. He took a breath and looked away for a moment before he said quickly, as if he needed to be rid of the words. "The boss is going give you a week's notice, Stan."

Never had Stanley expected that. He gaped at Bert almost as if he could not understand what had been said. "But why, Bert? Ah've not done anything wrong have ah? Bloody hell ah'm sure ah work hard enough. Don't ah Bert?"

"Oh your work is without question. The boss himself has always said that you are the best worker he's ever had and the most skilled. But it's a matter of economics you see Stan. He's getting rid of all the cattle and the horses, and when he does that, we'll be overstaffed.

He knows that you are after a smallholding of your own and will probably be leaving at some time in the future. Then there is the matter of the cottage. Nobody knows better than you and Doris what state it's in. It's only a matter of time before it is condemned as unfit for human habitation unless there is a lot of money spent on it. "

Bert looked away and then back at him. "He told me to give you notice but I refused. I thought he was going to sack me on the spot but I stood up to him, and he knows he needs me to run this place when he's away on business so much. So you can expect him coming to see you to do the dirty deed himself. Be ready for him. Forewarned is forearmed as they say. That's the best I can do for you Stan."

Stanley gave him a wave and a choked, 'Thank you,' before he slipped the tractor into gear and continued his work. He could hardly speak and needed time to think. He dreaded telling Doris and was thankful there was an hour to go before he went home for his mid-day meal.

By the time he walked into the house his head was buzzing with plans and arrangements to be made. He let Doris put the food on the table before he told her, and her reaction was every bit as bad as he had expected it to be.

"Steady down, Doris," he said, as she threatened to go across to the farm herself. "Just remember we're not supposed to even know yet, and I've given Bert my word that we won't let on that he has forewarned us. We have to play this very carefully. First thing ah need to do is to start looking for another job."

He picked up the Farmer & Stock Breeder and turned to the situations vacant page and ran his finger down the page stopping at the only one that seemed suitable.

"Listen to this," he said "It's at a place near Pontefract." He began to read aloud. "Skilled stock man required for large farm. Must also have experience tractor driving, and using machinery. Newly converted accommodation available if required. Apply in writing or telephone."

Ripping out the page he pushed his plate to one side and stood up. "I'm going to go to the telephone box right now Doris. While I'm gone can you write me out a letter that says I wish to give one month's notice and address it to Mr Smith. I want to have it with me, just in case the boss turns up today. I want to make sure I'm the one that gives notice. I don't want to give him the chance to sack me; it wouldn't look good when I apply for another job."

Within five minutes Stanley was on the telephone speaking to a man who was destined to become his future employer. He explained that he had just seen the advertisement in the magazine and was very interested in the vacancy. An appointment was made there and then for the following Saturday.

Returning home he briefly he gave Doris the news of the interview, then putting the letter that she had written into his pocket he rushed off back to work.

On Saturday, Stanley and Doris set off once again up the Great North Road to attend an interview. This was getting to be a habit. As always, Stanley was there much too early and they spent an anxious half hour sitting in the car, waiting for the clock to tick around to the appointment time.

Stanley looked again at his paper with the address on and the name of his prospective new employer and told Doris once more that it was a Mr. McLain that they had to see.

"Do you think he's Scottish then?" asked Doris, "Did he sound Scottish on the phone?"

"No, ah don't think so." Stanley shook his head, "Very well spoken though, and very polite, but firm," and that was as much as he remembered from their brief conversation on the telephone. "We'll just have to wait and see, Dot. I hope to God that this works out." He tapped his hand on the steering wheel; he was feeling extremely nervous, so much depended on this interview.

They had found Ponte Hall easily enough and left their car parked on the road. As they walked down the drive they looked at the building in front of them and then at each other. Both gave a sharp intake of breath in admiration. It was such a graceful old house with a large oak front door and two long windows at each side.

"How would you like to live here Doris?" he asked quietly as she took his arm. He looked down at her. He always felt such a glow of pride when they walked arm in arm. She glanced up at him and gave him one of her brilliant smiles, "I think I could manage it, Stanley Dale, as long as you were with me." He grinned back at her and told her that he would buy it for her if he ever came up on the pools.

He rang the bell and listened as they heard its sound echo in the house, and within seconds they heard footsteps coming towards the door.

Stanley was about to meet a man who would have tremendous influence in his life and would prove to be a true friend in spite of their different backgrounds.

As the door opened they were face to face with Stanley's future employer and he greeted them with a smile and invited them in. He led the way to his office and called down the hall for a pot of tea to be brought.

"Sit down, Mr and Mrs Dale, make yourselves comfortable, we'll have a cup of tea before we get down to business." As they waited for the tea he began to tell them about the farm and the school and shops in the village of Brotherton. Then he got around to describing the accommodation and explained that the house that went with the job was actually part of Clamton Hall. It was almost ready to be lived in apart from the electricity being connected and that would happen well before the winter set in.

"Is there a bathroom?" asked Doris.

"Oh yes, Mrs Dale, and also a separate toilet. There is a new hot water system of course, heated by the back boiler behind the fire. I think you would find it quite satisfactory. It is very spacious.

Stanley could see that Doris was sold on it straight away and relaxed as the tea was brought in. There was something about Mr McLain that was straight and fair and instinctively he felt that he would be a good man to work for.

"Well, now then, let's get down to business. Can I call you Stanley? I assume you have brought your references?"

As he looked through them Stanley felt proud. He knew that they were a good record of his working life and evidently Mr McLain thought so too as he folded them carefully back into their envelopes.

"You are very highly recommended, Stanley, and obviously experienced at all aspects of farming. The job is yours if you want it. The wages are four pounds ten shillings per week and there is usually some overtime available. There is a rent of five shillings per week for the house. There are plenty of fallen trees about in the woods if you want to saw your own logs. You can use the tractor and saw bench if you want to do that. But don't feel you need to make your mind up immediately, let me take you down to the farm and show you around before you decide. It's a big decision."

Stanley looked at Doris, he could read what she was thinking. The house was what she was interested in and he knew she was keen to see it. "Yes, "he said, "We would like to see the house and the farm thank you."

Mr McLain stood up. "Right, I'll go and get the Land Rover and take you now." He moved quickly across the room and indicated for them to follow.

Within minutes they were sitting in an old Land Rover that looked as if it had not been swept out since the day it was bought. Stanley dusted the seat for Doris. Mr McLain sucked in his breath, "I do apologise for the state of this I would have taken you in the car but my wife has gone out in it," and he made an ineffective effort to brush the dashboard with a filthy duster and only managed to raise more dust. "I feel really embarrassed about this, Mrs Dale. This vehicle needs a good clean. We've just been so busy recently."

Doris reassured him that she didn't mind in the least and it was true; she was so excited about seeing the house that the state of the Land Rover did not worry her in the slightest. It was becoming obvious that Stanley's potential new employer did everything at top speed. They held on tight as they headed down Ponte Lane at speed and then without warning turned sharp left up a narrow road that was almost hidden from view by the belt of trees and rhododendron bushes.

As they cleared the trees they could see a long straight road ahead of them that stretched for what looked like half a mile, and at the end of it, there were the ruins of a large house. Stanley and Doris had never seen anything like it and sat speechless as they drew nearer.

Impressive carved stone pillars stood at what would have the entrance, and now that they were close, they could see the enormous pile of stones, and the skeleton of interior walls still standing, as if defying all efforts to remove them.

At each side of the ruins were two buildings that were still intact, and had originally been part of the older house. They were looking at what had once been Clamton Hall, a stately home of tremendous size. Mr.McLain pointed to the smaller of the buildings and told them that that would be their home if Stanley decided to take the job.

He came to a halt at the front entrance, and jumping from the Land Rover he bounded up the steps that led to the heavy oak door. Doris followed him with Stanley behind and they found themselves in a long corridor with another door at the end of it, which opened out into a recently constructed yard.

They would have gone to investigate it further but Mr McLain was leading the way into a large square room with a huge fireplace. Two long windows gave views out on to the fields that had once been part of the private estate. The walls were still decorated with wallpaper that had been grand and expensive many years ago but was now faded and sooty, with marks where pictures had once hung.

Doris could not help a gasp escaping her at the sight of the room and then quickly bit her lip, but Mr McLain smiled at her, "Yes. I know how you feel, Mrs Dale. it still has that effect on me even now. I wish I could have seen it in its hey-day, it must have been magnificent. It was originally owned by Sir John Ramsden. Most of the stonework and gateways have ram's heads carved into them. He must have been a very wealthy man."

He continued down the corridor and opened the next door

and instantly it was obvious that this would be the main living area. This was where some modernisation had taken place. It was slightly smaller than the last room and a cooking stove had been installed. A kitchen led off that room and then a bathroom which Doris inspected and nodded her head in approval.

Although electricity had been installed it was not yet connected, but they were assured that it would all be in working order by the autumn.

There were just the bedrooms to look at now and they climbed the curved staircase to inspect them. The long corridor downstairs was matched by the identical one on the landing upstairs and off it were two huge bedrooms and one just slightly smaller. Stanley opened a pair of large double doors and discovered a white sink that they were told would have been used by the maids when they were cleaning.

Doris was quite dazzled by the size of the house and the thought of actually having a bathroom, an indoor water toilet, and electricity. Her thoughts were already turning as to how they could find enough furniture to fill it.

Next they were taken on a tour of the farm attached to the hall, and also the one at the other end of the estate. There were over a thousand acres being farmed at the moment and Mr. McLain had plans to extend that by turning some of the woodlands into arable land.

He explained as they went around the farm that he had bought the whole estate just after the war. The army had occupied the hall and land during the war and he said bitterly that they had done tremendous damage to the buildings and walls around the lake and the woods.

"Sheer sacrilege it was, some of the deliberate damage that was done. If I live to be a hundred I still won't ever be able to repair it all," he said. "But on the good side that probably brought the price down in my favour. I'll take you down to see the lake now. It's a real beauty spot."

How right he was. As they turned the corner and the lake came into view he stopped to let them take a good look. At the far side of the lake, rhododendrons grew all the way down the steep banks to the water's edge and in the distance an arched bridge crossed the narrowest part.

As if to complete the picture, a lone swan glided across the water and Mr. McLain pointed it out and said that it may look elegant but it had a bad temper, and would attack anything or anyone that dared to venture on to the water.

"My son David crossed swords with him last week," he said. "He'd got a canoe and decided to try it out on the lake, but Billy, that's what we call the swan, by the way, decided he had no business trespassing on his territory, so he flew at David and tipped him out of the canoe and into the water."

With the tour of the house and farm completed they returned to Ponte hall and as they got out of the Land Rover Stanley looked at Doris and she nodded slightly. They were invited to come inside and then the big question was asked.

"Well, do you want more time to decide Stanley? I can give you a couple of days but then I would need an answer."

"No need for any more time to decide Mr. McLain. I would like to accept. When would you like me to start?"

CHAPTER 23

They drove home feeling completely stunned. Their heads were buzzing with plans of things to do and arrangements to be made. It had been decided that they would move in just over two weeks' time. Stanley's first priority was to make sure that he handed his notice in at Smiths and he quickly revised the one month's notice that he had been planning on giving.

Almost the first thing he did when he got home was to tear up the original letter that he had been carrying about with him, and draft out a new one that stated he wished to give two week's notice. When that was safely done and tucked away in his work haversack ready to present to Mr. Smith on Monday he felt able to turn his mind to other things.

His next concern was their stock. It would all have to go, with the exception of their sow who was due to have her litter in less than four weeks. She would be going with them and he had been promised the use of one of the stables to keep her in. The other pigs would have to go to market next Saturday.

Doris was fretting about how much it was going to cost to actually move. Stanley pointed out that they would have no alternative but to dip into their farm fund and they would try to make it up again later.

So Doris went shopping, and bought enough wood patterned linoleum for the two long passages and yards of cheap curtain fabric from Doncaster market for the big windows, a large square of coconut matting for the living room and even some bargain priced stair carpeting. That would have to do she told herself, anything else they would just have to manage without. She worried about the cost of it all as she travelled home on the bus and stared unseeing out of the window as she added up the cost of it all in her head.

Stanley was hoping to see Mr. Smith on Monday rather than have to give his notice in to his mother, Mrs Smith senior, at the Adwick farmhouse. He was in luck. At nine o'clock on Monday morning while he was working in the bottom fields near the willow garth he saw his employer's green Jaguar come to a halt at the gate.

He took a deep breath and got the letter out of his haversack. He needed to be sure to get in first. He was not looking forward to this. Although he could understand the financial reasons for sacking him, it did nothing to stem the simmering anger at the injustice of it.

He stopped the tractor and watched as his employer strode across the field towards him, carefully avoiding the wettest parts of the newly turned earth. It was a grass meadow that Stanley was ploughing up and was marshy in some parts. Personally, he thought it was a big mistake to plough the grass up. It was much too wet for crops and Bert had agreed with him but as he said, 'Orders are orders.'

As he approached, Stanley noted the expensive moleskin trousers the farmer was wearing, and the tweed jacket. Then he looked at his sturdy brown brogue shoes polished to a high gloss and thought that one day he would have some just like them.

Mr Smith lifted his hand in greeting to Stanley, "Good morning, I won't keep you long, don't want to stop you working but I do need a quiet word with you." He reached his hand into his inside pocket and as he did so he began, "I am afraid this is---,"

But before he could finish his sentence Stanley handed him his own brown envelope, "Ah'm glad you've come this morning, I wanted to give you this."

Mr Smith looked at the envelope and began to open it. "You'll find that my notice is inside. Will two weeks be alright for you Mr Smith?"

"Err well yes. This is a surprise, Stanley, I didn't know you were thinking of leaving."

Stanley told him briefly that he had found another job with a better house and better prospects.

"Oh very well. I will be sorry to lose you. It's a shame we couldn't improve the cottage for you. I take it that's the reason you've decided to go?"

Stanley so desperately wanted to let it all spill out, but he thought of Bert and the promise he had made to him, so he kept quiet, but gave a sort of non-committal toss of his head and rolled his eyes. "You can say that again. The winters have been an ordeal and have got worse every year. So we're glad to be getting out of it."

"Tch, yes I know it needs modernising, but it's just not worth spending money on. Are you staying local then, Stanley?"

He listened as Stanley told him who he would be working for and he nodded, "Ah yes, I've heard of Mr. McLain. He has a big farm up near Pontefract. He's got a good reputation. Best of luck," They shook hands, Stanley's bony calloused hand clasping his employers large red fleshy one and they looked each other in the eye.

Before he left, Stanley thanked him for employing him for the last six years and said he hoped they would remain on good terms. "

"I see no reason why not Stanley, no reason at all. If I see Mr McLain I will tell him that his gain is my loss. Best of luck." Turning, he left, and strode out across the field.

At home when Doris heard about the meeting she said incredulously, "What, you actually thanked him for employing you? You've been working yourself to death for him for the last few years and he was about to sack you."

"Aye Doris, but I haven't forgotten that it was him who actually gave us the chance to get out of Winifred Road, and besides you never know if we will need him at some time in the future so it's best to keep on the right side of him."

She put her arms around him and nibbled his ear, and said, "Ah you're right I suppose," then sat on his knee until it was time for him to go back to work.

Two weeks later at mid-day they were ready to set off. They had hired the local coal man and his lorry to take all the outdoor equipment that they had acquired over the years, including the shed that Stanley had made. They had heaved it on to the back of the lorry with the aid of long poles, ropes and the help of a few neighbours. Alongside it there were rolls of netting, tools, feeding troughs, dog kennels, and all kinds of paraphilia that would be essential for their future stock rearing and particularly if they ever got the small holding that they wanted so badly.

They had also hired a furniture van for all their household goods. It was packed to the roof and Doris said she could not believe that they had gathered so much furniture in the tiny cottage.

Stanley took one last walk around the garden where he and Doris had worked so hard. The crops he had planted last month were just beginning to push their way up through the earth and he paused briefly to admire the healthy beans and peas, and sighed as he thought that someone else would get the benefit of them. He checked the pigsty and the buildings and thought of the different animals that had occupied them. They were all cleaned out and swept up. He closed the doors and slid the bolts across to secure them, and then walked back down the garden path for the final time.

He reached the rough trellis archway that covered the earth closet and the smell of the strong Izal disinfectant that Doris sloshed around every day reached his nostrils, and he thought with satisfaction that whatever the future held, at least they would have the luxury of two indoor water toilets in the new house.

As he turned the corner he could see his elder daughter waiting at the side of the furniture van with their two dogs and a wave of love for her swept over him. He had caught her unawares and she looked sad and forlorn standing there. He watched her for a moment and thought how tall she was becoming. He knew she was unhappy at having to leave her school and friends at such short notice, but what could he do? Like him and Doris, she would just have to get used to it.

She turned as he called to her, "Come on then, love, time to go. Climb aboard." Eileen and the dogs were the last things to be packed into the van. A space had been left for them and a place to sit on the piled up rugs. When they were comfortably settled

Stanley smiled at her, "Now you'll be comfortable there. It won't be too dark as there's a gap between the doors when they're closed, so it will let a bit of light in. Me and your Mam and Frances will be there before you, we'll be waiting. Look after the dogs and don't be standing up to look out through the gap, stay where you are until the doors are opened for you again. Now, you're ok aren't you?"

As she nodded, the driver appeared and between them they lifted the bottom door into place and bolted it securely. Next, the top door was dropped down and just as Stanley had said, it left a gap through which a beam of light shone. Eileen swallowed and put an arm around each of the dogs. Meg snuggled up close and laid her head on her knee while Lassie sat up straight and gave a little whimper. She would have jumped down if Eileen had not held her tight.

The engine started up and the van began to move off, slowly gathering speed. The piled up furniture creaked as it shifted with the movement of the van and Meg looked up and gave a nervous woof. Through the gap Eileen could see the familiar street retreating into the distance until they turned the corner and then it was out of sight.

Before very long they were on to the Great North Road and she could see the traffic behind them. She knew that when they reached Wentbridge they would be half way there, and she tried to spot the signposts, standing up in the rocking van but keeping hold of a rope that hung on the side. She had a vision of the doors falling off the rickety old van and herself and the dogs falling out into the road. Quickly she sat back down on the rugs and pressed herself as far back from the doors as she could.

The brakes on the van began to whine and the van juddered slightly and she knew they were now going down the steep hill into Wentbridge. All the contents inside seemed to be leaning towards the front as they descended and she heard the sound of breaking crockery and pulled a face knowing how cross her mother would be.

She held her breath as in her imagination she saw the brakes failing and the van crashing into the stream at the bottom; but there was to be no such excitement as the road levelled out and the van crossed the bridge.

There was a change to the sound of the engine as it strained to carry the load up the hill out of the valley. Slower and slower the van went, and the furniture now seemed to be leaning towards her. She stood up again and peered through the gap. A lorry was following them, only yards behind and she wondered if the driver could see her eyes staring at him and quickly dodged back out of his line of vision.

It was becoming very boring sitting on the rugs in the dim half-light of the van. The dogs were restless and it was a great relief when the van stopped and the engine switched off. Thankfully the doors were now being opened and there stood her Dad, holding out his hand to help her down.

"Well, we're here. Have the dogs been ok? Ah hope they haven't been sick on the rugs. Come on, our Frances is nagging for her big sister."

As she jumped down she stood gazing at the sight of the ruins in front of her and the big house that was to be their home. It was like nothing she had ever seen before or could have imagined. The delivery men were already pushing past her to begin unloading and she knew better than to stand in their way.

Frances was running towards her as if she had not seen her for months rather than a couple of hours and she scooped her up and swung her round till she was dizzy, then hand in hand they went into the house to explore.

By any standards the house was big, but compared to the cottage that they were used to, it was massive. Frances ran up and down the long corridor that was their hall and then did the same on the identical one upstairs that was the landing. They were to have the middle bedroom that had a magnificent marble fireplace and two long windows either side of it.

Each one had wooden shutters that closed over the glass, then folded away into the casements when they were not needed. These delighted Doris as she pointed out how much cold they would keep out in winter. Privately Eileen hated them and felt they made the room seem like a dark prison and resolved never close them no matter how cold it was. However, winter was a long way away, the sun was shining today and they had exploring to do.

It had been decided before they left the cottage in Adwick that the most useful thing Eileen could do was to look after her young sister and keep her out of the way until the furniture was unloaded. So as soon as the old black pram was unearthed out of the van, they were ready to set off.

Stanley put his arm on Eileen's shoulder and led them to the gateway where he stopped, and pointing to the big beech tree down the road he told her to go straight past that and said, "Can you see that entrance with the red brickwork at each side?" without waiting for an answer he continued, "Go down there, just follow the road and that's where the lake is. Don't go letting Frances fall in. See you both later." He gave her shoulder a squeeze before he turned and hurried back to organise the unloading of the shed from the back of the coal lorry.

He was anticipating problems with it, but gravity was on their side and it seemed to be proving much easier to get it off the lorry than it had been to load it in the first place. With the aid of two strong batons propped on the back of the lorry to act as skids, they slid it down until the front end hit the floor. There it stopped and appeared to be stuck, but without any more ado or consultation with Stanley, the driver got into the lorry and putting it into gear set off quickly, allowing the back end of the shed to drop to the floor with a load crash.

Jumping out of the lorry he came to the rear of it with a big grin on his face to find Stanley examining the shed for damage. "Well that got it off didn't it?" he said.

Stanley was not amused, "Aye, it did and smashed the window and the hinges on the door. Stupid bugger," he said through gritted teeth, "Ah was going to use the jacks to lower it down slowly." He reached into his pocket and produced the money for the hire of the lorry. "Here take it and bugger off before ah deduct a quid for the damage tha's done."

The driver shrugged his shoulders and left, leaving the shed in the middle of the courtyard with the broken glass spread out around it and the door hanging loose from the one remaining hinge.

Stanley knew he would have no alternative but to leave it where it was for the time being and concentrate on getting the furniture van unloaded. They were paying for the van by the hour and Stanley was anxious to get them away as soon as possible. He took hold of one of the rolled up mattresses and carried it indoors and up the stairs, and it did nothing to pacify his temper when he discovered the driver and his mate standing in front of the window admiring the view while they each smoked a leisurely cigarette.

He dropped the mattress on to the floor raising a cloud of dust and the men turned towards him, both looking startled and guilty. "Just admiring the view, Stan," the driver said as he nipped out his Woodbine and placed it carefully in an old tobacco tin, and his mate hurriedly did the same. Between them they bent to pick up the mattress that Stanley had dropped, obviously intending to place in on the wooden bed frame.

"You can leave that, ah reckon if ah've carried it upstairs on me own ah can manage to put it on t'bed. Ah don't want you two wasting time. Just concentrate on getting t'furniture out of the van, then you can go. Ah can't afford to pay you to stand about smoking, so no more fags until you're smoking em in your own time and in your own place."

With his words the atmosphere changed, but at least they got the furniture out of the van and into the house in record time. Stanley whispered to Doris that he thought he had probably upset them, and added, "Ah'm not bloody bothered if they like it or not. We're not paying em to stand around puffing smoke into t'air."

Half an hour later they were on their own, surrounded by their belongings that looked woefully shabby and inadequate in such a big house. Between them they pushed and pulled the furniture into some sort of order by which time they were nearing exhaustion, and Doris declared she had better go and make the beds up while Stanley got the fire going.

"Just think," she said, "When the water's hot we can all have a bath, I don't care if it is sunny outside, get the fire banked up well Stan, I can hardly wait to get into a nice hot bath."

However, lighting the fire proved more difficult than they had anticipated. The minute he put a match to the kindling, smoke belched down chimney, filling the room with soot and smoke. Stanley hurriedly pulled the sticks off the fire and carried them outside. He tried again a few minutes later holding a sheet of newspaper up to the fire to see if it would draw the smoke away, but it was no use, and he sat back on his heels, put his hands on his hips and swore at it. Doris came into the room at that moment and held her hand to her mouth. "Bloody hell, Stan, the room's full of smoke, what have you been doing?"

"What do you mean what have ah been doing? Av been trying to light the bloody fire, but t'chimneys blocked. There'll be no bath tonight." He went outside and looked up at the roof, counting the pots until he located the one above the living room and as he watched, a jackdaw flew out of it."

Doris had followed him outside and he pointed at the bird, "There, look; there's jackdaws nesting in the chimney, we'll have to get them shifted. But it's too late to get it done today, we'll have to manage without the fire. Ah'll speak to Mr McLain first thing tomorrow."

"Well you'll have to get the primus stove going then Stan, it's the only thing we've got to cook on and I'll have to boil water on it for us to wash in tonight. I hope we've got enough paraffin."

While all this had been going on Eileen and Frances were having their own little adventure. They had followed the path as Stanley had directed, and soon came to the lake.

Eileen was awestruck, and thought she had never seen anywhere so beautiful. Large clumps of water lilies floated here and there and the rhododendrons on the hill at the opposite side of the lake reflected their beauty in the water below.

They could see the bridge in the distance and, totally entranced, walked along the road until they reached it. Up close Eileen discovered what bad shape the bridge was in. The elegantly scrolled wrought iron that formed the sides of it was intact, but more than half of the woodwork was missing.

Clearly there would be no way she could take the pram across so she parked it among the trees and put the brake on. Telling her little sister that she must stay there she examined the best way to cross the bridge. Alone she could do it quite easily, by striding across the main beams and as long as she kept hold of the wrought iron she would be fine. She turned and looked at Frances; she had her thumb in her mouth and was watching intently.

Would she tell her mother? It was too big a risk and Eileen decided to save the bridge for another day. The lake was roughly an L shape and at the end of the road they reached the point where the lake turned to the right and steps led down to the level of the water. At each side of the steps there were elaborate stone balustrades and curved seats overgrown with ivy. About fifty yards away they could see a swan, and were spellbound by how stately and graceful it looked.

They were about to make the acquaintance of Billy the swan! The very one, that Mr McLain had told Stanley about. Walking hand in hand they ventured down to the bottom step where the water lapped gently against it.

"Look at the swan, Frances. We'll bring it some bread tomorrow. Isn't it lovely?" said Eileen, not really expecting an answer from her young sister. Frances bent and dipped her hand in the water and laughed as she swished it about.

That was enough for Billy. His head swivelled round to look in their direction and he reared up and flew across the surface of the water the way that swans do when they are about to become airborne. He headed straight for them, going at a tremendous rate. Eileen grabbed her sister, took the steps two at a time, threw her into the pram and ran.

By the time Billy leaned back and came to a halt at the bottom of the steps with his huge webbed feet acting as brakes, Eileen was running up the road as fast as she could go with Frances bouncing about like a sack of potatoes in the pram.

Believing the swan to be following them she kept going until she had a stitch in her side, and in agony continued until they had rounded the next corner. Only then did she risk a look back. Thankful that he wasn't behind them she came to a halt and leaned on the handle of the pram holding her side. She looked at Frances expecting her to turn the waterworks on and start crying for her Mam.

"Again, Eileen," she said, "Do it again."

It had turned very warm and the flies had come out, buzzing around their heads and settling on bare skin whenever they got the chance. The two girls swatted at them constantly but they simply flew up in the air and came back down with a vengeance. Frances was beginning to cry now, she was hot and thirsty and tormented by the flies, but it was no use, they were supposed to stay out until teatime.

They came to a crossroads and by turning right they would have reached the other farm belonging to the estate, while to the left were just fields, but straight ahead, perhaps half a mile away there were woods. The road leading to them was little more than a rough track. Eileen stood and thought about it for a moment. She thought about trees and green leaves forming a cool shade and decided that there would be no flies there.

Telling Frances to hold tight she set off down the road trying to pick the smoothest path among the stones and pot holes and the rough grass growing in the middle of the road. The flies were still annoying her but she fixed her mind on the cool woods and thought of sitting under the trees, imagining her and her sister going to sleep under one of them and she plodded on.

At last they were drawing closer and now she could see that the trees were mostly what she called Christmas trees, not the huge oaks she had been hoping for. The track had deteriorated into little better than a footpath and the flies were much worse, Eileen suspected that the ones that had been following them were now being joined by their bigger, fatter, woodland cousins, and they descended on the girls with an evil ferocity.

Frances was now holding her hands over her face and crying while Eileen flapped her hand about round her head in an effort to keep the flies from settling, and she was forced to admit that she was wrong about the woods being a peaceful haven.

There was nothing else for it; she would have to get out of there quickly. Turning the pram around she shouted to Frances to hold on really tight and she set off, running again with the flies doing their best to keep up. On and on she ran with Frances clinging on to the sides of the old black pram until at last they were back at the side of the lake and she sank down on the short grass and wiped the sweat out of her eyes.

Frances climbed out and sat on her knee, put her arms around her neck and said she didn't like flies and she was hungry and wanted her tea. It was while they were sitting there that Eileen noticed the front wheel of the pram. It had a decided wobble on it and she spun it around several times hoping that by some miracle it would straighten itself up, but of course that was not going to happen. She pulled a face as she anticipated trouble when her mother noticed it, and decided she would say it was like that when it came out of the furniture van.

Her own stomach was rumbling and they set off back, hoping that tea would be ready and as they went, she told Frances about the lovely hot bath they were going to have before they went to bed. No more all over washes using the old enamel washing up bowl and a flannel. Not now that they had a proper bathroom like other civilised people. Oh she could hardly wait to sink into that hot water!

The end cottage with sloping roof is where Stanley and
Doris lived in Adwick-Le.St.
From 1947 to 1952

Stanley and Doris in
the garden shortly after
moving to Adwick-Le.St.
1947/ 48

Stanley
tending to one
of his pigs at
Adwick-Le.St.
1949 aprox

Pleasant View Farm at Rawcliffe

This is a photograph of Byram Hall where we lived
from 1952-55.

Part of
Byram Hall
where we
lived
Note: called
Clampton
Hall in the
book

Ruins of part
of the Hall

Stanley on his Fordson Major Tractor
1952

Stanley and Doris
1952

Stanley with Austin 7 and
Lassie at Byram Park
1952/ 53

Stanley and
Eileen
sawing logs

Stanley and Doris Dale at their small holding
1953 aprox

Stanley, Doris and Eileen in park at Adwick-Le.St.

Eileen aged 12 with baby sister Frances

CHAPTER 24

It seemed so strange to be walking through the once grand gateway and up the steps and through the solid oak door into the house that they would now call home. Frances clung to her sister's hand as if she would never let it go as they followed the sound of voices and the smell of food to the kitchen.

Doris was doing battle with the primus stove that hissed and spluttered on the makeshift table near the window. She had managed to cook a rough sort of stew and was now in the process of boiling the kettle to make a much needed pot of tea. When asked if they could get bathed later Doris gave a contemptuous laugh, "You'll be lucky, we can't light a fire yet so there's no hot water and no way to cook either." She didn't mean to sound so scathing but she was tired and had been looking forward to a bath herself.

"Come on, Doris, we can manage for another day or so," Stanley summoned up all his patience and cajoled her, "Come on and eat something. We'll all feel better then." He turned to his daughters and said, "Now then, what have you two been up to?"

Eileen began by telling them about their experience with Billy the swan and they were soon laughing as she described running for her life with Frances bouncing in the pram and then followed it up with a description of the flies in the woods. Somehow when they turned it into a joke it was all so much easier and even washing in a few inches of lukewarm water that night became funny and bearable.

It was two days before the jackdaw's nests were cleared from the chimney and at last a fire was lit in the living room. Doris built the fire up in spite of the warm weather outside, using two buckets full of their precious coal. She was determined that this would be the night when they could all enjoy the long-awaited baths. From time to time Doris turned on the tap waiting for the hot water to come gushing through but all it managed was a stream of lukewarm, brown-looking fluid.

It may have been a new hot water system but it seemed that the plumber who had installed it was sadly lacking in plumbing skills, and it proved to be woefully inefficient from the day they arrived to the day they left.

The house was wired up for electricity but would not be connected until late autumn so in the meantime they had to manage with candles and an oil lamp that had been loaned to them by one of their old neighbours in Adwick-le-Street. Thankfully it was June and the days were long and they were usually in bed before dark, so that apart from calls of nature they could stay there until it was light again.

Now their new home may have had two indoor toilets, but both of them were downstairs and involved a walk along the upstairs landing, down the twisted staircase, past the door of the cellar and another door that creaked in the draught which constantly blew down the long passage.

Doris had a horror of that cellar and agreed that they could continue to use chamber pots for the time being until they had working electricity. No one was more relieved than Eileen at this news, as the hairs on the back of her neck stood up every time she walked down the stairs.

It was taking time to get used to living there and all of Doris's home-making skills to make it feel comfortable. She laid the linoleum in the long passages and hung the curtains she had made, and gradually they became used to the rambling house and its echoing rooms. One evening as they sat reading, Stanley put down his paper and announced that when the electricity was connected they would see about buying a television.

Doris stared at him, "Are you sure, Stan? They cost a lot. We should be putting the money away in the farm fund."

"It's about time we got one Dot," he retorted. "We won't be able to go to t' pictures you know. It'll be very quiet here in winter. Nearest cinema is in Pontefract. What we used to spend on going to t'pictures will nearly pay for one. They've got some at that shop in Knottingly and you can pay for em on t'weekly."

Stanley had been at work for nearly two weeks when a chance of fate brought the past flooding back to him. The estate employed their own joiner, and he worked in one of the old stables surrounded by wood and sawdust, making fences, gates, doors and whatever other general maintenance work was needed. His name was Jim Baxter and he was one of those people who always looked as if he was about to burst into laughter. He was a gentle giant of a man, softly spoken, and good natured.

The first time that Stanley came into contact with him he was greeted with a handshake and pat on the back and asked where he had lived before. "Oh," replied Stanley, "We have been living at Adwick-le-Street for the last seven years," then added that he had been born at Wath upon Dearne.

Jim at looked at him. "Did you say Wath upon Dearne? Do you mean Wath near Barnsley?"

For some reason as he nodded, Stanley felt a shiver go through him, "Yes. Why? Do you know it?"

"A bit. I've been to Wath quite a few times. The wife's family lived there. It's a mucky hole isn't it? All that coal dust everywhere. Ah couldn't live there." He picked up the gate he had been repairing and leaned it against the wooden partition, then began to brush the sawdust from it. "Ah think this gate's past repairing, but the boss said to mend it. Look here, this top rail is as rotten as a bad egg." Using a screw driver he pushed it into the soft wood. "Ah well, orders are orders, and if ah slap a few coats of paint on it ah dare say it will last a while longer."

Stanley took his cap off, smoothed his hair and put it back on again. "What's your wife called?" he asked, making an effort to sound casual. He sat down on a pile of wooden stakes and waited until Jim replied.

"Mavis. Her name's Mavis. She was Mavis Fields before we were married. Do you know any families of that name in Wath? I'll try and remember their address. Let me see. Ah, I remember. Her family lived in Oak Road."

For a moment Stanley was silent as the past came rushing back to him. Mavis Fields was the girl who had been engaged to Herbert, his step brother, who had been killed in a mining accident. In a flash he saw him as he was the last time he had set eyes on him. He could see a vision of Herbert as he joined his mates walking to their afternoon shift at Cortonwood Colliery.

Stanley was not a man to show his feelings. He swallowed hard and fought to keep his voice steady, "Aye, ah do know Mavis." Then he hesitated wondering how much Jim knew about his wife's past.

As Jim continued his work on the gate he said, "That's a coincidence you knowing Mavis. Did you know she was engaged to a man that got killed just before they were due to get married? Poor bloke got crushed in an accident down t'pit. Dangerous job down them pits. You wouldn't catch me doing it. "

"Well you'll not believe this, Jim, but that lad who got killed was my step brother. Ah knew Mavis very well. She was at our house nearly every day. She used to do me Mam's hair for her. Well bloody hell, what a coincidence."

Again in Stanley's head came the picture of Herbert, and he saw him as clear as if he had been standing there, and then he looked at Jim, and thought what a contrast between the two men. It would have been hard to find two so opposite in every way. Mavis certainly had not tried to replicate Herbert, who had been quite slight in build, but hard as nails, quick witted and full of fun. Jim on the other hand was like a big, cuddly bear, soft and easy going and Stanley thought that he had probably made Mavis a very good husband.

Doris was the one who did most of the letter writing, keeping in regular touch with the different members of the family, but that night Stanley sat down with pen and paper and wrote to his parents himself, telling them the news.

When his mother, Ada, opened the letter, she read it through, and tears trickled down her face as she remembered Herbert and the terrible time after he had died in Cortonwood Colliery.

She thought of Mavis and had a longing to see her and made up her mind that they would go the following Saturday. Stanley had said in his letter that they had a spare bedroom if they wanted to come and stay for a few days.

Ada looked at the clock. If she wrote a letter now she could catch the mid-day post and Stanley would get it the next day. She thought about her husband Harold. No doubt he would make a fuss and say he didn't want to go. More than likely he would say he had made arrangements with his mates to meet at the British Legion this weekend. 'Well, he can just jolly well unmake his arrangements this time,' she thought, as she reached for the writing pad.

The letter had been in the post box for half an hour when Harold arrived home from his early morning shift. Ada took his snap tin and Dudley from him, rinsed them out, then sank them into a bowl of hot soapy water and left them to soak. She had already run him a hot bath and she handed him a mug of tea as he sank gratefully into it. He ran his hand up her leg and smiled at her. He looked tired out, but his blue eyes were twinkling as he said, "Eh, thanks, love. You know how to spoil me don't you? You look nice today love. Are you going to come to bed with me for an hour after dinner?"

"No I am not, Harold Corker. I am going to give you some dinner then you can go and get some sleep," she said, as she picked up the flannel and began to wash his back. Ada was playing her cards carefully, knowing that it was best to let him get his bath and eat some dinner before she broke the news about going to visit Stanley and Doris.

For once they were alone in the house and Ada served their dinners out and passed a glass of beer over to Harold. He was half way through his second pork chop when Ada pulled the letter out of her apron pocket.

"Look," she said, "We got a letter from our Stanley today, and you'll never guess what he wrote to tell us," and she went on to read the first part of his letter.

Harold put down his knife and fork and stared at her, "Well, ah'll go to hell and back. What a coincidence. Fancy meeting up like that after all this time." A sad look passed over his face and a tear glinted in his eye. "Ah'll never forget our Herbert. Poor lad. What a way to go. He always wanted to work down t'pit didn't he?"

Ada put her hand on his knee, "Ah know, he was such a grand lad. Ah still miss him. Our Stanley's asked us to go and stay for a few days this weekend. Ah thought it would be nice to go and stay with em and see Mavis. Ah'd love to see her again."

Harold straightened up at her words, "Oh, ah don't know about this weekend, Ada. Ah've arranged to go to t'legion with Albert Nuttall."

'Ah knew he'd say that,' thought Ada, and without hesitating she played her trump card. "Well, our Stan says he's going to drive to you to the pub in the next village. You have to go the back way through the woods to get to it."

Harold finished his glass of beer and wiped his mouth, "Ah, going to the pub through the woods? That sounds interesting. It's about time we had a little holiday Ada. Ah think ah'll tell Albert that I won't be at the Legion this week. You write back and tell Stan and Doris that we will be on the bus on Saturday morning and tell him to meet us in Pontefract."

Ada smiled as said she would get the letter written while he had his afternoon sleep, and thought to herself that it had been even easier than she had anticipated.

On Saturday morning as they walked down into Wath to catch the early bus, Ada felt a shiver of excitement and was glad she had put her new coat on. It was the same shade of navy blue as her old one but a double breasted style with two rows of cloth covered buttons and a half belt at the back. She had trimmed her favourite hat with a new ribbon and felt very smart. She glanced at Harold and thought how impressive he looked with his watch and chain displayed on his waistcoat. As she looked he ran a finger round his collar and stretched his neck in an effort to make it more comfortable.

"This collar's a bit tight, do you think it's shrunk in the wash? What the heck have you got in this case Ada? It weighs a ton. We're only going for one night you know."

"Stop grumbling, Harold, we're nearly at the bus stop now. Your collar's fine, it's just a bit stiff that's all. Ah put some extra starch in when ah washed it, it'll soon soften. Come on, don't spoil things. We're going to have a nice weekend away. Ah'm really looking forward to it."

They caught the bus to Barnsley and from there they were just in time to catch the connecting one to Pontefract. As they sat together on the red plush seats with their thighs touching she turned to look at Harold and saw that he was staring at her.

"What's the matter?" she asked.

"Nothing. Ah can look at you can't I?" he replied with a wink, "Ah was wondering if you'd brought that nice pink silk nightie with ya."

Ada giggled as if she was a young girl and dug him in the ribs as she smiled at him. She thought back to the difficult time so many years ago when Stanley had been born before they were married. At that time they had despaired of ever being able to be together; and now look at them, just off to spend the weekend with their eldest son. Ada said a little silent thank you and looked up at the sky.

As they travelled towards Pontefract, Stanley was already there, waiting at the top of Horsefair for the sight of their bus arriving. He looked up at the clock; there were still twenty minutes to go before it was due. He paced up and down several times, then walked as far as the indoor market and took note of the prices of the fruit and vegetables. Doris would be interested, she had complained the previous night about how much the travelling greengrocer had charged her. He bought a bag of apples, another of oranges and as a special treat, four bananas. The sweet stall beckoned him but he resisted, thinking that he had spent enough.

Arriving back just as the green double decker bus was pulling to a stop he could see his mother in her navy blue coat making her way towards the door. She was the first one off the bus and her eyes lit up as she saw Stanley waiting for them.

He was wearing his Harris Tweed suit and although Stanley cursed it for making his legs itch, he knew it suited his tall, slim frame and he looked every inch a farmer. Ada looked at him proudly, and made everyone around them aware that this was her son. She hooked her arm into his while they waited for Harold to fight his way through the passengers who stood about on the broad pavement trying to get their bearings.

As Harold finally cleared the crowd he walked towards them, his hand held out and a smile on his face. As he clasped Stanley's hand he said the words that Stanley had longed to hear when he was a child. "Now then, son," he said, "Tha's looking well."

Stanley took the case out of his father's hand and led the way to where he had parked the Austin. Although they were walking downhill Stanley noticed how much worse his father's breathing had become and how flushed his face was as he struggled to keep up. Years of living among miners made the sound of laboured breathing familiar to him, and he knew that the coal dust was slowly but surely taking its toll on his own father.

"How's your chest, Dad?" he asked "Tha sounds a bit out of breath." It felt strange being able to talk to his father like that. In the past such an observation would have brought forth a caustic remark.

"Oh, it's all right, Stanley. Just a bit of bronchitis tha knows. It's all that fog we had in winter. It'll clear up in a week or two when the weather picks up."

As they drove out of Pontefract towards Brotherton, Harold talked non-stop. Stanley thought he had never had such a long conversation with his father. Soon they were passing the power station at Ferrybridge on the banks of the River Aire and it obviously impressed Harold greatly as he twisted his head around to see as much of it as he could.

"Did tha see that Ada? It's bigger than Mexborough. Ee, ah wish we'd got a camera. Albert Nuttall will never believe the size of it. When ah Cyril comes, ask him to take a photo of it will tha, Stanley? He's bought a fancy new camera tha knows."

From the back seat Ada piped up. "Aye and our Harold's got one. It's got a flash so you can take photos in the dark."

They were driving along Ponte Lane now and Stanley pointed out the cottage where Mavis lived. "Ah'll take you to see her tomorrow morning, Mam. Will you be coming as well, Dad?"

"Oh, aye, ah will that, ah were very fond of that lass." He

hesitated, wiping his face with his hand. "Ah can't tell thee, Stanley, how much we still miss our Herbert." He began to recall some of Herbert's little foibles and had just begun to describe again the way he ate kippers, when Stanley turned into Clamton Park.

Ahead of them, at the end of the long straight road, they could see Clamton Hall. Harold's voice slowly petered out as he gazed at the building they were approaching.

Stanley had often heard the expression 'their jaw dropped' but he had never expected to see it happen to his father. Harold was not often lost for words, but now it seemed he was speechless, as he took in the sight of the ruins with the tall central walls still standing, surrounded by the huge heaps of rubble. He gave a sharp intake of breath, and continued to stare at it even when Stanley had brought the car to a halt alongside the steps that led to their front door.

He gave himself a visible shake and climbed out, holding the front seat to one side so that Ada could get out of the car. He looked around at the part of the hall that was now Stanley and Doris's home, and then back at the ruined part of the building.

"Well," he began. "Well, ah'll go to hell. Ah never imagined it would be like this, Stanley. What do you think to this, Ada?"

Ada was equally stunned and nervous of the ruins. "Is it safe Stanley? Aren't you afraid of it all falling down on you? It looks very dangerous to me." She gave a shiver and moved back as if she expected the heap of stones to suddenly begin moving towards her.

"Ah reckon it's safe enough for now. My boss had his son here with the big tractor yesterday. He tied chains on to that highest wall and set about trying to pull it down with a winch. He couldn't budge it. Ah reckon he'll have to get dynamite to it."

Harold perked up at his words, "Aye, ah reckon explosives will be needed to shift that lot, Stanley. We've got some lads down Manvers that are expert with explosives, as tha well knows. We've got a couple of shot firers who would have that down in no time. Ah can av a word with em if tha likes."

Stanley shook his head, "Ee, its's nought to do with me, Dad. It's Mr McLain's property."

"Well you tell him, son, that ah can get them lads do it for him. They wouldn't charge. They'd do it as a favour to me and they'd think it were a novelty to work above ground for a change. They'd only want a few pints for doing it."

He noticed Stanley's look and said defensively, "They're experts tha knows. They could do it."

Stanley nodded, he didn't doubt for one moment that the men who fired explosives down the mine would be quite capable of blowing the ruins up. He just didn't think that Mr.McLain would go for the idea.

Doris opened the door at that moment and came down the steps to greet them, "Now then, Mam and Dad. It's good to see you both. You found your way to Pontefract without any trouble then? Come on, Mam, ah'll bet you're ready for a cup of tea. The kettle's boiled."

The smell of Lavender furniture polish wafted down the passage as they entered the long hall. The whole place gleamed. Doris always kept a clean home, but this week, in honour of their guests, she had gone into overdrive with the house work. She was a great believer in furniture polish and had polished the linoleum in the long downstairs corridor until it shone. It was also so slippery that it was like walking on ice.

Eileen had found that with a bit of practice she could slide on it in her stocking feet, but made sure she was out of sight of her mother when she did it. Frances tried to copy her but ended up doing a shuffle on her bottom from one end of the corridor to the other.

"What have you taught her that for?" demanded Doris. "Her clothes will be ruined." Stanley kept quiet and pulled a face as he gave his elder daughter a wink. They had spent ten minutes the previous day having sliding competitions while Doris was outside in the garden.

Leading her in-laws into the house, Doris began to show them around. Ada gasped as she saw the size of the lounge which, as yet, was empty of furniture. Next, Doris took them upstairs to show them the room where they would be sleeping. Their feet in their outdoor shoes clattered on the hard linoleum, and the sound echoed down the long corridor, making Doris wonder if she would ever be able to turn the place into a comfortable home with what few furnishings they had.

Ada stopped and looked through the landing windows at the ruins of the old part of the hall. She shook her head, seeing them from a different angle now that she was upstairs. They still terrified her. Taking hold of Doris's arm she said, "Don't go too near that lot, Doris, and keep our Eileen and Frances away from them. They could be buried underneath all that stone if it collapses. I've got a bad feeling about it."

Doris laughed it off, told her not to worry, and promised she would make sure that they kept away from it, then added, "Mr. McLain is going to arrange to get it pulled down and cleared away very soon. Stan asked him about it yesterday."

At that moment they reached the bedroom door and as they entered Doris pointed out that she hadn't had time to paint the walls yet. The old fashioned wall paper must have been there for many years and would have been the height of fashion when it was first hung.

Brightly coloured, exotic birds sat on the branches of trees eating unrecognisable fruit, but it was now faded and scuffed and Doris was desperate to cover it up with several coats of distemper.

While Ada stared in amazement at the wallpaper, Harold crossed the room to look out of the window. "Look at this, Ada," he said, pointing to the attractive view across the fields and the woods. "It's like being in a posh hotel."

He sat on the bed and continued to stare out at the scenery. "By heck, ah never expected it to be like this." He took off his suit jacket and hung it carefully on the back of a chair, then loosened the top button of his shirt and sighed with relief as he stretched his neck and ran his finger round the inside of his collar. "That's better," he said and slipped his braces off his shoulders.

Downstairs in the living room, a stack of logs burned sulkily in the fire grate. Doris had lit it that morning in the hope that it would heat the water. Harold looked at it and held out his hand towards it.

"By heck, Doris, these logs don't throw much heat out. I'll

bet they don't get the oven hot. You could do with some of our 'Manvers' coal."

Doris looked at him and resisted pointing out that they didn't get free allocations of coal like the miners. Instead she simply said, "Aye we could do with some Dad, but coal's expensive for us to buy. We brought a few bags with us but it's nearly all gone now. So we'll just have to manage with logs."

In the afternoon Stanley took his parents out for a ride around the estate, and ended by taking them to view the other wing of the hall that was still standing. It was almost a mirror image to their home but was not occupied or even liveable in. Although structurally sound it was still in the same state that it had been left in many years ago and originally had been the servant's quarters.

The rooms were large with high ceilings and tall windows that were covered in grime and cobwebs. Their footsteps echoed eerily along the passages and little clouds of dust rose as they passed through the rooms. Two dead jackdaws lay crumbling in the fireplace and Ada shivered.

She took Harold's arm and whispered as if she was afraid of being overheard, "Ah don't like it in here much, ah think we should go back. It's really creepy. "

"Come on then," agreed Stanley, "But before we go, ah just want to show you something." He led the way outside and round into the courtyard of the stables. There he opened a massive door and took them into several semi basement rooms that had evidently been the kitchens. Along one wall in the central room was a range of rusty ovens, with broad mantle-pieces, all crumbling away around the central fire grate.

On the other wall under the windows were four flat stone sinks and a pump with a rotting wooden handle. Ada ran her hand along the sinks and as she held the handle of the pump a tear escaped her eye and trickled down her cheek.

Stanley came close to her, saw the tear and took her arm, "What's the matter, Mam?" he asked.

She shook her head, "Ah were just thinking of all the poor folks who spent their lives working and slaving down here. Ah could see em as clear as day."

Harold gave heavy sigh. There were many times, when he repeated the same opinions that his own father had voiced years earlier when talking about the owners of the mines, and as Harold spoke now it could have been his father speaking.

He looked around and nodded in agreement, "Aye, bloody grafting their lives away for the rich buggers upstairs."

Stanley didn't often see eye to eye with Harold but on this subject he agreed with him completely. Today, however, he hadn't intended to awaken such feelings and he thought he had better draw the sightseeing to a close.

The big event that Harold was waiting for was the trip through the woods to the pub in the next village that evening. He disappeared into the bathroom straight after tea, and emerged much later with his face scrubbed until his cheeks shone. Looking at his complexion, no one would ever have guessed that he had been collier working down the coal mines since he had left school at thirteen.

"Are you ready then, Stanley?" he asked. Stanley gave a sideways look at Doris and winked. He was under no illusion that the visit to the pub was the highlight of the visit for his father.

"Aye, ah'm ready. Right we're off now, Doris. We'll not be late back."

Harold settled back in the car as if it was a limousine instead of a tiny Austin Seven, and waited for his son to start the engine. He'd never learned to drive himself, and saw no need for it now. After all, he had plenty of off-spring to ferry him about whenever the need arose.

The little engine fired up without so much as a cough, and Stanley pushed the starting handle into the back, eased himself into the driving seat and slipped the car into gear. They drove down to the lake and along the tree lined road, eventually reaching the rough track that led down to the woods. This was where it began to get interesting.

Stanley looked at his father; he was sitting on the edge of his seat staring intently through the windscreen. "What's that, Stanley? Is it a fox? It is. Well, ah'll be blowed. Look there's two of em. Cheeky buggers, they're not scared of us are they?"

Stanley shook his head, "No, the estate's over-run with em. They're into the poultry if we don't lock em up every night. You'd think they'd go for the rabbits. There's enough of em. Look across there, at that crop of wheat, the bloody rabbits have eaten half of it. The boss is organising a shoot next week. There'll be plenty of rabbit meat about. Doris doesn't care much for it but we'll have it if it's free."

They reached the woods and the track seemed too narrow to allow car access. Harold sucked in his breath. Stanley enjoyed his reaction and played up to it, pretending to be unsure if the track was negotiable. He had in fact actually walked it the previous day to check it out and had decided that it was usable with care, but he had no intention of making the trip less exciting for Harold.

As they entered the wood, the nettles and brambles that were almost as tall as the car, brushed against the sides and the wheels dropped into ruts making them lurch from side to side.

"Bloody hell, Stanley, Ah hope we don't get stuck," and then came the comment that Stanley had been waiting for, "Wait till ah tell Albert Nuttall about this. He'll never believe it."

The words had barely left his mouth when they reached a part of the track that was waterlogged. With the wheels spinning, Stanley crossed his fingers and kept his foot on the accelerator. The Austin valiantly kept going and they emerged onto dry ground.

Harold laughed, "That's it, son, go on, keep her going." Stanley had never seen him so exhilarated.

The trees were clearing now and they reached a fence that closed off the woods from the fields beyond. Stanley switched off the engine and turned to Harold. "This is where we get out and walk. We have to cross that field then follow a footpath into the village."

It was another half hour before they reached the village, entering it from the little used footpath, and Harold said he was in dire need of a pint or two after all that walking. It was a tiny village where everyone knew everyone else, and from the reaction they received as they opened the door and walked in, they might as well have come from Mars.

It was a tiny place, no bigger than someone's front room. Every head swivelled towards them and they were scrutinised from head to foot until the landlord took charge of the situation.

"Good evening," he said from behind the bar. He gripped a bottle as if it were a weapon. He was obviously of the opinion that strangers would be up to no good in their village on a summer evening "Can I help you?"

Harold was not a man to be intimidated when he was in need of a pint, and he walked straight up the bar. "Two pints of your best bitter please. Ah don't suppose you carry Barnsley bitter, so ah'll av whatever you've got in the barrel."

Recognising the authority in Harold's voice the landlord picked up a large enamel jug and descended down the cellar steps, slowly disappearing out of sight. With the landlord away there was an atmosphere so strong it made the hairs stand up on Stanley's neck, but Harold didn't seem to be affected by it, and he turned around, gave them all a nod and said, "Now then, lads, what are you drinking?" That put a different mood on things and the sullen suspicion that the four men had been displaying, vanished as they finished the ale in their glasses.

The man nearest to Harold stood up and joined him at the bar. He held out his hand, and put his half pint glass down. "I'm Jake," he said, "I'll have a half with you. Oh, actually, I usually drink pints."

Harold leaned back on the bar and introduced himself. He was in his element. Stanley gave an inward groan, realising that there would be no chance of getting his father home early now. The rest of the men, sensing free drinks, were rapidly turning into Harold's best buddies and Stanley was very thankful that there were only four of them in the bar.

"You're not from round here are you?" asked Jake. Harold shook his head and began to regale them with details of Manvers Main colliery.

The landlord returned from his trip down the cellar with a full jug of ale which disappeared down the throats of the group in seconds.

Stanley smiled to himself, thinking that the landlord would be up and down the stairs many times before the night was over.

As the drinks went down, the stories became more and more improbable, until Stanley decided enough was enough. He had been keeping count on Harold's consumption and was sure he was now on his eighth pint, and he had no doubt that he could easily keep going for much longer.

He nudged Harold's arm, "It's nearly dark, Dad. Ah think we should be going. The lights are not too good on the car. It's going to be a bit rough driving through the woods."

Harold held up his hand and said, "My son says we've got to go. Let's have one for the road, then ah will have to leave you lads." The 'lads' gave a united groan. They were now all mates together, united by the ale they had consumed.

"Well that's a shame, Harold," slurred Jake as he rocked back on his heels. Stanley guided him to a chair and plonked him down in it.

"No, Dad. None for the road, we've got to get going now." He was beginning to get irritated. As much as he enjoyed a beer himself he never overindulged, and he also knew that Doris would be none too pleased if he took his father back home the worse for drink.

As they walked out of the village pub Harold was only the slightest bit unsteady on his feet and Stanley marvelled that he could drink so much and suffer no effects from it. 'But then,' he reasoned to himself, 'He's had years of practice.'

But if Stanley had not been with him there is no doubt that Harold would have wandered around the village half the night trying to find the lane they had walked down. He stared around and claimed that coming out of the hot pub into the cooler air had made him disorientated.

Stanley shook his head and guided him down the lane and across the field to the car. Although he said nothing to his father he had a bad feeling that the car might refuse to start. He retrieved the starting handle from under the seat and said a little prayer to the saint of old cars as he cranked the engine. There was a slight kick from it and Stanley tried again and got a stronger kick that bent his thumb back.

Harold had emerged from the car and stood beside him breathing out beer fumes. Stanley stood up straight and counted to ten. He was tempted to kick the car, but instead he walked around the back of it, swore a few times, and tried again. This time it coughed, backfired weakly and burst into life.

Harold got back into the car smiling. As he patted his son's arm he lapsed into his broadest Yorkshire and said. "There tha is, Stanley. Tha's done it. Tha alus did av a way wi engines. Tha takes after me Dad. Eee tha's a grand lad. Ah don't know what me and thee Mam would do without yer."

Stanley smiled and thought, 'The beer's talking now.' But he'd never heard his father call him a grand lad before, and beer talk or not it was good to hear it said.

Although it was mid-summer and almost the longest day, it was now ten thirty, the light had faded out in the open and under the canopy of the trees it was very dark. The car's headlights were hopelessly inefficient, showing only a weak beam of light for a few yards ahead. Stanley leaned forward, peering through the windscreen, and as if it would be of some help his father did the same.

Dozens of sparkling dots of lights began to appear on the track in front of them, but disappeared as they drew close. "What the hell is that, Stanley?" asked Harold

Stanley was tempted to claim that they were some sort of woodland spirits and thought that his father, under the influence of the ale, might just believe him. But not wanting to spoil the new relationship they were now enjoying he said, "It's rabbits Dad. Their eyes are reflecting in the car lights. Ah told you, the estate's over-run with em."

"Bloody hell, Stanley, tha's not kidding, there must be hundreds of em." The words were hardly out of his mouth when a fox ran directly across their path, with its bushy tail held out straight, then another one followed closely behind. They disappeared into the undergrowth, and Harold pointed his finger at the spot where they had been seconds before. "Did tha see that Stanley? There were two foxes."

"Aye," said Stanley, trying not to lose his concentration as he drove along the narrow track, "We're over-run with them an all."

It was just after eleven when they arrived back home. As they got out of the car the ruins of the old hall loomed above them, vaguely outlined in the dark sky. They could hear faint shuffling from the dozens of jackdaws that had nested in the stonework. Apart from that there was total silence. The only light came from the candle flickering in the hall window and Stanley led the way up the steps to the front door, thankful that they were home and looking forward to supper and a warm bed.

Two things happened as he put out his hand to grasp the brass door knob. An owl, out hunting, swooped above their heads screeching out its ghostly call, as it glided by on out-stretched wings. At the same time Doris opened the door, her face white in the light of the candle she was holding.

Harold pushed in front of Stanley, eager to get indoors. As he went through to the living room he gave a shiver and told Ada, "By hell, lass, av ad more frights tonight than ah get in a month down t'pit." Then he turned to Doris and added, "Tha wants a bloody medal living here love. Ah'm a nervous wreck."

Next morning Ada was up early, washed and dressed in her long black skirt and white blouse. Over the top of them, as usual, she had put on her flowery patterned pinafore to keep her best clothes clean until it was time to go out. Harold appeared downstairs half an hour later, wearing his navy blue striped trousers with his braces hanging loose. As always, his face was smooth, clean and shining, with not a sign of the effects of the ale he had consumed the night before.

Doris had battled with the primus stove and managed to produce bacon, eggs and 2 slices of greasy fried bread. She placed them in front of her father-in-law, half expecting him to refuse on account of a queasy stomach. But Harold picked up his knife and fork and ate the lot, wiping his mouth afterwards as he said, "By that was grand, Doris. Ah don't know why our Stanley's not as fat as Billy Bunter if tha feeds him like that every day."

Doris shook her head. "No, I don't either, Dad. He never puts an ounce on no matter what he eats." She turned to take the pots away but found Ada had already whisked them into the kitchen and was busy washing up.

It was now time to set off to visit to Mavis and her husband Jim. Stanley brought the car round to the steps. Ada and Doris squeezed themselves into the narrow back seat, leaving the front for Harold. They travelled down the long straight road that led out of the estate, through the thick belt of trees and out on to Ponte Lane.

Jim and Mavis had a cottage set back off the road among tall conifers and rhododendron bushes. It was situated almost directly opposite the exit to the estate. Smoke was drifting gently out of the chimney and as Ada looked at it she was reminded of the cottage where Doll and Stanley had been born in Carlton. She fell silent as she thought of those far off days.

"We're here, Mam, this is the cottage where Mavis lives." Doris's words interrupted her thoughts. and she gave herself a little shake, and smiled at Harold, saying, "It's just like a picture postcard isn't it?" Taking his arm she walked with him down the path to the open door.

Before they reached it Mavis appeared in the doorway. Ada would have known her anywhere. She still had the same chestnut brown hair worn in a short bob, and the same smile that lit up her face. True, she had put on weight but it suited her, and she had a look of calm contentment. Seeing Ada she held out her arms and pulled her close, holding her for a long time.

"I can't believe I'm seeing you after all this time," she said, and then hugged Harold who reddened and for a moment became lost for words.

Jim stood watching them, nodding and laughing in his good natured way, then led them into his home and sat them down in the most comfortable chairs. It must have seemed strange to Jim to have the parents of his wife's deceased fiancé sitting in his home, but he took it all in his stride and joined in the conversation. Doris glanced at him and noticed a tear in his eye when they spoke of Herbert's death down in the depths of Cortonwood Colliery.

Then their reminiscences turned to happier times as they

recalled Herbert's sayings and habits. Harold trotted out again, his way of eating kippers, "Does tha remember Mavis, when he used to put a whole kipper between two slices of bread and eat it all, skin, bones, the lot? Everything went down."

Mavis agreed and gave only one big sigh before she took hold of Jim's hand, and looked up at him. "I've been so very lucky to have found Jim. I was broken when I met him, but he put me back together and we have been very happy. Haven't we, love?"

Jim managed to look pleased and embarrassed at the same time and hastily asked Stanley if he would like to take a look at his garden and his chickens.

They left an hour later and as they drove slowly back up the road towards the Hall, Ada commented that she somehow felt they would both be more at peace over the loss of Herbert now that they had seen Mavis.

At three o'clock Stanley saw his parents safely onto the bus and heading home to Wath. As he waved them goodbye he had a lump in his throat, but he walked back to the car thinking how good their visit had been.

For the first time in his life he actually felt quite close to his father. He remembered many occasions when he had hated him. But times were changing. He now felt that he had his father's affection, and even admiration, and it felt good. It felt very good.

CHAPTER 25

Their nearest neighbour was Hans. He lived in a tiny apartment above the stables in the next courtyard. Like the two Toni's whom Stanley had worked with at Adwick le Street, Hans was German. He had been a prisoner of war and employed on farms in the area for almost four years. His was a tragic story.

During the war he had lost all contact with his wife back in Germany, but as soon as peace was declared he travelled back, and spent a long time trying to trace her. When at last he succeeded in finding her, he discovered that she had believed that he was dead, and since then had remarried and had a young daughter. The rest of his family were now in what had become East Berlin.

Devastated, Hans had wandered about in war damaged Germany, and eventually decided to return to England, heading back to the part of the country that was familiar to him. There, he answered an advertisement for a general farm worker on the Clamton estate.

It was Mr McLain who had placed the advertisement, and he gave Hans a job and a place to live above one of the stables. The accommodation was very basic. He had a water toilet but no bathroom, just a cold water tap above an old stone sink. Hans said he managed very well and proudly showed Stanley around his home.

Stanley was impressed. It was spotlessly clean with not a thing out of place. The little fireplace where he did his cooking was shining. A copper kettle and two pans stood beside it at exactly the right angles. His glass oil lamp was placed on the centre of the table and a small bookcase held a dozen or more books. Hans pointed to his radio on a shelf, and said that he was now able to enjoy music in the evenings.

He was of average height with light brown hair, and pleasant but quite unremarkable looks, until he smiled; and then, he showed his beautiful white even teeth, his eyes sparkled and his whole face lit up.

He came to have supper with Stanley and Doris a couple of times, always thanking Doris with beautiful manners and never overstayed his welcome. After he had gone Stanley felt quite sorry for him and remarked to Doris that he led a very solitary and isolated life after the day's work was done.

Eventually, however, it became clear that Hans did not lead quite such a solitary, isolated life that everyone thought he did, and evidently that smile of his had worked its charm.

It was almost two months later in the middle of July when Hans confided to Stanley that he had just become engaged to a girl called Polly. She worked on the Home Farm at the other end of the estate. She was a very attractive girl. There were several young men who were eager to court her, but it was Hans who had caught her eye. They had been going out for quite some time and she had now agreed to marry him.

Stanley punched his arm and shook his hand. He congratulated him and told him he was a dark horse. Hans looked at him as if he didn't understand, and said, "I don't know what you mean Stanley. Why am I dark horse?" but his eyes were twinkling and he kept bursting out into a German love song for the rest of the day.

Their only other neighbours on the estate lived more than a mile away on the Home Farm. The nearest school and shops were in the village of Brotherton almost two miles away. At weekends and in the evenings, once the workers who were employed on the estate went home, they seldom saw anyone.

In fact, Stanley often joked that they had reached the stage when they actually ran outside if they heard an engine in the hope that it was someone to talk to. There was no doubt that Clamton Park could be a very lonely place at times. It could also be a dangerous place especially if you didn't look where you were going.

There had been a vast labyrinth of cellars beneath the old hall and following the demolition of the building, the cellars were gradually caving in, leaving gaping holes several feet deep. The holes would appear without warning and there were several at the rear of the two courtyards.

They had developed overnight at the side of a footpath that was used daily by some of the workers as a shortcut. It wound round the back of the stables and over some of the piled up rubble and into the part of the hall that was still used for storage. Although they were all aware of the holes it was an accident waiting to happen.

An serious accident almost happened on one particular Friday afternoon. Stanley, assisted by a workmate was on his way to collect some animal feed and they took the shortcut, both intent on getting the job done as quickly as possible so that they could finish half an hour early.

Stanley called out to Freddy, his workmate, to watch where he was walking and stepped carefully around a manhole sized opening in the ground before beginning the scramble up the rough path over the rubble. Realising that he was alone he looked back and for a moment could see nothing.

Then among the long grass he caught sight of Freddy's head and shoulders. His legs and body were dangling down into the abyss, while he was just managing to hold himself up by his elbows which were outstretched.

Grabbing him by his collar Stanley hauled him back up through the hole. "Bloody hell." Freddy gasped, "Ah thought ah'd had it then. Ah never saw it." He had stepped into the hole and would have fallen right through it if it had been just a little bit wider. Stanley sat on the ground beside him and dropped a stone into the hole. It seemed to take a long time to hit the bottom and they heard the splash of water. Freddy was still shaking and kept repeating that if he had been on his own he could have died.

Gradually he calmed down and said, "By heck, Stan, ah'm glad you were there. Them there holes want filling in. What the hell did you think when you saw me dangling there, Stan?"

"Well," Stanley said slowly, "Ah wondered where tha was, until ah saw your head sticking up out of t'ground."

Then they looked at each other, and as relief eased their shock they saw the funny side of it, and rolled on the floor laughing. As they described it later to the rest of the workers it sounded like something from a cartoon, and poor Freddy had to endure many jokes about his near mishap. But it could have had a very different ending if he had been alone.

That evening after work Stanley went back over the shortcut, and dragged several corrugated sheets over the holes, and weighted them down with stones until they could be filled in. He took Eileen with him and showed her how dangerous they were and instructed her never to take that path.

At the beginning of October the power cables were connected. At last, electricity had reached them. It was a momentous day when Doris flicked a switch and a light came on. For the first time in their lives Stanley and Doris had a home with electricity.

There was great excitement that weekend when Stanley reminded Doris that they were going to get a television. Doris was still reluctant about spending the money, but Stanley insisted, and they set off in the Austin to go to the shop in Knottingly. There they bought a television with a tiny screen and arranged to pay for it on hire purchase.

Doris worried about the expenditure all the way home, but when it was delivered and connected the following week she declared it was worth every penny. They watched the single BBC channel until their eyes ached. It was like a miracle to see the moving pictures appear on the box in front of them.

So now they were living in a large house with indoor toilets, a bathroom and even electricity. Their living standards had certainly improved. The same could not be said for their finances.

Although Stanley was on the same weekly wage as he had earned at Adwick, there were not the same amount of perks, like free milk, potatoes, and whatever else was grown on the farm. Nor was there the opportunity for Stanley to earn extra money taking on piece work. No longer could Doris sell eggs and home grown vegetables at the back door, but still they struggled to put a little away each week towards a farm of their own and Doris became even more careful with her housekeeping.

Their dream of having their own farm still burned brightly. Details of smallholdings to rent from the West Riding council dropped regularly through the letter box, and they continued to apply, but they had one knock back after another and it seemed they would never be successful.

For Stanley, as far as work was concerned, the move to Clamton had been a success. He was gaining in experience, especially with the new machinery that was now coming into farming. He respected his new employer more than any man he had ever met. Mr McLain was a hands on employer, who was not afraid to work alongside his employees when the need arose, and yet, everyone was very much aware that he was in charge. No one took liberties with him.

He spent a lot of time talking to Stanley, telling him about the early days when he had first bought the estate, and how, at times, he had wondered if he had bitten off too much. He had worked hard and now at last it seemed that the estate was beginning to pay for itself.

What Stanley did miss was his garden at Adwick and the stock he had kept. He missed the trips to Doncaster market and the camaraderie that he had enjoyed among the people there. To his surprise he also missed the village and chatting to passers-by who stopped to admire his garden. But Stanley had learned never to look back, his motto in life was to keep moving forward and make the most of the situation he was in at the time.

For Doris the move mainly meant a better house to bring up her family in. She loved the views out of the windows and was fascinated by the history of the place, often imagining the people who had been lived there in previous centuries.

When Stanley was away at work however, Clamton was a very lonely place for her. One of the things she missed most was the library. Doris had a huge appetite for reading and had been used to borrowing several books every week.

The nearest library and shops were a couple of miles away in Brotherton. The first time she went there she walked the full length of the village street, pushing Frances in her old black pram, looking into the shop windows. The few people she passed stared at her curiously, and ignored her smile. Feeling shunned Doris made her purchases and returned home.

Indignantly she told Stanley that night, "They looked at me as if I had just landed from the bloody moon Stan. Ah won't be going again. Our Eileen can go on her bike if we need anything, but we'll do our shopping in Pontefract in future."

As far as Eileen was concerned the move from Adwick was a disaster. It had happened at the worst possible time as far as her education went. Like many of her friends she had not passed the eleven plus examination but was happily settled at Woodlands Secondary Modern School.

Modern, was the best description for the school. Under a young headmaster who was full of innovative ideas, the school and its pupils were flourishing. There were clubs and activities of all kinds going on within the school. They had football, netball, cricket and hockey, athletics and even a fencing team. They put on a drama every year and from time to time had visiting orchestras. It was in general a very happy school, full of enthusiasm and Eileen loved it.

By contrast, Brotherton School must have been one of the worst in the area. It was a tiny village school with only four classes. Because the standard of education at Woodlands was so much higher than theirs, the Brotherton headmaster placed Eileen in the top class with pupils older than herself. She was a target from day one.

She was hated because she was a stranger, an incomer. She was bullied because she was taller than all the other girls. They didn't like the way she dressed, they didn't like the way she spoke, and probably most of all she was bullied because she seemed to know more answers to questions than they did.

Time in the playground was a nightmare. The boys in the top class regularly groped the girls who pretended to run away and acted coy. The teachers saw what was happening but simply turned a blind eye. Eileen was horrified.

If only she had had the confidence to tell her parents what was happening, but she didn't, and dreaded each day that she had to spend at school.

The teacher they had was a Mr Wilton. He took them for every subject except cookery and woodwork. His method of teaching was to take a text book, and copy a page from it on to the blackboard. He would then instruct his pupils to copy it into their exercise books.

If they failed to do it correctly he would resort to violence. His usual technique was to throw things. If he was in a reasonable mood it would be chalk, or the rubber or books, but if he was really annoyed he would swipe the offending pupil across the back of the head.

One day he erupted into such a temper, and dragged the offending boy out of his chair by his hair and proceeded to knock him from one side of the classroom to the other, while the rest of the class cowered at the back of the room. When he had exhausted his temper, he walked out of the classroom, shouting as he went that they were to get the classroom back in order.

When he returned smelling of the cigarette he had smoked, he acted as if nothing had happened. If he noticed the expressions of fear and hatred on the faces of his pupils he gave no sign of it.

The boy who had been attacked sat silent and cowed, his head was bent over his books but from time to time Eileen saw him glance at the teacher when his back was turned. On his face was written pure loathing.

Over tea that evening she told her parents what had happened. Stanley stopped eating. "He can't get away with that," he said. "Giving the cane for bad behaviour is one thing but what that teacher did was criminal. It'll serve him right if the lad's father turns up at school and gives him a dose of his own medicine. But don't you go saying I said so to your mates at school."

Quietly Eileen said she didn't have any mates, and told him that the lad didn't have a Dad, as he lived with his granny. Stanley said nothing for a while and continued with his tea. Then as he pushed his plate away he drew in a breath through tight lips. He was remembering some of the bad times when he had been on the receiving end of beatings as a lad.

250

"This Mr Wilton or whatever he calls himself should think on. What he wants to remember, is that the young lads he is knocking about now, will soon be men and stronger than him. One of them might repay him."

He was shocked to see his elder daughter suddenly burst into tears. She left the table and ran upstairs throwing herself on to the bed and sobbed.

Doris ran after her and sat beside her stroking her hair. "What's the matter love?" she asked.

Between sobs Eileen told her how awful the school was and how much she hated it.

"But you've got to go to school love, you know that."

"Can't I go to Pontefract School instead, Mam?"

Doris thought for a moment and then decided. "We'd have to pay bus fares, love, and find dinner money every day. We can't afford it."

"But Mam, I could get a bus pass and free dinners or take sandwiches. I wouldn't be bothered about dinner anyway I could manage without it. You'd just have to fill some forms in for the bus pass."

"We'll see what your Dad says. Come on, wash your face, it can't be that bad at school, you'll get used to it."

Eileen knew it would be no use. If she asked her Dad he would say that it was up to her Mam, and they would be going round in circles. If only she could gather up enough courage to describe to them what it was really like in the playground, if only she could tell them about the boys abusing and groping the girls they would have taken it seriously. But for some reason she could not put it into words and so her daily ordeal at school continued as before.

So far because she was so skinny and considered unattractive she had escaped the boy's attention as far as the groping went. It was the following week that Eileen had the feeling that this was about to change. Snide grins and looks in her direction between the boys in the classroom made her nervous, and fear that she was about to be their next target.

It was on the Friday morning break that it happened. Advancing

251

towards her was Jack Robinson, the boy she hated more than any other in the class. A solid wall of girls had gathered behind her blocking off any chance of escape. Grinning at her Jack put out his hand to touch her chest and as he did he shouted so that everyone could hear.

"Come on then, you skinny cow, let's have a feel at your tits." There were sniggers from the girls grouped behind her.

Something snapped inside her head and her fist shot out hitting him full in the face. Once she had let go, it was as if a tide had turned. She followed up the blow with more punches to his face and kicked him on the shins.

He was so shocked at her attack that he turned and ran. Eileen stood still, not knowing what to do next. She was shaking. The girls behind her suddenly began to pat her on the back. She walked away from them and sat on the low wall fighting the need to cry. She would not let them see how upset she was and she acted tough.

No one ever touched her again. The word went around that she could stand up for herself, and she gained a degree of respect. Several of the girls suddenly decided they would like to be her friend, but Eileen hated the school, the building, and everyone in it and could not wait to leave it behind.

CHAPTER 26

Although Edith wrote to them every week, it was no substitute for actually seeing her. They all missed her. So when her letter arrived telling them that she was coming to stay they were all delighted.

Stanley looked at Doris and together they said, "She'll get lost." How right they were.

Doris wrote a letter that afternoon explaining very carefully which bus she was to catch and told her to be sure to ask the conductor to put her off at Butterfields Garage in the village of Brotherton. She wrote that part in large capital letters. Once she was there she was to go to the garage and tell them who she was and they would drive her down to Clamton Hall.

As Doris walked up to the post box she went over what she had written, and felt she had made it as clear as she was able to. She called in at the garage and spoke to the owner who assured her that, yes, he would watch out for her mother on the arranged day.

'Surely nothing can go wrong now,' thought Doris, trying to reassure herself, but knowing her mother as she did, she was full of doubts.

Edith was so looking forward to her little holiday. Her brother William had grumbled about her going away, but on this occasion Edith had stood firm. She had not seen her daughter and family for months and she needed this break.

Her mother insisted that she could manage for a week as long as Willie got the coal and sticks in every night and emptied the slop buckets every morning. The washing could wait until Edith got back.

The night before she set off Edith studied her daughter's letter and the instructions about the journey. It seemed simple enough, and she could always ask someone if she was in doubt. After all, she reasoned, that had always worked for her before.

Edith was down at the bus stop in good time the next morning wearing her belted gabardine mackintosh and jaunty, brown felt hat. It was a little warm for a long coat but Edith was taking no chances and reasoned that she could always take it off and carry it if need be.

She caught the bus to Barnsley with no problem; after all she did that almost every week. The bus for Pontefract was waiting in the station. Edith double checked that it was the right one and just to be on the safe side she asked the passengers sitting on it if the bus was going to Pontefract.

When she was reassured that it was, she began to worry about needing to go to the toilet. Settling her case on the rack above her seat, she whispered to the passenger next to her that she was just going to slip to the toilet.

"Will you watch my case?" she asked. "Don't let the bus go without me will you? I'll only be a couple of minutes." Without waiting for an answer Edith hurried across the narrow road, and into the ladies toilets, and reached into her purse for a penny.

Dismayed, she realised she had no loose change. Feeling a flutter of panic beginning, she wondered what to do. If she went back to the bus now she would never last all the way to Pontefract without going to the toilet; but what if the bus went without her? She cursed herself for leaving her case on the bus. Whatever had she been thinking of? If she lost her case she would never hear the last of it from Doris and her brother William.

Just as she had made up her mind to go back to the bus and retrieve her case the door nearest to her opened. Edith could hardly believe it when she saw a bus conductress coming out. She put out her hand and held the door to prevent it closing and at the same time said, "Oh, excuse me, are you the conductress for the Pontefract bus?"

The young woman nodded as she went to the mirror and began applying more lipstick to her already bright crimson lips.

She combed her blonde hair, checking to see that no black roots were showing and applied spit to her eyebrows. Edith stammered a little as she explained her predicament. The conductress lifted her eyebrows and rolled her eyes.

"Well you'll have to hurry up missus. My driver won't wait for late passengers. He'd go without me if I was late." She turned her head and checked that her stocking seams were straight, then made a big show of looking at her watch. "You've got exactly three minutes missus. Then we'll be off. We've got a timetable to stick to you know."

Edith needed no second warning; she was in the toilet and locking the door behind her before the conductress had left the building. She arrived back at the bus just as the driver started up the engine. The conductress rang the bell as Edith got on and said in a superior voice. "You're only just in time."

Edith settled herself back in her seat, put her hat straight and relaxed. So far so good, she thought to herself and took out her instructions. The next part of the journey would be more complicated. She had to catch the bus that went through Brotherton. Doris said in her letter that it would be a blue bus and she was to catch it at the top of somewhere called Horsefair, near the Dog and Duck public house.

'That should be easy enough,' thought Edith, 'There can't be many pubs with that name.' Even so she was beginning to feel nervous, and wished that one of her family had been able to come and meet her.

It was almost eleven thirty when the bus arrived in Pontefract. Edith stepped off and looked around her. It appeared to be a pleasant little town and the first thing that caught her eye was a café. She looked at it longingly; a cup of tea would be more than welcome.

She tried to resist, telling herself that she should go and find the bus to take her on the next stage of her journey, but her feet steered her in the direction of the café for a cup of tea with a ham sandwich to keep it company.

Half an hour later, feeling refreshed, Edith paid the bill and asked the waitress for directions to the Dog and Duck public house. She discovered it was just around the corner from the café and wondered why she had been so nervous about finding it.

The bus was waiting, engine running, and ready to set off. Edith now felt full of confidence and stepped aboard, double checking that she was on the right bus before she requested that the conductor put her off at the garage in Brotherton.

The conductor with his cap set at a slightly rakish angle rattled the change in his bag, rang the bell, and agreed that he would tell her when to get off. Edith was now feeling very pleased with herself. She was well aware that she was considered a bit dizzy when it came to travelling but she would now be able to prove them all wrong.

The bus lumbered and rocked its way along the outskirts of Pontefract and down the hill towards Ferrybridge. The conductor had disappeared up the stairs and she could hear him chatting to a couple of teenage girls. Tension began grip her again and she called up the stairs, "Don't forget you are going to tell me when to get off."

There was no answer, just high pitched girlish giggles, and a deeper male laugh. Edith questioned the one remaining passenger seated across from her. "Would you tell me when we get to the Brotherton stop? The conductor's supposed to be telling me but it sounds like he's busy up there."

The woman looked at her with such anger that Edith was taken aback, "It's nowt to do with me," she snapped. "Ah'm not doing his bloody job for him. I'm getting off here," and she rang the bell herself and jumped off the bus almost before it drew to a halt. With no passengers waiting at the stop it set off again immediately, and Edith's tension levels were rising.

She got up from her seat and holding on to the rail, made her way to the staircase, intending to go up the stairs, but the bus rocked from side to side and she almost fell over. There was no way she that she could climb the stairs while the bus was moving. Sitting down again she looked out of the window hoping to see the garage where she should be getting off.

They were now in open countryside and Edith knew, she just knew, that they had gone beyond her stop. The conductor came downstairs with a grin on his face, and a smear of lipstick on his cheek. Edith glared at him, "Have we gone past the Brotherton stop?" she asked, hoping he would say no.

He looked at her and bit his lip, "Ah thought you'd got off ages ago," he said. "We passed Brotherton four stops back. I'll ring the bell, you'll have to get off at the next stop and catch a bus back."

It was rare for Edith to lose her temper, but something snapped inside her at his casual, unconcerned words and she stood up glaring at him. Having lived all her life in a mining area Edith had a good knowledge of uncomplimentary swear words although she never normally used them. But now, she was so angry she couldn't help herself and she fired a choice selection at the conductor.

He stared at her as she got off the bus and said in an injured tone, "Well there's no need for that, missus."

Edith shouted at him that there was every need for it, and added that she hoped a certain part of his anatomy turned septic and dropped off. She shook her fist at him as the bus drew away, and then noticed the girls on the upper deck were all pressed against the window watching her.

Once the bus was out of sight there was total silence. Edith stood at the side of the road looking around. There was not a house or a person in sight. Her temper drained away leaving her shaking and wondering what to do.

But Edith's guardian angel was never far away, and he was about to turn up now in her hour of need. From a distance she could hear the squeak of a wheel in need of oiling, and round the corner came a man on a bicycle.

As he came closer Edith put out her hand and called to him. Tears were not far away when she asked him if he could help her. As she explained what had happened there was a shake to her voice and a tear brimmed over from her brown eyes and trickled down her face.

"Ee. Don't get upset, love. Look, tell me where you need to be and I'll see what I can do."

Edith delved into her bag and took out Doris's letter. She

showed him the address and said that her daughter would be very annoyed with her.

"Well it's not your fault is it, love? Look this is no problem. You wait here. There's a telephone box just up the road, I'll go and ring the operator, she'll find the telephone number and get someone to come and pick you up. Have you got some change for the phone, love. I've got no money on me."

Edith would have happily given him every penny in her purse in her gratitude but he insisted he would probably only need tuppence. It was Mr McLain himself who answered the phone and he listened patiently while the situation was explained to him. "No problem," he said, "I'll come and pick her up. Tell her I'll be there in half an hour."

Edith never did manage to find out the name of her guardian angel. He delivered the message, and then said he had to go as he was due back at work. He set off on his bike riding away with the wheel still squeaking. Edith called out her thanks and received a sort of salute and a muffled shout of. "You're welcome."

Doris could hardly believe it when her mother turned up in Mr. McLain's Land Rover, and from the look on her face it was clear she was not pleased. The moment the door closed, Edith could see that she was about to get the sharp edge of her daughter's tongue. As she tried to explain what had happened Doris interrupted her.

"What were you thinking of, Mam. Ah've been worried to death about you. Ah expect you went off to the café as usual, and then got on the wrong bus. I feel so embarrassed. Fancy you having to get Stanley's boss to bring you. What will he think of us?"

"No I did not get on the wrong bus. If you shut up and listen, ah'll tell you what happened, but can I have a cup of tea and a sit down first, I'm tired out. You should have come to meet me then it wouldn't have happened. I'm worn out Doris."

Doris was pulled up short by her mother's words, and realised how pale and tired she looked. "Ah'm sorry, Mam. Ah've been worrying about you all day." Full of remorse she hugged her mother tight. "Oh ah do love you, Mam," she said. "Ah miss you. It seems ages since we last saw you. Come on and sit down. Have a rest, then ah'll show you round the house."

By the time Stanley returned from work Edith was her usual self, happy and glad to see her son-in-law. "Now then, Mam," he said, "I've been hearing all about your adventure and having to be rescued by Mr McLain."

Edith pulled a face and said his employer was a gentleman. She went on to give Stanley an account of what had happened. "Ah, never mind about it, Mam, you're here now. We'll go for a quick walk after tea and I'll show you the lake before it gets dark."

The nights were beginning to draw in and it was already dusk as they left the house. Edith looked at the ruins outlined in the darkening sky and shivered. Stanley put his arm around her, "You get used to them, they'll all be cleared away soon. Come on lets hurry up or it'll be too dark to see anything."

Doris took her hand and together they all walked down the hill, and through the tunnel formed by the trees, until they emerged at their favourite point where the lake came into view. Eileen and Frances had gone ahead and waited for them.

Edith gasped as she saw the scene. The lake stretched into the distance with a light mist hovering over the water and they could see the wrought iron bridge arching across at the narrowest point. In the dusk the scene had taken on an almost ethereal beauty. They gazed at it in silence as they walked along the road towards the avenue of trees and the bridge.

It was Edith that spoke first. "Well I never imagined anything like this. I've never seen anything like it. Your grandma would love to see it, wouldn't she Doris? Do you think we will be able to go over the bridge? I don't mean now, it's getting dark, but perhaps tomorrow?"

"Oh no, Mam. The bridge needs repairing. It's too dangerous to use at the moment, isn't it, Stan?"

Stanley nodded, " Aye, ah think Mr McLain is going to get the joiner on to it soon but it's not safe for us to use just now."

Eileen looked at Frances and hoped she would remember to keep quiet. They used the bridge regularly unknown to anyone. It was possible to get to the other side of the lake by walking the long way round but it was much more exciting to use the damaged bridge.

They usually left the old pram in among the trees and Eileen lifted her little sister on to her back and instructed her to hold on tight. Frances needed no second telling. She wrapped her arms tight around Eileen's neck and held her breath as they made their way across. In the very centre there were several planks missing, but by holding on to the rail and taking long strides it was just possible to make it across.

"Don't tell your Mam. It's our secret," Eileen always urged her little sister. "No don't tell Mam," came the echo from Frances.

She looked at Eileen now and a smile lit up her face. She put her finger to her lips and made a shush sound behind her mother's back. Eileen thought it prudent to divert her sister's thoughts and suggested that they go and look for the swan.

It was completely dark by the time they arrived back at the house and the owls were calling, making the ruins seem more eerie than ever. Even Stanley, who claimed to be unaffected by the atmosphere, was glad to go inside and close the door behind them.

Doris was worried about her mother. She had aged since the last time she had seen her and was not her usual cheerful self. Life was hard for Edith at that time. She had lived with her mother and her brother William for many years. Their home was a stone-built cottage that may have looked pretty and picturesque, but it lacked any modern conveniences.

The only utilities were one cold water tap and gas lights in two of the downstairs rooms. They did have a water toilet but using it meant a seventy yard walk. The coal house was the same distance away from the house.

Edith's mother was now in her mid-eighties and becoming frail, so Edith had taken over all of the washing and most of the housework. In addition, she did a full time job working in the kitchens at a nearby hospital.

As if all that was not enough, her brother William was extremely difficult to live with, and Edith dreamed many times of living in a little house all by herself. She swore that when her mother had gone she would invest all her savings in a place of her own, and William, she said to herself, could fend for himself.

Gradually, after a few days' rest, Edith began to relax. The weather was warm for late September and she spent hours sitting on the stone seat at the end of the garden, looking at the view and enjoying being able to do nothing at all.

At the weekend Stanley said he had a surprise for them all. He absolutely refused to tell them what it was, but insisted that they all had to get in the car. It was certainly a squash to get everyone in but Stanley said it wouldn't matter as they wouldn't be travelling far.

He drove slowly along the road at the side of the lake, stopping several times so that they could get out and peer over wall to try to spot some of the large pike that lived in the shallow water.

At the far side of the lake there was an opening that was well overgrown. It led on to a path that went all the way around the lake, ending up at the far side of the bridge. Stanley had walked the path several times and knew that it was wide enough for the car. As they approached the opening Stanley suddenly shouted, "Hold tight," as he turned sharply through the bushes, then down a fairly steep slope and on to the path.

At times Stanley could have a wicked sense of humour, and he laughed as his passengers cried out in alarm. Doris punched his arm, told him he was a daft bugger, and warned him she would get even with him. But once through the bushes it was worth any fright they might have had. It was like being in another world. The path opened out into a flat, even, area surrounded by trees and the lake stretched out before them.

They continued slowly driving until they were almost at the bridge. Stanley stopped beneath a horse chestnut tree whose branches curved down until they reached the floor, leaving an arched space underneath that was almost like a cave. A layer of leaves covered the ground and rustled under their feet as they all walked to the water's edge. They stood in silence soaking up the beauty of the trees that were changing into their autumn colours and watching the leaves gently falling around them.

It was then that Billy the swan glided into view. His head swivelled towards them, his neck straight up. His whole attitude was one of anger and he obviously viewed them as trespassers on his property.

"Get back in the car quick," Stanley shouted as Billy reached land and began climbing out of the water. There was a mad scramble for the car. Edith was first in, climbing into the back seat as fast as a twenty year old. Doris practically threw Frances in and followed her slamming the passenger door behind her. Stanley pushed Eileen in at the driver's side, but then found that the swan was already right behind him. He dodged round the side of the vehicle with Billy following him. He would never have thought a swan capable of moving so fast on land. As he dodged around the car again he reached the door and dived inside, closing the door just in time. "Bloody hell," he gasped, "That was a close call." Billy was staring at them through the windows. His head was on a level with theirs. He may not have been able to speak but his eyes said it all.

With the engine stopped there was no chance of driving away. The only way of getting the engine going again was to crank it with the starting handle. Stanley stared the swan in the eye and decided they would stay where they were. He gave Billy a little salute as he said, "We'll just have to wait until he gets sick of staring at us."

Billy was now at the front of the car and stretching out his wings he flew at it and struck the radiator. It seemed that striking that blow had satisfied his honour and he now considered the enemy beaten. With one more warning glare he returned to the water and glided swiftly away.

As Billy sailed off into the distance Stanley retrieved the starting handle and got the engine going. It was then that he discovered the dent in the radiator where the swan's wing had struck it. His respect for the bird grew and he warned Eileen not to take Frances too near the water when the bird was about in future.

Edith went home the next day. She said she would have loved to have stayed longer but was worried that her mother might need her. To make sure she got home safely, Doris walked to the top of the estate and continued with her as far as Pontefract. There, she saw her on to the Barnsley bus. Once she was there Edith would be on familiar territory and unlikely to get lost.

There was a lump in Doris's throat as she waved her mother off. She felt sad as she realised how vulnerable her mother looked and how much older. Doris sighed as her thoughts went back to the days when they had lived together, just the two of them, in the little cottage in Sandygate. Anger sparked inside her as she recalled how her mother had told her about the difficulties she was having, living under the same roof as her brother William.

"He's getting worse Doris. He is so bad tempered. There's no pleasing him," she had said. "God only knows what it will be like when he's retired and at home all day. He could do with a shed in the garden then he could sit in it on his own when he's in a mood."

Doris had agreed. She had often crossed swords with her uncle, "Well he always was a cantankerous bugger at the best of times. The way he talks to my Grandma is a disgrace."

"Yes it is, Doris, but you know, he thinks the world of her. It's as if he can't help himself. It irritates him because she can't hear very well, and he ends up shouting at her. Then he storms off into the garden. But there's nothing to be done about it just now. I'll just have to put up with him for the time being." and as Doris thought about it she knew that her mother was right.

With winter just around the corner Stanley was anxious to get a good stock of logs cut. He had permission to borrow one of the tractors and go down into the woods to collect as much fallen timber as he liked.

So on Saturday afternoon he hitched the tractor on to a trailer and with Eileen sitting on the mudguard they set off. There was an area of woodland that had recently been felled and the timber carted away, but there many branches that had been left behind and were an ideal size for cutting into logs. Within an hour they had the trailer loaded and were on their way back home.

Stanley had also borrowed the saw bench. It had a fearsome looking blade and turned Eileen cold as she imagined her father falling on to it and being cut to pieces. Stanley looped the heavy belt that ran from the saw bench to the pulley on the tractor. He tightened it up and started the engine. As he slipped it into gear and increased the revs the belt began to move, slowly at first, then increasing in speed until the saw blade was spinning so fast it was no longer possible to see the teeth on the blade. Stanley wiped the dust from an old pair of goggles, put them on and they were ready to begin.

It was to be Eileen's job to select branches and pass them to Stanley, who would push the wood on to the blade and cut it into logs. Doris was waiting at the opposite side to load the logs on to a barrow, then wheel them into an outside store and stack them.

Eileen swallowed hard and passed the first branch to Stanley. He gave her a grin and shouted over the sound of the engine that this was going to be a lot easier than sawing them up by hand. Standing with his legs firmly planted he moved the timber forwards on to the blade. As it bit through the wood it gave a high pitched whine and sent sawdust flying in all directions.

Working as a team the whole load of timber was reduced to burning sized logs by teatime. Stanley slowed the engine and brought the saw bench to a halt. Doris shared her daughter's fears of the saw and they were both relieved when it was over. But their relief was to be short lived when Stanley announced that they would be doing the same thing all over again the following day. By the time they went to bed on Sunday night, Stanley was feeling very pleased with their weekend's work, and he fell asleep thinking of their huge stock of logs that hopefully would see them through most of the winter.

He woke up next morning to find that a massive hole had opened up in the ground exactly where the tractor and saw bench had stood the previous day. More of the network of cellars had collapsed.

For days afterwards, and nights when he should have been sleeping, Stanley pictured what could have happened if the ground had caved in whilst they had been working there.

CHAPTER 27

There were only a few trades people who were willing to make the trek all the way through the estate to Stanley and Doris's home and to the two families who lived and worked on the Home Farm. The milk man delivered every morning and a baker came twice a week. Every Friday evening a greengrocer called, announcing his arrival with two loud blasts on his horn as he drove through the gateway.

He had a small truck with his name emblazoned on the side doors in gold and black lettering. Fredrick Shufflebank, purveyor of fine fruit and vegetables; the writing declared. The back of the truck had a tarpaulin covered roof and his wares were displayed in wooden boxes.

Fredrick or just plain Fred as he was more usually known, was a tall middle aged man, with a broad face, large mouth and dull complexion. He wore a flat tweed cap with matching overcoat and had a very masculine appearance.

Once he moved or spoke however, all hint of masculinity vanished. As he got out of the driver's seat, he minced, rather than walked around the truck to his customers; he spoke in a soft, effeminate voice. The first time he called on Doris she thought that he was joking and almost told him to stop messing about, but pulled herself up short just in time.

Stanley insisted it was all an act to draw attention away from the fact that he was slipping rotten fruit into the bottom of the bags, and giving them short measure. In wintertime it was always dark when he arrived and the only light came from the lamp above the door and the paraffin Tilly lamp that hung in the back of the truck just above the fruit.

If Doris complained about any previous bad produce that he had sold her, he put on an injured look, and gave every sign that he was about to burst into tears at the thought that she could suspect him of cheating her.

"But Mrs Dale, you are one of my favourite customers. I would never intentionally do anything like that." He stood looking at her, his eyes wide and brimming with tears.

Doris said she would give him another chance and went back into the house laughing, declaring that he should have been an actor. But her patience was running short and Doris was not a lady to mess with. It was only a matter of time before she lost her temper completely with Fred.

Stanley had long suspected that there was more to Fred than met the eye and he was soon to be proved right. Fred's usual routine was to go down to the Home Farm after he had been to them. The families there had had similar experiences with Fred and like Doris they were sick of him but dependent on his deliveries.

It was on the second Friday in December that Stanley caught him out. It had been a threshing day at the Home Farm and they were late finishing. Stanley walked out of one of the buildings with his bike just as Fred left.

He followed the truck, easily keeping pace with him. Fred was driving slowly down the track that was full of pot holes. He was approximately fifty yards in front of Stanley when he reached the crossroads. There was really only one way he could go and that was to the left but to Stanley's surprise he turned right which only led down into the woods. There was, of course, the rough track to the next village through the woods but he would never get through there with his truck, it had barely been wide enough for Stanley's little car.

'So where is he going?' Stanley wondered. He was curious enough to wait and see. Just past the crossroads was the hidden path that led around the lake and Stanley wheeled his bike carefully out of sight and leaned it against a tree. Then going back to the side of the road he settled down to wait, thinking as he did so that no matter how long it took he would stick it out. After all there was no other way for Fred to go. Unless he was thinking of camping out for the night, he had to come past him.

The temperature had dropped as night fell, and as he stood still, the cold began to creep through his clothes. He rubbed his hands together and twiddled his toes inside his boots to keep his circulation going. All around him there were the quiet sounds of animals going about their nightly business. Stanley listened, trying to identify them. When the long grass near him began to shake he stamped his feet hard and whatever it was scuttled away.

The clouds slid away from the moon, making everything more visible. Stanley looked up at the sky hoping the clouds would keep clear for the next hour at least. He pulled up his collar and drew his cap down as low as he could, wondering if he was wasting his time standing about here in the cold when he could be back home with his feet in front of the fire.

After another half hour the faint sound of an engine reached him. With his head on one side he caught the sound again and it quickly became louder; obviously coming closer.

As the lights appeared, Stanley drew himself back into the bushes and watched carefully. Fred's truck came into view, and increased in speed as he reached the tarmac road. He changed into top gear and swept quickly past Stanley; but not too fast to prevent him from seeing what was strapped to the roof of his truck. It was piled high with Christmas trees and as it passed him he could just make out the large bundle of holly wrapped in sacking and tied to the back.

'So,' thought Stanley, 'That's your game is it? Been pinching Christmas trees have you? I've got you now Fredrick Shufflebank.'

Retrieving his bike he rode quickly home. His hands and feet were freezing cold, but he smiled all the way as he thought of telling Doris what he had just seen.

He agonized for a full week, wondering what course of action to take; and by Friday he had made up his mind. As Fred came sweeping into the courtyard sounding his horn to announce his arrival, Doris picked up her purse and her shopping bag.

As she walked down the steps Fred came tripping around the

corner of the truck greeting her in his usual manner. He stopped short as Stanley followed his wife and stood with his hands behind his back apparently intent on looking at the produce piled high on the van and the sign hanging up above the apples.

The sign simply said, 'Christmas trees, varies sizes available. Order now.'

"Ah, Mr Dale." began Fred, "It's not often that I see you." Stanley decided he would come straight to the point.

"No," he said, "But I've seen you very recently; last Friday to be exact. You were on your way back from the woods. I wondered what you were doing down there in the dark."

Fred glanced at him then looked away. "I think you must be mistaken Mr. Dale. I've never been on that road."

"Come off it Fred. I saw you going to the woods and I saw you coming back with the truck piled high with Christmas trees."

Fred stood gaping at him, stuck for words; several different expressions passed over his face until Stanley said, "I'm prepared to forget that I saw you, so long as we get no more rotten fruit and no more overcharging. That goes for them down at the Home Farm an all."

There was no other comment made and Fred avoided eye contact with Stanley as he picked Doris's fruit out with great care.

Deep inside Stanley there was a chunk of admiration for the wily greengrocer. As he said to Doris later, when they went back indoors, "You've got to give him credit for his bloody cheek, haven't you?"

In the days that followed Stanley wondered if he had taken the right action, but as Doris pointed out, if he had gone straight to Mr McLain, Fred would have been kicked off the estate and they would all have lost their travelling greengrocer.

CHAPTER 28

On the estate there seemed to have been a population explosion among the foxes. They were also overrun with rabbits. Now if the foxes had been content to live off the rabbits all would have been well. But foxes always did have a taste for poultry and that spelt trouble.

The young poultry that were being reared to become next year's laying hens were kept on grass land. They lived in large purpose built arks, which were moved every few days so that the poultry always had nice fresh grass to run about on. The main part of the arks were covered with wire netting, but at the end they had enclosed sleeping quarters, with wooden, slatted floors.

Now chickens, may not be very well endowed with brains, but they have an inbuilt instinct for their own safety. The minute the sun went down they all trouped through the little doorways into their sleeping quarters and settled down for the night.

Stanley was in charge of the poultry and the last thing he did every night was to close the little doors to the sleeping quarters and secure each one with a bolt that even the foxes could not unfasten.

But as many poultry breeders know only too well, Mr and Mrs Fox are clever, cunning, and determined when it comes to gaining access to their favourite food.

By early light the poultry were clamouring to be let out to begin their day, scratching for worms and doing whatever chickens like to do. At the weekends it was usually Eileen's job to let them out, and it was a duty that she enjoyed. The grass land that was now used for the poultry had once been the beautiful gardens of the estate in years gone by and was surrounded by rare, flowering trees.

But on this particular Sunday morning there was something wrong. There was an eerie silence. Not a sound came from the chickens. It was when she got close to one of the arks that she could see soil scattered over the grass, and a hole that was dug underneath one of the arks. A splattering of blood and a collection of feathers surrounded the hole.

With her mouth dry she opened the little door and prayed to see the chickens come rushing out as they usually did. There was nothing, no sound, no chickens. She went to the large door that opened the roof of the sleeping quarters, unfastened the bolt and lifted it up.

An appalling sight met her. Every chicken was dead and covered with blood. Being unable to get into the poultry, the fox had pulled their legs though the slats, and eaten them off. Some of the chickens had been smothered by their companions in their efforts to get away from the fox. They were the lucky ones. The rest had died a horrible death.

The other arks had not been touched but the chickens in them were strangely quiet and subdued as if they knew that Mr Fox would be coming for them next.

It was decided that the foxes needed to be culled, and a shoot was quickly arranged for the following Sunday morning. Stanley was invited to join them. As he had no firearm of his own he had to borrow the old double barrelled gun that was kept in one of the out buildings and used at harvest time to shoot rabbits. It was covered in dust from the ground-up wheat and barley that was used as animal feed, but Stanley took it home and cleaned it thoroughly. Using an oily rag he pulled it through the two barrels and polished the wooden stock until there was not a speck of dirt anywhere on it.

He took it out into the fields and had a bit of a practice with it, trying to shoot rabbits. It seemed to shoot slightly to the left and he missed every one. Stanley took off his cap and looked at the rabbits casually feeding in the field as if they knew they were safe.

He took a deep calming breath, put his cap on again and raised the gun to his shoulder.

This time he looked down the barrel, lined up with the sights and aimed just a fraction off centre. He was more successful, and the rabbits scattered in all directions heading for their burrows, all except one, and that was destined to be dinner the next day. As Stanley picked it up and carried it home he felt more confident about the shoot.

When Sunday came around he was up extra early and had done all the feeding and been home for his breakfast before the shoot was due to begin.

The Land Rovers began arriving at nine o'clock and the men gathered about in groups with their guns casually hung over their arms. They were obviously all known to each other. Stanley stood on the edge of the group observing the clothing they were wearing. Each and every one of them appeared to have visited the same outfitters and was dressed for the occasion in tweed jackets, cavalry twill trousers and highly polished, brown leather boots

Stanley's clothing was the same as he wore for work every day, threadbare corduroy trousers and an old Harris Tweed jacket that had once been part of his best suit. It was now frayed at the cuffs and sported rough patches on the elbows. The pockets were stuffed with baler twine, a rather grubby looking handkerchief, his pocket knife and a handful of cartridges. On his feet were his usual black working boots from the Army and Navy stores.

The one thing he did have in common with the rest of the group was his flat tweed cap, although Stanley's had seen a considerably more wear and tear.

Mr McLain's son David arrived in their rather scruffy Land Rover and beckoned Stanley to join him. He laughed as Stanley got in beside him. "You look like a fish out of water among that lot, Stan." Like his father, David was very much a working farmer and today he was only slightly better dressed than Stanley.

"There's some money's worth of guns knocking about, we should get some results with this lot on the job," he commented, then added, "I see you've cleaned the old blunderbuss up, but you'll be lucky to hit ought with it. I've had a go with it and it pulls to the left."

Stanley agreed with him, "Aye," he replied, "I've had a bit of a practice with it. It'll be a bit of sport. We could do to get rid of some of the foxes. Have they got some beaters organised?"

"Oh yes, a gamekeeper that Dad knows has got it all sorted. I think we'd better stick together, Stan," and with that he revved up the engine and set off like a rocket towards the woods, with all the rest following and trying to keep up. Stanley clung on to the strap above the door, while they bounced around. He'd driven with David before and often referred to him as the farmer's answer to Stirling Moss.

They pulled up a good quarter of a mile away from where the shoot was going to begin and they all walked quietly towards the woods. Stanley said softly to David, "Ah'd like to bet there are at least a dozen foxes watching us right now."

David agreed, "Aye, they're a lot smarter than people give em credit for."

The gamekeeper had stopped at a large area of land that had been cleared of trees. Many stumps were still in the ground, surrounded by rough grass and self-sown plants that were flourishing. It was an ideal habitat for foxes,with plenty of places to hide and breed undisturbed.

They were organised into a line, guns at the ready. Stanley found himself the last man in the line with David next to him. He looked around; he knew this area of ground well. He had walked it many times with Eileen by his side and had pointed out the places where the grass had been completely flattened, "Look here," he had told her, "This is where the foxes play. They look very cute when they're playing and chasing each other, but they're not very cute when they are out killing the poultry."

At a signal from the gamekeeper they began to walk slowly forward until he held up his hand and they all knew they should wait now for the foxes to break cover and dash for safety. The sound of the beaters carried in the still air. Suddenly a gun was fired by someone in the centre of the line, then another and another. Stanley waited, gun raised to his shoulder. He was expecting the fox they had shot at to come racing past him.

Taking shallow breaths he concentrated, keeping his eye on the clumps of grass that moved. It looked like it would break cover any time now. There it was; a big dog fox streaking into view with his tail held straight out behind him. As he followed the movement of the fox, Stanley chose his moment and pulled the trigger letting both barrels go. The fox dropped and a cheer went up.

Suddenly Stanley went from being regarded as something of a joke in his working clothes and using an old gun, to being a champion. He accepted the praise quietly and said little, but deep inside he was cheering himself, and as he said to Doris later, "Well that was one up for the working man, Doris. Just shows that fancy outfits and expensive guns are not everything."

Another shoot was scheduled for the next Sunday and followed the same pattern. It was almost embarrassing when once again Stanley was the only man to shoot a fox. The praise was a little strained that day and Stanley had to turn his face away to hide his grin.

On the third Sunday the gamekeeper placed Stanley at the opposite end of the line, saying apologetically to him, that some of the expert gunmen had complained that Stanley had obviously had an unfair advantage. They claimed that he had been given the best position and someone else should have a chance.

Shrugging his shoulders he said he didn't mind at all and took up the position pointed out to him. He raised the gun to his shoulder and looked down the barrel just to get his eye in.

It was at that moment, when no one else was ready, that two foxes came out of hiding and ran, cutting right across in front of him. A shout went up and guns were raised, but they were too late. Stanley, who already had his gun to his shoulder, let fire and the first fox fell. The second one reached the cover and disappeared. A few shots whistled harmlessly where it had been a moment before but the fox was away to freedom. The shoot was abandoned early when no more foxes were seen.

Stanley could barely believe it. Incredibly, for the third Sunday in a row he was the only one to shoot a fox. As they walked back to their vehicles David slapped him on the back and in a loud voice said, "Well done, Stan. That's how you do it. All you gentlemen should take lessons off him."

There were some strained polite smiles and half-hearted

congratulations. Stanley couldn't wait to get home and tell his family how he had triumphed. "I bet they don't ask me to go on the shoot again," he said to Doris.

And he was right, they didn't.

The dog fox who had met his end on the first shoot had been staked out between two posts among the poultry arks. It had been put there by the gamekeeper as a message to any other marauding foxes that they could meet the same fate. It was left there looking gruesome until it stank to high heaven and the maggots were falling off its carcase.

Eileen gave it as wide a berth as possible when she went to check on the poultry and hoped it would soon be taken down. Every now and then the chickens stretched their necks and looked through the netting at the rotting fox and let off a loud, collective clucking that sounded remarkably like laughter.

Who says that chickens have no brains?

CHAPTER 29

June had come around again. They were all thankful that the long, cold winter was now just a memory. The estate was looking at its loveliest and as Doris admired it out of the bedroom windows she felt a glow of happiness.

Just last week Mr McLain had offered her a job. Granted, it was only for an hour a day and paid just one pound per week, but that pound would make all the difference to their living standards. The job entailed washing and grading all the eggs produced on the farm; then packing them in crates ready to be collected. This was to take place in an old prefabricated hut that was left over from the time when the army had occupied the estate during the war. As it was situated just outside the gates it was ideal.

As Doris went about her housework, she planned what she could do with the extra one pound that would soon be in her purse every week. It was while she was in this happy frame of mind that there was a loud knock on the door.

She pushed her duster into her apron pocket and hurried down the stairs and along the hallway. As she opened the door her face fell. A telegraph boy stood there, and in that instant she knew what would be written. Her normally rosy cheeks lost all colour as she took the telegram from him and closed the door

With shaking hands she opened it. It was brief as all telegrams were. It was stark message and read.

'Grandma died last night. Letter to follow. Mam.'

Doris burst into tears and sobbed. Her beloved Grandma had died just a few days before her eighty fifth birthday. For the first time Doris wished she was living back in Wath and able to go straight to her mother.

The promised letter arrived the next day and told how her Grandmother had woken up during the night feeling unwell. With her daughter Edith and her son William by her side she had stared past them and spoken the names of her long dead husband and son, before she quietly breathed her last breath.

'Try not to be upset, Doris,' her mother said in her letter, 'She was ready to go and went peacefully.' Her words were some consolation to Doris but she found it hard to believe that she would never see her grandmother's lovely face again, nor ever hear her straight forward advice.

The funeral was arranged for the following Wednesday. It was decided that Eileen would have the day off school and stay at home looking after Frances as they would not be attending the funeral. Stanley and Doris set off early on Wednesday morning in the Austin dressed in their sombre funeral clothes, with a wreath on the back seat and several trays of food for the mourners.

When they arrived at the house in Sandygate Doris jumped out of the car almost before it had stopped and ran up the uneven cinder covered path that led to the cottage. She passed Mrs Chappel, the next door neighbour, giving her only the briefest of greetings in her hurry to see her mother. As always, in summer, the cottage door stood wide open, everything looked just as it always had, but yet there was a strange hollowness about the room.

Doris called out for her mother and she appeared at the kitchen door carrying a tray of cups. The moment she saw her daughter she burst into tears. Doris took the tray from her, placed it on the table, then took her mother in her arms and they cried together.

As she dried her tears Doris nodded towards the door that led into the tiny front room, "Is Grandma?" she asked, but before she could finish Edith took her arm and led her into the front room.

The coffin filled the centre of the tiny room and was surrounded by flowers that had been cut from the garden that morning. Their fragrance filled the room. Photographs of her Grandmother's husband were placed close to the coffin as if he was watching over her. At the other side were pictures of her son and two baby grandsons. All three of them had all died within a fortnight of each other from meningitis many years ago.

Hesitantly, Doris walked to the coffin and stared down at the body. The deep lines on her grandmother's face were smoother now and she looked at peace. Doris touched her face and it felt firm, cold, and smooth. Her lovely silver hair was brushed back at the sides, with a deep wave in the front slightly covering her forehead, just the way she had always worn it.

Doris sensed someone beside her and turned to find Stanley there. He put his hands on her shoulders and kissed the top of her head. "She looks lovely, Doris," he said with a catch in his voice. "Come on, love, come and have a cup of tea."

The mourners began to arrive, among them her Grandmother's only living brother. He had not seen his sister for several years but had made the journey from Derbyshire to pay his respects. He sat by her body until the undertakers came to prepare the coffin for burial, and he cried, heartbroken as he stood at the door watching. "If I could just have held her in my arms once more; just once." he said as he wiped his tears

As the body was carried down the path and out to the hearse that was waiting on the road, a long line of mourners stood waiting to follow. Doris's Grandmother was well known and respected in Wath upon Dearne and Doris felt immensely proud of her.

It was a relief when the last of the mourners bid their goodbyes and Stanley and Doris were able to set off home. They had tried to persuade Edith to come and stay with them at some time in the near future but she had protested, saying that she couldn't leave her brother William on his own so soon after the death of their mother.

Doris had said "Well, Uncle Willie can come too."

Stanley, who had overheard the remark, gave an inward groan, and under his breath said, "Oh bloody hell. Ah'll look forward to that then! He'll take some putting up with," and he hoped that it would never happen.

With every week that passed it was becoming clearer that the car would have to go. The tax and insurance were an expenditure that they could not afford, and no matter how carefully Stanley maintained it, the car was no longer road worthy. The brakes, which had always been a problem, were now almost non-existent and Stanley joked that they would soon have to put their feet out and slide them along the road to stop the car.

If they had lived on a bus route it would not have been such a problem, but they faced a two mile walk to the nearest bus stop. Stanley and Eileen could use their bikes, but no matter how hard she tried, Doris was never able to find her balance and could not learn how to ride a bike.

As he thought about it one evening Stanley suddenly came up with a solution. "I've had an idea, Dot, ah can't think why I never thought of it before."

Doris looked at him expectantly, wondering what he was going to come up with.

"We don't need tax and insurance for the car if we stay on the estate. They are all private roads. We can use the car to go up to the main road, park it up and catch the bus. It won't matter about the brakes. I can cope with them when we are not in traffic. It'll just take longer to stop that's all."

Doris looked at him doubtfully, "Are you sure we won't need tax and insurance?"

"No. No. Of course not. We've got a couple of old vehicles that we use around the farm. Mr McLain doesn't pay tax or insurance for them. Besides, we won't get anything for the car if we try to sell it. It's had it. It's worn out. It would cost more to repair it than it's worth. We'll be better off keeping it for our own use."

He looked at Doris, waiting for her verdict; he knew that she had been hoping that they would get a few pounds for the car if they put it up for sale. Then he played his trump card.

"What would we do without a car when your Mam comes to stay?

And so Doris was persuaded, although she did point out that they would still have to buy petrol. He tapped his hand on the chair arm and was obviously in deep thought, then he said, "Ah don't know about that Dot. Maybe I can get it to run on paraffin. I can get that free. We've got a five hundred gallon tank full of it for the tractors. Be quiet a minute. Let me think"

The tractors ran on paraffin, but the engines had to be started on petrol. As soon as the engines were running they were then switched over to paraffin which was much cheaper than petrol.

The driver just had to remember to switch the engine back to petrol before the it was stopped.

Stanley reasoned that he should be able to do the same with the Austin, but he had to come up with a way to switch the engine between petrol and paraffin. He took the car up to Butterfields garage and explained the idea to the mechanic. He looked at Stanley for a minute with his lips pursed, turning it over in his mind.

"I don't see why it shouldn't work in principle, but it won't do the engine much good." he said, as he lifted the bonnet up and stared at it. He touched the pipe that led to the carburettor. "We could put a little tap on here, but it's your responsibility, Stan. If it doesn't work, or it ruins the engine, it's nothing to do with me."

Stanley nodded and held out his hand. As they shook hands he asked what the charge would be.

"Give me ten bob." the mechanic said, "No I'll tell you what, bring me a couple of rabbits up next time you catch some. I like a nice rabbit stew."

The job was done that very afternoon. Stanley bought a gallon of petrol in a can and went home to put his plan into action.

As it was a Saturday afternoon there were no workers about, and he filled a five gallon drum with paraffin from the big tank in the farmyard, and stashed it away under an old blanket in the garage out of sight. Then taking a deep breath and crossing his fingers he half-filled the car's tank with the tractor paraffin.

The carburettor was already full of petrol and the engine started as usual. When the paraffin began to feed into the engine it coughed and spluttered a little, as if it wondered what on earth was going on, and then it began to run normally.

It was just as well that there was no one about as Stanley did a little jig and patted the roof of the car. He drove straight round to the house and picked Doris up. She protested that she was just going to make some buns for tea but Stanley insisted.

"Just get in the car, Dot, we're going for a little drive."

He drove down the lane, past the lake, turned around and back again. As he pulled up by the steps to the front door he looked at her, "Well, what do you think, Dot?"

"What do you mean, Stan? We've just been for a ride down by the lake. What about it? There's nothing unusual about that, we're always going there."

Stanley sighed, "Yes, Doris, but the car is now running on paraffin. It won't cost us anything. There will be no need to buy any more petrol apart from an odd gallon now and then to start the engine."

Anything mechanical was lost on Doris, but she understood the financial part of it and smiled as she kissed him and told him he was a genius, but she now had to go and get her buns made.

CHAPTER 30

It is true that you can get used to anything, and in time the Dale family had become used to living next to the huge pile of rubble that had once been the old part of the hall. They had even grown used to the flock of jackdaws that had taken up residence in the remaining central walls of the building that were stubbornly still standing. They accepted that the birds rose up in the air squawking and protesting every time they opened their front door.

The jackdaws had become a family joke and they no longer found them creepy, except on autumn nights when the mist swirled around the upper ruined walls, and then they still sent shivers down their spines with their ugly calls as they flew, circling around in the air until they settled back into their nests.

The family had grown used to being isolated, and finding their own fun and entertainment. Eileen's favourite pastime was to scramble around among the rubble looking for differently coloured pieces of decorated plaster that had once been part of the elegant house. On one particular day as she climbed higher up the heap she reached the central wall and stared closely at it. That was when she noticed a small piece of paper protruding from the edge of the plaster.

Curious, she picked at the crumbling, weather beaten plaster until a chunk fell away. It revealed part of a sheet of paper that was covered in writing. Excited by her find she slid and scrambled back down just in time to see her father on his way across the courtyard.

"Quick, Dad, come and look at this." Stanley was in a hurry to get indoors for his tea, but his daughter was so insistent that he followed her, climbing up the heap and reminding her that she was supposed to keep away from the ruins in case of any falling masonry.

"But, Dad, look at this," and she pointed at the writing. Stanley examined it and pulled away at the edges of the plaster, exposing more writing. He was now as excited as his daughter.

"We need some tools," he said, "Go and fetch my small crow bar and a shovel, and tell your Mam to come and look at this."

With the crow bar Stanley was able to prise off the outer layer of plaster that was a false wall. Hidden underneath were many sheets of paper covered with pages of writing. They had been pegged to the wall with round wooden nails. The sheets were dusty and faded but it was just possible to decipher references to Oliver Cromwell and battles that had been fought nearby.

They were obviously historical documents. The find was reported and they were removed and taken away, presumably to some museum, but their whereabouts remain a mystery to this day.

Stanley still kept up his membership of the farm workers union and attended the monthly meetings whenever he was able to. He was voted on to the committee, but as he told Doris, it was not really any great honour, considering the small number of members in their branch. He laughed as he told her, "There's the committee and about six members. Ah don't think we're going to make the farmers stump up many pay rises."

Little did he know that in a roundabout way, it was his involvement with the union that would prove to be a turning point in life for him.

When an annual general meeting was called that included the farm workers union, Stanley was very keen to be present, especially when it became known that the politician Hugh Gaitskell was to speak.

Hugh Gaitskell was one of the few politicians that Stanley had any time for. He had read about him in the newspapers and heard some of his speeches on the radio and he agreed with many of the things he stood for.

The meeting was held in Pontefract, and this time, as he was dressed in his best suit instead of cycling, Stanley drove his car up to the edge of the estate just opposite the Brotherton Fox Inn, parked the car and caught the bus into Pontefract.

As always, he was there early and able to get a seat near the front. He took off his cap, smoothed his hair down with his hand and settled down to wait. The hall filled up rapidly and the speakers took their places on the stage. As Hugh Gaitskell joined them a ripple of clapping broke out. It was obvious that he was the one that most people had come to hear, and they were not disappointed. As he ended his speech and sat down there was not a single person that did not applaud him.

Later, the speakers mingled among the audience while refreshments were handed out. Hugh stood in the centre of a group casually holding a glass of beer. Stanley made his way over to them. As he stood on the edge of the group he caught Hugh's eye and nodded. He came towards him and Stanley spoke up, thanking him for the speech.

Hugh smiled at the praise and commented that he hoped that Stanley had found it interesting, "Are you from Pontefract, Mr --- ?" He questioned.

Stanley held out his hand, "Stanley Dale," he said, feeling self-conscious, and then he explained where he lived and worked and where he was from originally. Then he told him about his burning ambition to have his own farm.

Hugh took another drink from his glass, then he patted Stanley on the back, and as he looked around at the crowd surrounding him, he said in a loud clear voice, "This is just the sort of young man I like to meet, hard working and full of ambition." He shook Stanley's hand again and wished him luck.

Stanley's face coloured up under his tan and he said another thank you feeling very self-conscious but at the same time pleased at the praise.

Knowing he needed to catch the last bus he made his way out of the building and found himself walking through the door at the same time as a man who looked familiar. As Stanley held the door open for him to follow, the man spoke to him. "It's been a very interesting meeting don't you think?" he said. "Hugh Gaitskell obviously thought well of you. Praise indeed from someone in his position."

Startled, Stanley looked closer and recognised him as Mr. Tingle one of the committee members on the West Riding Council. He had sometimes been present at his interviews when he had applied for farm tenancies.

He continued, "You know who I am?" As Stanley nodded he went on to say "I'll watch out for you, Mr Dale, at the next lot of interviews. Make sure you keep on applying. Good evening to you,"

As Stanley ran to catch the bus he felt as if he could fly. The bus was ready to pull out just as he reached it and grabbing the rail he jumped on to the platform and climbed the stairs to find a seat on the upper deck.

He was still in high spirits when the bus reached the Brotherton Fox Inn. At the back of his mind the whole evening, there had been a niggling worry about his car, but there it was, safely parked behind the wall and positioned at the top of the slight slope.

He unlocked the door and taking off his jacket he carefully folded it and placed it on the passenger seat. At the other side of the rough track was a disused quarry with steep sides that dropped away some twenty or thirty feet and Stanley gave a little shiver as he imagined going over the side in the car.

He retrieved the lemonade bottle filled with petrol from under the seat and filled up the carburettor, then wiped the outside of the bottle and wrapped it in an old cloth before replacing it under the seat.

With the door open and his hand on the steering wheel he took a deep breath and began to push. As the car gathered speed he jumped into the seat, put his foot on the clutch, pushed the car into gear and released the clutch. The engine fired into action and Stanley patted the dashboard.

"Good girl," he said, "I knew you could do it." On this road into the estate, he was travelling along rough tracks which divided the fields. They had been carved out of the parkland and as he rounded the spinney of trees he could see the hall. A light was shining in the middle room and Stanley knew that Doris would be waiting at the gate for him.

Every year farming was becoming more mechanised and there was excitement on the farm when Mr McLain announced that they would be taking delivery of a brand new combine harvester. It meant an end to the old fashioned way of harvesting. There would be no more cutting the corn with the binder, no more long days of standing the sheaves of corn up in the fields to dry and no more threshing days in winter.

The corn would be cut and the grain removed right there in the field. The machine could be worked with just two men, one to drive and one to stand on the platform at the side of the harvester and fill sacks with the grain as it came down the two chutes. Once the sacks were full they were tied up, then pushed off the platform and collected later.

It all sounded too good to be true and of course it was. The snag was that the grain almost always had a high percentage of moisture in it and could not be stored in sacks just as it was. The grain had to be dried. So in addition to a new combine harvester they were also going to get a grain dryer.

In one of the huge Nissen huts that were left over from the days when the army had occupied the estate, work began on building a dryer. Builders were brought in and hundreds of bricks arrived. A square roughly thirty yards by thirty was marked out and the work began.

Walls were built on the marked out square until they reached the height of four foot. As soon as the walls were finished, a concrete top was constructed, leaving oblong holes the size of sack of corn when it was laid on its side. The holes had metal bars across them making them into grids that would support the sacks. If it had not been for those grids the whole thing could have been mistaken for a stage.

It was now time for the electricians to fit the massive electric heater and blower. A metal pipe went from the blower into a hole in the side of the brick platform.

These were soon in place and were switched on to test them. As the heater roared into life, the blower blasted the heat through the whole construction and out through the grids. Mr McLain nodded his approval. It all looked exactly as it should. When the sacks of corn were laid across the grids they would soon be dried to the correct level of moisture.

Stanley was put in charge of the dryer. It was to be his job to keep it going day and night. Two other men would be working on the dryer and they would operate a shift system. It was to be a harvest time like none they had ever experienced before.

The first load of sacks came in from the fields. There were approximately twelve stone in each sack. The first snag in the design of the dryer soon became evident when it was discovered that not enough room had been left between the grids to use a sack barrow, so each and every twelve stone sack had to be manually carried and placed over a grid.

After several hours each sack had to be turned over. That involved lifting each sack in turn and flipping it over. As the sacks were lifted, hot air, dust, and spores from the grain were blasted into the atmosphere, giving the person who did the turning of the sacks numerous chances to breathe it deep into his lungs.

Stanley had worked through many harvests in his working career and had always looked forward to it in spite of the hard work. Bringing in the harvest was the culmination of the season's work growing the crops.

This work however seemed nothing like farming. He worked twelve hour shifts without a break for several weeks in unbearably hot conditions and it took its toll on his health.

No one was more relieved to see the end of that harvest than Stanley and his workmates, and as if to celebrate it, a letter arrived stamped with the County Council address.

Eagerly Stanley and Doris read about the smallholding that would be available to rent at the end of the year. They were invited to send an application in. It was far from what they had been hoping for but they had reached the stage when they were prepared to accept anything they could get.

It was on Doncaster Road at a place called Woodlands, barely three miles away from the cottage where they had lived in Adwick le Street. To a stranger, the name Woodlands could have conjured up a picture of woods and trees, but if there had ever been any they were long gone. Stanley was very familiar with the area and knew that there were in fact eight of the small holdings. All of them were semi-detached houses spaced out along the length of Doncaster Road; and each one had ten acres of land and a couple of brick built outbuildings that were described as stables.

He and Doris decided to apply. They had now been to so many interviews that they were well acquainted with the routine and as usual Eileen was given the day off school to babysit her sister. They were back home by mid-afternoon feeling more confident than they had ever been before. The man who Stanley had met at the union meeting had been present and although he gave nothing away it was clear it was Stanley that he favoured.

So now they were back to waiting and in the meantime they had news that Edith would like to come and stay with them for a week. The fly in the ointment was that her brother William would be coming with her if they could accommodate them both.

Doris looked at Stanley knowing only too well what he thought of her uncle. He shrugged his shoulders and sighed as he said, "It's fine by me, Dot, I'll be out at work all day, it's you that'll have to put up with him." As he went across the courtyard to work he had to smile, thinking that it would be a wonder if Doris didn't lose her temper with William before the week was out.

They arrived the following Monday and already Edith looked harassed and stressed, but at least they hadn't got lost on the way as Stanley had expected them to. Doris took them upstairs and showed her uncle his room, pointing out the old fashioned wallpaper with the exotic birds posed on trees. He looked at them and gave no comment but sat on the bed and said it was a bit lumpy. He did admire the views from the window but then said there was a draught blowing through it.

Edith had used that room when she had stayed previously and had loved it, old fashioned wallpaper and all, but this time she would have to sleep in the same room as the girls. Doris looked at her mother and they pulled a face at Willie, (as he was usually known) behind his back, then linked arms as they walked down behind him. As they reached the bottom of the stairs Stanley arrived home for his mid-day meal and Doris could see right away that he was in a mischievous mood.

While they ate their meal Stanley managed to put the idea across to Willie that the room he was to sleep in might be haunted. "Ah don't believe in that rubbish," he replied.

"No ah don't either," replied Stanley, "But ah have to admit it's always much colder in there than any other room." He turned to Doris, "Didn't me Dad say he was sure that during the night he had been woken up by someone stroking his face. But then of course he had drunk best part of ten pints. Ah shouldn't worry about it, Willie." He got up from the table saying he had to get back to work and winked at Edith as he left.

Doris went to the door with him, "Bloody hell, Stan, you've frightened him to death now, you shouldn't have told him that." But she was laughing as she said it.

"Well it serves him bloody right, he leads your Mam a right dance; she looks harassed to death with the cantankerous old bugger." He kissed her and ran down the steps calling that he should be finished early that afternoon.

When she went back indoors her mother was already busy washing up the dinner pots, and as always had a half smoked cigarette balanced on a saucer, she took a drag at it from time to time and with each puff it became wetter until it drooped and threatened to go out. Edith picked it up, took one last pull at it then nipped it out and dropped it in the bucket beneath the sink.

Doris shook her head in exasperation; she had long since stopped trying to prevent her mother from indulging in that little habit. It was the only time she smoked but it still irritated Doris.

With the pots dried and put away she was about to suggest that they all went for a little walk, but Willie was nowhere to be seen. Then she caught sight of him standing in the middle of the courtyard. Just standing perfectly still staring at the ruins. She tapped at the window to attract his attention then went to the door and called him. There was still no response, whatever he was looking at was totally fascinating him.

She walked right up to him and took hold of his elbow, "What's the matter? What have you seen? Do you want to go for a walk?"

Without taking his eyes away from the ruins he said almost in a whisper, "Look up there, Doris, right at the top. There's something moving about. There's something black up there. Ah don't like the look of that, Doris, have you ever seen it before?"

Doris followed his gaze, "It's only the jackdaws Uncle Willie. There's a whole flock of em up there. Can't you hear em?" She gave a little laugh but it was a nervous one, she had to admit that the birds often unsettled her as they nested and hung about among the crumbling walls. She pulled his arm, urging him to come inside and get ready to go for their walk.

He followed her but kept glancing back and declared that the birds were bad luck. "You want to get out of here, Doris," he said, "It's bad luck is this place."

However, the walk around the lake did a lot to change his opinion. The bridge had now been repaired and they were able to walk over to the far side of the lake. Willie leaned on the wrought ironwork of the bridge looking down into the water. Below the bridge it was so clear that he could see a large pike, motionless, basking in the warmth, waiting for a smaller fish to swim by.

Edith and Doris waited for him in the shade of the silver birches and Edith commented that she wished he was always as contented as he was at this precise moment. She sighed and said to her daughter that she didn't think she could carry on living with him much longer. "He's getting worse, Doris," she said, "He's more moody than ever since your grandma died."

Doris replied straight away, "Well pack your bags, Mam, and go and rent somewhere on your own. You've got your own furniture. You could afford it couldn't you?"

Edith looked away to hide the tears that had sprung to her eyes, and she bit her lips before replying, "Yes," she said, "I could just about afford it while I am working but when I retire it would be a struggle. I'll think about it, don't worry, I'll be ok."

Throughout her life Doris had often wondered what her uncle had been like before he had gone away to fight in the First World

War, and before the time when his baby son, his brother Harry and his nephew had all died from meningitis; but most of all, before the tragic events that had resulted in him serving a six month sentence in Armley jail.

When she had asked her mother what he had been like before those events she had painted a picture of a happy young boy who had grown up to be handsome, hard working and caring. The kind of son any mother would be proud of.

Well, thought Doris, he had certainly changed. For the last thirty five years his mother and sister had pandered to his every whim in an effort to placate him and in return they had borne the brunt of his bad moods and temper. Now that her mother was gone, Edith was on her own with him, and if anything, he had become more cantankerous than ever.

Now, while Stanley understood the terrible times that Doris's uncle had been through; in his opinion it was many years ago and there was no excuse for him taking his bad humour out on his sister.

Usually when Edith came to stay the house was filled with fun as she played games with the girls and chatted with her daughter. She would talk to Stanley for hours, listening to his plans for the future, but this time her face wore an anxious look and she was as tense as it was possible to be. Willie had reduced her to tears during two separate meal times and she had left the table and gone to the bathroom to wash her face.

The next day was a Saturday, and by seven thirty everyone was up and about, everyone that is, except William. Edith said how unusual it was for him to stay in bed as he was usually an early riser and she went upstairs and knocked tentatively at his door. "Are you ok, Willie?" she called.

"Course ah bloody am," came the grumpy reply, "Can't a man have a bloody lay in without daft women waking him up?"

Edith pulled her tongue out at him through the closed door and went downstairs to relay his comments to Doris. Eventually Willie arrived in the kitchen and sat down at the table. "It's bloody haunted is that bedroom," he declared. "There's been someone watching me through the loft hatch all night. I've hardly had a wink of sleep."

Stanley had walked in just as he said the words and a grin broke out on his face. "Is that why you're late up then? Were you frightened to get out of bed?"

"It's no laughing matter, Stanley. Ah'm telling you, that there bloody loft is haunted. You want to get the ladder and take a look. Ah bet there's skeletons up there."

It was a Friday and they had only a few days of their holiday left. Doris said she would like to take her mother to Pontefract to do some shopping. Now, if there was one thing that Edith enjoyed it was a good day going around the shops, and she clapped her hands as she said she would love to go, "I'll buy you your dinner Doris. Oh ah' m so looking forward to that. Its such a long time since we went shopping together."

Edith ran upstairs like a woman half her age to get ready. Doris smiled at her uncle, "We'll leave some dinner ready for you and Stan, Maybe you'd like to go and have a walk, it's a lovely day."

Willie scowled at her, "You women, you're all the same. You're always spending money. Your mother buys all sorts of rubbish."

Doris had had enough, "Well, if she does spend money it's hers to spend. She earns it, not you. God only knows how she puts up with you." She turned away feeling so furious with him and went to find Frances who would be going with them.

Stanley was able to give them a lift up to the bus stop in the old farm car. It was a Ford that was just about managing not to fall apart and was used for carrying pig food out to the fields where the pigs were kept. They had taken all the doors off the car for easier access and Stanley had to wipe the grubby seats before they could sit on them. Edith took it all as a big adventure and held tightly on to the frayed rope that hung from the ceiling.

He could only go as far as the edge of the estate in the old untaxed car but they were very close to the bus stop and he walked the last few yards with them. Giving them both a quick kiss on the cheek he warned them that he might not be able to collect them when they were on their way home.

"Oh we'll be fine, Stanley," replied his mother in law, "A bit of a walk won't hurt us will it, Doris?" At that moment she saw a bus at the other side of the road and grabbed her daughter's arm, "Come on quick, Doris, there's the bus."

Doris looked at Stanley and raised her eyebrows, her expression said, 'Here we go again.'

"No Mam, that's going in the other direction, you'd end up in Castleford if you got on that one. Come on, we have to stand here, our bus will be here soon. Really, Mam, our Frances has a better idea on travelling than you have."

Edith looked as if she was not convinced, "Are you sure, Doris, it looks as if it's going to Pontefract." She started smiling as her daughter looked exasperated, and then she began to laugh.

Doris stopped and shook her head, "You crafty devil. You said that on purpose just to get me going didn't you? You get worse , Mam." She slipped her hand into her mother's and whispered, "Love you."

While Doris and her mother were away shopping, Stanley found that he had the afternoon off. It came as a complete surprise to him.

Friday afternoon was also pay day and Stanley looked forward to receiving his, with the extra money included for all the harvesting overtime. When Mr McLain handed it to him he thanked him for all his hard work and said as a bonus he could have the rest of the afternoon off.

Stanley needed no extra telling, he said thank you very much, picked up his haversack and headed for home. He always had work of his own to do and today was an unexpected opportunity to finish the chicken run that he had been building.

He found Willie sitting in the living room reading an old copy of the Farmer and Stockbreeder. He dropped it on the floor as Stanley walked in. They had little in common but Stanley decided to make an effort for his mother-in-law's sake.

"Now then," he said, as their eyes met. "Ah see Doris has left us some dinner ready. Ah'll just boil the kettle and make a pot of tea."

They sat down at the table to eat and Stanley racked his brains to think of something to say, anything to drown out the sound of the sandwiches being eaten. When they started on the celery the sound seemed magnified, and in the end, in an effort to turn it into a joke Stanley compared the sound to bullocks chomping turnips.

Willie lifted his head and looked at him dolefully and made no reply. Suddenly Stanley had an inspiration and began to tell him about the manuscripts they had found in the walls of the old hall.

"You want to keep off them ruins. Them there walls could collapse at any time," replied Willie.

This was something that Stanley agreed on, and he nodded his head. "Still," he said, "It was a good job we found them."

Willie ignored what Stanley had said, and got up from the table leaving his food half eaten. "What time can we expect them back?" he said, referring to Doris and Edith. "Ah think me and Edi should get off home this afternoon. Ah don't want another night spent in that bedroom"

"But ah thought you were staying until Sunday morning? It'll be too late to set off home when they get back from Pontefract. Edith will be too tired to start packing and travelling back today," Stanley reasoned.

"She'll be alright. She shouldn't have gone shopping. She's just like all women, always spending money."

Stanley was losing patience, but he bit his tongue and decided to try and humour him. He gave up on the idea of working on his chicken run and suggested that they go and have a ride through the estate. He added that later he would take him to have a look at the kitchens in the part of the old hall that was still standing.

There was a glimmer of interest in Willie's face as he agreed, and they walked across the courtyard where the car was kept in one of the outbuildings that had once accommodated the carriages.

Usually the car started with just a little coaxing but today it coughed and spluttered before the engine finally decided to burst into life. Willie stood at the doorway, hands in his pockets looking morose; he gave a loud 'Hmmm' as Stanley got the engine running smoothly and backed the car out.

It soon became obvious that the car ride was not going to be a success. Willie made little comment as Stanley pointed out places that he thought might be of interest but the only thing Doris's uncle wanted to talk about was what time the women would get back from shopping. In the end Stanley gave up, drove back, and stopped trying to make conversation with him. So it came as a surprise when Willie reminded Stanley that they were going to look at the old kitchens.

"Ok then. This way," said Stanley, once the car was back in its garage. The kitchens were situated only thirty or forty yards away and Stanley pushed open the heavy door and held it ajar. Willie walked past him and stood still, looking around at the cobweb-covered sinks and the rusty ovens. "That must be the pantry then," he said, pointing to a door in the corner.

"No, it leads to the cellars." Stanley pulled the door open. "Do you want to have a look?" he said, "Ah've got a torch in the car, I can go and get it." Taking a nod as a sign of agreement, Stanley ran back and collected the torch.

He shone it down the steps into the cellar. The beam flickered. As usual the batteries were in need of replacing, but they were always at the end of the shopping list, and were never replaced until they had given up altogether.

Stanley set off down the steps holding tightly on to the rail. He could hear Willie behind him and was so close that he could almost feel his breath on his neck. He was astonished that he was actually following him.

"We're at the bottom of the steps now, be careful, the floor's damp, it might be slippery."

Then Willie spoke, and for the first time in the whole week he actually sounded quite impressed. "Bloody hell, Stan, its cold down here, and dark as a bloody tomb. How far does it go?"

"It's like a warren down here," replied Stanley in a low voice. There was something about the place that made him feel he should whisper. "There's more cellars below us, you know, one layer on top of the other. But some of them have collapsed. Come on. Ah think we had better go back."

He turned around, and then some mischievous devilment

gripped him and he decided to play a trick on Willie. He knew very well that he shouldn't, but he just could not resist it.

As they passed a corridor that led to another part of the cellar he stepped aside into it and switched off the torch. There was complete silence for a moment, and then Willie's voice called "Stan, Stan. Where is tha?"His voice started off low and gradually got louder as he continued to call "Stan. Where is tha?" He brushed past Stanley's hiding place several times, going back and forth in his efforts to find him.

But Stanley was enjoying the joke, standing out of sight with his back to the wall, and his handkerchief stuffed in his mouth to stop himself from laughing out loud. Finally, he decided enough was enough and he slipped back out into the main passage, switching the torch back on as he did so.

"Come on, Willie. What are you hanging about down here for? Ah've been looking for you," declared Stanley as he led the way towards the steps and the doorway out of the cellars.

Back home he did have a little twinge of guilt and he put the kettle on for Willie to make himself a pot of tea, before he set off to see if Doris and her Mam were on the next bus .

  Willie took his coat off and sank gratefully onto the sofa. "I'll get me case packed in a minute," he said, "Me and Edi will be off home as soon as she gets back."

Stanley sighed in exasperation. "Ah've told you, Willie. It's too late to travel home today." He turned and went out of the room before he lost his patience completely.

"And I've told you," came Willie's voice, raised loud enough for Stanley to hear as he walked towards the front door, "Ah'm not sleeping another night in that bedroom."

Out of sight, Stanley put two fingers up at him and forgot any feelings of guilt he might have had about playing a joke on him.

He got to the top of the estate just as the bus was stopping. He waved when he saw Doris and Edith getting off. Doris was carrying Frances who had gone to sleep with her head on her mother's shoulder. Stanley ran across the road and picked up the bags.

"Hey up, Edith, been buying Pontefract up have you?" Edith

smiled happily at him, "Yea we have, and I'm spent up, it's a good job we are going home on Sunday."

"Well ah don't know about Sunday, Willie's got it in mind that you're going to go home today."

Edith looked at him. "Are you kidding, Stan?" As he shook his head, she went on, "But it's too late to go home today. Well, if he wants to go home he can go on his own. I'm staying," Her voice was determined, but the anxious look had returned to her face.

Edith stood firm when Willie informed her that they would be going home that evening, refusing point blank to even consider it. She insistred that Sunday was the day they had planned to go home, but in the end, worn down by his nagging, she agreed that they could set off first thing in the morning and catch the early bus, provided that he made no more fuss about sleeping in the bedroom that he insisted was haunted

As they washed the pots up in the kitchen after their evening meal, Edith whispered to her daughter that it would be the last time she would bring him with her, to which Doris replied, "Thank the Lord for that."

Stanley was up early the next morning and he crept quietly down the stairs to avoid waking the rest of the household. The swinging door at the bottom of the stairs creaked and he eased it closed very gently. Lassie had been sleeping in the hall and she sidled up to him with her tail going mad with joy and she gave him a doggy smile while she tried to get a grip on the highly polished linoleum and stand on her hind legs.

"Get down, Lassie" said Stanley softly. He walked along the passage and let her out into the garden. Her mother, Meg, looked up from her comfortable position on the pegged rug beside the door, her tail wagged but she stayed where she was and Stanley thought how old she was looking now. He bent down to stroke her head and said, "Come on Meg, out you go and get some fresh air."

With both dogs outside he went into the living room and was surprised to see that Willie was already up. He was washed and dressed with his case at the side of the sofa. His long, brown mackintosh was carefully folded and draped over the back of a chair. He had lit the fire and now sat beside it, holding a slice of bread on a toasting fork towards the glowing embers.

"What time can you take us up to the bus stop, Stan?" Willie was obviously not wasting words this morning.

Stanley sat down at the table and pulled the loaf and the bread knife towards him. As he cut a thick slice ready to toast it, he said that he had to go into work to see to the animals then he would probably be free at about eleven o'clock.

Willie put the bread he had toasted on to a plate and handed it to him, "Here you have this. I'll make some more. The sooner you get to work the sooner you'll be finished. Ah want to catch an early bus."

Stanley thought to himself that he wanted him on an early bus too, the earlier the better. He was pleased to see Eileen appear ready to help him with the feeding and cleaning out of the animals. Working together, they were finished in record time and Stanley started the car and drove it round to the front of the house.

It had been arranged that Eileen would go with Willie and Edith to Pontefract and see them safely on to the Barnsley bus. Their cases were packed and standing at the foot of the steps. The car had barely come to a halt before Willie had installed himself in the passenger seat with his case on his knee.

Edith said goodbye to Doris and Frances, then turned to Stanley. He took her arm and pulled her to the rear of the car. Leaning towards her he said. "Don't let him bully you, Edi. Stand up to him." He put his arm round her and gave her a hug. "Come back and stay with us again soon. Only next time see if you can leave that miserable bugger at home. A dose of his own company will do him the world of good."

Edith was close to tears, but she blinked them back and with a wobbly smile, said she would get her elder sister Anne to sort him out. Doris, who had come to stand beside them, agreed that would be a good idea. "You want to take a leaf out of her book, Mam. Aunty Anne puts him straight."

Anne was their eldest sister. She lived two miles away from them in Wath and didn't mince her words when talking to her brother.

Edith nodded, "Aye she's about as sharp as you Doris. I wish I was more like her."

"Are you coming then?" Willie's voice interrupted them, "We're going to miss the bus if you don't get a move on." Edith pulled a face and struggled into the tiny back seat with Eileen. Stanley pushed Edith's case in after them and somehow they found a space for it.

The little car struggled up to the top of the estate, with its engine protesting at the extra load. They had just climbed out of the car when Eileen spotted the bus coming and Stanley put his hand up for it to stop. There was no time for more goodbyes and before they knew it they were seated on the lower deck of the bus and Stanley was watching it disappear down the road towards Ferrybridge.

He sighed with contentment at the thought that he didn't have to put up with Doris's uncle any longer, turned the car round and trundled slowly back home.

The post office van followed him into the courtyard. Stanley got out and took the letters from him. The postman looked at Stanley's car and put his head on one side listening to the engine. "By, your car sounds a bit rough Stan. Is it firing on all cylinders?"

Stanley nodded but didn't enlighten him about it running on paraffin. "Aye, she's getting old now, but ah hope she'll last a bit longer. Probably needs some new plugs. Ah'll give em a good clean."

He glanced down at the letters in his hand and shuffled them. He forgot to reply to the postman's next words as he recognised the long brown envelope with the County Council stamp on the top. He turned away, gave a quick wave and opened the front door, still staring at the letter. This was what they had been waiting for.

He called Doris, and she came from the kitchen drying her hands on her apron. "What's the matter? Did they catch the bus?" Stanley held the letter up in front of her, then slowly took his pen knife from his pocket and slit the envelope neatly across the top. He drew the sheets of paper from inside it and unfolded them. The words were a blur for a moment and then he saw the only ones that really mattered.

'We are pleased to inform you that your application for the smallholding has been successful. We are happy to offer you the tenancy of Number 10, Doncaster Road, Woodlands.'

CHAPTER 31

They were ecstatic at the thought of finally having a small holding and they were brimming over with hope and confidence for the future. It was true that the small holding was far from being Stanley's first choice. He would have liked more land, and more buildings. He had hoped that they would finally be able to move right away from the mining areas but he was philosophical and said to Doris that this would just be a start.

Immediately they began making plans. They were to take over the smallholding in a month's time and Stanley said his first priority was to let his Mr McLain know that he would be leaving.

Stanley approached his employer first thing on Monday morning and broke the news. Mr McLain's face fell. "Oh I'm very sorry to hear that, Stanley. What's the problem? I thought you were happy here."

When Stanley explained about the smallholding his hand was grasped and shaken firmly. "Congratulations. I know you have been hoping for a place of your own for a long time. I'm disappointed to be losing you but I wish you the best of luck." He turned to go, then came back, and added, "Remember, there is always a job here for you if ever you should need one."

Full of excitement, Stanley and Doris set off to view the smallholding the following weekend. It involved driving to the top of the estate and leaving the car just across from the quarry while they caught the bus to Pontefract, then one to Doncaster.

Five miles before they reached Doncaster they got off the bus at Woodlands where Doris used to do most of her shopping when they had lived a few miles away in Adwick le Street. They were on familiar territory now and walked down the road through the housing estate that had been the built to accommodate miners who mostly worked at Brodsworth Colliery.

They were so accustomed to this type of housing that they could have been in any of the mining villages. Stanley was silent. Had they made a mistake? Were they returning to the kind of place they had previously strived so hard to get out of?

He thought of the beautiful surroundings where they lived in Clamton Park but then had to admit that even there, the coal mines were only a few miles away. Wherever you were in this part of Yorkshire there was bound to be a coal mine close by.

It was just that Clamton Park was an oasis of beauty and tranquillity among the industrialised areas. They had been privileged to live there for a while. He gave himself a mental shake. At least there were no pits actually in sight. Then they reached Doncaster road and could see the smallholdings spread out at the opposite side of the road.

They were unremarkable looking houses built in pairs and spaced out evenly along the road. Each one had in the region of ten acres of land that stretched out behind it as far as the railway lines at the bottom end.

Number ten was the last one and as they stood in front of it, they looked at each other. "Well, what do you think then Doris?" asked Stanley. Even as he waited for her answer he thought how lovely she looked. Her dark hair had grown much longer and she now wore it brushed away from her face at the sides and curled under at the back. The deep wave at the front fell slightly over her forehead accentuating her deep brown eyes.

"I think it will do fine Stanley," she said, "I can't wait to get here. If we rear some chickens I can sell the eggs at the door and we could grow vegetables to sell. There'll be plenty of customers with all these houses here. Frances will be starting school soon, and look, the primary school is just along the road. The library's just at the top of the avenue. The bus for Doncaster passes right by the door. What more could we want?"

"It means leaving all the lovely scenery behind, Doris, are you sure you'll be happy here."

Doris, ever practical, quickly replied, "You can't live on scenery Stan. This is a step up. Let's grab the chance with both hands."

Stanley smiled at her. He took her hand, "That's what I hoped you'd say. Come on, let's be cheeky. We'll go knock at the door and introduce ourselves as the new tenants who will be taking over from them."

The next month flew by with preparations being made to move to the small holding. With just two days to go Stanley borrowed the old lorry that was used on the farm. It was an ex-army vehicle that always started first time but was determined never to go faster than twenty five miles per hour.

The windows in the doors had long since stuck in the down position so there was no lack of fresh air in the cab, but Stanley cared not in the slightest as long as it carried all their worldly goods to their next home. It would need several trips to move everything.

He started with the outdoor sheds, dog kennels, and other outdoor equipment that they had acquired over the years. With his elder daughter as mate they loaded the lorry and set off.

It began raining when they reached Ferrybridge and the wind blew straight through the open windows carrying the rain with it. Before they had gone far they were both wet through. Eileen huddled at the back of her seat, pulled her collar up and put her hands in her pockets trying desperately to keep warm. Stanley looked at her shivering and pulled a sack from the back of his seat. He passed it across to her and she draped it over her knees wrinkling her nose at the smell of it.

"That'll keep your knees dry, love." He said encouragingly, as he held the steering wheel with one hand and put the other one under his arm, then swapped them over in an effort to stop them going numb with cold. "Just our luck isn't it? It would rain when the windows won't close."

Eileen nodded and didn't try to speak over the sound of the engine. She was trying hard not to show how miserable she was. While Stanley and Doris were thrilled to be moving, their elder daughter was not.

Just a month previously she had left the school that she had hated at Brotherton and moved to an all-girls school in Pontefract. She was beginning to settle in and had made a group of friends. Now it was all change yet again.

It was less than thirty miles to their destination but it seemed much longer as they trundled along in the old army lorry. Stanley remarked that if they went much slower, bikes would be overtaking them and the words were no sooner out of his mouth than two cyclists flew past them downhill into Wentbridge.

Father and daughter exchanged looks and burst into laughter. "What did ah tell you?" exclaimed Stanley, and suddenly everything seemed different; the journey became a challenge that they would overcome and they made more outrageous jokes about the lorry.

It was mid-day when he drew the lorry to a halt outside the smallholding. The rain had stopped and a faint glimmer of sun struggled to break through the clouds. Eileen got out and opened the five barred gate for the first time and Stanley reversed the loaded lorry down the drive.

Stanley stamped his feet and rubbed his hands together in an effort to get some circulation going in them then put his arm around his daughter's shoulders and said they would go and look at the stables.

The previous tenants had already left the day before, and Stanley's plan was to stack all the tools and implements they had brought in the stables. He unlatched the top half of the door and peered over, "Bloody hell, look at this Eileen. The dirty buggers have not cleaned it out." He shook his head in disgust. "We're going to have to clear this lot out now. Come on, we're going to have to get the muck forks and the barrow off the lorry."

The stables had obviously been used to keep pigs in and had not been cleaned out for months. They had simply kept adding more straw on top of muck, layer after layer until it was almost knee deep.

The stable was one brick built building but was divided into two halves. One half was to be temporary accommodation for the chickens they would be bringing the next day. Both halves would need to be cleaned out; but first they would eat the sandwiches that Doris had packed up for them, and they climbed back into the lorry and opened the paper bag.

It seemed that Doris had been a bit short of filling for the bread, and had had to resort to jam. Stanley opened his and looked at it, he had been hoping for cheese, but he had never been fussy about his food and would willingly eat almost anything. So he slapped it back together and took a bite. He looked across at Eileen who was nibbling at hers.

"What's up?" he asked, "Don't you like jam?"

"Well its ok Dad, but I wish Mam would get a different sort for a change. She always gets blackcurrant."

Stanley laughed, "Aye, she does, that's because she likes blackcurrant best. Get it down you, it's fine," and he picked up the bottle of water and took a long drink before wiping the top and passing it over to his daughter. "Hurry up. I'll go and make a start on this lot. We'll make a muck heap over there," and he pointed to a spot on the edge of the field.

It took almost two hours to clean out the stable, and as they took the last barrow load Stanley remarked, "That's the one we've been looking for, Eileen, the last one."

Stanley was now becoming worried about getting back before dark. The lights on the lorry were one more thing that didn't work. He calculated that they had just over one and a half hours to unload and be home before lighting up time.

In spite of both being tired the sense of urgency gave them the energy to unload the lorry in record time, and they were soon back on the road with Stanley pushing the lorry as fast as it would go. Without its heavy load he managed to coax it up to thirty miles per hour and even faster going down-hill, even though it meant ignoring the weak brakes.

They chugged back up the hill from Ferrybridge just as the street lights were coming on and Stanley breathed a sigh of relief when they turned off Ponte Lane and on to the estate.

"Well, we made it, love," commented Stanley. Eileen smiled, anticipating some food and a warm fire but then her heart sank as her father added "We'll just have to get the chicken shed on to the back of the lorry ready for tomorrow before we have tea."

Knowing it was going to be a long day Stanley was up extra early next morning. He had managed to get the shed loaded on to the lorry the previous evening and rope it securely into place. He now sat planning out the day while he finished his morning mug of tea.

Eileen came downstairs with her sister clinging to her hand, she was wearing the same grubby jeans that she had had on the day before and an old jumper that was now much too small for her.

"Good, you've put your old clothes on. Hurry up and get your breakfast," urged Stanley, "We've got a few more things to load, then the chickens can go into the shed just before we set off."

Trying to make conversation Eileen commented that she hoped it wouldn't rain through the windows in the lorry today.

"Well it won't matter to you if it rains today, love, you won't get wet."

"Why not?" she asked, "Have you managed to mend the windows?" She picked up the bread and began to cut off a slice.

Stanley shook his head. "No, the windows still don't work, but you will be travelling in the shed with the chickens to keep them from crowding into corners. So you'll be nice and dry."

Now anyone who has ever kept young chickens will know that they have a death wish. They will try to murder each other or commit suicide by any means available. Their favourite method is to pile on top of each other in a corner and smother as many of their companions as possible.

Travelling in a moving lorry was bound to put them into panic mode and send them dashing for the corners. Stanley had installed some curved boards to round off all the corners but there was really only one sure way to prevent disaster, and that was to have someone travel in the back with them, watching them all the time.

Eileen was the person who had been appointed as their saviour.

"You'll be all right; I've put a seat in there for you. It'll be nice and warm. All you have to do is make sure they don't start trampling on each other."

Eileen gaped at him, she could hardly believe it. She would actually have to ride all the way in the shed on the back of the lorry. She sat down to eat her breakfast, dreading the day ahead.

The chickens had been kept overnight in one of the old wooden arks at the front of the house. Before their work began, Stanley stopped and looked along the long expanse of grass that had once been a beautiful lawn and the setting for elegant gentry to parade and socialise. Now it was reduced to a rough grass paddock. He stared at it, imprinting the scene on his memory.

But, there was no time to stand and stare, not with a long day ahead. They carried the chickens to the shed on the back of the lorry, six at a time, three in each hand, holding them by their legs, while the chickens made protesting squawks from their upside down positions.

Once in the shed they shook themselves, stretched their necks, and settled down among the warm dry straw. As the last six went in to join their companions Stanley held the door of the shed open for his daughter.

"Right," he said as she climbed up on to the back of the lorry, "Look, there's a seat there at the front end of the shed. Whatever you do don't let them crowd on top of each other. They might panic a bit once we start moving."

Eileen gave a weak nod of her head and stepped around the chickens that were all lying down with their feathers fluffed out. They looked very calm and comfortable. She sat down on the upturned oil drum with the sack on top of it that served as a seat. She managed a smile as Stanley asked if she was all set. When the door was closed, the only light came from a small window which was mostly obscured by several corrugated metal sheets that made up part of the lorry load.

As her eyes became accustomed to the gloomy light she could see the chickens more clearly and they seemed to be asleep; and then the lorry engine started up. As it throbbed into life, a vibration went through the shed.

Instantly half of the chickens stood up and looked around in alarm. They set up a disturbed chirping sound and Eileen spoke quietly to them trying to make them calm again. She wondered what some of her ex-classmates at Brotherton would say if they got to hear of this little trip. She could imagine their ridicule and the names they would call her. 'Chicken woman' sprang to her mind and she could almost hear their cruel jibes.

However, she soon found that when the lorry began to move she had no time to worry about the comments from anyone as she struggled to prevent the chickens from panicking. If she let these stupid birds die she would never hear the last of it.

Dust rose from their feathers and the smell in the confined space was foul. But in spite of that the time went quicker than she had expected and she could hardly believe it when they came to a halt and the noise of the engine stopped.

She could hear her father let down the back door of the lorry and then the shed door opened and he was looking at her anxiously and asking if she was ok before he ran his eyes over the chickens to check that they had all survived.

He held out his hand to help her down and told her she had done well. Nothing else mattered then. She glowed with pride. Praise from Stanley was praise indeed and all the more valued for its genuineness.

They moved into the smallholding the next day. Once again all their household goods were packed into a furniture van and once again Eileen was travelling in the back of the van but this time Stanley was with her. The blue Austin had finally come to the end of its days and he had left it there at Clamton for one of the young farm hands to tinker with. Stanley had felt a pang of sadness at parting from his little car but consoled himself that he would get a replacement as soon as the smallholding was running profitably.

The house that went with the smallholding had an odd layout, having been altered over the years as cheaply as possible by the West Riding Council.

It had been given a bathroom which had a bath and a sink, but it had not been considered necessary to put the toilet in there. That was still outside, across the small back yard.

There was no proper kitchen as such, just a large white sink and a few shelves beside the back window of the living room. Cooking was done on the old fashioned fire stove in the same room.

But Doris made no complaint about it and soon adapted to the strange set up. Like Stanley she was more concerned with the grounds of the smallholding and what kind of stock they could rear.

To begin with, having ten acres of land and a stable block to work with seemed marvellous, but it was not long before it became obvious that it was inadequate if they wanted to make a living from it. The lack of any machinery to work the ten acre field was also a stumbling block.

They could have employed a contractor to work the land, but Stanley had another idea, and it was one which would not cost him anything. It was time to renew his acquaintance with Smiths, his previous employers at Adwick le Street.

He went to see Bert Dunning, his old friend who was also the foreman at Smiths. Bert was pleased to see Stanley again and shook his hand warmly before he brought him up to date with recent happenings on the farm. Gradually Stanley broached the subject of him taking on some acreage of turnips to chop on piece work, as he had done in the past.

Bert paused before he answered, and Stanley knew that he was working out a price to bargain with. Friend he might be, but Bert had to come up with a figure that would satisfy both his employer and Stanley.

"Well, aye, ah could offer you some piece work Stanley, we are a bit short staffed at the moment. We just need to agree on a price. How would six pounds an acre sound?"

Stanley in his turn also paused before replying. As if he was a little reluctant he made a 'tch' sound and sucked in his breath as he said slowly. "Ah, I had been hoping for a bit more to tell the truth, Bert. The rate should have gone up a bit more than that"

He looked down at the ground then met Bert's eyes. "Ah've just had an idea. If I do it for that price can we have an arrangement that I can borrow the plough and the harrows to get my land worked?"

Bert smiled and clapped Stanley on the shoulder, "Crafty as

ever, Stan. Aye, you can borrow what you need. Ah know you'll look after it. Don't forget though, to apply the same rules as before concerning Sunday working. You know that Mrs Smith will not allow any work to be done on the Sabbath."

Stanley cycled home a happy man. He had got some piece work to bring in some extra cash and solved the problem of working his land.

Within weeks a chicken run had been built and they had two expectant sows in the stable block. An area of the land to the right of the smallholding had been allocated to market gardening with the idea that eventually they would have vegetables to sell at the back door along with the eggs that the hens would be laying.

Eileen had gone back to Woodlands School and found it a big disappointment. Nothing was as she remembered it and there was a huge gap in her education from the time she had attended the school at Brotherton.

There was nothing else for it but to do her best and hope the time passed quickly to the end of the next summer term when she could leave school and get a job. In years to come she was often to reflect that the only useful thing she had learnt when she had attended the village school at Brotherton was how to stand up for herself.

Stanley spent most days chopping turnips as fast as he could, sometimes taking Eileen with him to help if it was not a school day. With two working they got the acres done much faster. In addition to his days spent chopping turnips Stanley also went out to farms that were having a threshing day and worked for them on day work but still they struggled financially.

This was an interim time which they had to get through. It would take time to get their flock of hens laying, their pigs ready for market and crops ready to sell. So for the time being they had to tighten their belts and manage on as little cash as they could.

And then, just a week before Christmas, Doris found an egg when she went to feed the chickens. Full of excitement she saved it to show Stanley. "Look Stan," she called, "They've started laying." That one egg boosted their morale no end. To them it meant that their enterprise would soon begin to pay off.

The following morning Stanley was up first as usual. The moment he opened the door and walked down the steps he had a feeling that there was something wrong.

He began to walk down the yard towards the chicken run and as he drew closer in the half light of early morning, he could see that the wire netting was lying on the floor trampled into the mud. The shed door was open and he could see the clasp that held the padlock had been prised off.

By now he feared that all his poultry would have gone, and he peered inside the shed. It was still dark too dark inside to make out how many were missing, but the perching rails were tipped over and what birds he could see were crouched on the floor.

In that moment Stanley would have given anything to have come face to face with the thieves. He closed the shed door and hurried back to the house. Doris raged when he told her, "They'll have been after fat chickens for the Christmas market. What bloody use will point of lay pullets be to them? They have no meat on them. Bloody hell, Stan, just when they are about to start laying. We were depending on them. I wish I could get my hands on them."

"Aye. Me too. Ah'd like to bet they've come over the railway lines from Adwick Lane. The thieving swines. Ah'll call at the police station on my way to work and report it. There's nothing else we can do."

Before he could set off to work though, the netting had to be repaired, and it was almost dinner time when he walked into the police station. The constable on duty looked disgruntled to see him. He had been about to each his lunch and hastily stuffed a greaseproof paper bag out of sight as Stanley approached the desk.

He drew himself up to his full height and said "Yes, what can I do for you?"

As Stanley gave his name and explained, the constable began to look more interested and picked up his pencil. "Yours is not the only report of chicken theft last night, Mr Dale. I think my sergeant will want to come and see you about this. It will probably be this evening."

All the rest of that day, as he chopped turnips with his back aching and his hands freezing, Stanley seethed with anger towards the thieves. He wielded the sharp knife he was using and imagined chasing them across the fields with it held in his hand putting the fear of God into them. The rage inside him must have lent him extra strength and he was almost shocked when he realised he had completed the field he was working on in record time.

That evening just as they had settled down to relax after the day's work there was a loud knock on the front door. Stanley got up from his armchair and went to answer it. As he passed Doris on his way he said, "That'll be the coppers." He winked at Eileen, "I can tell from the way they knock."

He was right. As he opened the door he could see two policemen standing at the front door. "Mr. Dale?" asked the one of them. Stanley nodded and replied that he was, and invited them in. Although Stanley was over six foot they seemed to tower above him and filled the small living room.

He recognised the younger of the two as the constable he had spoken to that morning. The other one was obviously his sergeant and was definitely in charge.

"We've come about the theft of your chickens, Mr Dale. Do you think we could have a statement from you?" As he spoke he took off his helmet and placed it on the table and indicated for the constable to do the same.

"We've had a few reports of chickens being stolen the last couple of days. We are keen to catch the thieves so anything you can tell us will be a help. In confidence I can tell that we do have our suspicions, but as yet, no proof."

Stanley and Doris exchanged glances; they too had their suspicions but were not keen to put them into words at this point. "Would you like to sit down," said Stanley and he pointed to the arm chair. Doris pulled out a dining chair for the constable and asked if they would like a cup of tea.

"That'll be very welcome, Mrs Dale," he replied as he fished about in his pocket for a pen and proceeded to sit on the arm of the chair that Stanley had indicated.

As he lowered himself down Stanley knew what was going to happen. Doris knew what was going to happen and so did Eileen, but there was no time to prevent it.

Why he had to choose to sit on the arm of the chair rather than in it no one knows, but as his considerable weight rested on it, the chair tipped to one side, sending him sprawling onto the floor. He landed on his back with his legs in the air and as he went down he tried to save himself by clutching at the new, green brocade curtains that Doris had hung up that very afternoon. The spring rod that supported them gave way, pulling a chunk of plaster out of the wall with it. Curtains, spring rod and plaster settled on top of him, and for a second or two everyone stared in horror before the comedy of the scene hit them.

Stanley turned his head to one side, biting his lips to stop the laughter bursting out of him and his shoulders shook while Doris bent over the sink and held the tea towel to her face. The constable struggled to keep a straight face and with a massive effort managed to say in a high pitched voice. "Are you ok Sergeant? Have you hurt yourself?"

To make matters worse Doris had polished the floor to a high gloss with her favourite wax polish and the sergeant's boots skidded on it as he struggled to get up from his position where he was wedged between the wall and the armchair.

Eventually he managed to sit up and as he looked around he saw the absurdity of his situation and began to laugh himself. Great booms of laughter came from him and his face became redder and redder until at last he pushed the chair to one side and clambered up.

"Well," he said as he pulled his uniform straight and tried to regain his dignity, "I'm sorry about the curtains, Mrs Dale. I'll repair them of course. I'll come tomorrow when I'm off duty. You know, you need to have a look at that chair. It's really not safe."

Stanley shook his head and said it didn't matter, he would sort the curtains out. Privately he was thinking that the sergeant shouldn't have sat on the arm of the chair but decided he had better not say as much.

The statement was taken hastily and Stanley saw them out through the front door. Just before he closed it after them, he distinctly heard the sergeant say to his constable. "I don't want any of this getting around the station. Do you understand me? Not a word about it to anyone."

311

Just as Stanley had expected, the theft of the chickens was never solved, although he personally suspected a certain family who lived in the rougher part of Adwick le Street and were regular visitors to the local magistrate's court. However, suspecting and proving were two different matters and he could only console himself with the thought that at least they hadn't managed to get them all. Now instead of a flock of fifty laying hens they would only have thirty two.

All their surplus savings had been used up paying for the valuation on the smallholding and buying the sows, so if he wanted to have a flock of fifty laying hens he would have to find some extra cash.

With all the available piece work finished at Smiths farm in Adwick he took on five acres of turnip chopping at their Hooton Pagnall farm although it meant a very long cycle ride to get there.

Stanley and Doris decided that Christmas this year would have to be a very lean affair. What presents they had were cheap and basic and only Christmas Day would be a day off work. First thing on Boxing Day it was business as usual. At eight am Stanley and Eileen set off for Hooton Pagnall on their bikes, with their sharpened chopping knives in their cycle bags.

It was bitterly cold with a smattering of sleet in the north wind. They rode hard, peddling as fast as they could up the hill to Brodsworth in an effort to get their sluggish circulation going. Hands and feet were the worst. The old socks they wore on their hands as gloves were no protection at all, and long before they reached their destination Eileen was suffering and wondering how she was going to get through the day.

Stanley's hands were equally cold but his skin was harder and he seemed to stand it better. He encouraged his daughter as best he could. They began work the moment they arrived, leaving their bikes propped against the stone wall that surrounded the field.

They took two rows each, first pulling the turnips out of the frozen ground with their left hand, then chopping off the root with a large knife held in their right hand. Then they slashed the stalk and leaves away before they threw it to the ground. With practice and a sharp knife the top could be cut off while the vegetable was still in the air on its way down to join its neighbours in a neat row.

Pull and slash, pull and slash, one after the other, row after row with backs aching and extremities freezing. The only relief came when their knives needed sharpening and they took a breather while Stanley ground the blade against the sharpener.

It was while they were at the start of a new row that they heard the sound of a hunter's horn and the baying of the hounds. They stopped their work for a while and watched the hunt pass by in the next field in pursuit of a fox.

Stanley thought it was a novelty and pointed out the fine clothes they were wearing and the way they rode their magnificent horses but Eileen was too miserably cold to be impressed in the slightest, and could only concentrate on enduring the pain until it was time to go home.

As she bent to begin the new rows of turnips Stanley suddenly grabbed her arm and pulled her towards him. Shocked she looked at him.

"Look," he said pointing up the row of turnips. For a moment she could see nothing. Then a fox streaked into view, running straight towards them through the turnips. It looked up and for a moment they saw the sheer terror in its eyes. It almost swerved but at the last moment carried on straight past them and through a gap at the bottom of the wall. From there it instantly disappeared into the woods.

Stanley was no lover of foxes. He had seen what they could do, and would shoot them as vermin without a second thought if the need arose. But he thought little of any animal being torn to pieces by the hounds, while people with too much money watched and applauded.

Privately he called them called the 'court jesters,' and sometimes much less complimentary names, as they rode out dressed in their red jackets, to gallop across the countryside on their expensive horses, in pursuit of one solitary little animal; and all in the name of sport.

Today he was feeling very much on the side of the fox. In the next field he could see that the hounds had lost the scent and were milling about around the master of the hunt, while he stood up in the stirrups, looking, to see which way the fox had gone.

Throwing his knife down on the floor, Stanley put his hands around his mouth like a loud speaker and called out to the hunters. "He's gone that way," he shouted, pointing in the opposite direction to the one taken by the fox.

The master of the hunt touched his cap with his whip as a salute, and rallied his hounds to go where Stanley has indicated. As they galloped away across to the adjoining field Stanley looked at Eileen and softly said, with his blue eyes sparkling, "Well that's round one to the fox," then added even softer that it would serve em right if they broke their bloody necks.

The day seemed to go easier and faster after that as they worked side by side. They finished the field much earlier than they had expected to, and rode the five miles home on their ramshackle old bikes feeling that it had been a Boxing Day to remember.

Stanley had made a decision, and he fully expected Doris to oppose it. He waited until New Year's Eve to broach the subject.

"Doris," he said, and had to repeat it as she was lost in the book she was reading, "Doris, I've been thinking."

"Oh aye," she replied, reluctantly tearing herself away from the story she was lost in. "What's that then?"

Taking a deep breath he said," Ah think ah need to get a regular job." Instantly he had grabbed her attention. "What do you mean? You've got a job, getting the smallholding running."

"Aye, ah know that but it's not making any money at the moment and won't be for several months. We can't keep going on as we are."

"Well, I'm not complaining. Ah can manage the housekeeping on what you get from the piece work. We always said we'd work for ourselves once we got our own place."

Stanley sighed; she had that stubborn look on her face. "Doris, ah don't want you to have to keep managing. You've been doing that ever since we got married. It's time to have things a bit easier. I can earn a regular wage for a few months until we start making this place pay."

Then he added, "There might not be much more casual work

314

going, and you know as well as I do that we haven't got enough land to be able to make much money. We'll be dependent on being able to sell enough from the market garden to make a wage. No, it's no use, we need regular money coming in."

Doris however, was still opposed to the idea and raised the subject every day. Stanley let her continue but he had made up his mind. He was on the lookout for a steady job, and he didn't have long to wait.

On Friday morning as he cycled past the council offices he saw a sign in the window advertising job vacancies. He turned around in the road and headed back to read it. They were advertising for a driver for the dust bin lorry. The hours were from seven thirty in the morning till three thirty in the afternoon. That was perfect for him. He went straight in to the office and asked about the job. He was directed to the lorry depot at the rear of the offices and told to ask for the foreman.

Stanley could not believe his luck when he found that the man in charge was Tom Duncan, an old friend of Bert Dunning.

"Now then, Stan, What are you doing here? Ah thought you had moved to somewhere up Pontefract way. Was you home sick?"

Stanley laughed, "Aye you could say that, Tom. It's a long time since I last saw you. How's the family?" He then went on to tell him about the smallholding and his need to get a regular wage coming in.

By the time he went home half an hour later he had been appointed as a lorry driver and would start the following Monday morning.

Arriving home Stanley crossed his fingers that there would be no big row when he broke the news to Doris. To his surprise she said she had been thinking, and he was quite right. He sat down at the table and began to eat his meal as he waited for her explanation. As she poured him a mug of tea she shrugged her shoulders and said she had had a good think and could see that it was the only sensible solution.

He squeezed her knee as she sat down and told her that she was bloody contrary but he loved her.

CHAPTER 32

Stanley's new career as a dustbin lorry driver began promptly at seven thirty on Monday morning. He very soon found that apart from an unsavoury smell that hung about the lorry it was by far the easiest job he had ever had.

He had been appointed as a driver, and he was in charge of the lorry, Driving it was all he had to do. The three men who worked with him were the dust bin men and emptied the bins into the back of the lorry.

Each of them wore a belt and strap which had a thick leather pad on one shoulder. The dust bins were round metal containers with a handle at each side. They collected the bin from wherever it was kept, removed the lid and hoisted the bin on to their shoulder which was protected by the thick pad. They then carried the full bin to the lorry and emptied it. It was a dirty, unpleasant job.

Everything went into those bins, rotten meat, stinking fish, paper, tins, bottles, sometimes the contents of babies potties, and the whole horrible cocktail was often topped off with hot ashes from the fire which then set the rest of the trash alight.

Whenever that happened, the men would tip the bins upside down and leave the contents for the owners to clean up themselves. Back in the cab on their way to their next collection point they would laugh and joke about the reaction of the owners of the upturned bins.

But sometimes the bin men themselves were on the receiving end of nasty tricks.

One of the men had very bad eyesight. It was so bad that the spectacles he wore resembled the bottoms of glass bottles. His name was John Rickard and he, like Stanley had the tenancy of one of the smallholdings on Doncaster Road.

He was a pleasant enough man but was, as you might say, a bit slow on the uptake, and very hindered by his poor eyesight. Stanley marvelled everyday about how he had managed to get the tenancy of one of the prized smallholdings when he seemed unable and unwilling to do very little with it.

One morning not long after Stanley had started work at the council they went to collect the bins from a council estate. It was a bitterly cold day and the ground was frozen hard. It was made colder by the slight mist that floated about eerily at ground level.

John went to collect the bin from the end house, and found it among a patch of winter cabbages. Grumbling aloud about having to retrieve the bin from the garden, John took off the lid and threw it to the ground before he picked up the bin and hoisted it on to his shoulder.

Given that he was so short sighted, he failed to see the length of thin wire that had been tied to one of the handles of the bin and the other end tightly knotted around the stem of a cabbage which was frozen solidly into the ground.

He began to move forward but could make no progress. Something was holding him back. He looked but could see nothing. He pulled harder and dropped the bin. Again he hoisted it on to his shoulder and set off almost at a run, only to be brought to a sharp halt as the wire reached its limits. Again he dropped it. John was not a man to be beaten and more determined than ever he repeated the performance until an audience of children began to gather and cheered him on.

It took five more tries before his workmates saw what was happening and went to his rescue. It took a long time for John to live that one down.

Emptying the bins was certainly not the worst job that the bin men had. More unpleasant by far, was cleaning out the earth closets and emptying the boxes full of human excrement!

There were still quite a few houses that had no water closets.

They were mostly out in the country on farms or farm cottages, and usually down long lanes. Sometimes the earth closets had a sturdy wooden box with handles on each side. They were usually full and brimming over by the time the bin men arrived to empty them. The boxes were carried out to the lorry by two men and then the foul mess was tipped into the back of the lorry with the rest of the rubbish. As could be expected, a disgusting stench arose when it was tipped into the lorry.

But even worse than that were the places where the contents of the closets had to be dug out manually every week and shovelled onto the lorry.

Thankfully for Stanley, as a driver, he was never called upon to take part in emptying the earth closets, which was just as well as he would never have done it.

In his lifetime he had cleaned up after many different animals and never flinched, but he drew the line at clearing up human excrement and would never have agreed to do it.

He held a handkerchief to his nose as the stench became unbearably strong and urged the men to wipe their hands thoroughly before getting back into the lorry cab.

All in all it was not the most congenial job, but at the end of the week when he was handed his first wage packet from the council, he looked at the ten pounds folded up inside and knew he had made the right decision.

Now, with a regular wage to take care of day to day living expenses Stanley and Doris would be able to reinvest all their profits back into the smallholding.

Not only was Stanley happy to get a regular wage he soon discovered there were other perks to the job. If he had not seen it for himself he would not have believed some of the things that were thrown away.

In the first week he glanced out of the rear window of the lorry and watched one of the men bring out a bin. Rather that tipping it over into the lorry, he began to rummage through the contents. Curious, Stanley got out and took a closer look. The bin was full of clothes, some of them still folded as if they had just been taken out of drawers. Hands reached in and the clothes disappeared in a flash, rolled up and stuffed into the men's dinner bags. By the time Stanley had elbowed his way to the front, the only thing remaining was a pair of green shoes in soft leather with small heels, and as Stanley picked them up knew exactly who they would fit.

That evening when Eileen tried them on she could not have been more delighted if they had been Cinderella's slippers delivered by Prince Charming himself. They were the nicest shoes she had ever owned.

After that Stanley kept a sharp eye out on what was being dumped. He found lots of brasses for Doris to add to her ever growing collection, which hung on nails above the fireplace and were polished lovingly every week, but he never found anything else to compare with the green leather shoes.

One other advantage to being on the bins was the early finishing time. Each day they had a certain area to cover and once all the bins from that area were collected they had finished for the day. With Stanley driving they had cut their time down drastically and were on their way home an hour before their official finishing time.

That suited Stanley down to the ground. He was working every spare hour on the smallholding. By the end of March he had built another shed and pen for more chickens. This time they had cockerels for fattening up, hopefully, in time for the Easter market. He had already taken orders for twenty without even advertising.

Remembering the break in that they had had before Christmas when eighteen of their point of lay pullets had been stolen, Stanley installed Lassie in a kennel just inside the chicken run every night. She was tethered with a long chain that would allow her to reach every corner of the chicken run. Stroking her head, he talked to her, "Now then, Lassie, you're here to look after the chickens, don't you let any bloody thieves in."

She looked at him quizzically and wagged her tail. Stanley had no doubt that she would spring into action if the need arose, but knew she was unlikely to bark. 'Oh well,' he thought, 'She won't change now.' Lassie had always adopted a silent but deadly approach as far as being a guard dog went. She had never wasted time barking, in fact, he had often wondered if she was incapable of it. Whatever the reason, Lassie just went right in and bit the ankle of whoever she took a dislike to, and he had never been able to cure her of it.

He patted her head, and went away leaving her in charge. As he walked up the yard he thought that maybe it was time to start thinking about another dog. Lassie was past her prime now and her mother Meg was old and classed as the house dog. He thought back to the day he had collected Meg from Barnsley when they had lived in Wath upon Dearne.

What a long time ago it seemed. As if she knew what Stanley was thinking Meg appeared on the steps to greet him. She was as beautiful as ever but there were grey hairs on her muzzle and her coat was not as shiny as it had once been. She made an attempt to stand on her hind legs and lean on his chest the way she always had when he came home, but she gave a little yelp and sat down with her head hung low.

"What's up with you then, Meg? Come on let's have a look at you." He sat in his chair and stroked her head as she laid it on his knee. With his thumb he wiped under her eyes and felt at her ears, then her stomach. He looked up at Doris as she went about preparing their meal. "Ah think she's ok don't you, Doris?" he said, "She's just feeling her age aren't you, Meg?"

As if she understood and agreed Meg went to her rug just inside the front door where she liked to sleep and laid down with her head on her paws. Only her eyes moved as she watched Doris put the dinner on the table.

At bed time, Meg still lay there and refused to go out even to relieve herself. Doris warned her not to soil the rug and went up to bed. Stanley switched off the lights and followed her, yawning, and looking forward to a good night's rest.

He woke very early the next morning, long before it was time to get up, and for some reason he felt uneasy. He lay there for a while, unable to get back to sleep, then with a sigh he slipped out of bed, picked up his clothes from the chair and tiptoed downstairs intending to get dressed and go outside to catch up on some chores.

He opened the back door and he could hear a robin singing. He stood for a moment or two listening to it, before he walked gingerly across the yard in bare feet to the outside toilet, wincing as he stood on loose grit in the concrete.

As he went back indoors and filled the kettle he wondered why Meg had not followed him outside as she usually did. "Meg," he called softly. When there was no response he walked across the room to the tiny hallway and peered around the door, expecting her to look up at him.

She lay in exactly the same position that he had left her in the previous night and in an instant he knew that she was no longer alive. He held his breath as he bent down and stroked her. Her fur was as soft as ever and she lay with her head on her paws. Her eyes were open slightly as if she was just waking up. A tear crept down Stanley's cheek as he acknowledged to himself that she was never going to wake up again.

His first thought was to get her out of the house before his daughters woke up. He found an old, grey ex-army blanket outside in the shed and wrapping it around her he lifted her up into his arms, complete with the pegged rug she had been sleeping on. He felt the damp soaking through and realised that she had wet herself as she had died, and he thought how upset she would have been.

In all the years they had had her; never once had she made any mess in the house. From the first day that she came to be their dog she had stood at the door and asked to be let out. Somehow, that really touched Stanley and he swallowed as a lump came into his throat.

Giving himself a shake he carried her outside and walked down the yard, and as he did so he wondered where he could lay her while he dug a hole for her grave. He decided on the stack of straw bales that had just been delivered. Laying her down on them he turned to go to find his spade and suddenly felt a nudge on his leg. He looked down to see Lassie staring up at him. He shook his head at her. Once again she had slipped her collar over her head, and jumped over the wire netting that surrounded the chicken run.

Before he could prevent her she sprang up on to the straw bales and sniffed at the body of her mother wrapped up in the blanket. She began to scratch at it with her paw and as she did so she gave a low whine and the fur on the back of her neck stood on end.

"Come on now old girl, your Mam's gone." Stanley spoke to her, and he knew instinctively that she had understood him. Lassie came close to him and snuggled up just as she had done when she had been a puppy. Stanley put his arms around her and stroked her fur and thought how rough it was in comparison to her mother's. They had always been as different as chalk and cheese in every way, but yet, they had been as close to each other as any human mother and daughter.

It was still early morning and just beginning to get light when he locked Lassie in the shed and dug Meg's grave in the front garden. He placed her in it and covered her over before he went indoors to break the news to Doris and his daughters who were just getting up.

When he set off for work at seven fifteen he felt as if he had already done a day's work and was thankful that his job driving the dustbin lorry was so easy. He often said that he went to work to have a rest, and he was very thankful this morning that it was true.

It was now less than three days to Easter and all the cockerels that they had been fattening were ordered, apart from one which they had kept back for themselves. Stanley and Doris had planned to kill the birds on Good Friday and spend the day plucking and preparing them for their customers to collect on Easter Saturday. Stanley was very pleased with the birds and already had plans to reinvest the profits from them into more stock and hopefully put some money away towards a tractor. They had no fridge of course but as it was mid-April the weather was still cool. There was a long, narrow room at the rear of the house that Doris called the back kitchen. The room was, in fact, nothing more than a store room but the one useful thing it did have in its favour was that it faced north and was always cool.

So Stanley had fitted boards over the old copper to form a long table and Doris had covered it with a white sheet. They were all prepared for their marathon plucking session. Eileen was part of the team and quite frankly was dreading it. It was one job that she hated above all others; not that that mattered, the job needed doing and that's all there was to it.

Frances could play outside while the work was going on. Since Stanley had rescued an old three wheeler bicycle from going to the tip, she spent all day on it, riding up to the gate then down to the bottom of the yard.

Yes, everything was organised, everything was under control. There was however, one thing he could not control and that was the chance of another break in and the poultry being stolen.

He had made the chicken shed as secure as he could, and extended the wire netting pen. Finally, he had installed Lassie in her kennel right inside the pen next to the door of the shed. He went to bed that night feeling that he had done everything that he could, but nevertheless spent a restless night worrying about the poultry. He eventually fell asleep in the early hours of the morning and then, ended up waking later than usual.

He got up straight away and dragged his working clothes on before he went downstairs. He opened the back door and stepped outside. He almost fell over Lassie, who was laid on the top step.

Instantly he thought about the poultry and began to run, with his boots still unlaced and flapping with every step. Down the yard he ran and across to the chicken shed.

As he ran he was saying to himself, "Please don't let them have pinched the poultry. Please don't let the thieving bastards have taken them."

The door to the run was open, the lock thrown on the grass at the side of the wire netting, but to his relief the shed door was still locked. He could hear the cockerels inside clamouring to be let out.

He looked back and could see Lassie coming towards him. She was limping slightly, and he knelt to look at her foot. It was while he was in that position close to the ground that he noticed the speck of blood. Looking closer he saw another and could then make out footprints coming towards the pen and some leading away. He followed them to where the ten acre crop of winter wheat began.

Quite clearly he could see tracks made through the young corn, going at an angle across the field to the bottom corner where there was a gap in the hedge. Beyond that there was the railway line.

Stanley clenched his fists, he had a very good idea who the

culprits were, but proving it was practically impossible. He only hoped that Lassie had managed to do them some damage.

Thankful that they had not managed to get away with any of his poultry he went back to the house, eager to give Doris the news. Lassie walked so close behind him that she was almost touching his heels.

Normally she stayed outdoors but today he allowed her inside and she would have sat close to him as he sat down to his breakfast but that was behaviour that Stanley would not stand from any dog. He pointed to her to go to her mother's old position behind the front door and she gave him a look of reproach before she went and lay down, watching them eat with her nose resting on her paws and her ears slightly raised.

As he finished telling Doris about the attempted break in he looked at Lassie and said, "If only she could talk and tell us what happened." The words were hardly spoken when there was a loud knock on the door.

It was Doris who opened it and found the young boy who delivered their papers standing there. With him was his father who stood with his arm around his son's shoulders and appeared very irate. Doris gave a sharp intake of breath and went pale. This was obviously trouble. She pulled herself up straight and looked him in the eye before she called Stanley.

The man came straight to the point. "Your dog has bitten my son. Just look at him. He's still shaking. What the hell are you doing having a dangerous dog running about loose?"

Both Stanley and Doris began to apologise together but the man shouted above them "I'm going to report this to the police. I'm going to sue you, and your bloody your dog wants putting down."

Stanley tried again, "I'm really sorry," he said, "The dog is usually fastened up, she's not normally running about loose," As he spoke Lassie came up behind them and the young boy saw her.

"That's the dog, Dad," he cried, and ran toward the gate and slammed it shut behind him.

His panic transferred itself to his father who backed away saying that they were to keep that savage animal away from him, he turned and ran to join his son on the other side of the gate.

Following him Stanley tried to appeal to him to be reasonable and discuss it but it was no use, he was not prepared to listen.

Eating humble pie was not something that came easy to Stanley, but he would have been happy to have a double helping if he could have placated the boy's father. But there was to be no reasoning with him and to be honest Stanley did not blame him. He would have felt the same himself if one of his girls had been bitten. He looked at Lassie and deep inside he knew what the outcome would be.

Having such a busy day in front of them should have taken their minds off the matter, but it didn't. Stanley gave himself a mental shake and made a determined effort to concentrate on the work that had to be done, but every few minutes the words of the boy's father came sliding into his brain and he began to worry all over again.

Doris was just as bad in her own way, and kept saying the same things over and over again until they had an argument that began when Stanley snapped and said, "For God's sake shut up about it, Doris. Don't keep going on and on about it. Give me a chance to bloody think won't you?"

They had planned their strategy for dressing the chickens the night before when they had not had this all-consuming worry occupying their minds. Now they began to put the plan into action. They tackled the birds in batches of five.

Stanley went into the shed with Eileen beside him to help. He picked out five birds, wrung their necks one by one and passed them to his daughter to hold. By the time they had carried them across to the outhouse they had stopped flapping and were ready to be plucked.

Doris had decided that scalding the birds made them much easier to pluck, and one at a time they were placed head first into a large bucket and boiling water poured over them.

She handed the first, still steaming bird to Eileen and instructed her to begin. Working together they soon had the first five birds plucked and ready to have their innards removed. Doris took them into the kitchen to do this while Stanley killed the next five. By early afternoon they were all finished. It had not taken them as long as they had anticipated. All the birds were now laid out, clean, oven ready and wrapped in greaseproof paper, with price tags on them waiting to be collected by their customers.

Stanley went out to the chicken shed and began cleaning it out. He piled all the soiled straw bedding on to the heap of manure knowing how valuable it would be to spread on the field next spring.

As he worked he turned the scenes of the early morning confrontation over and over in his mind and by the time the shed was clean his decision was made. Deep inside him he knew there was no other solution. Lassie was becoming more dangerous. They could not keep her. She would have to be put to sleep. There was no avoiding the issue, and there was only him to do it. Taking a deep breath he hardened his heart and thought about the consequences if she attacked a young child. She had to go.

Afterwards he buried her in the front garden alongside her mother and raked the ground smooth. Then he walked alone down the full length of his field and stood for a while leaning on the fence at the bottom end near the railway line. He gazed at the narrow strip of land that divided his field from it and pictured the poultry thieves walking across it and climbing through the hedge.

Half a mile away at the other side of railway line there was a housing estate. It was well known as a rough area and there was one family in particular who had a bad reputation. At any moment in time there was usually at least one member of the family enjoying Her Majesty's hospitality. The galling thing was that they openly boasted about it in the local pub.

He sighed and began to walk back towards the house. He felt better for his half hour of solitude and in the right frame of mind for the next thing he had to do. He could see Doris looking for him and she waved as she saw him.

As he joined her he put his arm around her shoulders and pulled her close. "Can you hold tea for an hour Doris? I'm going to see the paper lad's father."

"Do you know where he lives? I'll come with you; I'll just go get my coat."

"No, Doris," he said firmly. "I'm going on my bike. They live at the top of Fourth Avenue."

He could see her mouth set ready to argue but won when he pointed out that someone had to be at home to see to the customers coming for the chickens.

Before she could say any more he wheeled his bike out of the shed and set off. As he rode he rehearsed what he was going to say. He was prepared for a repeat of the scene he had had this morning but was determined to try and make the man change his mind about taking the case to court.

He swallowed hard as he knocked at the door and looked around at the well-kept garden as he waited. He noticed the red geraniums in pots on the kitchen window sill and the clean step and he wished he was anywhere else but here.

He had the words right there on his lips as the door opened, but he forgot what he was going to say as the boy's mother stood in front of him.

"Yes?" she said. Her face was hard and hostile. "You're the man whose dog bit my lad, aren't you?"

"Yes," Stanley's voice faltered a little, "I've come to say how sorry I am about it and see how he is. I can understand you being angry. I would feel the same. It won't happen again."

"He's in a bad way. Ah wouldn't be surprised if it's gone septic. My husband's going to the police as soon as he gets home from work."

Stanley's face was flushed; he had forgotten all the rest of his rehearsed speech and was almost on the point of turning round and going home. There seemed little point in trying to appease the mother. He was getting no further with her than he had with her husband that morning.

At that moment the young paper boy himself dodged around his mother with a football in his hand. "Hiya, Mr Dale," he said, and to his mother he called, "Ah'm off to play footie on the rec. Mam," and with that he was off, running up the road to join a gang of other budding football stars.

Stanley looked at the woman, "Oh," he said, "I see he's feeling better now." There seemed to be nothing else to say at that moment and he turned and walked back down the path pushing his bike.

That evening the boy's father came to see Stanley. There was a short discussion between the two men, and although they didn't exactly part as friends they came to an understanding that there would be no more talk of dangerous dogs or reports to the police.

Later when Stanley and Doris were alone they talked the whole matter over, and they came to the conclusion that sad as it was that Lassie had gone it had been the right course of action to take.

By the middle of 1955 Stanley and Doris were moving forward fast. With Stanley earning a steady wage from driving the dustbin lorry they had more than enough to live on. The coal shed had been cleared out and whitewashed and was now used as a little shop for their market garden produce. The neighbours who lived nearby were soon regular customers and Doris never minded how many times she was disturbed from her housework as long as she was taking money. Their flock of hens was in full production and the profits from them were reinvested into new stock.

Stanley was a regular at Doncaster market. He was now recognised and respected among the farmers and the auctioneers. It was a matter of great pride to Stanley that when he sent in a litter of store pigs he was named as their breeder.

By now Stanley was used to negotiating prices and he considered himself able to strike a good bargain but he met his match one day when a travelling salesman called.

He was a very tall, imposing man, obviously of the Sikh religion judging by his immaculate white turban, and had a magnificent black beard. He had called several times over the past few months carrying his large suitcase as he went from door to door hoping to sell the goods in his case. Doris had always said no thank you, very politely, but firmly.

This time, however, before she had time to speak he held up his hand, "Today, madam, I am not selling. I wish to buy from you." It was at this point that Stanley arrived home from work. He came around the corner wheeling his bicycle. He looked at the man standing on the steps with his suitcase in his hand and was not in a mood for having his time wasted. "Now then," he said curtly, "What can I do for you?"

Immediately, the man put down his case on the top step and turned to face Stanley. He came down the steps and said he wished to buy a chicken. That put a different light on things as far as Stanley was concerned.

Although he did not approve of the way the Sikhs slaughtered their animals he was prepared to overlook it if it meant he could get rid of one of his old hens. He looked at the man in a more tolerant way.

"Alas," the man said, "I do not have much money today. Business is very bad. I have walked miles and sold very little. Would you be prepared to trade for the chicken sir? Come, I will show you my goods. They are very high quality."

As he began to open his suitcase it started to rain and Stanley invited him inside. Doris gave him one of those looks that said, 'What have you done that for? We'll never get rid of him now.'

Quick as a flash the suitcase was open on their living room floor and he was pulling things out of it. There was a mixed selection of household items and clothes. Stanley looked across at Doris. He could see that she was not impressed. Frances had wedged herself behind the armchair and was staring at this foreign gentleman as if he was a visitor from outer space and her eyes were like saucers.

Reaching down into his case he rummaged about and brought out a white blouse with embroidery on the front. He shook it and beckoned Eileen to him. Cautiously she moved towards him and he held up the blouse against her.

Maybe it was an accident or maybe it was deliberate but his hand touched her left breast and she backed quickly away, blushing as she did so. Neither her father nor her mother noticed anything and Eileen was certainly too shy to say anything.

"Look how it suits your daughter, sir. Surely she would love such a garment. I would be prepared to trade this wonderful blouse for one of your chickens."

Looking at his daughter, Stanley asked if she would like it. Of course Eileen said yes. Actually she would have said yes if it had been made of sacking as she was always short of clothes.

So Stanley agreed and led the man with his suitcase outside. Instructing him to wait near the gate, he went to his chicken run and selected a hen that lay in a corner looking very sorry for itself. It had not been well for days and he was glad to get rid of it. As he picked it up he could feel its chest bone and thought to himself that it was really only fit for making into soup.

The Sikh gentleman went off up the road with the old hen tucked under his arm and Stanley congratulated himself on having made a very good deal.

Eileen was thrilled with her new blouse but sadly, it fell apart the first time it was washed.

They had a crop of wheat growing in their ten acres of land. It had already been planted when they took over the smallholding and they had paid valuation on it as incoming tenants. Stanley criticized it as being badly sown and grown from poor quality seed but he coaxed it along, pulled all the wild oats out of it and worried when they had heavy rain in case it was flattened.

It would be ready to harvest in late August and Stanley thought that he would probably have to employ a contractor to harvest it for him. This was not something that he wanted to do due to the cost, which he considered far too high.

More than once he had said in all seriousness to Doris, that he would cut the bloody corn himself with a scythe rather than pay that much, and she did not for one moment doubt that he would do it if he had to.

In July he heard of a second hand tractor for sale. It belonged to the local greengrocer who had used it for his regular weekly delivery rounds. It was one of the very versatile little grey Ferguson tractors. Eagerly Stanley pointed out to his wife that it had never done any heavy work and it also had a cab on it.

The one disadvantage was that it had a petrol engine which made it more expensive to run, but that was offset by the low asking price.

"Well, Doris, what do you think? Can we afford it? He wants £100. But he might take £90 if I offer him cash."

Doris was reluctant for them to part with that amount of money and Stanley grew impatient with her. He took his cap and stormed out of the house and went to check on the livestock. Then picked up his hoe and began to weed the cabbages. He knew from experience that the best way to handle his wife was to give her some thinking time. She was sure to come round thought Stanley, but no matter what she said he was determined to have that tractor.

Before he reached the end of the row of cabbages he heard Doris call him. He looked up, his face a picture of tight-lipped determination and gave her his grimmest glare. But Doris was now compliant and said that she thought the tractor was good buy and he should go and see about it immediately.

Stanley shook his head in exasperation as he put his arm on her shoulders in the familiar way that he had. "Are you sure then, Dot? You're not going to change your bloody mind again in the next five minutes are you?"

She looked at him with an injured expression on her face as if to say, 'What me?' before Stanley pinched her bottom and chased her back to the house.

The greengrocer, appropriately enough, was named Ben Green and Stanley knew him slightly. As he walked into his shop in the centre of Woodlands, he breathed in the fragrant aroma of the fresh fruit and vegetables. Ben was standing behind the counter and greeted Stanley as he saw him. "Now then, it's Stan Dale isn't it? What can ah do for you? You've only just caught me. Ah was about to close the shop."

Stanley smiled at him and came right to the point, "Well, I've heard that your tractor is for sale and ah'm looking to buy a one."

"By heck, word soon gets around, ah've not really advertised it yet, but yes, it is for sale. Would you like to have a look at it?"

He beckoned to Stanley to come through to the rear of the shop and called for his son to go and stand behind the counter. It seemed that his son was not inclined to do as he was told and he remained seated at the table with a drawing book in front of him.

That was when Stanley saw a different side to the outwardly good natured Ben Green.

He repeated his instructions quietly enough but there was a definite menace in his voice and the son got up without any argument and disappeared into the shop.

"Sorry about that," he said. "My lad needs straightening up now and then. He could do with a kick up the backside. All he thinks about is drawing pictures. Wants to be an artist he says. Huh, ah can't see him making any money at that. Got his head in the clouds he has. He could take over the business in time but he's not interested."

Stanley nodded but made no reply. He thought it better not to be drawn into family arguments. He could see the tractor parked in an open fronted shed, and went towards it.

From the first glance he could see what a good buy it would be. The wheels had obviously never seen soil or mud. It looked brand new.

"There it is, as you can see it's in good order. It's never really done a proper day's work all the time I've had it. Hardest thing it's ever had to do is pull that little trailer with a load of fruit and veg on it. I'm only selling it as I've bought a van to do the rounds in. What do you think to it?"

Stanley walked around it, opened the cab door and felt the gear stick. It moved as smooth as silk. He tried his best to look disinterested. It didn't do to look too keen if you wanted to strike a bargain. At Ben's invitation he sat in the cab and started up the engine. He revved it up a few times and could find no fault with it. He switched it off and got out.

"How much do you want for it?"

Ben Green laughed, "Ah come on, Stan. Ah'm sure whoever told you about it will have told you the price too. It's £100. Take it or leave it."

Putting his hands in his pockets Stanley looked at the ground, then at the tractor. He pursed his lips as if he was considering the matter. "Will you take £90? It'll be cash."

At the cash word Ben smiled, "Tell you what. £95 cash and we've got a deal. But it won't be available until after the weekend." He held out his hand and they shook on the deal.

Stanley then allowed himself to show how pleased he was. It was all he could do not to start grinning from ear to ear.

"Ah'll send my daughter up with the money." he said," She'll be here within an hour, then ah'll come and collect it on Monday evening."

It was a downhill ride home and Stanley freewheeled most of the way. He felt so excited. At last he had got his own tractor, and a good one. It would be perfect for working the smallholding. 'This is just the beginning.' he thought, and he felt such confidence in the future.

In late July at the age of fifteen Eileen left school. She left on a Friday evening and began work at Woolworths in Doncaster on the following Monday morning. Having another worker in the household would increase the family's prosperity.

From her wage of two pounds five shillings Eileen gave her mother one pound. With what was left she would buy her own clothes, pay her bus fares and her dinners, then save any money that was left over. An agreement was made that with every rise she got she would contribute half of it until it was considered that she was paying enough to cover the cost of her keep. Until then she would be expected to work on the smallholding in the evenings and at weekends.

CHAPTER 33

With the wheat in the field almost ready to harvest, Stanley went to see Bert, his friend and ex-foreman at Smiths farm. They now had a combine harvester and Stanley hoped he would be able to borrow the old fashioned binder that lay unused and gently rusting at the back of one of the cart sheds.

He felt embarrassed at asking to borrow it now that he no longer worked there, but he swallowed his pride, gritted his teeth and went ahead. Bert, to be truthful was beginning to think that Stanley had used up all his favours, but as the binder was virtually now just scrap and never used, he said yes he could borrow it.

Stanley thanked him and tried to say that he understood the position that Bert was in and knew that he was being a nuisance, but at that stage in his life he was still sometimes clumsy and brusque in his manner.

Thankfully Bert understood what he was trying to say, he held out his hand and Stanley took it and simply said, "Ah won't forget this Bert."

"Aye," Bert replied, with a laugh, "When tha's a rich farmer, ah'll come to work for thee, and I'll expect top rate of pay. Now take the binder and clear off. Ah wish you best of luck with it, and believe me you'll need it. It's given me plenty of headaches. You can expect to have trouble with the tying mechanism. Oh and by the way, go out of the top gate will you? What they don't see at the farmhouse won't cause any problems."

Hooking the old binder on to the back of his little Fergie, Stanley set off. He took a chance and cut through the field at the top of the park, hoping the gateway had not been closed off. It was a short cut that would save him a long trek through the village.

He was in luck, the field was soon to be made into a playing field and joined on to the park, but for now, it was still open. It was fairly easy going on the grass but once he reached the road it was a different matter. The iron wheels were never meant to travel on tarmac roads and they crunched and rumbled every inch of the way.

People rushed out to see what all the noise was about and stood at gateways watching him pass. The flails at the front of the old machine flapped about and looked as if they would collapse at any moment but Stanley nursed it along and reached home safely.

He spent the next three evenings after work greasing the old machine, tightening up bolts, and testing every moving part. The only thing he couldn't test was the tying mechanism. That would have to wait until he actually got started. He filled the string compartment with a huge ball of rough string and crossed his fingers.

Every day he tested the wheat. Breaking off an ear of corn, he rubbed it in his hands then bit and tasted it. All the while he watched the weather, and there came the day in the middle of August when he judged it was just right.

He had taken a few days off work and began as soon as the early morning dew had dried. It was time to open up the field. A strip right around the perimeter about eight foot wide would need to be cut by hand to allow room for the tractor and binder to access the corn without flattening it.

In 1955 Stanley was thirty six. He was probably at the peak of his strength. He was as lean as a greyhound and could work from dawn to dusk with scarcely a break. Cutting a swathe of corn around a field was well within his capabilities, he had done it many times before.

Taking his scythe he carefully sharpened the blade, running the filing stone expertly along the full length of it. Once he was satisfied that it was sharp enough, he began. Standing with feet well apart he swung the scythe just the way he had been taught all those years ago when he had worked for Downings in Wath upon

Dearne, and as he did so he thought of those days and wondered what Teddy Downing would say if he could see him now working on his own crop of wheat.

Doris and Eileen followed him scooping up the wheat until they had enough to make a sheaf then tying it around the middle. Once they had made six they stood them up, leaning them against each other into what was called a stook. They would stand there until they were fully dry.

It was backbreaking work and the wheat straw was rough and sharp. In spite of wearing old long sleeved shirts their hands and arms were soon scratched and sore. Occasionally Stanley stopped to sharpen his scythe again and straighten his back for a couple of minutes. Doris returned to the house to make sandwiches and tea to sustain them at dinnertime and the same again at tea time. Sweating and exhausted they carried on, until the end was in sight. It was a great relief when Stanley swung the scythe for the last time and declared it was all done.

Frances had long since tired of trailing after them and had gone to sleep on their coats in the hedge bottom. Stanley put his tools away and started feeding and bedding down the animals while Doris gave Eileen money to fetch fish and chips for supper.

In spite of the heat, the fire had been lit in the early morning and had been burning low all day, so thankfully the water was hot. Doris filled the bath and sprinkled in a generous amount of Daz washing powder. Frances had the privilege of being first in, followed by Doris. Eileen was next and finally Stanley who got to soak in the only slightly grubby water for as long as he wanted.

The next morning Stanley was awake early and even before sleep had left his brain he was thinking about the day ahead. At regular intervals throughout the night he had woken up with the harvesting on his mind and he had fretted about the weather and worried about the old binder's capabilities. Would it actually work properly? Would it tie the sheaves or just dump the wheat in an untidy heap?

He decided it was pointless to stay in bed any longer, he might as well be up and doing something. He slipped out of the bed as quietly as the old spring base would allow and went to the window.

Parting the curtains slightly he looked out. The view from the front of the house was not one to be admired.

Just across the road on a piece of waste ground there was a large, communal air raid shelter left over from the war. The local youths of the area tended to hang out there, but only the bravest or the least particular ventured inside the dark, stinking interior that was often used as a toilet.

Someone had drawn a picture of a wall on the side of the shelter, with a huge head above it and an enormous nose that hung over the wall. Painted below it was the slogan 'CHAD WAS HERE' in large letters. Who the hell was Chad? thought Stanley as he pulled his clothes on.

Doris awoke, yawned and asked him what time it was. On hearing it was ten to six she said she would have another half hours sleep and turned over. Once downstairs, Stanley made a mug of tea and drank it standing up while he looked out of the rear kitchen window.

The view was better from this side. He could see down his field and his neighbour's land as far as the railway line. In his mind's eye he was already planning the lay out of the field for next year. There would be no more wheat. Instead, he planned on setting half the land to potatoes and on the other half he would have six young calves that he would grow on and fatten up for the market. But, he thought, no time for dreaming just now. There was a long day ahead.

He emptied the tea leaves down the sink and rinsed his mug. Doris would get the breakfast ready later, after he had fed and cleaned out the pigs. As he walked down the yard he breathed in the fresh early morning air. There was a slight mist hovering just above the ground that promised an ideal day for harvesting.

He broke off another ear of corn and tested it. This was the day when it was at a perfect stage, he hoped and prayed that he would be able to get as much as possible cut while the weather was just right.

The dew was particularly heavy and it was almost ten o'clock before it was dry enough to begin. Stanley had been pacing about for an hour before that in an agony of impatience; he had never been much good at waiting.

Well, at last it was time. The dew had all disappeared. The tractor was already hooked up to the binder and in position. He pulled down the lever that lowered the cutting blade and the flails which pushed the straw on to it.

Taking a deep breath he put the tractor into gear and set off. Keeping going at a nice steady pace he watched the binder through the wing mirror and constantly kept looking back, while at the same time made sure that he was going in a straight line.

He could have cried with relief as he saw the straw being cut and carried along the conveyor. Into the machine it went and the metal arm flew over and tied the sheaf of straw just the way it was supposed to; then flicked it off the edge and on to the ground. It was working like a well-oiled sewing machine and Stanley dared to begin estimating how long it would take to cut the whole field.

All was well until he was half way down the field and then in the mirror he saw a sheaf of straw being dropped untied on to the ground in a tangled mess. He kept his nerve and carried on, hoping against hope that it was just one malfunction of the machine and that it would right itself. It did.

Stanley held his breath, fearing it would happen again, but all was well and the tied up sheaves dropped with precision in a line behind him. He allowed himself to relax a little and even began to hum quietly.

Then the blade which moved from side to side as it cut the straw, suddenly stopped working. On examination, he found that a bolt had sheared off so he spent the next half hour rummaging through his tool box to find a replacement.

By dinnertime only two rounds of the field had been completed and many of the sheaves needed retying before they could be stacked into the traditional stooks. Stanley's temper and patience were becoming very short and when one of the wooden sails snapped he blasted and cursed the old machine.

Just at that moment Doris came to see how the work was going and received a very curt, "Well how the bloody hell do you think its going? Can't you see for yourself?" Anyone else might have tried to cajole him but Doris had a fiery temper and before long they were having a raging row in the middle of the field.

Doris stormed off telling him that he could shove the binder somewhere painful, and it was his own fault for not getting the contractors in to cut the corn.

Stanley fumed and shouted at her as she walked away, reminding her that she had been as reluctant as him not to pay for the corn cutting. She responded by putting two fingers up at him and carried on back to the house.

He knew there was no alternative but to mend the machine again and he spent more valuable time finding a piece of suitable wood and bolting it into place. 'Surely now,' he thought, 'surely nothing else could go wrong with the damned thing,' and he got back on to the tractor seat and set off.

The first sheaf off the back of the machine was not tied. Stanley swore again and shouted into thin air that, he 'must have killed a bloody robin.' The temperamental old machine then decided to work, and for three whole rounds of the field it threw out perfectly tied sheaves.

It was well past dinnertime and Stanley's stomach was rumbling. He was loath to stop the machine when it was working well, but he needed food and now that his temper was cooling he wanted to make things up with Doris. He stopped the tractor leaving it ready to begin work again after he had eaten, and made his way up to the house.

He climbed the steps and opened the door slightly. All was quiet and there was a rich smell of food. He took off his cap and threw it into the house. For a moment there was no response, then the door opened fully and Doris appeared wearing his cap with the peak to one side. She looked beautiful even in his old cap and Stanley took her in his arms and said he was sorry for shouting at her. Doris in her turn said that she was sorry about telling him what to do with the binder. They were friends again.

As he ate his dinner Doris stood close to him and poured his tea into the pint mug. Stanley ran his hand up her leg and all was well.

The field was still waiting to be cut and as much as Stanley would have liked to linger in the house there was no time to spare, so he bolted the food down as quickly as he could, jammed his cap back on and returned to do battle once more with the old binder.

Thankfully, the afternoon was more successful than the morning but it was still a very slow process. The binder for whatever reason would throw out an untied sheaf about one in every ten. Unable to cure it Stanley decided to carry on and simply go back later and tie the loose ones up by hand. Doris turned out as soon as the dinner was cleared away and began standing the sheaves up into the stooks. It was work that she was not very good at and the stooks she made kept falling over, but she carried on valiantly until it was time for her to go and meet Frances from school.

Stanley carried on cutting. He would do so for as long as he was able. The sheaves would have to stay where they were on the floor until he had finished the job. Help would arrive in the shape of his elder daughter at six thirty when she arrived home from work.

Doris was watching out for her. Eileen had gone to work on her bike today, choosing to cycle the five miles into Doncaster to save on bus fares. The moment she wheeled her bike into the shed Doris was outside urging her to hurry and eat her tea before joining them out in the field.

Eileen nodded but gave her mother a sulky look. She was tired. It had been extra hot in Woolworths today, her feet were aching, and the ride home had been exhausting. As she went indoors she could see the meal her mother had left for her drying on top of the oven. It had been there for over four hours and looked unpalatable but as there was nothing else she carried it to the table, and ate what she could. Her relationship with her mother was volatile at times and there was an argument most days.

Going upstairs she changed into her old working clothes and went outside to help with the harvest. Frances was outside playing on her three wheeler bike and called out to her elder sister to come and watch her but Eileen shook her head. "No, I can't just now, Frances, I've got to go and help."

Frances pulled a face and said, "It's not fair." Eileen agreed with her and as she walked down the yard towards the field she thought enviously of her friends who were not expected to work all day then work at night too.

But the work had to be done and it would only be completed by using every available pair of hands. Stanley carried on cutting until the light began to fade and the dew was beginning to settle. At last he called a halt, threw an old tarpaulin sheet over the binder and helped Doris and Eileen to stand up the last few stooks.

They looked at their arms. They were scratched by the sharp ends of the straw and stinging. Eileen pulled a piece of straw out of a particularly nasty cut and dabbed at it as it began to bleed.

Stanley and Doris stood for a moment or two looking at the scene of their field that was half harvested. It looked charming and rural, almost feudal, in the evening light. But Stanley certainly didn't see it that way. It had been an exhausting day for them all, and it would be the same again tomorrow and the day after until all the wheat was cut. Then, they had to bring all the sheaves into the yard and build them into a stack ready for the threshing machine to come later in the year.

Stanley said, "Never again will I attempt anything like this. Ah must have been mad. This way of harvesting went out with the ark. In future it will be the combine harvester no matter how much it costs."

It took another day and a half before all the corn was cut and the sheaves stacked into their pyramid shaped stooks. It was a Sunday evening but Stanley had no alternative but to take the binder back right then no matter what day it was. He was due back at work the next morning and Bert had said he should have the machine back as soon as possible.

Stanley was glad to see the back of it and felt great relief when he replaced it back where he had got it from. He kicked it as he left it and said under his breath that he hoped it rusted away to nothing in the very near future.

After a week of good weather Stanley decided that the sheaves were ready to be led off the field and stacked. Having no trailer of his own he was forced to go to see Bert again and hope to take advantage of his friendship.

As he explained what he had come for, Bert looked at him with a long suffering expression on his face, and took a deep breath. With it being harvest time all the trailers were in use, except one. Bert pointed at it.

"That's the only one that we won't be using, Stan. If it'll help you out you can take it." Stanley knew exactly which trailer he meant. He remembered it well from when he had worked on Smith's farm several years ago. It was a rusty, old four-wheeled trailer that was awkward to handle and difficult to reverse, but Stanley recalled the old saying that, 'Beggers can't be choosers,' and said thank you very much.

He hooked it up to his tractor and slowly pulled it out from among the long grass that had almost overgrown it. Bert looked on as Stanley got the oil and the grease gun out of his tool box and set about getting it ready for the road. Parts of the wooden floor were missing but Stanley was confident that it would do the job for him.

Back home Stanley could hardly wait to get started on leading the corn into the yard and see it all safely stacked. It was not however, a job that he could do alone. Ideally it needed three people. So he waited impatiently for Eileen to get home from work. The moment she walked through the gate she could hear Doris shouting to her to hurry up. They needed her help.

The three of them made a good team. Doris drove the tractor, Stanley lifted the sheaves on to the trailer with a two-pronged fork, and Eileen was on the trailer stacking the sheaves as they were thrown on by her father.

It had always been a tradition in farming that when the tractor was moved, the driver would call out, "Hold you," in a loud voice. This was so that the person on the back of the trailer would be aware that it was going to move.

Now Doris had learned to drive the tractor only a few weeks previously, and although she was beautiful, clever, and good at many, many things, driving was not one of them. She had never mastered the skill of letting the clutch out slowly and setting off without jerking.

After Eileen was nearly shaken off twice, Stanley shouted up to her, "Eileen. When your mother says, 'Hold you,' she really means it, so you'd better throw yourself down flat and hold tight."

They managed to get one load led off the field that night and Stanley began building his stack of wheat in the yard. He had decided to make a round stack and had carefully marked out a large circle, then proceeded to lay the first layer of sheaves very carefully within the circular markings.

This was Stanley's first stack from his own crop of wheat, and it was going to be a show piece. It was a matter of great pride that it should be perfectly round. It would start out just fractionally within the circle then very slowly increase in circumference as it got higher. That way the rain would run off the sides not down into it the centre of it.

Before he left the stack that evening it was covered with a tarpaulin sheet in case of rain. The same was repeated the following two evenings until all the wheat had been led out of the field.

With some of the sheaves Stanley constructed a circular pointed roof that rose to a conical shape in the centre, and then thatched it just as he would if it had been the roof of a cottage. He was the last person off the high stack and slid down the roof, dropping the last six foot on to the back of the trailer. He walked around the stack and looked at it critically before he nodded his approval. All that remained to do then was to lay a net over the top and rope it down.

Stanley was extremely proud of his circular stack and it was admired by many, but it was not destined to be there for very long. Wheat prices were good and Stanley decided that now was the right time to sell, but of course before he could do that he needed it threshing.

He knew that Trevor Dickinson who owned a threshing machine lived at Skellow which was ten miles away. At first he thought he would cycle the ten miles and then thought to himself, 'Well what's wrong with going on the tractor?' and then another thought occurred to him, 'Why not take Doris with me?'

He found a piece of wood and fixed it at the rear of the tractor just behind the driver's seat to form a bench. He called Doris to look at it and asked if she fancied going with him. Before Stanley knew what was happening Doris had gone into the house and pulled on an old pair of his trousers and tucked her skirts inside them. She settled herself on the improvised seat with her feet on the drawbar and held on to the mudguards with both hands.

Stanley came out of the house carrying his jacket and stared at her already sitting there. "Blimey, Doris, you didn't need telling twice. Where's our Frances?"

"Oh, she's playing with the little lad from up the street. His mother's going to keep her eye on her."

To Doris it was a welcome outing. She regularly caught the bus to Doncaster to go shopping but this was something different. Sitting with her back to Stanley she enjoyed every minute of the ride. When they arrived back home she said they should go out again on the tractor but next time she would take a cushion to sit on. Stanley smiled and agreed but said nothing. He was only waiting for the right moment to suggest that they bought another car.

CHAPTER 34

The threshing day had been booked for two weeks on Saturday. Trevor Dickinson would arrive with the threshing machine at eight am and the arrangement was that Stanley had to provide the staff.

There was always someone glad to earn a bit of cash in hand and Stanley had no difficulty finding the necessary workers. They would need a minimum of seven. Two of his smallholder neighbours had agreed to help out in exchange for help in kind later on in the year. Eileen and himself made another two. Trevor would be one more member of the team.

A young lad who lived in the miner's estate just across the road had jumped at the chance to earn some pocket money. Eagerly he had told Stanley that his name was Alex and that he was not going to be a miner like his father, he claimed that he wanted to be a farmer. Stanley had smiled, remembering how he had felt at his age. He told him to be there at eight o'clock promptly. Alex said, "Yes, Mr. Dale, I'll be here on time," and suddenly Stanley felt as if he had aged twenty years.

That only left one more worker to find. Maybe word had got around on the farming jungle telegraph or maybe it was just chance, but that same day a man turned up at the door and asked for casual work. He said that his name was Tom Smith and that he was between jobs, but was used to farm work. He was a burly man with a mouth that never quite closed. He looked clean but had the foulest of breath and sent out little balls of spit whenever he spoke.

There was something about the man that Stanley didn't quite trust but as he needed one more for the threshing team he agreed to employ him for the day and pay him one pound ten shillings.

345

On the appointed day, bright and early, Stanley was waiting at the gate. Eileen stood beside him, she had agreed to go sick from her shop assistant job for the day and work on the threshing machine.

They heard it before they saw it. The distinctive chug chug of the Field Marshall tractor and the rumble of the iron wheels of the threshing machine were unmistakable. As it came trundling slowly into view Stanley nudged his daughter.

"Listen to that engine," he said, as he cocked his head on one side. "It's a Field Marshall tractor. Best thing out for the threshing machine. They make em in Gainsborough, near where your Aunty Edith and Aunty Sarah live. I'll show you one day when we get another car."

Eileen looked at him at the mention of a car. His face was giving nothing away but he winked and said, "Don't say anything about cars to your mother."

As the tractor towed the machine into the yard Stanley walked alongside and indicated where he should set it up. The driver beamed a toothless grin at him, and Stanley thought to himself that as usual his teeth must be in the tool box. No doubt he would get them out at dinnertime.

It was four years ago on a threshing day at Smiths that he had discovered Trevor's false teeth in the tractor tool box. He had gone to get a spanner and opened the box to find the teeth staring up at him from their position nestled in an oily rag. He had carefully picked up the required spanner and handed it to Trevor, unable to hide his amusement.

Trevor had looked at him and said, "What's up with you then? Can ah share the joke?"

Stanley had said that it had been a surprise to see his teeth in there. At the time Trevor had stared at him dead pan, and said, "Well they didn't bloody bite you did they?"

As Stanley got to know Trevor better he discovered that he always took the teeth out of the toolbox at dinnertime, wore them to eat his food, then carefully wiped them on a duster and put them back among the tools till the next mealtime.

Today, as he pulled the machine into place, he looked at Stanley's circular stack, and he commented that it was a grand job. "Is this the first one of your own, Stan?" he asked.

"Aye," said Stanley, "And ah can tell you it'll be the last. It'll be the combine for me in future. Tha wants to find another business, Trevor. This machine will be obsolete soon."

Trevor nodded, "You're not wrong there, Stan. Next year ah'm going to buy a fancy combine harvester and do contract work. Got to keep up with the times tha knows."

That was the end of any social conversation. It was now down to business. The machine was in position beside the stack. Trevor quickly backed his tractor into line and looped the long belt from the fly wheel on the side of the threshing machine and on to the one on the Field Marshall tractor. Testing that the belt was at the right tension he then looked around to see if everyone was in position.

Stanley was on the stack ready to begin forking the sheaves across to Trevor who would cut the string and feed the wheat into the open top of the machine.

Eileen was in charge of the bag end, where the grain would come gushing down the two chutes. Hessian sacks were hung on each of them and as one filled she would remove it, tie it up securely, drag it to one side and replace it with an empty sack.

The man called Tom Smith was to take the filled sacks of grain up the yard and place them in the open-fronted stores. All the sacks of grain were to stand clear of each other in order to allow the air to circulate, but for now he had nothing to do except wait for the threshing to begin and he lolled against the wall scuffing his feet in the dust giving everyone sidelong glances.

Once the grain had been removed from the ears of wheat in the depths of the machine the remaining straw passed along a conveyor belt out on to a baling machine which packed the straw into tight oblong bales and tied them up. The neighbouring smallholders who had come to help, would take care of these and build a new straw stack a little distance away from the circular one.

Alex was given the unenviable task of dealing with all the chaff, which was the waste from the threshed corn. It came out from the bottom of the machine and was raked on to a huge hessian sheet, then tied up corner to corner, carried away and dumped in the chicken run. In spite of it being light in weight it was considered the worst job of all, due to the dust and the sharp pieces of straw that managed to find their way inside clothing.

So now they were all assembled at their posts around the threshing machine. The engine of the Field Marshall tractor was chugging away steadily, solid and reliable. Trevor eased the fly-wheel into gear and slowly at first the long belt began to move. Gradually, as he increased the power, the great threshing machine came to life. Wheels turned, wooden chutes rattled, belts spun with increasing speed and the whole thing shook. A great rumbling came from deep inside as if it were a giant waiting for food.

Trevor climbed the ladder and stood on top of the machine at the edge of the gaping, hungry mouth. He signalled for Stanley to begin throwing the sheaves to him. With a experienced hand Trevor caught them, cut the string and dropped the wheat into the depths. Dust began to rise and slowly the grain began to trickle down into the sacks.

They were soon all working in unison, each playing their part, carrying on regardless of aching backs, sweating bodies, sore eyes and the irritation of spiky bits of straw sticking to tender places where spiky bits of straw should never reach.

At ten o'clock Doris appeared with a tray of mugs full of strong tea and Trevor climbed down the ladder and slowed the engine until the threshing machine stopped. Now that there was only the sound of the tractor's engine it seemed almost deathly quiet and they were able to speak to each other. But the respite was not meant to last long. Eileen drank her tea and ran to the back yard to use the toilet, while the men discreetly disappeared behind the hedge one at a time.

Their next break was at dinner time. Again Trevor stopped the machine but left the tractor running quietly, Its engine chugging away as smooth as a sewing machine. As Stanley and Eileen walked up to the house for dinner he whispered to her to watch out for Trevor retrieving his teeth out of the tool box. She stared at him disbelievingly and gave a glance back. She was just in time to see him wipe his dentures on a dirty handkerchief, give them a quick check and pop them into his mouth.

They were finished by mid-afternoon. Stanley was pleased with the amount of wheat that was now stored in the shed ready to sell. He handed the wages out and paid Trevor for the use of his machinery. He was now moving on to a neighbouring small farm ready to begin work there on the following Monday.

As he began to move off he gave Stanley one of his gummy smiles and said "Well, ah'll see you next year then, Stan."

"Not with a threshing machine, you won't. That's my first and last threshing day on this place. From now on it's the combine harvester for me"

As he watched Trevor rumbling up the road with his outdated machinery he thought to himself that it was the end of an era, and he felt nostalgic and a little sad, but not for long.

Farming was entering an exciting new phase, with machinery that would ease the back-breaking manual labour and Stanley looked forward to the future.

CHAPTER 35

Since they had moved to the smallholding Stanley and Doris were prospering. He had kept his job as dustbin lorry driver and joked that when he was at work it was the only time he got a rest. The moment he arrived home he worked non-stop, building up and improving their smallholding; making use of every square inch of his land

By the end of the third year, they had five sows who produced litter after litter of young piglets. He had fenced off a section of his land close to the house and built a shelter in the corner of it. His sows ran outside until they were ready to farrow and then they were brought indoors into the brick built stables.

Almost other every month he had a litter of young pigs ready to go to Doncaster market where he had become well known and respected for the quality of his stock. With so little land Stanley decided that the best use for it would be to rear stock on it rather than trying to grow crops.

He put half of his land down to grass and fenced it off. Then in the spring he bought six young calves at Doncaster market with the intention of fattening them up.

In the remainder of the field that year he planted potatoes to sell in their little farm shop along with the eggs and vegetables.

In April, out of the blue, a letter arrived from the West Riding County council informing Stanley and Doris that the committee would be calling on an inspection visit the following week.

Making a good impression on the committee was essential to Stanley and Doris. They had ambitions to apply for a bigger place at some time in the future. A proper farm was what they aspired to with a decent amount of land.

If royalty had been expected they could not have made more of an effort to make sure that everything was in good order. Between them Stanley and Doris had lime washed the stables yet again and any rogue weeds that dared to appear had been pulled up. The yard was swept, and the grass was cut.

On the evening before the committee was due Stanley stood at the gate and took a long look at the place. He knew they had improved it immeasurably and felt very proud of their achievements.

The committee were due to arrive at ten o'clock. Stanley had arranged to have the day off work and at ten minutes to ten he was pacing the yard looking at cars that passed the gate. He felt exactly as if he was on trial and couldn't wait to get the inspection over.

They all arrived on the dot of ten in a large, black Austin Princess. Mr. Tingle was first out of the car and walked quickly towards Stanley holding out his hand. He had been present at the union meeting when Stanley had met the politician Hugh Gaitskell.

"Now then, Mr Dale, How are you?" He glanced around him. "I can see you've put some work in here," and he waved his arm in the direction of the crops growing in the market garden patch.

He turned as Mr. Wainright joined him then looked towards the gate to see Mr Molton, the chairman of the committee standing at the gate looking around. Stanley had taken a dislike to the man from the moment they had met and now as he noted the expression on his face his lips tightened and his jaw clenched.

The chairman walked slowly down the yard taking in the crops growing and carried on straight past Stanley as if he did not exist. He looked over the stable doors and made no comment at the sows in there or the pigs contentedly rooting about in the fenced off area at the far side of the market garden plot.

It seemed to Stanley that he was looking for something to criticize and he was right. Suddenly turning to face him the chairman said almost triumphantly. "Still trying to farm without any tractor then are you, Mr. Dale?"

It gave Stanley great satisfaction to lead him and the other two committee members further down the yard and show them his Ferguson tractor parked neatly behind the straw stack and at the side of it the single furrow plough that he had acquired only two days previously. Also from there they could see the six young bullocks in the grassed off part of the field.

Mr Tingle was genuinely impressed and said so. "My word, Mr Dale, you have made great progress. The place is a credit to you." He nudged the chairman's arm, "Don't you agree, Mr Molton?"

Without waiting for a reply he continued, "I wish all our tenants had your standards." He looked across at the neighbouring field and the sparse crop growing in it.

Still Mr. Molton made no comment. His mouth seemed to be firmly clamped shut, until they returned to the back yard and Stanley thought they were on their way out. It was at that moment that the chairman turned to Stanley and said with a smug look on his face. "You do realise that this is a smallholding?" Wondering what he was getting at Stanley nodded and said of course he did.

"Well in that case, what are you doing running a shop from here?" as the remark left his lips Stanley could quite happily have smacked him right between the eyes and he clenched his fist behind his back.

Doris had joined them at this point and her hot temper flared at his words but before either of them had chance to reply Mr. Wainright stepped forward, "Oh come now, Mr. Molton, the smallholders are permitted to sell their own produce. That has always been the case."

The chairman glared at him but knew he had to back down, and he gave a grim smile as grudgingly he muttered, "Very well, if my two colleagues are prepared to turn a blind eye to it I am sure I can do the same."

Both Stanley and Doris were relieved when the committee left to inspect the other smallholdings, and over a cup of tea they discussed their visit. They laughed as they recalled the obvious discomfort of the chairman as he was corrected by one of his own committee members, but Mr Molton was a dangerous enemy and would be a thorn in Stanley's side for years to come.

Later that day they had another visitor. Stanley heard the creak of the gate but assumed it was someone coming for something from their little farm shop. He carried on hoeing his vegetables, expertly slicing out the weeds with the sharp blade of his hoe and was deep in thought when he heard a familiar voice.

"Now then, Stanley, I see you've lost none of your expertise with a hoe."

Stanley looked up to see his former employer, Mr McLain striding towards him. Pushing his cap to the back of his head Stanley went to meet him holding out his hand and smiling a welcome.

As they shook hands Mr McLain looked around at the market garden patch and explained, "I had a bit of business in Doncaster and thought I would see how you were going on. It's not an inconvenient time is it?" as Stanley shook his head he continued, "Well you certainly look as if you're thriving, Stanley."

He walked to the fence and admired the pigs running free in the field and scratched the back of one of the sows. She shook her head and her ears flapped before she began to rub against a post.

"Are you going to show me round, Stanley? I'd like to see what you've done here."

"Aye, ah will with pleasure. Ah'm used to showing people around today," and he told him about the visit from the committee earlier that day and the comments from the chairman.

As they walked around he looked at everything, remarking on the young calves and the potatoes that were just beginning to show through the earth. He nodded his head in admiration. "You've done well here, Stanley. You've used every square foot of ground. What a grand job you've made of it."

Stanley flushed at his praise but said that he could not have done it alone, Doris had worked equally hard. As if she knew she was being talked about she appeared around the corner coming towards them. Recently, to keep her clothes clean, she had taken to wearing a flowery cotton apron with a cross over front. It was probably one of the most unflattering of garments she could wear, but even in that she managed to look alluring and Stanley felt so proud of her.

Her hair was brushed back behind her ears and held in place with a couple of hair grips. It was as dark and shiny as ever and her cheeks glowed with health. As she came to stand beside him she shook hands with Mr McLain and asked how his wife and family were.

"They're fine, Mrs Dale, and I can see how well you two have done. It's a real credit to you both. I can see you're happy here. So I don't think there's much chance of you wanting to come back to Clamton is there? I would love to have you back, Stanley, the place is not the same without you."

Stanley thanked him while Doris returned to the house to put the kettle on, and he went on to tell him that they both hoped to be able to move on to something bigger with more land in the future.

He left half an hour later repeating his offer. "Don't forget, Stanley, you have always got a job at Clamton if ever you need one. But I wish you both every success now and in the future. Keep in touch." And with that he was off, walking briskly to his car, and gave then a wave as he set off.

As they watched him drive away Stanley said with genuine feeling, "There goes a true gentleman, Dot. They don't make many men like him."

Thankfully they had not had any more visitors of the thieving variety but that did not mean that the area was free from crime.

At the end of the road there was a tiny shop. It had been run for many years by an old man called Mr. Mattershaw. In earlier days it had been run by both him and his wife and had been a thriving little general store, selling everything from bread to reels of cotton.

It was situated directly across the road from the housing estate and was quite an unusual spot for a shop as it was fairly isolated. After his wife died, Mr. Mattershaw had continued to run his shop and he had a loyal customer base, even when it was evident that the business was slowly fading away as he grew older.

It had got to the point where there was little stock on the shelves but still Mr. Mattershaw kept going and customers continued to buy from him just to help him keep the shop open.

Every week he went on the bus to the cash and carry in Doncaster and came back with two shopping bags full of goods that he carefully arranged on the shelves. Every tin and packet was placed precisely on the shelves with the labels facing forwards and a price ticket alongside. When he had arranged his goods each week he would stand back and look around with pride, then take himself off into his back room and settle down in front of his fire.

Customers often had to call twice and rap on the counter when they entered the shop to attract his attention. In addition to ageing he was also becoming increasingly deaf. When his callers eventually drew his attention he would appear from behind the curtain that covered the door and demand to know what they wanted.

If by some chance he had what they wanted he would hand it over almost reluctantly and inform them that that particular commodity was in short supply and they were lucky to get it. He would then proceed to charge them an extortionate fee. They seldom bought more than one item.

As the months went by he became frailer and his appearance deteriorated. He was a local character and treated with affection by almost everyone. But there were a few who claimed he was actually a very rich man and had thousands of pounds stashed away in his bedroom. It was mostly beer talk, but evidently it reached the ears of the wrong person.

One day someone called on Mr. Mattershaw and beat him up so badly that he died from his injuries. The community mourned him and many of the miners swore they would deal with the person responsible in their own way when he was found; and no doubt they would have done, but they never discovered who had beaten the life out of the old man.

CHAPTER 36

For some time Stanley had been had been waiting for an opportune time to suggest to Doris that they should get another car. He had been dropping hints, and trying to get the notion across to her for a couple of weeks before he finally brought the idea out into the open.

To his amazement she said straight away that she had been thinking the same. Taken aback that she should agree so readily he pressed on, "We should be able to get a decent one for a couple of hundred pounds,"

Before he could go on any further she shook her head, "No, I think we should get a new one. Then there won't be any problems with it. I've seen some advertised at £600 in the Doncaster Gazette."

She had taken Stanley completely by surprise. Now it was his turn to question if they could afford it. Without a word she got up and took their bank book out of the top drawer and opened it up in front of him.

He grinned, "Bloody hell, Dot, we're doing ok aren't we? We can buy a car and still have a good balance left."

Before twenty four hours had passed they were the owners of a new Ford Anglia car. A very basic model and the cheapest in the showroom but at least it was new and it was theirs. When it arrived the following week Doris wasted no time in attacking it with her tin of Mansion furniture polish.

Inside and out it received a good coating of wax until it shone like glass. When Stanley proudly showed it off to his brother Cyril, he ran his hand over the roof, and with a grin said Doris had done a grand job, and that flies would never settle on it as they would never get a foot hold.

Cyril had called unexpectedly on his motor bike and Stanley was always glad to see him. Although they led such different lives, they had always been close, and he was especially happy to see him today as it had given him a chance to show off his new car.

As they walked around the smallholding Cyril admired the stock and the produce growing in the market garden corner. Stanley had a feeling there was something that his brother wanted to say. It was not like him to be reticent, and he was about to ask him what was on his mind when Cyril said casually, "Ah see tha hasn't got a dog now, Stan? Ah was wondering if tha wanted Glen back?"

Glen was one of Meg's sons from a litter she had had early on in her life. He had gone to live with Cyril when he was just a pup.

He was now almost six years old and was very like his mother. He had the same long silky black fur and white ruff with touches of tri-colour on his face. He was a very handsome dog. At Cyril's words Stanley looked at him sharply and waited for him to continue.

"Well it's like this, Stan. We haven't really got the time to look after him. Ah never have chance to take him for a walk and he makes a hell of a mess in the garden. We're at it every day cleaning up dog muck. So ah wondered if you would like to have him back, seeing as you haven't got a dog now."

Stanley was actually quite willing to have the dog back and he knew that Doris would be too, but he had got his brother squirming and was not about to let him off the hook just yet.

"Oh," he said slowly, "What tha means is, tha's got fed up of cleaning up after him. Course he's going to make a mess in t'garden. Poor dog's got to shit somewhere hasn't he?"

Cyril coloured up at his elder brother's words until he saw his mouth begin to twitch.

"Is tha kidding Stan? You bugger you. Tha had me going then." Stanley couldn't keep a straight face any longer and burst out laughing.

"Aye, we'll have him back," he said, "We'll come on Sunday afternoon and collect him.

They set off just after one o'clock on Sunday afternoon dressed in their best clothes. It was their first real outing in the new car and Stanley felt incredibly proud as they drove out of the gates. He had always been very critical and disparaging of the modest little Ford Anglia cars, but since he had become an owner of one, he had unashamedly reversed his opinion and he was now full of praise for them.

"She quite nippy isn't she, Dot," he stated, "Although I have to admit, I could do with a bit more room for my legs."

Doris smiled happily and waved to a neighbour as they went along Doncaster Road. She ran her hands along the dashboard and made a mental note to apply a little more wax as soon as she had the time.

As if he had read her mind Stanley pointed out that she had again been polishing the dashboard when he had specifically asked her not to. He shook his head and gave up.

When they arrived at Wath, Stanley parked the car carefully at the side of the road alongside the stone gateway and path that led to Edith's home. As he got out of the car he stood still for a few moments gazing down the road. His memory flashed back to the days when he had worked at the farm just a few yards away, and he smiled at Doris who had just linked her arm in his. He knew that she was remembering too.

He squeezed her arm, and together they began to walk up the cinder covered path that led to the cottage where Edith lived with her brother William. Doris walked on tip-toes trying to avoid damaging the heels of her best court shoes and swore under her breath as she almost twisted her ankle.

They were nearly at the cottage when Edith appeared at the open door and it was plain to see the delight on her face as she saw them, but she stepped quickly out of the house, put her finger to her mouth, and pointed up at the bedroom window. Instantly Doris knew what she meant and nodded her understanding. She whispered to her husband that her uncle was in bed so they must talk quietly.

Edith led the way up the stone steps into the garden and they sat on the old wooden bench near the wall. Now that they were out of earshot Doris leaned over to kiss her mother and said, "Is misery guts in bed then?"

Edith pulled a face, "Aye, it's the best place for him. I'm hoping he's in a better humour when he wakes up. It's a lovely surprise to see you both. You look well, Doris," but then she looked at Stanley and tapped his knee, as she told him he had lost weight.

Stanley shrugged his shoulders said he was fine, and then added that they had something to show her. Doris interrupted and looked pointedly at her mother's flimsy slippers. "Change into your shoes, Mam, we've got to walk down the path to the road and those slippers are just about falling to bits."

Curious, Edith entered kitchen through the back door and changed into her gardening shoes before following them back down the path. As they reached the road Stanley stopped and looked at Edith expectantly, waiting for her to comment on the car. Edith stared up and down the road not sure what she was supposed to be looking at. Doris nudged her from behind.

"The car, Mam. That's what you're supposed to be looking at. The car. It's ours. What do you think to it?"

Edith stared at the car. "What? It's yours? But it's lovely Doris. Is it brand new? It's so shiny."

Stanley laughed out loud, "There's no wonder it's shiny, Mam, you know what Doris is like. There's nearly five full tins of furniture polish on it."

Edith pushed him, "There is not, Stanley Dale. Stop trying to kid me." She walked around the car, shaking her head in wonderment. Then she stopped, and a worried look crossed her face, "You haven't got into debt buying it have you? You wouldn't do that would you?"

Doris pulled herself up straight. "No, Mam," she said proudly, "It's all paid for." Stanley opened the passenger door, and as if he was a chauffeur, he indicated that she should get in.

"Oh, ah can't get in the car like this Stanley, I've got my old clothes on, and what's our Willie going to say if he wakes up and finds I've gone out and left the door open."

Stanley however, was not about to take no for an answer, and ushered her into the car, saying as he did so, "Let's not worry about that cantankerous old bugger. What he doesn't know won't hurt him; we're only going down Sandygate and back up New Road."

As they set off down the road, Edith sat up straight , looking left, then right, hoping that she was being observed riding in her daughter and son-in-law's new car, by as many neighbours as possible

She gave a sigh of content as Stanley drew the car to a halt after their little circular tour, and put her hand over Stanley's. There were tears in her eyes as she said she had always known he would be successful.

Unused to being paid compliments, Stanley's manner was a little brusque, but he did manage to say that it was thanks to her loaning them the money for their first pig, that they had been able to get a start, and he quickly leaned over and kissed her cheek.

Declining Edith's offer of tea, they said a quick goodbye and set off to pay a visit to Stanley's parents in Oak Road. In comparison to Edith's quiet house this one was full of noise and Stanley had to shout twice from the kitchen doorway, in order to make himself heard.

He turned and looked at Doris, "Nothing changes does it," he said with a smile. His mother Ada came into the kitchen and at the sight of Stanley and Doris came towards them, her arms outstretched. "Well, look who's here. Well ah don't know. What a surprise."

This was Ada's usual welcome to everyone in the family, followed by, "Ah'll get the kettle on." Stanley smiled at his mother and put his arm around her. "No, don't bother with the tea Mam, we only stopped in to say hello. We've got to go to our Cyril's and pick the dog up."

"But you must have time for a cup of tea, Stanley, and our Cyril's here." No sooner had she said the words than Cyril appeared in the doorway. His face was flushed, partly from the heat of the fire, and partly from the best Barnsley Bitter he had consumed during a dinnertime session with his father down at the Royal Oak.

"Hey up, our Stan. How is tha? Come and have a sit down for a bit. Then tha can give me a lift home so tha can pick our Glen up. Ah give him a good brushing last night and told him he was going back to live with you and Doris. Eeh come here and give us a kiss Doris, tha gets bonnier every time ah see thee."

Cyril was obviously in fine form and taking Stanley's arm pulled him into the living room. "Sit thee-self down, Stan. Come on, Doris, thee sit here next to me." As Stanley looked around he could see that every chair was occupied and two of his sisters sat on the hearth rug beside their father.

Only his mother's chair remained empty until she reappeared with the large brown teapot and poured two cups of tea out. Handing them over, she indicated the sugar bowl and the slices of fruit cake on the table.

While they helped themselves, Stanley's youngest sister, Laura, nudged Cyril, "Tell our Stan and Doris about your window cleaning job."

A beaming grin spread across Cyril's face, and he settled himself back in his seat. "Well, its' like this, Stan. Tha knows my mate who has window cleaning round?" Stanley nodded and waited.

"Well," began Cyril, "Ah decided to do a couple of days working for him to earn a bit of extra money. But he didn't tell me ah would be doing the upstairs windows did he? Tha knows ah'm not too keen on heights doesn't tha?" Again Stanley nodded.

"On t'first day wasn't so bad, and ah were getting used to it, but the second day it were blowing a gale. Ah nearly packed the job in, but ah thought to meself, 'He's depending on me helping him, so ah can't let a mate down.' The first house were one of them big places wi three stories. Ah got to t'top of ladder and bloody hell it was high up. Then just as ah started to wash the window a great gale blasted round me, and the ladder slipped to one side. Eeh, ah grasped hold of that t'windowsill and dug me nails into it. Ah'm not kidding thee, me fingers were like claws. Anyway, me mate saw what had happened and he ran, grabbed the ladder, and hung on to it." Cyril paused here for effect, then continued.

"He shouted up to me. Is tha all right, Cyril?" Here Cyril paused again, before he delivered the punch line. "Aye," ah said, "But don't stand underneath, cos ah'm shitting meself."

As the whole house erupted again into laughter, Cyril joined in, looking very pleased at the reaction. He loved to make people laugh.

Stanley wiped his eyes and exchanged glances with his mother who shook her head in mock exasperation at her youngest son. Slowly the level of noise and laughter subsided to a normal level and Stanley took the chance to remind Cyril that they had to go to Bolton to collect his dog.

Before they could start though, the new car had to be viewed and admired, and Stanley was becoming edgy. He was mentally calculating how long it would take them to complete the journey to Bolton and be on their way home again.

"Come on, Cyril. Get a move on will you? We've got animals to feed when we get home. We're not all bloody miners tha knows, with big wages and all weekend to do nothing but stand at t'bar supping beer."

Cyril took no offence at his remarks, he was in too good a mood to be rattled and simply said 'ok,' as he got into the back seat. With Stanley in an impatient mood, they were soon in Bolton and pulling to a halt in front of Cyril's home. They could see the dog beside his kennel at the bottom of the garden and he greeted them with a bout of loud barking.

"Come on, Glen," Doris called and the barking instantly stopped to be replaced by a low whine and a frantically wagging tail. Bending down Doris stroked his soft fur and spoke quietly to him as she unfastened the chain from his collar. "Now then, Glen," she murmured, as he rolled on the floor with his legs in the air. "Are you coming back with us?"

As if he grasped her meaning, he stood up and shook himself, then looked from one person to another, before he ran down the path and sat waiting beside the gate.

Cyril looked a little downcast at the dog's eagerness to leave him, but said he would be better off with them. He gave the dog one last stroke before he opened the car door.

With one bound Glen leapt straight onto the blanket on the back seat. He lay down with his head on his paws and gave Doris a doggy smile as she turned to look at him.

Once they were on their way home all Stanley's tension drained away and he smiled as he remarked to Doris that it felt good to be having the son of their old dog with them.

From the back seat Glen wagged his tail and gave a little woof of agreement.

CHAPTER 37

1960 was to be another time of great change for Stanley and Doris. They had had nearly seven good years at the smallholding. Years when they had grown immeasurably in experience, and they had prospered; but now it was time to move on. Ambition was driving them forward to reach for a real farm with more land.

Eileen was now married and living in Doncaster. Frances was nine years of age and attending the local school. The time was right. They began looking out for a suitable farm to apply for.

Within weeks, details came through of a farm in Rawcliffe, near Goole. The black and white photograph on the front of the application form showed a solid, square built house, and immediately Doris was drawn to it. As they read the details they discovered that there were sixty acres of land that went with the farm.

The land was spread around in separate fields on the outskirts of the village. Attached to the farmhouse was large yard surrounded by a barn, a granary and a fold yard. To the rear of the buildings there was a further extensive yard, backed by a large orchard.

They looked at each other and they needed no discussion to know that they were going to apply for it. Even before they had been to view the farm, Stanley had filled in the forms and posted them off to Wakefield.

At the weekend, full of excitement, they set off to view the farm. The most direct way to Rawcliffe would take them through Doncaster which was a notorious bottleneck so Stanley had worked out an alternative route that took them through the countryside.

As they passed by Askern, Stanley pointed out a field surrounded by a high hedge.

"See that field, Doris," he said, "Do you remember me telling you that me and my mate had walked some of Downing's cattle to Askern? It was before me and you were courting. Teddy Downing had us walk four bullocks from Wath to Askern."

He glanced at her and she looked at the hedge and nodded. "Well," he continued, "That was the field we took them to." Stanley reflected that it seemed like a lifetime ago but he had never forgotten that marathon journey with the cattle.

As they drew near to Rawcliffe they could see the pointed spire of the church standing tall above the village. Doris gripped the edge of her seat waiting for the farmhouse to come into view, and there it was, on the first corner as they entered the village. It stood back behind a hawthorne hedge and a sizeable garden and was exactly as she had expected it to be. Stanley pulled the car into the wide drive and sat for a minute or two looking at it.

"Well come on, Doris," he said, "Let's go and see if we can have a look round." As if he had been overheard a man appeared at the gate. He walked towards them and took off his cap.

"Morning," he said as he smiled at them, "Are you prospective new tenants?" He shook hands with both of them and informed them that his name was Bill Lawson. "You can come and have a look round the buildings if you like. We had a couple here yesterday, but I don't think they were really interested. He said there was not enough land for him. If that were the case I can't think why he bothered to look when he knew how much land there was from the papers."

Stanley nodded in agreement. "Well, I'll be glad of sixty acres," he said, "We've only got ten at the place we have now. There's a good range of buildings." He entered the barn through the double doors and looked around. It was a substantial building, built of a mixture of brick and stone with a concrete floor. At the left hand side a set of wooden stairs led up into a granary.

Then they looked at the fold yard and the separate buildings within it that had evidently once been used as stables. In his mind's eye Stanley could see them converted to accommodate his sows.

Doris was right beside him and he turned and raised his eyebrows in a questioning manner. She smiled and nodded and Stanley knew that she was as excited about the place as he was.

The farm yard was much bigger than they had expected. There were a couple of tractors and some machinery lined up neatly along one side. Stanley admired the almost new Massey Ferguson tractor and complemented Bill Lawson on it. As they walked to the top of the yard they came to the orchard.

It was an orchard in name only. There may at one time have been many fruit trees, but now there were just a couple of bent and twisted apple trees. The orchard covered well over an acre and extended right up to the back of the village school playground. It was enclosed on all sides and Stanley remarked to Doris that it would be an ideal place for the pigs to run free range.

After that there was the land to see, and Bill gave them directions where to find the various fields. "I'd come and show you but I have an appointment to keep, and the wife is out at the minute or she would have shown you round the house." Doris's disappointment must have shown on her face and he quickly said, "Come on, ah can show you the kitchen but then ah must go or I'll be late."

He led the way to the house and opened the back door to show off the big square kitchen. It had a large table in the centre, and a deep white sink under the window that overlooked the farmyard. There were no built-in cupboards, but there were several open shelves for crockery in an alcove beside the range. In addition there was a pantry just off the kitchen. Doris thought it was perfect and was already planning where she would hang her collection of horse brasses.

A fire glowed in the range even though it was warm outside, and Bill explained that they kept it lit for the hot water. Doris nodded in understanding. "Yes," she said, "We have to keep a fire going all day in our house for cooking and hot water. It's a nice big kitchen. Your wife keeps it lovely."

"Oh aye, she's very house proud is my missus," agreed Bill, but Stanley could see that he seemed tense and guessed he was worried about being late for his appointment. They left quickly not wanting to inconvenience him any longer.

As he waved them off he wished them luck and hurried away. Stanley and Doris got back in the car and set off to look at the land. As they drove slowly through the village they counted the shops. As far as food was concerned they would be well catered for with two butchers, four grocery shops, a post office, a chemists shop, a couple of fish and chip shops and a bank. They were all spread out fairly evenly around the village.

They admired the picturesque village green with the church almost in the centre of it and the set of stocks still preserved from a bygone age. The River Aire meandered its way along the outskirts of the village and best of all as far as Stanley was concerned there was not a coal mine anywhere in the area.

After inspecting the land, they set off home. Stanley tried to control his excitement, and did his best to get Doris to do the same. "Don't build your hopes up, Doris." he said. "If you bloody know who is still chairman of the committee we might as well forget it, cause we won't stand a chance."

A worried frown wrinkled Doris's forehead. She knew he was right. For some reason the present chairman of the committee seemed to have taken a dislike to them both, and to Stanley in particular.

Despite Stanley's words of caution it was difficult not to imagine themselves living on the farm at Rawliffe, and planning what they would do with it. On Monday Stanley set off for work as usual and slipped back into the routine of driving the dustbin lorry from one stopping place to the next. As useful as the steady job had been in helping their finances it was not something he wanted to do indefinitely, and he allowed himself to plan a little.

He would need another tractor if they got the farm, and also a trailer to take the pigs to market. Oh, and they would need to buy a boar pig to service their sows, and they would need a bigger plough and several more farm implements. The list was growing longer and the cost higher but it wouldn't matter, if they got the farm they would manage it somehow.

At the end of the shift he cycled home and he felt despondent. What was he planning for? They would never get it. Then he saw Doris standing at the gate waiting for him. She had an envelope in her hand. As he came to a halt she rushed towards him. "Hey Stan, We're on the short list. The letter came this morning. We're in with a chance."

The interviews were to be held at Wakefield in two weeks' time. Stanley thought he had never known a fortnight to pass so slowly, but eventually the day came around and they set off.

The previous day Doris had polished the car inside and out. Nothing had escaped her tin of furniture polish. The dashboard had received special treatment and was now so shiny that the sun reflected on it.

Stanley was in a tense mood and not happy to have to drive with the sun bouncing off the dashboard and dazzling him.

"What the hell have you done, Doris? You're going to have to go easy on the polish you know. This is ridiculous. Whatever did you polish the dashboard for?"

"Well it's leather," she replied. "The polish will preserve it."

There was a loud exhale of breath from Stanley, "It is not bloody leather, Doris. It's plastic."

"Well it looks like leather."

"Course it looks like leather. It's imitation leather. Ah'm telling you, Doris, its plastic. Don't polish it again. Ah can hardly see where I'm going for the sun reflecting on it."

Doris's face took on a mutinous look and her expression said she would do what she liked. Stanley glanced across at her and gave a 'tch' sound in exasperation.

The journey continued in a simmering silence until they had almost reached Wakefield. Thankfully the clouds had slid over the sun and some of the tension had left him.

"Nearly there, Dot," he said tentatively and gave a sigh. "Ah hope someone up there's watching out for us. We could do with a bit of luck today."

By the time they reached the County Hall, harmony reigned again, and Doris checked that her hair was in place, peering into the little vanity mirror on the back of the sun visor. She nudged Stanley and asked if she looked all right.

"Aye,"he replied, "Tha looks like a fifty bob horse, love. Come on. See if you can charm the committee, Doris, especially that swine of a chairman."

Doris laughed, "I don't think I'll be able to do that, Stan."

Stanley took her hand as they began to walk up the stone steps, "What do you mean, Dot?"

She gave him a knowing look and said quietly, "I don't think he likes women much."

They had reached the top of the steps and their conversation came to a halt as they entered the hall through the magnificent doorway, but Stanley was to recall her remark many years later.

After attending so many interviews they were now familiar with the layout of the County Hall and made their way straight to the waiting room. As always they were the first there, and they sat on the hard wooded benches in the big room. Their voices echoed in the empty room and they spoke in whispers.

Stanley gazed around the room and stared at the elaborate coving and the carving of roses around the light fittings. He didn't have to say anything. Doris had a very accurate idea of what he was thinking, and she was right. The thoughts going round in his head went along the lines of, 'Aye, that's where all the rates money goes.' But he refrained from putting his thoughts into words there and then. Instead he said very quietly in Doris's ear. "Have you kept count of how many times we've sat in this room, Dot? Ah hope it's the last time. Fingers crossed eh?"

Five other couples gradually filtered into the room over the next few minutes, each giving slight nods and furtive glances at the people already assembled there. One thing that they all had in common was their nervousness.

The man seated next to Doris took out a packet of cigarettes, and after handing one to his wife he flicked open his lighter and applied the flame to the end of it. Taking a deep drag at it he gave an almost audible sigh of relief as the nicotine hit his lungs.

His relief however, was to be short lived as Doris drew his attention to the large NO SMokING sign hanging on the wall.

He gave Doris a bitter glance as he stubbed out his cigarette , and his wife glared at her but Doris was not a woman to be intimidated and said curtly. "If you want to smoke go outside."

Stanley squeezed her arm and she looked at him and shrugged her shoulders. Her whole attitude said that she didn't care if they liked it or not, and Stanley smiled to himself.

Promptly at ten o'clock the interviews began. Applicants were called in alphabetical order. Stanley and Doris were the third to be called. As they walked in through the double doors Stanley took a deep breath, and reminded himself to be extra polite to the chairman in an effort to get on the right side of him.

As he closed the doors behind him he looked towards the long desk where the committee members sat. There were four members present, and immediately, he recognised Mr. Tingle and Mr Wainright but he had never seen the other two men before, and he could see no sign of Mr. Molton, the chairman.

Mr Tingle was the first to speak. "Good morning Mr and Mrs Dale, very nice to see you both again. You know Mr Wainright of course. This is Mr. Goode, and Mr Smith, they are new members of the committee." He paused as he indicated them, and then said as he looked directly at Stanley,

"You will note that Mr Molton is not here today. I'm afraid he has a bad bout of influenza. So we will have to conduct the interviews without him."

Stanley managed to keep a straight face as he said, "Ah hope he is soon better."

The committee got straight to the point, and began by questioning them about their financial position. Papers were shuffled on the desk, and Mr Tingle looked up and smiled at Stanley and Doris. "I can see you have improved your finances considerably since you were last here, Mr and Mrs Dale."

He leaned forward and addressed the new members, "The committee visited the smallholdings on Doncaster Road a few weeks ago and we were all impressed with the progress made by Mr and Mrs Dale. It is an example to the rest of the holdings, don't you agree Mr Wainright?"

"Yes indeed. The smallholding has been greatly improved." He looked back at his colleague and a few whispers were exchanged.

"Thank you, Mr and Mrs Dale," he said, "That is all we need to know for now. Would you wait outside until all the interviews are concluded? We won't keep you long."

Back in the waiting room Stanley and Doris sat stiffly on the hard seats until all the interviews were over. They kept exchanging glances, but felt unable to speak when their voices echoed so loudly in the large room.

When the last applicant came out and sat down, Mr. Tingle followed them. Raising his voice he said, "Thank you, everyone. You will be informed on the results of your interviews in due course. We have all the information we need now. Have a safe journey home."

Stanley and Doris got up and were about to follow the rest of the candidates when Mr Tingle approached them. Very quietly he asked them to return to the interview room. Exchanging looks they followed him.

This time the atmosphere was much more relaxed, and suddenly Stanley had a good feeling wash over him as they sat and waited expectantly.

"In the absence of our chairman," said Mr Tingle slowly, "We are adopting a slightly different method of informing our candidates of the results of the interviews. I am pleased to tell you that we are offering you the tenancy of Pleasant View Farm in Rawcliffe."

Stanley and Doris looked at each other, then back at the committee, they were both lost for words, but their smiles said all that needed to be said. Stanley suddenly found his voice and thanked them.

Speaking for the committee Mr Tingle said, "You will receive confirmation and legal documents in the post next week, Mr Dale. Congratulations to you both."

As they drove home they began to make plans. Stanley's head was buzzing with things to be done and arrangements to be made. It took two days for the realisation to really sink in, and even then they half expected to be told that it was a mistake.

It wasn't until the paperwork arrived in the middle of the week that they actually believed they had succeeded in winning the tenancy.

They would be taking over the farm at Rawcliffe in early autumn, so they had a few weeks to make all the preparations. One of Stanley's first requirements for the farm would be a larger tractor and as luck would have it there was a farm sale being held at Carcroft the following Saturday. It was advertised in the Doncaster Gazette, and Stanley scanned down the page looking at all the machinery that was to be sold.

"They've got a Fordson Major for sale, Doris," he called as she disappeared upstairs. Her muffled voice came from the bathroom, "We'll go and look at it shall we?"

Stanley had already marked it in his diary when he realised that she had said, "We will go and look at it."

As she came back into the room he asked, "Did you say you were going to go to the sale with me?" Doris retorted that of course she would, and carried on clearing the table. Stanley thought about it for a minute.

"But Doris, you always said looking at machinery was boring. Ah thought you would rather take our Frances to Doncaster." What he really meant was that if he was looking at machinery he would prefer to go alone.

"Ah was going to go on my bike, Dot, then if I buy the tractor I can put my bike on the back of it and drive home. It'd save going back to collect it later." Doris thought about it, then decided to go to Doncaster, but told Stanley not to go spending a ridiculous amount of money on the tractor.

Stanley glared at her over the newspaper but bit his tongue, there was no point in entering into an argument. Getting up, he stretched and picked up his cap, "Right, love. Ah'm going to get the pigs mucked out and some potatoes dug up for tomorrow. See you later."

He walked down the yard and thought about the sale. He was looking forward to it. He had often attended farm sales but had never been in a position to buy a tractor from one before.

On Saturday morning he was up even earlier than usual. The sale began at ten o'clock and he was determined to be there well before it started so that he could inspect the tractor. He ate his breakfast quickly and went out to feed the pigs.

Each of the stables had been divided by wooden hurdles to make two separate enclosures. At the moment there was one sow in each of them. They were still asleep and lifted their heads and looked at him as he opened the outer door. They clambered to their feet almost reluctantly and their whole manner said, 'What on earth is he getting us up at this time for?' but they gamely scrambled to their feet, and lumbered their way across to their troughs, their bodies heavy with unborn piglets.

They slopped and slurped at the food Stanley had poured out for them and he watched them for a few minutes and reflected, as he often did, that pigs were quite similar to people in some ways.

Here he had two sows, both the same age and same breed, but they were as different in nature as it was possible to be. One of them was clean in her habits, keeping an area in her pen to use as a toilet, and her bedding was kept in the opposite corner. Her trough never needed cleaning out, and she was gentle and amiable.

The other one soiled her pen wherever she happened to be when the urge took her. Even her trough was full of excrement every morning, and had to be cleaned out before her food could be put in it. She was unpredictable, and more than once she had come at Stanley with her mouth open ready to bite. He regularly called her uncomplimentary names but it made no difference of course.

He scratched the back of their ears and patted their backs, "There you go girls, early breakfast today. That's your lot until tea time." From there he went to the chickens, checked that their feeders were full, and topped up the water trough. Doris would collect the eggs later.

By eight thirty he was wheeling his bicycle out of the gate. He had the cheque book in his jacket pocket along with a pen and a few of his favourite Mintoe sweets He took one out of its wrapper and popped it in his mouth, welcoming its sweet, minty warmth on his tongue.

It was a fine morning and Stanley was in good spirits as he

cycled down Doncaster Road, through Adwick Le Street, and over the railway bridge. The sale was being held at a farm a little off the beaten track. As he rode along the rough track dodging the worst of the pot holes he could see the machinery all lined up in the field ready for the sale, and straight away spotted the blue Fordson Major tractor.

He parked his bike in one of the cart sheds and removed his cycle clips. As he slipped them into his pocket a familiar voice called his name. He turned and groaned as he saw Eric, who used to work at Smith's farm several years ago.

At the time, Stanley and Doris had nicknamed him Harry Basskin, (who was actually an unsavoury character in a book they had read) and they often joked about his dirty, unwashed appearance and filthy clothes. He was now scruffier and dirtier than ever. Stanley had never made any secret of the fact that he disliked him, but it made no difference. Eric never had taken the hint, and now he almost broke out into a run in order to catch up with him.

"Hey up, Stan. Ah've not seen you for a long time." He was panting as he came close, and Stanley backed away trying to avoid inhaling his stale breath and the rank smell coming from his unwashed body.

"Oh aye, and ah see that tha's just as much a stranger to soap and water as ever. Good God man tha stinks. Stand back a bit will tha?"

Eric laughed and said, "Ah couldn't get bathed last week, there were no hot water tha sees. Anyway what you doing here? I heard you've got one of them smallholdings on Doncaster Road. Tha's a lucky devil. Ah was thinking of applying for one, Will tha put a good word in for me, Stan?"

"Tha must be bloody joking," Stanley was doing his best to insult Eric in an effort to get rid of him, but he just could not shake him off. As he turned and walked away Eric was just two steps behind, following him. In the end there was nothing else for it.

Stanley turned, his eyes were fierce. "Now look. Ah don't want thee following me. Go take thee stink and torment somebody else. Ah'll not tell thee again. Bugger off."

"Oh all right, Stan. Ah'll see thee later," and with a wave Eric went off in the opposite direction. Stanley almost smiled to himself as he thought, 'Well I can't insult him no matter how hard I try.'

He had been so distracted by Eric that he had not really been taking notice of the implements for sale, but now he came up to the tractor, and stood for a moment casting a critical eye over it. He walked round it and ran his hand along the mudguard.

The old Fordson Major had obviously seen many hours of work and small patches of rust dotted the engine casing, but judging from the fresh mud clinging to its wheels it was still in good working order. He climbed aboard and sat on the iron seat. It felt very familiar. He pushed in the clutch and tried the gears. They worked smoothly and the tyres seemed to be in a reasonable state. He examined the engine and moved the throttle. He really couldn't fault it, but he needed to see it working before he would be prepared to bid on it.

"Aye tha can start it up, son." Stanley looked in the direction of the voice and nodded to the man who had just approached him. "I'm the owner." he said, "Go on, start it up. Are you interested in bidding for it? It's done some mileage but it's got plenty of work left in it yet. You'll not go far wrong with this old girl." He patted the tractor as if it was a horse and added. "It's a good tractor. You have my word on it." With that he turned and walked away.

Stanley's mind was made up, and it was just as well as the auction was starting. The tractor was lot twenty nine and the auctioneer was working at quite a speed. Stanley joined the crowd and watched, noting the prices the machinery made.

Right next to the tractor was a long flatbed trailer, lot twenty eight. An idea came into his head. He could do with the trailer. It would be invaluable for moving equipment to Rawliffe. Should he bid on it? But if his was the winning bid and then he didn't manage to get the tractor it would create problems. Of course, he reasoned, he could always come back and collect it with the little Fergy the next day.

The auctioneer was now starting the bidding on a set of harrows, lot twenty five. Without having time to think about it Stanley put in a bid. He swallowed hard as the harrows were knocked down to him for four pounds. He forced himself to stay calm, and took a deep breath, and told himself not to let auction fever get a hold of him.

He was used to bidding for livestock at the market but this seemed different somehow. He had to hold his nerve, his palms were sweating and he wiped them down his trousers. It didn't do to let other bidders know how nervous he was, nor did it do to let them know what he was interested in buying.

Now the auctioneer stopped at the trailer and wasted no time in starting the bidding. Stanley kept quiet, waiting to see how high it would go. At twenty pounds it stopped and just as the hammer was going to go down Stanley called twenty one and the trailer was his.

The tractor was next and the bidding was slow to begin with. The auctioneer cajoled and teased his audience. "Come on now, gentlemen, don't play coy with me. You know this is a grand piece of machinery. Let's have your bids. All right then, we'll play silly games. Let's start at a silly price. Twenty five pounds. Who'll bid twenty five pounds just to get us started?"

A hand went up and they were off. As before, Stanley stayed quiet and waited. He was prepared to go to one hundred. Any more than that and Doris would be bending his ear for a week or more.

The bidding built up to seventy then faded out. As the auctioneer held up his hammer Stanley offered seventy two. The previous bidder shook his head and turned away.

He could hardly believe his luck. A tractor, trailer and set of harrows for less than one hundred pounds! He made his way to the make-shift office that had been set up in one of the stables and wrote out a cheque for the required amount. With the receipt in his pocket he went to collect his bargains.

First of all he loaded the heavy harrows on to the back of the trailer, and then checked the fuel in the tractor. There was more than enough to get him home, and he started the engine before he climbed up and seated himself on the cold, iron seat, thinking as he did so that one of his first jobs would be to make a straw filled cushion for it.

With the ease that came from years of working with a tractor,

Stanley reversed to the trailer and hooked it up. He loaded his bike on to it and set off down the narrow cart track that led to the road. Reaching the gateway he noted how narrow it was as he lined up the tractor and long trailer. He negotiated his way through it, cringing when one of the wheels dropped down into a large pot hole and tipped the trailer to one side, almost scraping the post that marked the gate way.

As he pulled out on to the road and straightened up he noticed he had an audience. A group of elderly men standing back out of the way gave him a little cheer and doffed their well-worn flat caps. Stanley smiled at them, recognising that they were retired farm workers, every one of them. He saluted them with respect, feeling a connection with them.

Sitting aloft on the tall tractor Stanley saw the cyclist a long way in front of him. There was no mistaking who it was. No one else he knew rode with his heels on the pedals and his knees splayed. It was Eric. He was battling in a head wind and at the speed he was going it would be a long time until he reached home.

As he pulled alongside Stanley leaned forward and caught the expression of pure misery on Eric's face. In that moment Stanley felt sorry for him and realised that he was getting on in years. He slowed down and waved to Eric to stop. He couldn't leave him to struggle on in the head wind.

"Does tha want a lift, Eric?" he called to him. Eric's face lit up and he nodded, almost too out of breath to speak.

"Put your bike on the trailer, ah'm going past your house." Stanley waited while he dismounted and lifted the bike up on to the trailer. Then he came round to the back of the tractor. "What are you doing?" asked Stanley.

Eric wiped his nose on his sleeve, "Ah'm going to ride at the side of you on the tractor, Stan, just a minute while ah climb up."

Stanley held up his hand, "Woah," he said, "Ah can't do with you up here with me. You stink too much. Get on the trailer."

With a grin, Eric did as he was bid, and seated himself on the side of the trailer with his legs dangling over the side. Stanley shook his head, 'Bloody hell,' he thought, 'He'd be sitting on my knee given half a chance.'

He knew well enough where Eric lived. He lodged with his sister. Everyone recognised that it was the dirtiest house in the whole street. As he drew to a halt outside the house, a swarm of snotty-nosed children appeared from inside, every one of them filthy. The door to the house seemed to be permanently wide open. Stanley took a glance inside and shivered as he saw the wallpaper hanging in strips from the walls, the blackened remains of curtains at the windows and the suspicious brown filth on the floor.

He remembered Eric's statement that there had not been any hot water for a bath last week, and decided that there had probably never, ever, been any hot water to wash in. Stanley had been brought up in the poorest of households himself, but his mother had kept her home and family clean no matter how hard up they were.

He could hardly believe the squalor he was looking at, and Stanley began to feel sympathy for Eric. He got off the tractor and lifted the bike down for him. "There tha is, old lad." he said. "Thee look after thisen."

As he got back onto the tractor, he looked again and saw several of the younger children standing with thumbs in mouths staring back at him, while some of the older ones were heading towards him intent on climbing onto the back of the trailer.

He shouted at them while he revved the engine and set off as fast as safety would allow, just managing to outpace the oldest child, who stood in the middle of the road loudly mouthing foul obscenities at him.

Stanley smiled with relief as he left them behind and couldn't help picturing Doris's face if he had arrived home with a few of Eric's nephews on the trailer.

As it happened Doris was at that moment sweeping the pavement in front of the house. Her rigorous housekeeping extended as far as the road, and as she finished sweeping she heard the sound of a tractor approaching. She stood on the edge of the pavement, with the brush in her hand, and peered down the road. As Stanley came into view she began to smile and wave.

He pulled into the yard, a triumphant look on his face, and jumping down from his uncomfortable seat he put his arm around her shoulders. "What do you think then, Dot? How much do you think ah've paid for this lot?" She looked at him trying to sum up what figure to say. "Go on, guess." he insisted.

"Oh ah don't know, Stan. I hope it wasn't more than we agreed. I hope you didn't get carried away with the auction."

He sighed as he said, "How does £98 sound? Plus auction fees of course. Come on, get up and sit on it. Let's see if ah can teach you to drive it."

She laughed, but declined, saying that his tea was on the table and maybe she would have a go on the tractor later. As they ate their tea, Stanley told her about Eric and the state of the house where he lived.

"Well why doesn't he leave and find lodgings somewhere else? He's working."

Stanley folded a piece of bread around a chunk of ham and dipped it in the juice on his plate. Just before he popped it in his mouth he said, "Ah reckon his sister and that fat husband of hers take all his wages every week. Her husband's never worked for years. He reckons he's got a bad back. It doesn't seem to hinder him in the bedroom though. Eric's sister keeps churning another baby out regular as clockwork every year."

"Still, you'd think Eric would get out of there if he is as miserable as you said. "

"But Doris, where would he go? Who would take him in looking as he does? Would you have him in the house? Ah tell you, for the first time I actually felt sorry for him today. If only he was able to get a wash now and then he'd be a lot more popular." He shook his head and drank the rest of his tea

"That was tasty, Dot. Ah'll just go and have a look at the pigs, then we'll call it a day shall we? Are you coming with me? You haven't had a good look at the new tractor and trailer yet." He picked up his cap and pulled it on his head as he went outside to admire his new acquisitions.

CHAPTER 38

Moving day was coming closer and there was so much to do, but he intended staying on at his job driving the dustbin lorry until the week before they were due to move in order to keep the wages coming in, so everything had to be done in the evenings and weekends.

The young bullocks that Stanley had been growing on were sent into market a little earlier than he had planned, but they made a good price and he decided he would buy more young calves in at a later date, once they had got settled in at the farm.

The first task was to move all the farming equipment that they had acquired over the years. It was impossible to move everything on the same date so they gradually began taking a load at a time and storing it in the orchard.

They planned on taking their three best breeding sows and all the chickens with them, but they would not be going until the very last minute. The first of October was their date for taking over the farm and they would give up the tenancy of the smallholding on the same day. The new tractor and trailer were proving invaluable at transporting loads but even so it was slow work moving one load at a time. Doris came up with an idea to speed things up a little.

"Why don't I take a load at the same time? I could drive the little tractor and trailer. All I have to do is follow you." Stanley pondered on her suggestion for a minute two. Doris had a provisional licence which meant she could drive a tractor on the road so long as she had L plates on.

He had got her the licence a few months previously with the idea that he would teach her to drive the car, but the lessons had not gone well. Lesson five ended with an argument that would have rivalled gang warfare. It erupted when he lost his patience and declared that Doris was incapable of learning to drive. He had added that he was doing the general public a favour by not teaching her as she was a danger to herself and anyone who happened to be on the road.

Doris refused to speak to him for a full day but gradually peace was restored and she forgot about driving. Until now!

He could see the advantages of them taking two loads at once and also the potential problems, but Doris was insistent and so he gave in. "But don't forget, Dot, to follow me closely and watch my signals. We'll go through Askern, Sykehouse and Fishlake and come out at Cowick, that way we will avoid the heavy traffic. It'll take us longer but it will be safer."

He looked at her and had his doubts. "Are you sure about this, Dot? If we get split up are you going to be able to cope?"

Doris was full of confidence and had never lacked courage. "Of course I can do it. I can drive the tractor easily. Ah don't have to bother about all that gear changing like I had to do with the car. We'll set off early tomorrow morning. Let's get the trailer loaded up now."

Before they set off the next morning Stanley gave her long instructions, particularly stressing that she must follow him closely, but not so close that she would run into the back of him. Doris was full of the pioneer spirit and impatient to be on their way. "Oh shut up, Stanley, you've already told me that. Let's go now." Dressed in the Macintosh that she wore to feed the pigs in and a pair of Stanley's old trousers, she climbed on to the little Fergie and started the engine.

Stanley was not a religious man, but he looked up at the sky and sent out a prayer just in case someone was listening. As he set off he glanced back at his wife and waved to her encouragingly. She waved back and let the clutch out too fast and stalled the tractor. To himself Stanley uttered, 'How the hell did she manage to do that? It's practically impossible to stall it.' But he stopped at the gate and waited patiently while she got herself organised again.

At last they were on the road and making steady progress. Stanley began to relax. He had to admire Doris for tackling this when she knew that driving was not one of her skills. They went through Adwick, over the railway bridge and past the cinema. They had to turn right at Carcroft and Stanley viewed the cross roads with some trepidation. He slowed down and put out his arm to signal that he was turning right, then glanced back to check that Doris was following.

She was close behind him with her arm out signalling her intention to turn, and kept it out all the way around the corner, somehow managing to negotiate the turn with one hand. The moment they were on the straight she put her arm down again and gave him a big triumphant smile as he looked back at her.

He signalled to her to stop when he reached a wider part of the road, and explained that she didn't need to keep her arm out all the way round the corner. "Well I know that, Stanley," she said patiently. "But I was just making sure that the cars behind knew what I was doing. There was one right behind me and I was sure he was going to overtake me."

Stanley took a deep breath and said, "Ah well in that case you did right, Doris, but in future, just signal what you intend to do, then keep both hands free to turn the steering wheel"

Doris admitted it was a bit difficult trying to turn the corner with one hand and his way was probably better, then she kissed him quickly on the lips before he went back to his own tractor.

The rest of the journey continued without incident and they arrived at the farm in Rawcliffe just before it began to rain. They stood inside the barn and sheltered for a while enjoying the sensation of being in what would be their barn. There was no one at home today and it appeared that Bill Lawson and his wife (the outgoing tenants) were busy moving into their new farm at the other end of the village.

It was the first time that Stanley and Doris had been at the farm on their own, and they wandered around holding hands, taking in what would be theirs in just a couple of weeks. Stanley rarely showed his emotions, but today he felt overcome at the realisation of what they had achieved since they left Wath upon Dearne.

In the privacy of one of the stables he looked at his wife and thought how much he loved her. He wrapped his arms around her, kissed her slowly and told her in a voice full of emotion that he could never have done it without her at his side.

Then he announced that that was enough of sentimentality and normal service was going to be resumed right now. Doris gave him a playful punch before she asked him how she had done with driving the tractor. He replied that she had done great but not to let it go to her head, and they began unpacking the trailers.

As they stacked all the tools, feeding troughs, and assorted paraphernalia into a heap in the orchard Doris paused and said. "You know, Stanley, I really think I'm getting the hang of driving now. It's not very difficult. I've got confidence now. I think I'll have another go with the car.

Stanley froze for a moment, remembering what a fiasco the driving lessons had been. Biting his lip, he said, "Ok, Dot, but we'll leave it until after we've moved shall we?"

Back at the smallholding, they loaded the two trailers with all the rest of their outdoor belongings, in preparation for their last trip on the following day. After that there would be just the animals to move and the household goods. They loaded the wooden chicken shed on to the biggest trailer with some help from their neighbour and went to bed that night congratulating themselves that everything was going according to plan.

Evidently, they were tempting providence in thinking that things were going smoothly. As Stanley was shaving the next morning he glanced through the open window. He could just see the Fordson tractor and immediately he felt there was something wrong with it. He opened the window as wide as it would go and leaned out.

"Oh bloody hell," he said, and then called out louder, "Doris, the tractor's got a puncture."

Doris was by his side in a minute, still wearing one of her husband's old shirts that she slept in. She pushed to the front of him and peered out of the window. "How can you tell from here, Stan. It looks ok to me."

"Well it's not. Can't you see how the tractor is lower down at one side. This would happen today just when ah thought we'd got nearly all the outdoor stuff shifted. Of all the luck. Damn and blast it."

He was right. The tractor did have a puncture and on closer examination he could see that the tyre showed signs of being perished. He leaned against the wheel and gave it some thought. There was no way round it; he was going to have to buy a new tyre and inner tube.

Returning to the house for breakfast he explained the situation to Doris. "We're just going to have to abandon the trip to Rawcliffe today," he said. Doris made a sympathetic sound then replied, "Well there's nothing to stop me taking the little tractor and trailer is there?"

"What, you mean, go on your own? Oh ah don't think that's a good idea, Doris." He laughed, and of course that was like a red rag to a bull as far as Doris was concerned.

"Oh don't you think I'm capable then? Of course ah can do it and what's more I'm going to." Stanley closed his eyes and blew out his breath while mentally kicking himself. He really should have phrased that more tactfully and certainly should have known better than to laugh.

He tried again, "But Doris, you'll have to unload it on your own at the other end, and how are you going to reverse the trailer out of the orchard? You know you're not very good at reversing."

Of course Doris had an answer. "Well, I'll just drive round in a big circle then I won't have to reverse. My mind is made up, Stan. Don't try to stop me."

He sighed, "I wouldn't dream of trying to stop you, Dot. Ah'd have more chance of stopping a steam train with one hand. Do it if you must then, but remember, if it all goes wrong, it was your idea."

Doris was still fairly bristling with indignation as she went upstairs to change into the old pair of trousers that she had worn yesterday. Very quickly though, doubts were setting in, and even as she walked back down the stairs she began to worry about the trip.

However, Doris was not a woman to give in and there was no

way now that she would back down and admit that Stanley had been right.

Tying a scarf round her head she went outside. The Fergie stood waiting, already filled with fuel and facing in the right direction. She climbed up and sat astride the sturdy little tractor and started the engine. Stanley appeared at her side and eased the throttle so that the engine ran slower. "Now are you sure you want to do this, Doris?" he asked, and took her hand. "We can leave it till later in the week and go together when I've got the puncture mended. I could get a day off work. We could go on Tuesday."

Doris considered it for only a moment before she swallowed and replied yes, she really wanted to do it. Stanley nodded, "Ok then. You remember the way don't you? If you're not sure, stop and ask someone for directions."

With a lot more confidence than she actually felt Doris revved the engine and put it into gear, "I'll get off then, love. There's some bread and potted meat in the cupboard, our Frances has gone to play at John's, but she'll be back for dinner."

Stanley stepped back as she put the tractor into gear and set off. He watched her as she disappeared out of sight; he had to admit his wife had some nerve. She had no way of contacting him if anything went wrong, but Stanley didn't doubt that Doris would cope. Nevertheless he knew he would spend the rest of the day worrying about her.

With the tractor in top gear and the throttle full out Doris sat up straight and gave the driving all her concentration. She was determined to get this right. As she turned every corner she visualised the route ahead that she had to take. She had travelled to Rawcliffe this way three times before, but her sense of direction was not good. Gradually though, as she recognised several landmarks her confidence grew, and she gave a little triumphant cheer when she reached the iron bridge that led on to the main road.

Licking her finger she made a sign of marking a point in thin air and congratulated herself. From there the rest of the journey was easy, and Rawcliffe church soon came into view. She remembered to signal when she turned into the gateway of the farm and drove slowly up the yard and into the orchard.

The contents of the previous loads were stacked neatly and

covered with a tarpaulin sheet. She drew up as close to it as she dared and debated if she should switch off the engine, but then worried about what she would do if it refused to start again and so left it running but slowed the engine until it was just ticking over.

It was not until she climbed off the tractor and found that her legs almost buckled under her that she realised how cold and stiff they had become. She stamped her feet and rubbed her hands together as she thought of Stanley and all the other tractor drivers enduring hour after hour working in the fields, ploughing in the coldest of weathers.

After taking off her headscarf and coat, she dragged the tarpaulin sheet to one side and began to unload the trailer. Over the sound of the engine she heard the church clock begin to strike and counted the chimes. It was twelve o'clock already and her stomach began to rumble.

In less than half an hour she was ready to begin the return journey. The tarpaulin sheet was replaced and weighted down with bricks the way that Stanley had instructed her to. She took one last look around, imagining their sows running free in the orchard before she prepared for the return journey, and tied the red tartan headscarf around her head, knotting it tightly under her chin.

With her coat buttoned up to her neck she climbed back onto the tractor and settled herself on to the seat, thinking as she did so that at the first opportunity she would make a more comfortable cushion for it. Remembering to increase the revs, she set the tractor in motion and turned in a large circle before heading down the farmyard and out on to the road.

Once clear of the village she reached into the haversack hanging on the tool box and retrieved the cheese sandwich that Stanley had insisted she take with her. She had stated that she would not need any food or drink to take with her, "Ah can wait until I get back, Stanley," she had said, but Stanley had insisted and put the tractor ignition key into his pocket until she agreed to do as he said.

Now, she was ravenous and glad of the food. Driving tractors was hungry work she decided, as she gratefully took a bite out of the rough cheese sandwich. By the time she reached the bridge where she turned off the main road, Doris had demolished the bread and cheese and she stopped at the far side of the bridge to take a drink out of the lemonade bottle.

It was full of nothing more exciting than lukewarm water, but it quenched her thirst and Doris packed the bottle back into the haversack, wiped her mouth, and took a deep breath. Then she put the tractor into top gear and opened the throttle wide. The little Fergie surged forward and Doris gripped the steering wheel tightly as she prepared herself for the long drive back.

She still felt tense and nervous about losing her way, but in just over half an hour she reached Askern and relaxed her tight grip on the steering wheel. One of the advantages of the Ferguson tractors was the simplicity of their mechanical workings, and with an empty trailer behind her there was no need to change gear. Doris simply slowed the revs as she approached the road junction in the centre of Askern, then signalled that she was about to turn left. Thankful that the road was clear she turned out on to the main road, and still in top gear opened the throttle fully again.

The Fergie reacted with a puff of smoke from its chimney and pulled away with the empty trailer rattling along behind it. She glanced across to the left to look at the lake in the centre of Askern and reflected that it was the mining village's one claim to any kind of beauty. It was then that she heard the wolf whistles coming from her right and without thinking, automatically turned her head to see where the sound was coming from.

A group of miners were just leaving the nearby working men's club and were obviously in a cheerful mood after their drinking session. Doris tossed her head and looked away but hid a secret smile at their whistles as she left them behind.

'Not long now,' thought Doris, and felt a renewed confidence as she kept the Fergie going at its maximum speed. Her hands were cold but she kept them clamped on the wheel and ignored the chilly wind finding its way up her trouser legs.

Back at the smallholding Stanley was anxious. The moment Doris had left that morning he had cycled to the telephone box and rang the agricultural engineers. When he stressed how urgent the job was they had obligingly turned up in record time. By noon the new tyre was fitted and Stanley had a bill in his pocket with an amount on it that made his pulse quicken.

Now, he was expecting Doris home and by his reckoning, she should have been back half an hour ago. With every minute that passed, his anxiety increased. 'Where the hell was she?' he wondered, and decided that he would give her five more minutes, and then he would go looking for her.

For the fourth time, he walked to the gate, and peered down the road. He was about to turn away when he heard the sound of a tractor in the distance. He walked to the middle of the road and to his relief he could a see her. He waited, his smile becoming broader as she rapidly approached. Doris had seen him and waved, feeling jubilant that she had completed the trip successfully. Her headscarf had slipped to the back of her head, her dark hair flowed around her face and her cheeks were glowing as she reached the smallholding.

Stanley's smile quickly disappeared as he realised that she was going much too fast to negotiate the gateway. "Slow down, Doris," he shouted, "Slow down." But Doris was euphoric, and slowing down never entered her head. She swung out wide into the road ready to turn into the gateway with the trailer rattling behind her, and Stanley would have bet his last penny that she would hit the gate post.

There was nothing he could do. He put his hand to his head and closed his eyes for a split second expecting to hear a loud bang. When he opened them again, Doris was safely through the gate and was travelling quickly down the yard. She stood on the clutch and the brake at the same time and screeched to a halt.

Stanley ran to her and reaching across he switched off the engine. She almost fell into his arms and said, "I did it, Stanley. I did it, and I didn't get lost." Stanley swung her round and hugged her.

"By hell, Doris," he said as his heart started beating normally again, "Tha had me worried then. Why didn't you slow down? God only knows how you managed to get through the gateway at that speed."

She just shrugged her shoulders nonchalantly as if it was something she did every day and smiled.

Stanley put his arm around her shoulders in his familiar way and together they walked to the house for their long overdue meal.

CHAPTER 39

It was on a Tuesday, two weeks later, that they finally moved into the farmhouse at Rawcliffe. Stanley's first priority was to get to know his land. So early the next morning, he started up his Fordson Major and set off to examine the fields. The closest one to the farmhouse was down a well-used lane that was deeply rutted with large pot holes. Even though he avoided the worst of them, the tractor rocked from side to side as the wheels dropped into the holes, and he made a mental note to find the time to fill some of them in as soon as possible.

He pulled on to the first field that was still covered with the stubble from the recent harvest. This one was in the region of ten acres. Stanley bent down and took a handful of the soil. To his surprise it was light and slightly sandy. He had been expecting much heavier soil and was pleasantly surprised. He took his notebook out of his pocket and wrote down all the details before he moved on to the next field.

This one was further down the lane and closer to the River Aire and was a different proposition all together. It had recently been ploughed and even from the tractor seat it was obvious to him that the middle of the field was wet. The ploughed furrows on the outside of the field were neat and straight with just the odd wisp of straw from the recent crop poking through.

But the centre of the field told a different story. Stanley climbed down from the tractor and began walking across to it, uneasiness building up inside him. As he reached the area he was heading for he could see that even though it was a dry day the ground looked wet and the twisted furrows were evidence that the ploughman had had difficulties working the land.

Stanley stamped the heel of his boot into the bottom of a furrow and exposed a slither of mud. In wet weather this part of the field would be unworkable. He turned and walked back to his tractor where he stood for a minute or two making more notes in his book.

He left the tractor where it was and walked to the next field. He stood and leaned on the gatepost at the entry to the field of eight acres. This field ran right up to the banks of the River Aire. Half of the field consisted of good, workable warp land while the other half showed signs of having had water standing on it.

With his face showing the dismay that he felt, Stanley recorded it in his notebook. Now there was just the grass field to look at and he strode along the headlands and found a way through the tall hawthorne hedge.

He stood and looked across the field. It was the only one belonging to his farm that was not arable. His practised eye took in the verdant green grass and his heart lifted. This was a good, useful field he thought. Already he was making plans to run a small herd of bullocks on it. Even though they would be a long way from the farm they would surely be safe out here. The grass had not been cut for some time and had grown long. He began to walk across towards the gate and looked at the hedges. He noticed that they needed cutting and stopped to write a note in his book to schedule the job for the coming winter.

It was when he started walking again that his boot sank into a ridge of boggy land disguised by the long grass. It sucked at his boot as he pulled it out and Stanley swore. He could see now that there were ridges running the length of the field. He tested them and most of them were damp and boggy. His lips tightened as he thought that if they were waterlogged now during a dry spell it meant problems in wet weather.

He could not help feeling despondent as he drove the tractor back towards the farm, and pondered how very different one field was from the next and how much the soil varied in such a short distance. He took a different track back to the farm this time, one that would bring him out at a lower point in the village.

When the track turned a corner he could see a large shed with its double doors wide open. As he drew alongside he heard a voice and he stopped, looking closer into the gloomy interior.

Leaning on a blue tractor with his cap slightly to one side was a man dressed in the usual working man's uniform of overalls and well-worn tweed jacket.

"Nah then. It's a grand morning. You must be Stanley Dale," he called as he came out of the shed wiping his hands on greasy cloth. Stanley got down from his tractor and shook hands with the man who was to become a good and trusted friend. He discovered that he was known locally as Stitchy Mann and ran his own business doing contract work with his very well cared for Fordson Major.

Stanley admired it, and said ruefully that it showed his tractor up. Basking in the praise, Stitchy brought the shiny tractor out of the shed and together they walked round it with Stanley making admiring comments at the superb condition of it. It was certainly the best looked after tractor that he had ever seen.

"Aye, I look after it. It's my living tha see's. Look at this," Stitchy indicated the engine, "Ah even keep this clean. I never leave oil on it. If I'm not working with it I'm usually here in me shed looking after it."

"Well," said Stanley, "It's a credit to you. I'd better get off now. I've just been to look at my land and it's a lot wetter than ah expected it to be. I've got a feeling I'll have problems with it. Ah hope I find the field down at the other end of the village in better shape."

"Oh you'll not have any problems with that field. We call that the Quay. It's grand soil is that, best in the country. It's a heavy warp but by heck its good growing land. You go and have a look at it. And remember me if you need any contract work doing." He waved as Stanley got back on his tractor and drove away.

His spirits had been raised by his new friend's words and he found him to be correct. The field down at the Quay was the best he could have hoped for. Stanley stood at the bottom end of it and looked at the even furrows left by the ploughing and knew that this was one field which would always produce good crops.

That evening, after tea, Stanley sat at the table with his diary and his note book. He had little to say that night. His head was filled with the problems of the land he had walked that morning. He had of course been warned that some of the land was wet, but he had not expected to find that so much of it would be too wet to work.

Stitchy had warned him that not only was the lowest lying land almost bound to flood in a wet winter, it was also affected by the tidal river that ran alongside of it. This was a problem that was out of Stanley's experience.

He felt downhearted but was determined to farm the land to the best of his ability. He looked at the list of crops that had been grown the previous year by Bill Lawson and began to plan next year's crops accordingly.

Once his plans were made he felt happier. He was optimistic again, and turned his thoughts to stock. At that moment in time they had just the flock of laying hens that they had brought with them and three sows.

He picked up the chocolate that Doris passed to him and broke off a piece. He put his hand on her knee and began to tell her about his plans for the land next year.

Doris was more concerned with the amount of stock they had, and said they should go to Doncaster market on Saturday to buy more pigs. Stanley nodded in agreement but said that first they had to make sure all the buildings were thoroughly cleaned and lime washed. "I'll start tomorrow," he said as he yawned. The last few weeks had been hectic and they were both exhausted.

Doris looked at her husband and noticed the lines around his eyes and how pale and drawn his face looked. She got up and put her arms around him, kissing the top of his head, "I'll go and run you a hot bath, and then we'll have some supper and watch the television for an hour before we go to bed."

"Oh, we're having an early night tonight are we?" he answered. His blue eyes twinkled in spite of his tiredness and he slapped her bottom as she turned around. She winked at him, "Well you never know your luck, Mr. Dale," she said, as she sashayed towards the door.

They began on lime washing the buildings the next day. Stanley poured a large amount of lime into the old tin bath full of water. As usual it bubbled as if it was boiling, and he turned his head away making sure not to breath in the dust and fumes as he stirred it continuously, until became a creamy consistency

He had put on an old boiler suit and wore his oldest cap turned back to front so that the peak covered his neck.

Doris was wearing a tatty old gabardine mac, belted round her waist with a length of frayed binder twine. A scarf was wrapped around her head turban style. Stanley wolf whistled as she came across the yard, "Wow you look fetching in that, Dot. Here you are, put these goggles on, and then no one will recognise you."

He had bought the goggles from the army surplus store years ago for a shilling a pair, and they had lingered on a shelf in his tool shed ever since. The lenses were so misted and discoloured that it was difficult to see through them. Doris put a pair on, then took them off again and cleaned them. She put them back on. They were no better, but Stanley insisted that they had to wear them. "You can't risk a splash of lime in your eye, Doris. We'll just have to manage, we'll get used to them."

He put his on and also tied a handkerchief around his mouth to prevent breathing in any of the dust. Doris did the same and they were ready to begin. Taking a wall each they slapped the creamy liquid on, lathering it into every crack and every hole. It was dirty, unpleasant work and they were both relieved when at last it was all done.

"Thank God that's finished, Dot," said Stanley, as they walked together through the buildings and admired their handiwork. Then they looked at each other. Both were liberally splattered with splodges of lime, and a lock of hair that had escaped from Doris's scarf had a broad white streak in it. She untied her string belt, removed the old mackintosh and dropped it along with the scarf straight into the dustbin.

"There," she said, "That's what I'm doing with them, and you can do the same with that old boiler suit and cap. I'm not washing them. I'm off to get bathed now. I'll leave the water in. I think we've earned an early finish today."

Stanley peeled off the boiler suit and dropped it into the bin along with Doris's clothes, although he couldn't quite bring himself to bin his old cap, and instead hung it up in the barn to dry, hoping to be able to brush it clean the following day. Stanley tended to have a special affection for his work caps and hated having to dispose of one.

He walked up to the orchard to check on the sows. As they saw him they rushed to the fence, grunting and jostling each other as if it was feeding time. He leaned over and scratched their backs and noted that one looked as if she was close to farrowing.

"I'll have you in your new quarters tomorrow, old girl," he told her, but unimpressed and disappointed at the lack of any treat she wandered away to the rough temporary shelter he had built for the pigs.

He stood for a while leaning on the gate contemplating the orchard and planning how he would divide it up as soon as he had the time. There was so much to do, but he had never been happier. He had got his farm and he would work until he dropped to make a success of it.

Darkness was closing in and a mist was gathering as he walked slowly down the yard savouring the satisfaction of a good days work done, anticipating a hot bath and an evening relaxing in front of the fire, watching the television.

CHAPTER 40

Acquiring the tenancy of the farm was a great achievement to Stanley and Doris. They had started out with absolutely nothing, and what they had accomplished was by sheer hard work and determination, and now, at last, they felt that they were on their way to realising their ambition.

When Doris wrote to friends and relatives giving them their new address she felt such a great sensation of pride wash over her as she wrote, 'Pleasant View Farm' at the top of the page.

The house was much bigger than the semi-detached smallholding they had just left, and one of the things that Doris worried about was how to fill the many rooms. What furniture they had barely filled a quarter of it.

Downstairs, besides the kitchen, there were three large square rooms, a long hall leading from the front door and a pantry. Upstairs, there were four spacious bedrooms and an equally spacious bathroom. The bath and hand basin were squashed into one corner, while the toilet had been installed in the opposite corner beside a large sash window.

The bathroom had once been a bedroom and the window still had plain glass in it. So any prolonged visit to the toilet could be entertaining, as the user could while away the time watching the goings on in the back gardens of the nearby street. The disadvantage of course was that whoever was using the toilet was in full view of everyone outside.

Doris quickly remedied that by fitting a net curtain which gave instant privacy while only partly obscuring the view out. Stanley said it was the best toilet they had ever had, it was an indoor toilet with a view. What more could anyone ask?

The shortage of furniture troubled Doris. She longed to be able to make her new home nice, but there was little money to spare for furniture to fill the farmhouse. Her problem however was soon to be solved.

There were many implements that Stanley still needed to work the land and so he began attending farm sales. They were a treasure trove for struggling farmers who wanted to pick up equipment at a low cost. The items for sale were usually set out in rows in a field, all numbered and itemised in a catalogue. A quick, almost casual note at the end of the catalogue sometimes mentioned that household goods would be auctioned at the end of the sale.

Doris's eyes homed in on that information, and she told Stanley that she would attend the sales with him. The moment they arrived at a sale, while Stanley examined the various farming implements, Doris headed for the household goods and cast an eye over the furniture that would be sold after all the farming equipment had gone.

By the time the auctioneer reached the goods that Doris was interested in, most of the bargain hunters had gone home, and Doris was often the only buyer left.

She had never bid before and felt nervous, but Stanley said she had to learn to do it herself and urged her not to put her hand up at the first figure that was mentioned. Standing behind her he bent down and whispered to her to wait. "Don't bid yet, Dot. He'll come down in price. You're the only one interested."

She could hardly believe it when she bought a three piece suite for two pounds. Admittedly, it was very outdated but had obviously been kept for best in a farmhouse parlour and was just like new apart from its slightly damp smell. Doris ran her hand over the plush velvet upholstery and cared not at all that it was old fashioned. Doris knew quality when she saw it.

She was now well and truly bitten by the auction bug and could hardly wait for the next sale to come around. Every day she scoured the pages of the Yorkshire Post for farm sales and urged Stanley to attend.

If the sale was not too far away they usually went on the Fergie, with the smallest trailer behind. That way they could load whatever they had bought on to the trailer and take it home the same day. Doris bought all manner of furniture for ridiculously small amounts of money.

Much of the furniture was only a few years away from being an antique. If it had been just a few years later many of the items would have been snapped up by designers and sold for high prices in the cities.

But as it was at the time, there was little demand for marble topped wash stands and old fashioned wardrobes, and so Doris was able to furnish the large farmhouse on a shoestring. One of her very best buys was a bureau with a locked drawer. She paid ten shillings for it and when Stanley eventually managed to get the drawer open there was great excitement when they found that it contained a book with carefully folded five pound note inside it.

A piano was another one of her finds, and of course it was very heavy. With great difficulty it had been loaded onto the trailer, then unloaded at the farm and dragged up the garden path and into the house. No one in the family could play, but that didn't matter in the least. It was a lovely piece of furniture, and as far as Doris was concerned, that earned it a place in her hall.

In time every room was filled, but Doris was still in the grip of auction fever and could not stop. Stanley was beginning to lose patience. "We've got enough now, Doris," he insisted, "The house is full of furniture. No more, don't buy any more."

Eileen arrived one day on a visit with her two young children and as she opened the back door she could hear raised voices. There was a crash and the corner of a wardrobe smashed the window on the landing. Signalling to the children to keep quiet, she backed out of the house and went for a walk around the village, hoping that peace would have been restored by the time she returned.

Later on she learned that her mother had bought a very large oak wardrobe. It was heavy and difficult to manoeuvre. It had got stuck as they had tried to carry it up the stairs, then slipped out of control and smashed the window.

"I wouldn't mind," said Stanley who was glad to have someone he could confide in. "Ah wouldn't mind, Eileen, but we've got at least two wardrobes in every bedroom. Your Mam's got to stop. Drop a few hints can you? Tell her the house is overcrowded. We could open a bloody second hand shop with the amount of furniture we've got."

In spite of Stanley's irritation he would have been the first one to admit that Doris had managed to create a very nice home on an extremely tight budget. She had a unique natural flair and put things together that really should have clashed, but somehow they didn't. She just ignored convention and did things her own way.

She did however, curtail her auction buying to please her husband, unless of course, something very special caught her eye, and then she would tell him that it was such a bargain they would be fools to miss it. Stanley would then sigh, shrug his shoulders and say, "Go on then, you'd better bid for it if it's that good."

Rawcliffe was a charming, historic village situated on the banks of the River Aire. The imposing church sat on the large village green in the centre of the village. With a school, library, bank, an assortment of shops and public houses, it had everything that anyone could need for day to day living.

It also had a very busy road that ran through the centre of it. The continuous stream of traffic shook the foundations of the old houses and was a danger to everyone. A bypass was continually demanded by the long-suffering residents, but it was to be several years before that happened.

In the meantime however Stanley and Doris saw the potential in all that passing traffic and wasted no time in setting up a stall with farm produce. To begin with Stanley made a table out of a couple of empty oil drums and a piece of wood, and laid out a few dozen eggs and some bags of potatoes. They were sold out on the first day and that evening, plans were made to further exploit the situation.

Pleasant View Farm was situated on the first corner as the road entered Rawcliffe, or the last corner depending on which direction you were travelling in, so they were in an ideal position to capture trade.

First thing next morning Stanley set out with money in his

pocket, and bought a load of potatoes from another farm, packed them into bags, and they were on their way to running a farm shop.

Another batch of point of lay pullets was ordered to take over from the present flock and Stanley made a more substantial stall to arrange their produce on. There was, at first, precious little own grown produce to sell on the new stall but that small fact would not deter them. Stanley made a tour of all the farms in the village and bought turnips, carrots, and any other vegetables that they had surplus and sold them on the stall for a small profit.

He had already prepared a seed bed and sown an assortment of vegetables in a portion of the first field, but as yet, they were still in the growing stage, and would not be ready for weeks. It was while he was working on his plot that his new friend Stitchy stopped to talk, and told him about a group of smallholdings near Carlton that grew and sold their own produce.

Stanley's eyes lit up and that afternoon he decided to take trip out there to investigate. As he set off he marvelled at the coincidence that had led him to get the tenancy of a farm just a few miles from Carlton, which was where his Aunt Lizzie had lived all those years ago. It was also where his sister Doll had been brought up. He had often visited them with his mother when he had been very young and had never forgotten those times.

He wondered if his mother realised how close he lived now to the village of Carlton that had played such an important part in all their lives. How he wished that his Aunt Lizzie was still there, and he imagined himself walking through her door and the look on her face as she saw him. What a greeting she would have given him, but sadly she had died several years ago while still a comparatively young woman.

He shook himself, and aloud said, "Forget the past, Stan, and get on with the future," but he could not help his thoughts from turning to his sister Doll, who was still alive and well. He had not seen her for many years and was not likely to as Doris would barely have her name mentioned.

As he thought about the circumstances that had brought about the rift he did feel some resentment towards his wife that she had taken such a stance. He considered that it had all been unnecessary and could have been smoothed over if only Doris had not been so dogmatic. But it was water under the bridge, he decided, it was all in the past, and better forgotten, it was now that mattered. He put away such thoughts and followed the directions to find the smallholdings that he was looking for.

By the time he was on the return journey deals had been made with two of the smallholders who were only too glad to find another buyer for their produce, and Stanley went home feeling well satisfied at the way things had turned out.

CHAPTER 41

That evening Stanley and Doris sat up long past their usual bedtime discussing their future plans. With so much of their land liable to flood it was clear that the income from it carried a fair amount of risk. They could not count on sufficient revenue from the land to pay the rent and give them a living. The answer, Stanley felt, was for them concentrate on building up a substantial herd of pigs which would bring in an additional income.

Stanley intended going to Doncaster market as soon as possible to begin looking for good quality sows. At a recent farm sale he had bought a small covered trailer suitable for carrying a sow or a litter of young pigs, but was worried that their car would not be powerful enough to pull it.

"We really need a stronger vehicle, Doris. Our car's not built for towing a trailer with a heavy pig in it. We'll probably have to go to market most Saturdays buying and selling. It's going to take a big chunk out of any profit we make if we have to pay a carter every week."

"Well in that case," said Doris," I think we should go to the garage and see what they'll offer us in part exchange. Are you thinking of a van? "

"Yes," replied Stanley, "But ah'm loath to spend that much money at this stage. We've got to keep enough in reserve for the rent. Ah'll tell you what, Doris, ah sure miss the regular wage that I had at the council. " A worried frown wrinkled his forehead and he sighed.

Doris, however, knew when to boost his confidence, and she did so now, reassuring him that they would manage fine and reminded him that they had a litter of pigs almost ready for selling.

By the time they went to bed it was agreed that they would go to the Ford garage the next day and see about trading the car in for a van. Stanley could hardly sleep that night. His emotions ranged between excitement at getting a new van, and the worry of spending the money on it.

When he eventually fell asleep it was to dream of a fleet of vans appearing in the farm yard, and a salesman standing in front of him demanding payment for them. He awoke with a dreadful headache and a strong conviction that they should not under any circumstances, go to the garage. But a mug of Doris's strong tea and a bacon sandwich brought things into perspective again and they set off to trade in the car as arranged.

They emerged from the garage two hours later the owners of a Ford Thames van. A deal had been done and a finance repayment arranged so that they had no need to spend any of their precious capital.

The cost of the repayments would go against their tax bill, or so the salesman had reassured them, and of course that made sense, but Stanley couldn't help thinking that would be all very well as long as they made enough money to be eligible to pay tax.

Stanley and Doris both had a deep, ingrained fear of being in debt, and it took some time for them to convince each other that it was better to use their capital to buy more stock, which would in turn increase their income.

Two days later they drove to the garage and collected the van, complete with a newly fitted tow bar for towing the trailer. Now that they had taken the plunge they were well pleased with their new acquisition and Doris stopped off at the shop to buy a tin of polish.

In vain Stanley protested, telling her that there was no need to waste her energy on polishing it. "For goodness sake, Doris," he said, "It's a working vehicle, there's no need to tire yourself out giving it so much elbow grease."

He might as well have told the birds to stop singing. Doris took not the slightest notice and began waxing the long expanse of cream coloured bodywork on the van. Stanley shrugged his shoulders and left her to it.

They were ready to set off for the market early on Saturday morning. Stanley had spread a generous amount of straw on to the floor of the trailer and hitched it on to the new tow bar at the back of the van. Seat belts were something that would be thought of at some time in the future, and for the moment Frances was able to squeeze onto the front seat with her mother and they were off.

Doris smiled happily at her husband, enjoying sitting higher up than she had done in the car, and she marvelled at what a good view they had of the road in front. A thought occurred to Stanley about Doris's intention to resume her driving lessons, and clearing his throat he broached the subject.

"What are you going to do about the driving lessons then, Dot? Are you going to renew your provisional licence?"

With no hesitation at all Doris replied, "I'm going to leave it. Ah couldn't handle this van, it's far too big for me. No ah'll leave it. Ah don't mind driving the tractor in the fields, but ah don't want to be driving a great big van like this on the road."

Stanley turned away so that she would not see his smile of relief and replied that it was up to her and it was her decision. Doris for her part was also relieved; she much preferred to sit in the passenger seat.

They arrived at Doncaster with just half an hour to spare before the livestock market commenced. In a hurry to view the pigs on sale Stanley parked the van and almost ran the distance between the car park and the market. He had already dropped Doris off and she was busy checking out the stock in the pens when Stanley reached her. Taking her arm he asked in a low voice if she had seen anything that looked good. She nodded and indicated the pen just behind them, and then whispered that number twenty five and thirty one were worth taking a look at.

"Ah'll get off now, Stan. Ah've got some shopping to do and our Frances wants to spend her birthday money. It's burning a hole in her pocket at the moment. The sooner she gets it spent the sooner we'll get some peace."

Stanley laughed and Frances, who was hanging as far away from the pigs as possible, pulled a face.

As she turned to go, Doris promised to get Stanley some tripe. That did nothing to improve Frances's mood, she hated it as much as her elder sister did, and asked if she could have something else. But Doris did not believe in pampering her children with different meals and told her abruptly that she would have what was on the table.

It was good to be in Doncaster again. Doris loved the hustle and bustle of the busy town. Not only was Doncaster livestock market one of the best in the county it also had a huge general market selling everything imaginable, all at bargain prices. In addition there was an extensive fruit, vegetable and fish market, where the vendors called out their goods for sale, each one competing to attract the customer's attention.

Anxious to get back to Stanley and see what he was buying Doris quickly stocked up on everything she would need for the following week, including a few treats to enjoy in the evenings. She stopped at the sweet stall where trays of home-made toffee were on sale. Asking for half a pound of walnut toffee she watched while the woman tapped at the toffee with a small metal hammer and broke it into manageable pieces.

"Fresh made this week, love," commented the stall holder. "I've got some liquorice toffee today. Here you are, love, do you want to try some?" She held out a saucer with some broken pieces of black toffee on it. Doris took a small section and popped it in her mouth. "Guaranteed to turn your teeth black is that," said the woman, "Can ah sell you some?"

With the toffee sticking her dentures together Doris could only nod and take out her purse. As she battled to get her teeth under control she handed out the money, took the paper bags and turned away from the stall. There was no doubt the liquorice toffee tasted delicious but it was better eaten in private thought Doris.

Frances was agitating to go to Woolworths to spend her birthday money and in the end Doris said she could go alone while she went to buy the tripe. "But," she said firmly, "When you've been to the toy stall, go and wait for me just inside the doors, near the big red weighing machine. Do you hear me, Frances? Do not go out of the shop."

Relieved to be free from parental restrictions Frances shot off, her birthday money clutched tightly in her hand, and quickly became lost from view among the crowds of Saturday shoppers. She knew her way well around this part of town and was soon entering the double doors of Woolworths. Straight up the stairs she ran, trailing her hand along the highly polished brass rail, dodging through the crowds until she came to the toy department in the centre of the upper floor.

Now she was here she could not decide on anything, and was aware that time was passing. Her mother did not like to be kept waiting and in the end, ignoring all the cheap, tin clockwork toys she went slowly back down the stairs and went to wait at the door for her mother.

Pleased to see her daughter waiting as instructed Doris asked what she had spent her money on, and without pausing to hear what she said, handed her one of her shopping bags to carry. "Come on, love, tell me about it later. Ah want to get to the pig market," and pushing her way through the crowds, she led the way back to see if Stanley had bought anything.

As luck would have it he had at just at that moment, put in a winning bid for a fine, large white sow. She had been sold as being in pig and due to give birth in three weeks' time. At first Stanley had been hesitant about bidding for her. Some instinct made him question why anyone would sell a sow so close to farrowing. He wondered if she had some habit that made her a bad mother. However, at the last minute he decided to take a chance. He was less doubtful once he had made the winning bid, and the man next to him commented that he had got a bargain.

The auctioneer recognised him and said, "Mr. Dale of Adwick-le-Street? " He gave him a questioning look as he said it, and Stanley proudly corrected him, saying that he was now at Pleasant View Farm, Rawcliffe.

"Ah'll remember that, Sir," replied the auctioneer. He tipped his cap with his stick and gave Stanley a nod before he moved on to the next pen.

They drove home, all feeling happy with the day's events and pleased with their purchases. All except Frances of course, who was going home with nothing, and the prospect of tripe for tea. Although she did cheer up considerably, when Doris handed the liquorice toffee around, and Stanley got his teeth well and truly stuck together.

CHAPTER 42

That day at Doncaster market set the pattern for most future Saturdays. Doris usually went with him but occasionally opted to stay at home and be there to sell their produce. It was on one of the days when Stanley went alone that he had a little adventure.

He had set off early with the boar pig in the trailer. This particular male had proved to be not very competent at his job. He had often shown a decided lack of interest in the alluring female pigs that Stanley had presented him with, and the few times that he had done the deed, the results were disappointing. So, over the fence, as the boar chomped his way through another bucketful of expensive feed Stanley had informed him that he had to go. It was time for him to be traded in.

All was going well; the boar had gone into the trailer with no trouble and settled down in the thick layer of straw. Stanley hummed as he drove towards Doncaster, looking forward to the day at the market.

It was just before he reached Thorne that he noticed several cars flashing their lights at him. He gave them a flash of acknowledgement in return, assuming that they were warning him of a police speed check ahead and he made sure that he was well within the limits.

A loud beep of a horn sounded right behind him and he was overtaken by a builders van. The passenger had wound his window down and was shouting something inaudible to him. He pointed towards the back of the trailer and Stanley stared back at him wondering what was wrong.

It was then that he caught a quick glimpse in his mirror of a pig's ear sticking out at the rear of the trailer. Slowing down, Stanley swore, and knew in that minute what had happened. Just above the rear door there was a gap to let fresh air in. This was filled by a small section of slatted wooden fencing made to fit exactly into the gap. By some means the boar had managed to lift it up until it had fallen off. Now he was standing on his hind legs trying to climb out of the trailer through the narrow gap at the top of the door.

Stanley pulled over on to the grass verge and could see that the huge pig already had the top half of his body hanging out. The moment the van came to a stop Stanley leapt out, leaving the door swinging, and ran to the back of the trailer; but he was too late. Somehow the pig had squeezed his way out and fallen head first onto the grass. Fearing that he had done himself some serious damage Stanley held his breath and put out his hand towards him.

Far from having sustained any injury the pig jumped up, almost knocking Stanley over as he rushed past him. He went down into the dyke, then up the other side and through the hedge. Once through the hedge he began running across the field. For such a large, clumsy looking animal he could run at quite a speed.

Before he gave chase Stanley had the presence of mind to lock the van door, grab his stick, and let down the rear door of the trailer which also served as a ramp. Following the path that the pig had taken through the hedge, he scanned the field in front of him and there he was, already a good fifty yards away and showing no signs of slowing down.

He took a deep breath and began to follow him. He set off running fast through the long grass but before he had covered half the field his breath was coming in gasps, and he had to stop. He bent over with his hands on his knees; taking in great gulps of air.

As if aware that his pursuer had given up chasing him, the boar pig paused, and began to graze on the lush grass. He looked back at his owner casually, knowing that he had the upper hand and casually began to root at the ground with his snout.

Under his breath Stanley was threatening him with all manner of punishments, but aloud he began to call him the way that he did when it was feeding time. "Come on then me old lad, come on." Slowly and calmly he walked towards him, approaching him in a wide circle so that he would come at him from the far side, and he kept the stick concealed behind his leg.

When he got to within ten yards of him the boar looked up at him. There was menacing look in his eye, and he tossed his head showing the tusks at either side of his mouth. "Come on then old lad, come on," chanted Stanley. "Come on." He rattled the paper bag of Mintoes in his pocket and wished he'd had the foresight to have a bucket of pig food with him. He also cursed himself for not remembering to bring the rope that he kept in the back of the van, but it was too late now. Getting the boar back into the trailer on his own was going to be difficult.

"Come on, me old lad," he said again and took his bag of Mintoes from his pocket. He threw one on to the grass in front of the pig who grunted and picked up the sweet, looking at Stanley as if to say, "Is that all?" But evidently he liked the taste and allowed himself to be steered back towards the trailer.

Stanley was sweating profusely now, partly from the heat of the day but more from the tricky situation he was in. They were almost back at the hedge, and the trailer was just at the other side of it. 'Just a few more yards,' he thought, 'and I could have the damned pig safely back where he belongs.' But there was still the tricky part of getting the pig to go up the ramp and into the trailer before he could relax.

He had never believed before that pigs could laugh, but this one gave a good impression of it as he turned towards him with his mouth open. He shook his head so that his ears flapped away from his face and gave Stanley a knowing stare. He looked at the hedge and Stanley could almost hear him saying that he wouldn't be going through it.

This was a time for being devious and Stanley decided to try to lead him rather than drive him. Bending down he forced his way through the gap in the hedge dropping another minty sweet on the way. Grunting and snuffling the boar followed him through the hedge and looked at him expectantly. The packet of sweets was almost gone now, but Stanley put his hand into his pocket, pulled it out again and pretended to throw one into the trailer. He held his breath as the boar put first one foot on the ramp then another.

For a moment he hovered and gave Stanley a sideways glance as he peered at him from under his ear as if undecided what to do next.

Quickly he pulled out the paper bag, took out the last sweet and threw it into the trailer. The boar lurched his way up the ramp and stopped. He made as if to back down again but Stanley had got the upper hand now and gave him a resounding slap across his rear end with the stick. It had the required result and the boar pig almost leapt the rest of the way into the trailer. The minute his weight was off the ramp Stanley lifted it up and slammed it into place. He secured it with the bolts and leaned against it, gasping with relief.

Now it was just a matter of filling in the gap left by the lost piece of fencing and he could be on his way. As if reading his thoughts the boar turned himself around in the narrow trailer and stood on his hind legs with his head up at the gap. For a moment he stared Stanley in the eye, before he was dealt a sharp rap on the nose from the stick, and dropped back down out of sight.

As a temporary measure Stanley covered the gap with an old car blanket blocking out the daylight. Then he retrieved the length of rope that he carried In the van and tied it back and forth across over the gap until it formed as sort of net. Satisfied at last that there was no chance of the boar escaping, he set off to complete the journey. He reached the market just as they were about to stop taking entries.

The policeman on duty at the gate was a regular and commented that it was not like him to be late. Stanley said he had been delayed but it was a long story.

"Ok Stan, off you go, see you next week." He waved him on, but then banged on the van roof for him to stop. He looked at the trailer tyres, shook his head and tutted.

He held up his hand and said, "Now then, Stan. Ah don't mind thee running over me feet, but not with a bloody bald tyre. Get it replaced before next week."

Thankful to have arrived safely with the pig Stanley nodded and promised that he would see to it.

CHAPTER 43

The busy road that ran through the Rawcliffe was a constant danger. It was feared and hated by everyone and yet for Stanley and Doris it sometimes gave a little bonus. Pleasant View Farm was situated on a sharp corner. From time to time lorries were prone to taking that corner too fast, sometimes with disastrous results.

They had only been living there for a couple of months when a lorry, heavily loaded with long planks of wood approached the corner. Stanley happened to be in the gateway at the time and heard the screech of brakes. He looked up, and watched as the ropes snapped and the entire load of wood rolled off the lorry, spreading itself across the farm drive, over the hedge and into the garden. The lorry came to a halt just before it hit the stone wall.

When the noise of the crash subsided, there was a strange silence as all the traffic stopped. The driver of the lorry got out of the cab and stood looking at it for a moment, clearly shocked by what had happened. The local shop owner rang for the police and crowds began to gather. Fortunately no one had been hurt.

Stanley looked at his smashed fence and then at the wood scattered all over his front lawn. Doris came and stood by his side. He looked at her. "Are you thinking what I'm thinking, Doris?" he said.

She looked up at him, "That's just what you need to build the shed you've been on about."

He nodded and said pensively, "It's bloody inconsiderate of them to put it on the lawn, but I'll move some of it tonight and stash it away in the orchard."

Valuable lessons were learnt that day. One of them was how to deal with insurance companies after their fences were smashed. They were destined to be destroyed several times over the next few of years. An even more important lesson was never to stand on that corner, it was far too dangerous.

They became ready to turn spilt loads to their advantage, although they never again had such a useful one as that load of wood which was used to build a new chicken shed.

Doris did however, once happen to be in the exactly right place at the right time. Coming out of the barn one morning with an empty wheelbarrow, she was just in time to see a couple of sacks of coal fall off a lorry and scatter across the drive.

Quick as a flash Doris grabbed a brush and a shovel, loaded the coal into a barrow, threw the empty sacks on top of the load and took it to her coalhouse. She then closed the gate and there was nothing left of the spilt coal apart from a sprinkling of black coal dust.

The following weekend, Stanley and Doris were enjoying a drink in the Neptune, which was their favourite public house. They got into conversation with a couple they had never seen before. As the man took a drink of his pint he looked around the crowded room.

Stanley asked if he lived in Rawcliffe. The man shook his head. "No," he said, "I pass through it now and then. As a matter of fact I passed through during the week. Ah lost a couple of sacks of coal from the back of my lorry on that bad corner as you come into the village. Do you know where I mean?" Stanley shook his head and nudged Doris's knee.

"Well," he went on, "Do you know, when ah discovered I'd lost them, ah went back, but they'd gone. Not a bloody sign of em, except for a bit of coal dust on the floor. What do you think to that?" Stanley gave a sympathetic tut, finished his pint and said they had to be going.

Doris had always had a great affection for her parents-in-law and now that they had plenty of spare bedrooms and all fully furnished she suggested to Stanley that they should invite them to come for a little holiday.

Stanley's father, Harold, had recently retired after working down the coal mine for fifty years. He was, at last, a gentleman of leisure. Not that he was pleased about it. He insisted that he should have been allowed to carry on working at the coal face for several more years, but rules were rules and he had had to take forced retirement.

"Look at me, ah'm plenty fit enough," he told his family and anyone else who would listen. "They've chucked me on the scrap heap just because I'm sixty five" He looked thoroughly miserable at the thought of not being able to go and spend eight hours hacking away at the coal face. The real truth was that he dreaded losing the camaraderie of his work mates and also the dip in income that would curtail his drinking at the British Legion.

"Silly old fool," Stanley said to Doris in private, "He's been slaving his guts out down the pit since he was a lad of thirteen. You'd think he'd be bloody thankful to get out of it." But in spite of his harsh criticism, Stanley hated to see his father so downright miserable, and agreed with Doris that they should invite his parents to come and stay.

Doris wrote asking them if they would like to come for a holiday and received a reply from her mother-in-law by return of post saying they would love to come. At the end of her letter Ada said she would find out the bus times and let them know what day and what time they would arrive.

"Well, there'll be none of that," said Stanley when he read the letter. "There's no need for them to get the bus, we can go and fetch them in the van."

The van, of course, only had seats at the front, but that was no problem for a resourceful couple like Stanley and Doris. They swept the interior of the van and carried two of the fireside chairs out of the house and placed them in the van as close to the front as possible.

The floor of the van was metal and the two chairs had metal studs on the end of the legs to protect the wood. Metal on metal provided as stable a condition as skates on ice, and as they set off on Sunday to collect Stanley's parents, the chairs slid from one side of the van to the other each time they turned a corner.

Stanley glanced back as the chairs did a sort of waltz around the van. They were now facing the opposite way to the one they had started. "Bloody hell, Doris," he said, "I'll have to do something about those chairs. I'll have to tie them down. My Mam and Dad'll be dizzy by the time we get them from Wath to Rawcliffe."

Doris pointed out that maybe when someone was sitting in the chairs their weight might hold them down and if he drove slowly it would be okay. Over the next few miles Stanley drove as if he had a load of eggs in the back; but it made little difference. Even when he set off very carefully the chairs slid to the back of the van, stopping only when they actually hit the back doors.

He had a nightmare vision of the chairs, with his parents in them, hitting the doors and ending up on the road. When he turned to the right the chairs hit the opposite side and vice versa. If he had to stop the van suddenly the chairs flew from wherever they happened to be and joined them at the front.

He stopped in a layby and found the rope that he always carried tucked away beside the spare wheel. He spent some time securing the chairs to each other and then tied them to the sides of the van. To his relief it seemed to have done the trick although the chairs still strained at the ropes from time to time.

Ada and Harold thought there was nothing unusual about sitting in the back of the van in a couple of fireside chairs and they laughed as the chairs tilted when they went around corners. From the back Harold called out, "It's a good job tha's tied the chairs down, Stanley. They'd be all over the van otherwise," just as he said the words they went around a sharp corner and he grabbed hold of Ada's chair arm, "Eh, come here lass, tha nearly got away then. It's better than being on t'fairground."

As they pulled into the drive at the farm, Stanley felt a surge of pride in showing his parents where they now lived and farmed. His father was greatly impressed with the farm and the village. The fact that there were three public houses in a small village definitely met with his approval. "Do you think we could try them out tonight, Stanley? Just to see what the beers like."

Stanley looked at Doris and winked before he agreed. "Don't want to be too late to bed though, Dad. It's a busy time on the land just now. Come on, you can have a look round while ah'm feeding the pigs."

Harold wandered around the farmyard. He had to admit it was far bigger than he had anticipated. He stood in the orchard and took in a deep breath just as his son walked up behind him.

"By heck, Stanley," he said "Does tha know, the air's like wine here. No coal dust in the air here. Tha's done well lad. Ah always knew tha'd do well."

Stanley could not help his thoughts going back to his childhood and remembering how hard his father had been on him in those years. He remembered those times so clearly and maybe that was why his father's words meant more to him than he could express.

He looked at Harold and could see that in spite of his boasting that he was still fit for work, the years at the coal face had taken their toll. Although his body was still stocky and muscular from a lifetime of manual labour, his lungs were damaged and would never recover from all the coal dust that he had inhaled over the years.

Suddenly Stanley experienced a feeling he had never expected to have for his father, suddenly he felt protective of him and he put his hand on his shoulder and said that tea would be ready.

The church bells began to ring at that moment and Harold smiled as he said they sounded grand. In his head he was thinking of those far off days before they were married, when Ada was due to have his baby and had gone to stay with her sister, Lizzie, in nearby Carlton, but he said nothing. Even all these years later it was much too sensitive a subject to discuss. Instead he just said that he was ready for his tea and looking forward to going for a drink later on.

Doris had set the table with her best tablecloth and there in front of Harold's place was a jug filled with crisp celery which was his favourite tea time treat. Next to it were plates of boiled ham and corned beef. There was a large plate of fresh crusty bread, thickly buttered and cut into triangular shapes. On the sideboard stood a glass bowl filled with trifle and at the side of it an apple pie liberally sprinkled with sugar.

As Harold washed his hands at the white kitchen sink he turned to Doris who was filling the teapot and said in his quiet, throaty voice that she had gone to a lot of trouble and it looked grand.

Half an hour later with a considerable amount of the food eaten they sat around the table chatting and drinking a second cup of tea. Ada brought them up to date with all the events in their large family, then, as always jumped up and began to clear the table despite Doris's protests that she would do it.

"No," insisted Ada, "You and Stanley go and get changed, Doris, I'll see to these."

It was useless to argue. Having brought up a large family Ada was programmed to clearing away the pots and washing up almost before the meal was over. Doris gave way and went upstairs to get bathed and changed.

Stanley followed her, whispering that his Dad was keen to get to the pub. "He just wants to try out the local beer, Dot, just to sample it and see if it's up to the British Legion standards, or so he tells me."

Doris laughed and whispered back, "Aye, ah bet he does. I wonder how many pints he'll have to test." Then louder, she informed him that his suit and shirt were laid out on the bed ready for him and began to get changed into her best clothes herself.

Harold had been looking forward to visiting all the public houses in the village that night, but once he walked through the doors of the Neptune with its windows overlooking the church, he sat down and forgot all about the other two pubs. He was utterly charmed by the old fashioned ambience of the main room and as he gazed around he declared this was his favourite public house ever.

Doris leaned towards him and said, with a mischievous look, "What, even better than the British Legion at Wath?"

Harold took a long drink out of his glass while he considered her question, then smiled as he said, "Oh now steady on, Doris, ah wouldn't go that far,"

Stanley was still drinking his glass of stout when his father emptied his pint of bitter and went for a refill. He stood leaning on the bar chatting to the regulars with an ease that came from years of practice. He looked as if he was in for a long night, but Ada had other ideas and beckoned Stanley towards her.

"Don't let your Dad drink too much, Stanley; he'll be here till closing time if he has half a chance." Stanley had been thinking the same himself and decided to take charge. At nine thirty exactly he stood up and walked to the bar, "We've got to get off now, Dad. It's an early start tomorrow. Are you ready?"

Harold gave him a sharp look then downed the rest of his pint, "Aye, ah am." He waved to his newly made friends and said, "Got to go folks, work to do tomorrow, see you later in the week." He followed his son without a word of protest and Stanley could hardly believe it. Outside Ada linked arms with him and they walked sedately back to the farm as the dusk began to draw in.

The next morning Stanley was half way through cleaning out one of the sows when he heard his father's voice at the gate to the fold yard. He poked his head out of the pigsty and held the brush in front of him to prevent the sow coming back in before he had finished. "Get back," he said, as he pushed her backwards out of the sty.

Harold watched his actions and seemed keen to help, "Aye up, Stanley, ah can give you a hand, what do you want doing?" he asked.

Early mornings were always hectic when it was cleaning out and feeding time. Being in the fold yard among the pigs was no place for someone not used to it. Doris was already busy doing the feeding, carrying the buckets of swill out to each pen. They had a routine which worked well. He did the mucking out as they called it, while Doris did the feeding. He considered for a moment then asked his father to take water up to the pigs that were running free in the orchard.

"You don't need to go over the fence, Dad, just pour the water into the troughs; Doris will be taking them their swill shortly."

As Harold nodded and picked up a bucket, he looked over the gate again at the huge sow rooting about in the fold yard. "Are they dangerous?" he asked casually. His son glanced at him. Harold had faced constant danger every day of his working life, but Stanley got the feeling that he was nervous of the sows.

417

"Not usually. This one's as quiet as a lamb," he reassured him, and rubbed the sows neck behind her ears to demonstrate, while she pressed against his hand like a dog asking to be petted. Then he added, "They can get a bit savage when they're giving birth if they're in pain, or when they're protecting their young, but it's the boars you have to watch." He noted the doubtful look on Harold's face, "You'll be ok with the ones up in the orchard, just pour the water through the fence into the troughs," he repeated, "Don't bother to go over the fence. Doris will be up there anyway. She treats em all like pets."

Reassured, Harold filled his bucket and walked slowly up the yard to the orchard and found Doris already filling the troughs with swill. He emptied his bucket of water and stood leaning over the fence watching the pigs gobble at the food, shoving and competing with each other to get the best feeding position. For a minute Doris stood beside him.

"Well," he commented, "I've often heard the expression, 'like pigs at a trough.' Ah know what it means now. Wait till ah tell my mates at the Legion about it."

Once all the feeding and cleaning out of the animals was complete it was their custom to have what Doris called, 'drinkings,' before Stanley went out to the fields to begin his days work. It consisted of mugs of strong tea and a couple of biscuits each and gave them time to have a breathing space after their early start and a chance to plan the rest of the day.

This was a busy time on the land with both the haymaking and a seven acre field of sugar beet demanding Stanley's attention. After due consideration, he decided that the hay was the most urgent. It had been cut and turned and was now almost ready to bring home.

He had bought an old rake from a recent farm sale. It was a simple, old fashioned design that had been converted from a horse-drawn implement.

It had relatively few working parts, but needed someone to sit on the hard iron seat situated above the curved steel prongs that gathered up the hay. While sitting on this seat, the operator had to lift the rake by means of a manually operated lever at the end of each row so that it deposited the collected hay in a heap.

On hearing of his plans, his father immediately offered to help. Stanley looked doubtful. Sitting on top of the rake was no job for an old man but when he began to express his worries Harold looked fierce and stated firmly that he could do the job easily.

"Ah'm not ready for t'scrap heap yet tha knows," he stated, and Stanley knew better than to contradict him.

The sun was shining when they drove out of the farm yard with Harold sitting on the mudguard of the tractor beside his son. For a man in his sixties he looked fine and healthy but Stanley could hear the rasping sound of his breathe and knew the true state of his health.

Harold however, was not thinking of his health at that moment, he was enjoying the sun and the slight breeze on his face. To him, this was a fresh new experience and one that he was thoroughly enjoying.

By dinnertime all the hay was raked into four long rows and Stanley planned to go back that afternoon and load it on to his biggest trailer. It would not be baled; he was doing it the old fashioned way to save the cost of baling.

How, he wondered, was he going to be able to go back out into the fields that afternoon without Harold? He could see that his father was more tired than he would ever admit to. It was his mother who solved the problem. She took one look at her husband and informed him that he was not fit to go back out into the fields that afternoon.

Harold sighed, "Can tha manage without me this afternoon then, Stanley? Thee mother says ah've got to rest." He tossed his head, and gave a 'tch' sound. "Women!" he stated indignantly, but Stanley was pleased to see that he didn't argue with Ada.

Doris stepped in, "I'll go back to the field with you, Stan, if your Mam and Dad will keep their eye on the potatoes and eggs on the trolley at the front," and so it was settled without hurting Harold's pride too much. While they went off to bring in the hay, Ada and Harold spent the afternoon sitting on chairs in the front garden enjoying the sunshine and watching the traffic go by.

On the way to collect the hay Stanley stopped to take a look at the sugar beet crop. It was in dire need of hoeing. Stared across the expanse of rapidly growing beet he said ,"Ah don't think ah'm going to be able to cope with this. It's getting away from me. It's growing faster than ah can deal with it."

As usual it was Doris who reassured him. "Look, Stanley," she said, "You can't do everything yourself. You're going to end up making yourself ill if you carry on as you are doing. Then what will we do? Why don't you get that young lad from down Bell Lane to help you for a few weeks, and while you're on with it, see if he knows a couple of women who want some casual work to get the sugar beet sorted?"

Stanley shook his head, "Oh ah don't know, Doris. Can we afford to pay wages? Ah could start doing an extra couple of hours every evening after tea." He got one of Doris's fierce glares in response. "Don't talk daft, Stan," she retorted, "You're working yourself to skin and bone as it is. If you don't go and see about getting some help, I will."

And so Stanley became an employer. Even though it was only casual labour he was using, in some way it made him feel more like a farmer and less like a farm labourer. Not that it made any difference to the amount of work he did. He toiled every available hour and Doris matched him. She took on all the feeding and cleaning out of the pigs while her husband was busy on the land and they fell into bed each night utterly exhausted, laying there holding hands, too tired to do anything else.

"Bloody hell," commented Stanley one night, "We're working so hard our sex life has gone out of the window." Doris made no reply as she snored softly. She was already fast asleep.

Ada saw how hard their lives were, and worried about them both, while Harold said he had always thought mining was hard, but he had come to the conclusion that farming was worse.

Their holiday was coming to an end, and as Stanley had no pigs ready for market that week they had opted to go home on the Saturday instead of Sunday. That suited Stanley as he and Doris had a plan.

They set off as early as they could. Despite Ada's protests, Doris had packed them a bag full of potatoes, vegetables and eggs to take home with them, but said nothing about the plan that she and Stanley had worked out the previous day

This time the fireside chairs were tied as securely as possible and a piece of old carpet had been laid on the floor of the van, which had cut down the chair's ability to slide considerably, and they reached their destination without any calamities.

Harold and Ada had recently moved into an old folk's bungalow on Barnsley Road in Wath and as they pulled up outside it Stanley indicated to Harold that he wanted him to stay in the van.

Doris accompanied Ada into the bungalow and it was not until they were inside that she realised Harold and Stanley were driving away. Turning to Doris she demanded to know where they were going. "It's a surprise, Mam," said Doris, "Stan's taken Dad to Barnsley to get a television."

"What? We can't afford a television; it takes us all our time to manage week to week now that Harold's retired."

Doris took her hand, "Don't worry, Mam. We're getting the television for you."

Ada became more agitated than ever, "You can't do that, Doris. Fetch him back. Go on, fetch him back."

"Ah can't, Mam, he'll be halfway to Barnsley by now. Come on, let's make a cup of tea. Think how much Dad is going to enjoy watching football on the television on Saturday afternoons." She didn't add that it would help to stop him feeling miserable now that he could no longer afford to go to the British Legion so often. That had been one of the main reasons they had decided to do it.

Ada was now only one step away from bursting into tears, and she declared that she would, 'Bray our Stanley when he gets back.'

An hour later however, when Stanley walked in through the door with his father, and informed her that a man would be delivering a television on Monday, she threw her arms round him and kissed him.

On their way home Stanley said it was worth the expenditure, just to see his Dad's face in the shop when they ordered the television. They smiled at each other as they enjoyed the glow it had given them to be able to do something for Harold and Ada.

"It's a pity," said Stanley, "That your Mam hasn't got electricity in the cottage. I'd save up and get her one too. She'd enjoy watching it."

"Yes." Doris agreed, "But can you imagine what Uncle Willie would have to say about it?"

Stanley gave a huge "Hugh!" and no more was said.

When they arrived home they changed into working clothes and while Doris set about feeding the animals Stanley headed down the lane to hoe a few more rows of sugar beet. With all his years of experience he was able to hoe almost at a walking pace but even going at that speed, he was not going to get the field finished before the beet had grown too big.

He was pleased now that Doris had persuaded him to get some help. He had found the young lad who had been recommended to him. His name was Jed and he lived with his mother and siblings in a cottage in Bell Lane. At only sixteen he had not had a lot of experience but he was strong and eager to work.

Stitchy had put him in touch with two ladies who often took on casual work. They were called Ivy and Renee, both were middle aged, and well used to farm work. He had knocked at Ivy's door and asked if she would like to come and give him a hand with the sugar beet. She had looked him up and down, adjusted her skirt and apron around her generous waistline and said. "Aye, and how much are you paying?"

When Stanley mentioned the figure she nodded and informed him that she would bring her cousin Renee with her. "We always work together you see. We'll be there at eight thirty on Monday, half an hour for dinner and we finish at four ready for the kids coming home from school. ok?"

And so it was arranged, and was to prove a good working arrangement. Just as she had said, Ivy turned up promptly with her cousin Renee on Monday morning. Jed was already there almost treading on Stanley's heels as he walked around the farm yard.

What a difference it made to have some help with the labour and as the fine weather continued they had the whole field of sugar beet hoed and singled by the end of the following week.

As they got to know each other, Ivy kept them entertained with her stories of characters in the village, and also had a tale to tell about her own little mishap the previous Sunday.

She had a young daughter aged seven and she had called out to her mother who was chatting to friends at the end of the road. "Mam," she called," Can I have a drink of pop?" or at least, Ivy understood her to say pop.

Ivy, easy going as always, waved her hand casually, "Aye, course you can. Finish the bottle if you like." Her daughter quickly disappeared inside and Ivy carried on chatting. Only trouble was, her daughter had said Port, not pop! She took her mother at her word and finished the bottle of port. Ivy found her fast asleep on the hearth rug with the empty bottle beside her.

"Bloody hell," commented Ivy, "She had a right headache next morning, ah think it'll have put her off drink for life."

Once the sugar beet was finished his workers moved on to another farm and Stanley was sorry to see them go. In the few weeks they had all worked together they had become friends and he looked forward to employing them again later in the year once the potatoes were ready.

CHAPTER 44

There was now a welcome lull in the farming calendar which allowed Stanley to catch up on some neglected jobs. There was his market garden to cultivate and some machinery in need of repair and Stanley set about them with his usual thoroughness.

Doris also was catching up on jobs in the house, and was keen to give some rooms a fresh coat of paint. Just as she did with most things, Doris had her own unique way of tackling the decorating. Plain white ceilings were not for her and it was probably just as well considering the many cracks and rough repairs that the ceilings had suffered over the years.

Remembering how they had used a rolled rag dipped in distemper to decorate the walls during the war, Doris adopted a similar method of her own. Fortunately emulsion paint was now available which made the job much easier than it would have been with distemper.

Taking an old cloth she screwed it up tight and dipped it into the paint, then dabbed it haphazardly all over the ceiling. Once she had covered it all over, she then went over it again with a different contrasting colour. Sometimes she did it three or four times over, each time with a new colour. It certainly hid all the lumps and bumps in the ceiling and people either loved it or hated it. If the clock could have been moved forward several years she might have been hailed as an innovator of interior design but at the time it was just considered very unusual.

Doris was at her most enthusiastic with a tin of gloss paint in her hands and she would keep going until every last drop of paint was gone. Anything that looked remotely as if it might benefit from a new coat of paint was sure to receive one. During the lull they were enjoying at this time, Stanley came into the house one day for his dinner to find every room reeking with paint fumes.

He ate his dinner quicker than usual, and was in a hurry to go back outside into the fresh air, but first he needed the toilet, and taking the newspaper with him he went upstairs to the bathroom. He sat on the toilet and glanced through the window at the view over the neighbours gardens before he opened his newspaper.

He allowed himself a few minutes then folded the paper and stood up, or rather, he would have stood up if he had not been stuck to the toilet seat that Doris had painted earlier in the day, and forgotten to mention. The paint had reached the very sticky stage, and afterwards Stanley swore that it almost peeled the skin from his backside as he tried to part himself from the seat.

To make matters worse the paint was a bright blue colour and it took a long time with a bottle of turpentine and a cloth to remove it all. There was a monumental row between Stanley and Doris, with all guns blazing, and it took until the next day for Stanley to see the funny side of it.

Harvest time was approaching and Stanley had a fine crop of barley that would soon be ready to cut. He drove down to the field on the Ferguson tractor to check on it and strode into the field, tested the grain between his teeth, and felt optimistic that it would yield well if only the good weather would hold out.

While he was there, and before he began work on the market garden, he drove to the bottom of the lane to take a look at the field of potatoes, and feeling content he began to sing softly to himself. As he came closer to the field his singing stopped abruptly. There was something wrong.

Even looking at it from a distance he knew there was something wrong, and his spirits were sinking. The foliage on many of the plants had a very slight, but definite yellow tinge that was not normal. With a sinking feeling in the pit of his stomach he took a spade from the tractor and walked to a patch of plants that looked wilted and yellow.

Placing the sharp blade of the spade in the earth he drove

it in as deep as he could and carefully levered the root of the potatoes upwards. Kneeling down he bent close to the roots and stared at them.

There was no mistaking the tiny round white objects on the roots of the plants. It was eel worm, the infestation that all farmers and gardeners dread. He had been prepared to lose some of the crop due to wet ground in the centre of the field where it was particularly low lying, but he had not expected this. He sat down on the grassy bank that surrounded the field and stared across the expanse of potatoes that were now just waste.

Stanley knew, as every farmer knew, that potatoes need to have at least a seven year gap between crops, otherwise any eel worm that lay dormant in the soil would begin to breed and infest all over again.

When he had taken over the farm, records of crops only showed what had been grown for the last five years, so he had no way of knowing where potatoes had been grown before that. He had had no choice but to take a chance and luck was evidently against him.

He sat there for a while coming to terms with the catastrophe. It would be a huge financial loss to them at a time when they could least afford it. It had been a costly investment to buy the seed potatoes and plant them in the spring and they had hoped to have a decent crop to sell, and bring in an income during the winter. Now, it was all wasted, and on top of that, they would have the work and expense of clearing the land of infested potatoes.

With a heavy heart he got back on the tractor and drove slowly back to the farm to break the bad news to Doris.

She took the news calmly as she always did when it was something serious and grasping his hands she looked at him with her large brown eyes and lifted her chin. "We'll manage, Stan." she said. "We always do,"

Unknown to them, there was an event lurking just a couple of weeks in the future, that could so easily have become a tragedy, and it brought the lost potato crop into perspective.

In Rawcliffe there were two ponds, both close to the banks of the River Aire. They had been formed several years earlier when earth had been excavated and used to repair and build up the waterways. They were known in the village as the big hole and the little hole. The larger of the two had become a fair-sized pond that was surrounded by bulrushes, and was used by local fishermen who dangled their rods in the water in the hope of catching something other than a cold.

The smaller pond was just a hole in the ground that had naturally filled with water and was used as a drinking place for animals and occasionally by the children of the village in hot weather to paddle and swim in.

Frances was strictly forbidden to go anywhere near this pond, but of course, when the sun is scorching down and all your school friends are off to the pool to cool off it is hard to resist, and Frances took little persuading to go along. They all trooped down the lane in the hot sunshine laughing and larking, all eager to get to the pond.

Once there, they all stripped off their shoes and paddled in the shallow water. They were treading where cattle had left their footprints and the cold mud squeezed through their toes delightfully. Three of the girls paddled back to the edge and sat on the grassy bank giggling at their mud covered toes.

Frances ventured a little further into the water enjoying the feel of the coolness on her legs. The mud at the bottom of the pond had now discoloured the water and Frances laughed as she shouted that she could not see her feet any more. Nor could she see that the shallow part of the water had come to an end, and she was approaching a steep drop where the water became much deeper.

Looking back, she waved to her friends, then took another step but went straight off the ledge, and into the deep, muddy water. Not being able to swim she sank immediately but thrashed about until she surfaced. For a few seconds she could see her friends all sitting chatting. Desperately she flailed her arms about and called, "I can't get out," before the water closed over her head again.

Terrified, she struggled, and came to the surface once more. Her friends were still there but now they were standing, and even in her moment of terror, as she scrabbled in desperation to stay afloat, she wondered why they were not saving her. But thankfully, help was on its way. Strong arms grasped her and pulled her back to the shallow part and out onto the grass.

It was a young man aged sixteen who had saved her On seeing her in trouble in the water he had bravely run straight in fully clothed, and pulled her to safety. Frances was so shaken by the incident that she barely said thank you to him.

Later when she went home she explained her wet clothes and hair by saying that one of her school mates had squirted water at her with a water pistol. Doris looked at her and suspected that there was more to her wet hair and clothes than she was letting on, but could get nothing else out of her and so no more was said.

Frances was shocked and traumatised by her experience and so worried that she would be in trouble for going to the pond. A few days went by and she still had not told her parents. Slowly she began to believe that they would never find out, but just one week later the Goole Times published a story on the front page of the local newspaper naming Frances as having narrowly escaped drowning and identified the young man who had saved her.

Even then Stanley and Doris did not hear of it straight away. It was the following morning when Doris went to the local butchers that she was made aware of what had happened.

As she walked into the tiny shop the queue of people went silent. All eyes turned towards her. The butcher bid her "Good Morning," then followed it up with, "By, your lass had a lucky escape, didn't she?"

Doris looked at him and then around at the rest of the customers, "What do you mean?" she asked. When a copy of the Goole Times was shown to her, she left the shop abruptly with the newspaper still in her hand and stormed back across the road to the farm.

Stanley was just about to set off to work in the fields when Doris practically ran into the yard.

He switched off the tractor engine and smiled a greeting, but his smile quickly faded as he saw Doris's expression. "What's up, love?" he asked. Without answering she thrust the newspaper at him

"Look at this," she shouted. "It's a bloody good job she's at school. Wait while she gets home at tea time. I've never felt such a fool as I did in that butchers. Why the bloody hell didn't she tell me?" Doris was in full flow, eyes flashing, cheeks flushed. She headed for the house, indignation bristling from her every movement.

Stanley, incredulous, read the article before he jumped off the tractor and followed her inside. Doris was pacing around the kitchen, barely able to contain herself. "Why didn't she tell me, Stan?"

Stanley struggled to sort out his feelings, "Well why do you think? Because she knew what you'd be like." He bent his head and read the paper again. "Calm down, Doris, do you realise we could have lost her."

Doris burst into tears, "I know," she sobbed, "I know. That's why ah'm so upset."

When Frances walked in at tea time the newspaper was laid out on the table for her to see.

"What have you got to say to that then?" Doris asked. She was still angry, but she had had time to get her emotions under control, and she held out her arms to her daughter and hugged her as if she would never let her go.

And then Stanley walked in. He was not a man to display his emotions but he gathered Frances into his arms and held her tightly without saying a word.

The atmosphere over the tea table was emotional and strained, but slowly Frances was coaxed into telling them exactly what had happened.

"Do you realise, Frances," Stanley said, "Why we said you were not to go there?" Frances nodded her head tearfully. He continued, "Ah don't have to tell you never to go there again do I?" She shook her head, "Ah'm never going near any water again, not ever."

In order to bring in a lighter note, Stanley joked "Well you'll be just like your Uncle Cyril then." He was speaking of his brother Cyril who was well known to be frightened of water.

Frances gave a sound that was half a giggle and half a sob as she wiped her eyes and blew her nose.

"Right. We'll say no more about it, but now I'm going to see the young man who saved you. We need to thank him"

Stanley had never been more grateful to anyone in his life as he was to that young man who had rescued his daughter. He thanked him profusely and wished he had been in a position to reward him more generously. As it was the only thing he could do was to buy him a new pair of shoes to replace his own that had been ruined when he had waded into the water.

CHAPTER 45

To begin with, Stanley had not planned to go to Doncaster market that Saturday. It was the end of August, and now that the two fields of barley were harvested he was anxious to get the fields ploughed. But as fate would have it, they woke up that day to hear heavy rain lashing at the windows.

Stanley got out of bed and looked through the windows. "Ah'm not going to be able to get any ploughing done today. It looks more like winter than the end of August. We might as well go to Donny after all. Ah'll see if ah can get another sow, we've got room for one more."

It was to be the worst decision he had ever made.

It was an unremarkable day at the market, an average sort of day, nothing about it that would distinguish it from any other, and yet it would be one they would never forget.

There were the usual number of pigs for sale and the one that Stanley bought was nothing out of the ordinary, just an average Large White sow that was heavily in pig and Stanley was well satisfied with his purchase.

When they arrived home they unloaded her from the trailer and installed her in the first sty just inside the fold yard. She went in like a lamb and rooted around in the clean straw before flopping down in it, grunting as she settled herself.

The rain had now cleared and Stanley changed into his working clothes before starting his tractor up and heading down to his land to get a couple of hours of ploughing done. As he drove down the lane, he thought how the look of the fields was rapidly changing.

With the corn all gathered in and most of the potatoes too, the land was taking on its winter look. The only green was the sugar beet and a few odd acres of turnips.

Stanley had just one field of beet to harvest, and he was intending to begin opening up the headlands on Monday morning in readiness for the contractor to get in with his machinery. As he drove past his crop of sugar beet now he thought to himself that next year he would try to have his own machine and save the heavy cost of the contractors. As usual when he was happy he began to sing softly as he continued towards the field that he was working on.

For a few days, life continued in the usual routine, until dinnertime on Thursday. Stanley had almost finished his plate of stew and dumplings when Doris said, almost casually, "That new sow has not eaten her food today."

"Oh," he said sharply, and stared at her. A pig not eating its food was unusual, and often a sign that something was wrong. "Ah'll have a look at her straight after dinner." Doris had made a rice pudding and she scooped out a large spoonful and dropped it into a round dish before passing it over to Stanley. He began to eat it automatically but Doris's information about the sow had worried him, and he ate without tasting.

He pushed his plate away and said that he would go and take a quick look at the sow. "Just pour my tea out, Dot, I'll be back in a minute."

He left the house and walked across to the fold yard. He opened the gate and looked over the half door at the new sow. She was lying stretched out on the thick pile of straw and raised her head briefly to look at him, then dropped it back down again as if she could not be bothered to hold it up. The food in her trough had barely been touched. It was that more than anything that troubled Stanley.

Quietly he opened the door and went across to her, talking softly. "Now then, old girl, what's the matter?" He bent and put his hand on her back and stroked it. Through the rough bristles on her back she felt hot and there was a niggling worry beginning in his head that he did not want to acknowledge.

Backing out of the sty Stanley walked across the yard to the house. Doris was washing up as he went back into the kitchen, she glanced at him, "What do you think to her? Do you think she's due to farrow earlier than we thought."

Stanley sat back down at the table and picked up his mug of tea. He made no answer for a moment or two. "No," he said, "There's no sign of that, Doris. To tell the truth, ah don't like the look of her. She's not touched her food. Can you send our Frances to Jack Tates fish and chip shop and ask him if he can sell us some off cuts of fish? If you boil them up with a few potatoes it might tempt her."

He got up, not wanting to discuss it any further at the moment. If he voiced his fears right away it would only worry Doris. He put his cap on and pulled it into position. "I'll be finished ploughing early today. Ah should be done by four," and picking up his jacket he went outside to begin the afternoon's work.

When he returned, having completed the field, he pulled the tractor under the shed, stopped the engine, and went straight down the yard to check on the sow. He had been hoping that she would have recovered by the time he got back, but she lay in exactly the same position as before. Doris came to join him and they stood together staring at her.

"We got some fish bits, Stan. Look, they're there in the trough. I cleaned all the old food out and put the freshly boiled fish in for her but she's just not interested in eating."

Stanley walked across to the barn and came back carrying an old tin bath in one hand and a large can of strong disinfectant in the other. He placed the bath outside the door of the ailing sow and poured half of the disinfectant into it.

"I've got another tin bath in the cart shed," he said, "I'll put that just outside the fold yard, Doris. We must disinfect our boots every time we come in or out. It'll be better if you feed all the other pigs and I'll look after this one. Ah don't want you to have any contact with this one in case what she's got is contagious, although it's probably too late now. Ah'd move this one if ah could but ah don't think we'd ever get her up on her feet."

Doris searched for his hand and gripped it, "There's something badly wrong with her isn't there?"

Stanley nodded. His face was grim, "Ah wouldn't have been so worried if it had been one of the other pigs, but as this one's just come from the market she could be carrying some disease. We'll just have to wait and watch her."

Doris looked at him, the concern in his eyes was matched by the concern in her own, "You think its Swine Fever don't you?"

"We'd better bloody hope it's not," replied Stanley, "We'll just have to wait and see. If ah was a praying man, ah'd be down on my knees right now."

There was to be little sleep for either of them that night and they were both relieved when dawn broke at last. Stanley was the first to throw the blankets to one side and begin to get dressed. Doris pulled on her old, blue dressing gown and went downstairs to put the kettle on to boil, then returned quickly upstairs and dressed while Stanley shaved.

The moment he came downstairs he headed straight for the door and looked behind him to find Doris almost treading on his heels. "Where you going, Dot?" he asked, with a note of irritation in his voice.

"Ah'm coming to have a look at the sow," she snapped back at him. Stanley gave a huge sigh of exasperation as he said, "Ah thought we'd agreed that you should not have contact with her?"

Doris continued following him, "I'll stay outside," she assured him. Stanley shook his head and gave up. "It's no good us falling out," she said, "It's bad enough without that."

He turned and put his arm round her. "Ah know, love, you're right. Ah'm sorry. Ah'm just worried out of my head at the moment. Come on, you wait at the gate and let me have a look at her."

He opened the bottom half of the stable type door and disappeared inside. Doris waited; her fingers crossed and her face anxious. She had not long to wait. Stanley was soon out again. His face was grim. He shook his head and said, "She's worse, Doris. She been sick and she's got diarrhoea. She's absolutely red hot. We're going to have to get the vet. I'll go up to the telephone box now and ring him."

They stared at each other, they both knew that Swine Fever was a notifiable disease, with heavy penalties if they did not inform the authorities, and they both knew what the outcome would be if the sow did have swine fever.

As always, Doris had laid the table for breakfast the night before, but it remained undisturbed this morning. Food could not have been further from Stanley's mind. His stomach was churning with nerves as he found a handful of small change and went to collect his bike out of the shed. Doris ran after him with the vet's telephone number on a scrap of paper and watched as he put his feet on the pedals and began to cycle out of the farm yard.

The red telephone box was situated at the back of the village green, near the Coop shop, and the deep dread inside him increased as he drew closer to it. Within seconds it seemed, he was pulling open the door, lifting the receiver and inserting the coins.

He dialled the number and almost immediately, Jim Grenfell, the vet answered. Stanley swallowed hard and said in a voice that sounded as if it belonged to someone else that he needed the vet to come and look at one of his pigs. "Ah need you here as soon as possible please." Then as he remembered that he had not told the vet who was speaking he quickly added. "It's Stanley Dale, Pleasant View Farm, Rawciffe."

The vet's voice came through calm and professional, "Ah, good morning Stan. Now then, you sound a bit upset. What's the problem?"

"One of my sows is very bad. Can you come as soon as possible, please. It's urgent." He put the phone down, not trusting himself to speak any more. As he left the phone box he passed one of his neighbours who greeted him cheerfully. He received just a curt nod in reply and Stanley wheeled his bike on to the road and began to ride home. The neighbour looked after him and said aloud, "Well what's up with him then?"

Back home, Stanley shoved his bike back into the shed and went indoors to tell Doris that he had spoken to the vet. "Ah think he said an hour, but ah can hardly think straight,Doris." He quickly drank the mug of tea she had poured out for him and took a couple of bites out of the slice of toast, but put it back on the plate and shook his head. "It's no use" he said, "Ah can't eat. Ah'll go out into the yard and wait for him."

Doris began feeding the animals while Stanley kept away from them as planned. He also kept away from the infected sow but could not resist peering over the door at her, hoping against hope to see a miraculous recovery, but far from recovering he could now hear that her breath was coming in short gasps and every now and then she gave a loud cough. Turning away he went back out to the yard and paced up and down.

He was sure now that the vet had said an hour. He looked at his watch, the hour was almost up. He went back into the barn and began to fold some sacks, hoping that the mundane, routine job would steady his nerves. And then he heard the squeal of brakes and the slam of a car door and knew it would be the vet.

He was a man who went everywhere in a hurry, a down to earth man, who was popular with all his clients. "Now then, Stan," he called out as he saw Stanley coming out of the barn. "Let's have a look at this sow of yours then, shall we?"

Stanley led the way and opened the door. The vet went silent at the sight of the ailing pig. He bent over and looked at the sow without touching her. He gave a sharp intake of breath. Then he stood up and said, "I'm sorry, Stan. I am certain as it's possible to be that it's Swine Fever. I'll have to take some swabs and send them away for testing. You know what it means don't you?"

In reply Stanley said, "You'll have to put the farm in quarantine won't you? How long will it be before we get the results?" He was amazed at how calm he was managing to sound. It was almost as if his emotions had been frozen. He heard himself asking what the procedure would be and was aware that Doris was standing beside him. He put his arm around her and they exchanged looks.

They heard the vet tell them that there was to be no movement of animals to or from the farm and more tubs of disinfectant were to be placed at the gates.

"I'll be as quick as I can with the results. The authorities will want to know where you bought the sow from and they will follow the trail back to the person who sent the pig to market."

After he had gone and the gates were closed with warning signs hung on them, Stanley and Doris walked into the house and sat in their chairs feeling totally drained and shocked. It was Stanley who broke the silence. "Ah'm sorry, Doris." he said, " It was me that bought the sow and brought all this on us. If only ah'd stayed away from the market that week."

Doris got up and stood beside him, "It might not be Swine Fever."

Stanley shook his head, "It's no good kidding ourselves, we both know it is and the vet knows. Sending the swabs away is just a formality." He could stand it no longer in the house and left the mug of tea that Doris had just poured out for him, picked his cap up and went outside.

Without really thinking about what he was doing he went into the barn, picked up a spade and walked up the yard. Behind the cart shed there was a small area of land that he rented from the chapel next door. Normally it was used for standing any spare implements on, but today he planned to turn it into a cemetery. Taking hold of his spade he began to dig a huge communal grave for all his pigs.

All day he dug, working with a steady determination, pausing only to straighten his back now and then. By evening it was almost finished. He had dug a deep channel that he judged would be big enough to take the bodies of all his stock.

He knew what was going to happen; there was not a doubt in his head that very soon he would be burying all his pigs here. He took several deep breaths but they could not alleviate the despair that seemed to have a grip on his heart.

He looked in at the sow that had brought them all the trouble and felt sorry for her as she stared up at him. His instinct was to put her out of her misery. He hated to see an animal suffer.

The rest of the pigs on the farm were making their usual commotion as they demanded their evening meal. They sounded so healthy and normal that it was almost impossible to accept that they would all be dead within the next few hours.

It was to be another night with little sleep as they waited for the results on the swabs that had been sent away for testing. The results arrived mid-morning the next day, and any tiny hope that they might have had, was soon squashed, as they were given the confirmation that it was as they expected.

The sow that Stanley had bought at Doncaster market was suffering from Swine Fever, and so, according to government rulings, every pig on their property must be slaughtered.

James Grenfell, the vet, was appointed to destroy them all. When he arrived, he was wearing protective green overalls and carried a brown leather case. Stanley looked at the case; he knew that inside it were the means to destroy all the pigs. James was not a young man. He had seen many things in his working life as a vet, but this morning he was as upset as Stanley and Doris.

He put his hand out to them and said, "I am so very sorry that I have to do this. What do you want to do Stan? Do you want to watch?" As Stanley hesitated he added, "If I were you I would go out of the way until it's all over."

Doris turned and went back into the house. Stanley followed her and they sat in the kitchen together, holding hands. As the sound of the first gunshot reached them the pigs began a panicky squealing and screaming that increased as more shots rang out.

They listened for the shots, as one by one they destroyed their stock and everything they had worked for. Afterwards, when it was over, when the gunshots had ceased,and the frantic screaming of the pigs was silenced forever, they stood up and went outside.

James was coming out of the fold yard, his face was as white as a sheet and Stanley thought he had never seen him look so haggard. He rubbed his hands on his overalls and looked back at the fold yard. "Well that's it, Stanley. This has been a bad day. Are you going to get some help burying the pigs?

Stanley's face was grim, "No," he said, "I've already dug a trench for them. They will all be buried by the end of the day."

"You'll probably have some officials coming around within days to check that the pigs have all been properly disposed of," pointed out the vet as he prepared to leave, "If there is anything you need to know give me a ring."

As he drove off they stood in the middle of the yard and Stanley put his arm around his wife as he did so often. The farm was strangely silent without the pigs grunting and snuffling in their pens. The only sound was the traffic passing by on the road and the odd cluck from the hens.

Stanley took a deep shuddering breath and squared his shoulders. He went into the fold yard and looked at the bodies of his sows, lying stretched out as if they were asleep. Now he had the heart breaking task of disposing of them. He decided to begin with the sick sow.

He had already fitted the bucket on to the front of his faithful old Ferguson tractor and he drove it as close to the fold yard as he could. Doris joined him dressed in her oldest clothes Taking hold of the back legs of the sow they dragged her out into the passage and on to the bucket. She was still warm and pliable and her body flopped over the sides.

Taking a length of rope he tied her on to it to prevent her rolling off, and then he revved up the engine and put the lifting mechanism into gear. He had been expecting problems but the little tractor gamely lifted the bucket high enough from the ground for him to move and he drove slowly up to the trench that he had dug.

He lowered the bucket slowly and carefully, positioning the sow so that she was lying as neatly as he could place her, and then returned to the fold yard and they did the same with the next one.

When the final one lay in the trench, Doris collected all the baby pigs into a barrow and wheeled them up to join their mothers. They laid them in the gaps between the bigger pigs and took one last look at them before they began covering them with the soil that he had dug out.

At last it was done, and he drove the tractor up and down on top of the trench and flattened the heap. Now all that remained of their herd of pigs was a long patch of slightly raised soil.

CHAPTER 46

Once again it seemed that Stanley and Doris were living in the wrong era. If they could have fast forwarded time just a few years the government would have compensated them for the loss of their herd of pigs.

As it was, at that time, they had been forced to slaughter all their stock on the orders of the government, but were not entitled to a penny in compensation. As Stanley said so bitterly, not only had they lost their herd of pigs, they had actually had to pay to have them destroyed. It was bitter pill to swallow.

The loss of their pigs had left them almost destitute. The Swine Fever could not have come at a worse time. Several of their litters of pigs had been almost ready to go to market, and the store pigs they had been fattening up were very nearly at bacon weight. Now they had all gone.

That evening they took out all their outstanding invoices, and laid them out on the table. Their financial situation was desperate. Their income now consisted of the proceeds from the seven acres of sugar beet that was yet to be harvested, and money from the barley. The two combined would just about cover the rent for the half year that was due in January and the outstanding invoices for animal feed.

The loss of the potato crop meant the only things they had to sell in the shop were eggs and the vegetables that Stanley had grown.

Stanley put his head in his hands at the table and was silent for several minutes. When he looked up he said, "It's no good, Doris. We're beat. We're finished. There's no way around this. There's no money to buy new stock."

In his entire life he had never felt so disheartened, so without hope, "We'll just have to hand in our notice, and I'll get a job again. All the bloody years of working and striving have been for naught." There was nothing Doris could say. She knew he was right and she felt as despondent as he did.

They slept that night from sheer exhaustion, and when Stanley woke the next morning, for a moment or two he had forgotten what had happened the day before. As the realisation hit him, he groaned. But somehow he was more accepting of the situation. He leaned over and drew Doris into his arms and they lay quietly together, each comforted by the presence of the other.

"Well, Dot," he said, and he heaved a huge sigh, "Ah'll start on getting all the places mucked out today, then ah'll lime wash them before we hand our notice in."

And then he thought of the chairman of the county council, Mr Molton, who had disliked Stanley from the first day he had met him and the feeling was quite definitely mutual. For some reason the chairman had never wanted Stanley to be given the tenancy of the farm

As he thought of him now Stanley commented, "Ah don't want that bloody 'Molton' coming round to inspect and having any reason to complain."

He swung his feet out of bed and began to get dressed. "Ah'll tell you what, Doris, if that bugger pushes me too far, the way ah feel just now, ah'll not hold back. Ah'll knock his supercilious nose flat to his face and enjoy doing it."

Doris could not help a wry laugh at his words, "Supercilious?" she said, "Where the heck did you find that word from?"

"Well." he said, "It describes that bugger perfectly doesn't it? He walks about with his nose in the air. One day he'll get what's coming to him. Ah bloody hate to think of the pleasure he's going to get, seeing us go down."

Straight after breakfast Stanley went out to the fold yard and walked around, looking into pens that now held nothing but piles of straw. It was eerily silent and empty now, almost as if the pigs had never existed.

He collected his fork and shovel, put them into the wheel barrow and began mucking out. He took each loaded barrow up to the orchard, tipped it into a heap and set it alight. By the end of the week everywhere was clean and washed. The walls had been painted with lime again and the wind blew through the empty buildings, drawing attention to the complete lack of any living stock.

The farm was now ready for inspection, it was now time to hand in their formal notice, and yet Stanley put it off, always hoping for better times.

They scraped a living as best they could from the sale of their eggs and vegetables. Stanley managed to get a couple of days helping with threshing on a neighbouring farm and with the wages he received they bought a ton of potatoes, bagged them up and resold them for a small profit and bought another ton with the proceeds.

Doris was running the house on a miniscule amount of money, they mostly ate their own produce and every week she worked magic with a tin of corned beef; turning it into a tasty stew and using the left overs to make a pie the following day.

They may have had very little money, but what Stanley and Doris did possess was more than their fair share of Yorkshire grit. Sheer stubbornness and refusal to be beaten kept them going.

Again and again Stanley said that if they once gave the farm up they would never get another chance. They had many dark days when they both felt thoroughly depressed and wondered if they would ever get back on to their feet.

But then, one day, out of the blue, they had a visitor.

CHAPTER 47

It was late November on a cold dreary day and Stanley was working on one of the farm implements that he had bought earlier that year. He was scrubbing at it with a wire brush to remove all the rust prior to painting it when he heard his name called. He looked up to see Mr McLain his old employer from Clamton Park striding across the yard towards him.

At that moment in time there was not another person that Stanley would rather have seen. He had always been a friend as well as an employer, and at the sight of him Stanley dropped his wire brush, wiped his hands, and hastened to greet him.

"Now then, Stanley. It's very good to see you, but I wish the circumstances had been different."

Stanley pulled a face, "It's very good to see you too. You've heard about our troubles then?"

He tried to sound as bright as he could, but there was no hiding the slight tremor in his voice. Pretending not to notice, Mr. McLain nodded and continued, "Yes , I've just been to see relatives of mine who farm at Balne and they gave me the bad news."

"It's been a bad time," replied Stanley, "It's just about got the better of us, but we're struggling through. Come inside and have a cup of tea, I know Doris will be glad to see you."

Doris had already seen them walking towards the house and had hurriedly taken off the turban that she often wore while doing the housework, brushed her hair and removed her pinafore.

By the time Stanley opened the door and announced that they

had a visitor the kettle was already on and Doris was looking good in spite of her flushed cheeks.

Once they were seated with cups of tea in front of them Mr McLain broached the subject of their recent misfortune. "You remember," he said, "That when you left Clamton I told you there would always be a job for you?"

Stanley nodded and began to thank him, but Mr McLain held up his hand, "No, no, I don't want thanks. What I am offering you now is a job and a house at the home farm at Clamton. You would have a better house than you had before and higher wages. You don't need to thank me. I would be more than happy for you to come and work for me again. It's up to you, Stanley. You don't have to give me your answer right away. Take your time."

Stanley looked across at Doris He could almost read her mind. She was looking at him with her dark brown eyes and her lips straight. She gave him a slight nod and said, "It's up to you, love."

Stanley swallowed. It was a tempting offer. No more worrying, no more uncertainty. He would have a regular wage and a house provided. But then he thought of giving up what he had been struggling to achieve for most of his life.

He looked his old employer in the eye and said, "Ah can't tell you how much I appreciate your offer and I am tempted, but I don't want to give in, we'll struggle through somehow. We want to keep the farm."

Mr McLain looked at him and gave a smile. "Do you know, I knew you'd say that, Stanley, and I understand, I would have done the same myself. But, you do need a hand to get back on your feet and I'll tell you what I'll do. If you are willing, I'll send you four sows from my herd. They are all in pig and they'll do well for you. You can pay me back whenever you can afford to."

Stanley was overwhelmed that someone would do such a thing for him, and for a minute he struggled to speak. He began to thank him but the words he found seemed so inadequate and he shook his head. "Ah can't believe that you would do such a thing for us. We will never be able to thank you enough. You can be sure we will pay you back."

Mr McLain got up to leave, "I'm only too happy to be able to help, Stanley," he said, "You can rest assured I will keep my word. The sows will be with you by the end of the week," and he shook hands with them both before he walked quickly back to his car.

As they waved him goodbye Stanley put his arm around Doris's shoulders and they slowly made their way back towards the house, barely able to believe what had just happened. As they reached the door they turned around and looked up the farm yard.

In his mind Stanley could already hear the sound of animals in the buildings again and see the farm coming back to life.

Stanley pulled her close and kissed the top of her head, and with hope filling his heart again he said, "We're not finished after all, Doris."

Just when Stanley had thought they were finished, Mr Mclain, his previous employer had thrown him a lifeline, and Stanley had grasped it gratefully.

Together he and Doris began the long hard struggle to recover financially and emotionally after losing all their stock. It was to take them years of back breaking work to get the farm running profitably, but they were rewarding years when they grew in knowledge and experience.

They were years that were filled with laughter, joy, despair, and some tears. Whatever life threw at them they continued onwards, always refusing to be beaten. Through it all their love and devotion to each other never wavered.

Stanley never forgot his former employer's kindness and when he spoke of him many years later it was still with a little tremor of gratitude in his voice.

One of Stanley's favourite and frequent quotations was, 'It's not what you know in this life, it's who you know.'

How right he was and it is that quotation which inspired the title of this book.